THE PRODIGALS

THE BOYARS

* *

The Prodigals

By Petru Dumitriu

Translated from the French

BY NORMAN DENNY

PANTHEON BOOKS
A Division of Random House
NEW YORK

CONTENTS

I

Country Life

9

I

On a warm evening in June 1915 Dimitri Coziano got off a slow train at the small station of Dobrunu, near his parents' estate. He was fifteen years old and was to spend his summer holiday in the country after reaching the fifth grade at the high school where he was a boarder. Dimitri was the son of Manuel Coziano, the grandson of Eustache Coziano and the great-grandson of Alexander and Sophie Coziano. He was the nephew of Madame Helene Vorvoreano and cousin to Elvira and Michael Vorvoreano, Serban Romano, the Apostolesco children, Cesar Lascari and Alexander Sufana and his brothers.

He stood waiting with his suitcase on the platform, letting his eyes grow accustomed to the dim light while he gazed at the leafy branches of a few dusty chestnut trees half hiding a building of grey brick. The word " DOBRUNU " shone in red letters on the glass of lanterns fixed to the wall, and an open door afforded a glimpse of a waiting-room dimly lighted by an oil-lamp. Vague forms were moving within, and a thin, small woman stood in the doorway looking out.

Peasants were jostling one another on the platform, while the women chattered or called to their children in shrill voices, seeming overtaken by panic. The train was due to leave in another minute. The engine gave a piercing whistle, and the departing passengers leaned out of the windows to say urgent last words to those who were staying behind.

" No one here," thought Dimitri. " Perhaps they're outside." After a last look round he walked past the end of the station buildings through a broken fence to the road, bordered with chestnuts and limes. Dogs were barking somewhere in the distance. Carts with canvas tops passed by with a faint rattle of chains and the sound of the oxen champing in their nose-bags.

11

Further off there was a sound of horses stamping, and Dimitri made out the shape of the carriage, recognisable by its two lamps. He walked slowly towards it, feeling his shoes sink ankle-deep in the dust. Two peasants, leaning on their staves, were talking to the coachman.

" You're being foolish. You can see he hasn't come," one of them said.

" How can one be sure? We must wait a little longer," said the coachman uncertainly.

Dimitri knew his voice. It was Nicolai with the moustache, who was married to the cook.

" You're only wasting time. I'll stand you a drink as well," said the other peasant.

Nicolai did not answer. Dimitri was incensed. Without waiting to see what would happen he moved abruptly into the circle of light cast by the nearest lamp.

" Good evening, Nicolai," he said coldly, and pushing past the peasants he jumped into the carriage.

" At your orders, master! " exclaimed Nicolai.

The horses started with a jerk which flung Dimitri back against the cushions. He recovered and looked round, but the peasants were already lost in the darkness.

" What did those two want? " he asked.

The coachman turned in his seat and bent amiably towards him.

" Which two, Master Dimitri? "

" The two you were talking to. Don't pretend you don't know."

" Oh, those. Why, nothing. We were just talking. They came from my village."

" You're lying, Nicolai. They wanted you to give them a lift. They were offering you drinks in exchange."

" Why, no, master, nothing of the kind. They'd never dare. A gentleman's carriage isn't for the likes of them. They have their carts and that's all they need."

" You're still lying. I heard what they said."

" They were only joking. You mustn't take too much notice of what they say."

Dimitri knew perfectly well that Nicolai was laughing at him. " I shall tell Father," he resolved, and propped himself firmly against the cushions with his legs crossed, a hand on his hip and an arm on the side of the carriage, in the attitude of a grown man and a master.

The carriage had settled down to a steady pace with no other sound than the deadened clop-clop of hooves on the dust. The moon was high in the sky, and the road, passing amid grey fields with a sheen of silver, disappeared between rows of round-topped trees, thick-leaved, heavy and compact, so sharply etched against the sky that even their smallest leaves seemed to be engraved upon it. Everything had a wonderful clarity, the haystacks, the carts loaded with straw, the meadows and houses, all of a grey tinged with blue amid the huge emptiness of the summer night. A thousand or ten thousand restless dogs, hungry and hostile to nocturnal travellers, howled ceaselessly over the countryside; but the schoolboy so comfortably installed in the carriage did not hear them. He was gazing in wonderment at the sky filled with stars, at the fields which seemed to have been touched up with the finest of brushes, and he was thinking about himself. He was conscious, in a confused way, of the fact that he was a person of importance. Snatches of phrases that he had read recently in some novel occurred to his mind. He was returning to the castle of his ancestors. (The Dobrunu house had twice been rebuilt: in 1907 it had been burnt to the ground.) He was the youthful Lionel, son of Lord FitzRobert. (His father in fact was plain Monsieur Coziano, landowner, a member of the Upper College of Electors and a barrister-at-law.) Seated beside him in the diligence bearing travellers from Edinburgh to Athlone was the ravishing Lady Margaret Rose. This figure was less easy to evoke amid the realities of the Danubian plain, but Dimitri pictured her as the girl with dark eyes and braids of brown hair coiled like a crown on her head who had gazed at him with a remote but disturbing smile through the window of a classroom at the girls' high school at N—— He had afterwards strolled several times past that window, but always, as luck would have it, at times when the teacher was present or when the girls were elsewhere. He knew the name of his Lady Margaret Rose: it was Julieta—Julieta Doicesco—and she was the daughter of a lawyer. Marriage was thus not out of the question. After the ceremony they would have a honeymoon in the country, travelling first by train and then by carriage from the little railway-station through the blue night to the manor; and the night would be passed in a fever of love-making.

Dimitri sought to picture these raptures in detail, but without much success, owing to his lack of experience. His imaginings were based on the revelations of day-boys at school who had been able to escape from their homes to pay furtive visits to the Grand Union Hotel, the resort of the town's few prostitutes, or to the dilapidated suburban dwelling inhabited by a lady called Iona, known as " Tin-Bottom," who entertained members of the police-force on night patrol. Mingling these gleanings with passages derived from romantic novels, and weaving them round the olive-tinted, childlike face of Mademoiselle Doicesco, Dimitri conjured up a dream of ecstatic debauchery which brought him to a state of almost unendurable physical tension as he travelled sedately through the warm, translucent world of the night.

He was still lost in this vision when they turned into the drive, with lighted windows gleaming ahead and all about them the barking of dogs which Nicolai sought to disperse with random slashes of his whip. They pulled up at the front door. Dense masses of wistaria and virgin vine were visible, and the cottages where the servants lived, and, beyond a row of poplars, the farm. Further away was the mill, now hidden in darkness. Dimitri jumped down from the carriage and entered the house. Wicker chairs, sporting guns arrayed in a corner, the tall, stained mirror in its old-fashioned frame, the bronze bust of some unknown lady, the photographs of bearded gentlemen rigid in high, stiff collars, the silver bell hanging above the door, the Ghiordez rug of handsome olive green but now worn threadbare, these things greeted him, accompanied by the familiar smell of woodwork warmed by the sun, wax floor-polish, dust and lavender, which was the smell of summer holidays. He took off his black cap with its square peak bearing in gold letters the initials of the Gheorghe Bibesco High School, and went into the big, empty drawing-room. Oil-lamps surmounted by green globes stood burning on round tables. The curtains parted to allow the passage of Victoria, the maidservant, carrying a tray loaded with plates. Plump, dark-haired and smiling, she was so startled at the sight of him that she nearly dropped it.

" Master Dimitri! How good to see you! "

He smiled at her and went on into the dining-room. But here

he paused, suddenly self-conscious, as the company turned to look at him. He stood uncertainly in the doorway, skinny and slender, his neck too long, a faint shadow on his upper lip, with dark, deep-set eyes which were handsome but seemed to shine more with the fevers of a difficult adolescence than with any exceptional intelligence. Tightly encased in his black school uniform, buttoned up to the neck, Dimitri Coziano stood holding his cap in his hand while the diners cried:

" It's Dim! Dim's arrived! "

There were a great many of them, more than he had expected. Some no doubt had come only to dine, and their carriages must be waiting outside. Why had he not noticed? This was what always happened when one wasn't expecting it. Why hadn't the wretched Nicolai warned him? Dim bowed awkwardly, then walked round the huge oval table to kiss the hand of his grandmother, seated in the place of honour, who had smiled fondly the moment he appeared. Madame Cléopatre Coziano, married after the death of Eustache, the brother of Davida, to Walter Apostolesco, was now in her sixties, and it was impossible to say whether she had ever been pretty. Her round cheeks with a slight fluff on them had begun to sag, and a double chin lent heaviness to her face. But the dark eyes still twinkled alertly beneath her greying brows. Brought up in an age when ladies did not redden their lips, Cleopatra had nevertheless fallen into the habit of using lipstick adopted by young ladies in the year 1910. Her thick mass of hair, almost white, was tightly bound in a chignon on the back of her head. Her whole head was an assembly of spherical contours bearing little relation to one another, the fleshy cheeks, the double chin, the two grey hemispheres of her coiffure, and the chignon, hanging in a heavy cluster above a high collar trimmed with lace.

She gazed fondly at her grandson as he blushingly approached, and held out her hand for him to kiss, a plump hand flecked with brown and adorned with a ten-carat solitaire diamond.

" Make room," she said. " The child must be starving. Stand still, Dim, I want to look at you."

Keeping his hand in hers, she looked him over so searchingly that he blushed still more. In particular, his ears turned a vivid red; he knew it and, growing increasingly shy and resentful, tried to withdraw his hand from that soft, firm grasp.

" You've grown. You're turning into a man," she said with a sort of gloating satisfaction. " Sit down, my love, and have your dinner. But first you must kiss your mother and father."

" I don't want anything to eat, thank you. I'm not hungry."

Dim's face was still crimson and his grandmother seemed delighted.

" Listen to his voice! He's like a young cock! "

The women at the table laughed teasingly and disturbingly, and Dim, very conscious of the fact that his voice was breaking, blushed yet again. He went on to greet his parents. His mother, sad-faced, her eyes sunken, smiled affectionately at him as she stroked his hair. His father, Manuel Coziano, welcomed him with a vigorous shake of the hand, after the English fashion, and a hearty smile in which there was no true warmth. Dim made the round of the table. He was ill at ease, because from the doorway he had noted the presence of several young women whose beauty he found dazzling. There was his cousin Elvira, married to Prince Ipsilanti, a general in the Army; she had come by herself, no doubt having matters to discuss with Dim's father. Elvira was about twenty-five, dark-skinned, with hair that was almost blue-black in colour and eyes that were almost green. She smiled at him, her lips heavily made-up, and offered him a slender, amber-tinted hand. As he touched it with his lips Dim caught her scent, as sweet and penetrating as that of carnations or tuberoses; and the contact with that cool, silky skin caused him for an instant to close his eyes. Recovering himself, he moved on and, still with a slight feeling of intoxication, kissed the hand of Madame Hagibei, who was also his cousin. Augusta Hagibei, then aged about twenty-eight, was more roundly shaped than Elvira. Her face, like that of a Greek statue, was the colour of Eastern ivory, with the bright smear of Paris rouge throwing the full lips into relief. Her eyes were clear and handsome, as brown as her hair, but with little expression. To the detached observer she might have seemed uninteresting; but Dim felt her hand melt with a hint of moisture into his own as she said:

" Well, young man, and how are you? "

This, accompanied by a smile and the studied gaze of her brown eyes, had the effect of throwing him into further disarray. No woman had ever smiled at him like that, looking deep into his eyes in that intent and lightly teasing fashion, which in Augusta was unconscious and quite meaningless, but which Dimitri at once credited with the force and impact of an avowal, a positive invitation. Escaping from her gaze, agitated, startled and flushed with delight, he hurried towards the next hand that was extended towards him. It was that of Aunt Olga, the widow of Prince Gheorghe Duca, killed two years before in a motor accident, who had come with her son Gheorghe Duca (Ghighi for short), another of Dim's cousins. Aunt Olga, on the verge of forty, had a slender figure, delicate hands and a cool, casual manner. Beautiful but always remote, she reached out her hand with an air of indifference, and Dim was afraid he might have offended her by first kissing the hands of his cousins. He passed over his cousin Alexandrina Romano, Augusta's sister. They were the daughters of Alexander Lascari, Davida's eldest son. Alexandrina was gentle and colourless. She smiled indulgently as Dim went by her with no more than a nod and hurried on to shake hands with the gentlemen. Monsieur Romano, President of the Tribunal of Justice in the capital of one of the mountain provinces, wore a high starched collar and had a thick crop of hair and a black moustache; like him, Monsieur Hagibei, who used a monocle, affected an air of calm superiority which irritated Dim. Then came Captain Michael Vorvoreano, the brother of Elvira and another cousin; he was dressed in mufti, in a suit of white tussore silk, and he had a clipped moustache, for he was serving under General Averesco, who maintained that all soldiers should have a martial aspect and did not permit his officers to be clean-shaven. Finally there were the younger cousins, Ghighi Duca, a tall, fair-haired boy of sixteen with blue eyes in a triangular face, elegantly dressed in a white linen suit with faint blue stripes, and Serban Romano, a sturdy youngster of about ten with a big head and a solemn expression. Dim took his seat with them at the bottom of the table. Ghighi said in a cool, superior voice:

" Well, young fellow-me-lad, are you glad you've got here? "

" I'm delighted. I note with satisfaction that there are women around," said Dimitri, anxious to display his male cynicism.

Ghighi glanced at him with interest but also with mockery.

" So you've started to notice women, have you? "

" My dear boy, I'm the local stallion. They bring them to me for service."

Ghighi Duca smiled tentatively, not altogether sure if this

were nothing but a boast. The ten-year-old Serban listened in open-mouthed admiration.

The meal had reached the dessert stage, and the grown-ups were talking about the war.

"France!" sighed Dimitri's grandmother. "Alas, poor France!"

Monsieur Hagibei declared: "Every man has two countries—his own and France."

"And where exactly was your second country?" asked his wife. "At the Moulin Rouge?"

The other gentlemen laughed loudly, and Hagibei, slightly disconcerted, replied: "You shouldn't despise ideals. France is the lighthouse of civilisation, and the Huns are the wave of barbarism that threatens to swamp humanity."

"No, really, you can't say the Germans aren't civilised," said Captain Vorvoreano. "Discipline, cleanliness, honesty, obedience, loyalty—those are the qualities you find in Germany. They're the finest soldiers in the world. And what's more," he added with a chuckle, "German women are the most accommodating on earth."

"Meaning that you don't care for Roumanian women," said old Madame Cléopatre. "Or is it that they don't care for you?"

"Oh, but they do. That's to say, they have a weakness for cavalry officers. It's the uniform that attracts them," said Vorvoreano, with affected modesty.

"The question is," said Manuel Coziano, "are we to come into the war or are we staying out?"

At this the gentlemen all began talking at once. "Of course we've got to come in! What's more, we ought to do it now . . ." "No, not before next year . . ." "We should have done it long ago . . ." "It would be suicide, Austria-Hungary would swallow us in one gulp . . ." "It's not the Austrians, it's the Russians who'll swallow us—the Austrians have been knocked out by the Serbs . . ." "Anyway, the King doesn't want war . . ." "Yes, he does, but the time isn't ripe . . ."

Dimitri was not listening. He was eating a pastry and glancing sidelong at his cousin Elvira, whose laughter disclosed a flash of gleaming teeth. As she talked her gaze kept straying to his end of the table, perhaps inadvertently or perhaps because she knew she was being watched. Their eyes met, and Dim, with a sudden feeling of giddiness, turned away his head. His state of perturbation alarmed him. After a moment he glanced towards her again, but Elvira was now looking elsewhere. Had she really smiled, and had the smile been meant for him? He was afraid to think so. Why should she have done it? But he was sure that she had smiled. She had been beginning to smile when, like an idiot, he had looked away; and now it was too late. As he sought to catch her eye again Dim encountered the earnest gaze of Augusta, another of those deep, intent glances that for a moment rested full upon him and then, slowly and indifferently, passed on. Dim felt a sort of anguish. Augusta had looked at him. How beautiful she was! She was like Julieta Doicesco, but much better; yes, incomparably more beautiful. He gazed in ravishment at her bosom moulded in a bodice of white lace, thrown into relief between her high black collar and the black silk sash round her waist. He tried to attract her gaze again but she paid not the slightest attention. Furtively and desiringly, Dimitri gazed at all the women round the table, but found that none was taking any notice of him. Except, that is to say, his grandmother, whom he caught watching him when he least expected it. Greatly abashed he lowered his head and did not look up again.

2

After dinner the company moved out on to the terrace, where there were wicker chairs and tables surrounded by plants in tubs. Moonlight flooded over flower-beds and newly mown, well-watered lawns, with clumps of oak and lime heavy with leaf. Beyond these lay the meadows, overgrown with rank grass and nettles, and further still the waste of stubble burnt brown by the summer sun, torrid as it always is on the Danubian plain. The servants brought trays of coffee and sweets and misted glasses of ice-water. For the gentlemen there were ice-buckets with bottles for their refreshment as they continued their heated dispute over whether Roumania should enter the war. The ladies meanwhile talked about their ailments and recommended doctors and remedies. Elvira had seated herself beside Augusta Hagibei. Smiling suddenly at Ghighi she said:

" My dear, will you fetch me my shawl? "

Ghighi Duca jumped to his feet, very slender in the white trousers which he wore with a cummerbund of blue silk. He ran into the house and came back with a large shawl which he wrapped solicitously about Elvira's shoulders. Augusta glanced at them, not without malice, and remarked with a faint smile:

" You must take care, Elvira, or you'll make that boy lose his head. Didn't you see the way he put that shawl round you—he's like a young tom-cat! You'll have trouble with him if you don't look out. Unless, of course, you mean to be nice to him." She added the last words lightly and without emphasis, so that they would have meant little to a casual listener.

" Why, you're absurd! We're cousins after all," said Elvira. " Am I supposed to behave like Lot in the Bible? " And she quoted in French a verse of the Chevalier de Boufflers:

> *"Il but*
> *Il devint tendre,*
> *Et puis il fut*
> *Son gendre!"*

They both dissolved in laughter. Ghighi, who had returned to his chair, said with great politeness:

" Would you care to go for a row on the lake? "

They decided that they would, and the little group moved off down the length of carefully trimmed box hedge. Beyond the oak trees there was a large pond flanked by sedge and willow which the overflow from the Danube filled every spring. Dim, who had overheard the ladies' conversation, stayed seated at the side of Serban Romano, watching them as they vanished in the darkness, their wasp waists encased in high sashes, their hips swaying beneath wide, white summer skirts, one on either side of the slim form of Ghighi Duca. Serban, who was also gravely and intently watching, suddenly turned his big head with its bulging forehead towards Dim and said in the most matter-of-fact of voices, using a word of extreme indelicacy:

" You know what Ghighi does to Elvira? He —— her.'

" Are you crazy? " asked Dim in utter amazement. " Didn't you hear what Augusta just said to Elvira? "

Serban nodded wisely. " All the same, I've seen them."

" What do you mean? What did you see? " demanded Dim, his throat suddenly dry.

" I saw Ghighi and Elvira together in the woods," said Serban in the same calm voice.

" Well, go on—tell! How did you come to see them? What were they doing? "

Serban did not answer, and when Dimitri pressed him he merely said: " I tell you I saw them. What more do you want? "

" You're lying. I don't believe it. You've got to tell me what you saw."

But Serban would say no more, even when Dim offered him a ball and a book by Jules Verne.

" I've got plenty of those," he said.

" Were you by yourself? "

" No."

" Well, who was with you? "

" Two of the village boys. We hunt hares together. They've got dogs." Serban seemed to be becoming more communicative.

" I want to come with you. You've got to take me with you," said Dim eagerly.

" I can't," said Serban, shaking his head.

" Why can't you? You mean you don't want to? Do you want me to give you a punch on the nose? "

" If you do you'll get one back from Ghighi. He has boxing lessons." Serban paused for a moment and then said pacifically: " It's the other boys who wouldn't want you. They don't mind me because I'm little."

" Blasted peasants," growled Dim. " Blasted cheek! " His thoughts returned to the hazy vision in his mind, which he so longed to clarify. " Look, if you'll tell me what Ghighi and Elvira were doing I'll let you shoot with my rifle."

Serban was unimpressed. " Ghighi said I could have his ages ago. I can use it for target-practice any time I like."

Dim fell silent, trying to imagine what Serban had seen. The tension which so often visited his body had returned with a painful, unbearable intensity. He got up abruptly and said angrily to Serban:

"I don't give a damn what you do, and anyway you're just a dirty liar and nobody believes a word you say."

He ran off down one of the paths between the box hedges with a vague idea of catching up with his cousins. But he was brought to a stop, as he moved silently across a lawn, by the sound of two gentlemen strolling along a gravel path while they smoked their cigars. They were Monsieur Hagibei and Monsieur Romano, clad in straw hats, white jackets, black trousers and laced boots. Dim could clearly hear what they were saying.

"She's an astonishing woman," said Monsieur Hagibei. "Amazing. She had her son, Manuel, by old Lascari, the grandfather of my wife and Alexandrina."

"My dear fellow, it can't be true! You can't seriously mean it?" exclaimed Monsieur Romano, chuckling, but still trying to keep his dignity as a magistrate. However, astonishment was too much for him, and he went on: "It's inconceivable! Are you really sure?"

"Well, I wasn't hidden under the bed. I'm only telling you what people say. Anyway, Zoë is undoubtedly the daughter of Boniface Coziano and Lascar Lascari's the father of Madame Duca. The old lady always had a weakness for public figures."

"Then, if I understand you rightly, both her brothers-in-law . . . !" Monsieur Romano, quite forgetting his accustomed gravity, was convulsed with laughter.

"I tell you she's a most formidable woman. As for her other children, she had those by the late Walter Apostolesco. Afterwards, when he died, she travelled a lot abroad. At home she was a pattern of decorum—*mais elle rôtissait le balai à l'étranger*. You can see it even now, that gleam in her eye! The fire still burns, my dear chap, although she must be getting on for seventy."

"You don't really mean . . . ?"

"Oh no, I wouldn't go so far as to say that."

Dimitri moved away, afraid of being caught listening to a conversation which was certainly not intended for his ears. He was in a state of profound perturbation. Whom had they been talking about? Could it possibly be . . .? But there was no one else. It was she who had had all those children—Manuel, that is to say, his father; and then Aunt Olga and Aunt Zoë with . . .

He put a stop to his thoughts, feeling lost, a stranger even to himself. Ghighi, Elvira and Augusta, returning at this moment, did not notice him. In any case they seemed preoccupied. Dim, starting at the sound of their footsteps on the gravel, watched them as they hurried past. The two young women had picked up their skirts and were staring straight in front of them, neither speaking. Ghighi was grinning and trying to keep pace with them. All three went towards the terrace, and after a few moments Dim followed them. What had happened? What had they all been doing? He could not imagine. He had caught a glimpse of another puzzle which for the moment distracted his thoughts from himself.

3

Dim slept restlessly. He had absurd and shameful dreams, and then a sort of terror assailed him. He woke abruptly and looked about him, expecting to see the dormitory at school.

But no, he was at Dobrunu. The windows were opened wide on the tranquil night, and little Serban was asleep in the other bed. Dim got up, crossed the room barefoot in his long night-shirt, and poured himself a glass of water which he emptied at a gulp. His body seemed to be on fire, although his skin was cold. Serban was sleeping soundly, both hands beneath his right cheek. Dim went to the window and looked down over the deserted terrace, the wicker chairs, the lawn that seemed tinged with blue.

A sound of whispering caused him to lean further out. In a corner of the terrace two shadowy figures, intertwined until that moment, were moving apart. He heard a woman's voice say in a passionate murmur: " Let me go! Let me go! "

One of the shadows ran towards the house. It was Elvira, in a white bed-robe, her feet bare. She passed under the window with her head raised, her eyes half closed like those of a person lost in thought, and with a queer smile of satisfaction on her lips. She vanished through the french-window into the drawing-room. The other figure also left the terrace and disappeared round the end of the house. Dim stayed a little longer at the window, then returned to his bed and sat down. Had the other person been Ghighi? It must have been. What had been going on? How pretty she was! He let his head fall on the pillow and for a few moments lay quite still, but then the excitement returned. Not a hope of getting to sleep again. He tried counting to a hundred, but wild images were flooding through his mind before he had reached ten.

Time passed, he had no idea how long, and presently a pressing need got him out of bed again. Putting on his dressing-gown and slippers he left the room. A single lamp was burning at the far end of the passage, and suddenly his heart began to beat tumultuously. Out of the zone of shadow he saw, coming rapidly towards him, the figure of his cousin Augusta, clad in a flowing gown with a lace collar. She stopped as she drew near him, smiled in a feverish, embarrassed way, and said in a low voice:

" Why aren't you in bed? Can't you sleep either? I've been trying for hours. I've tried counting and deep breathing and not thinking of anything, but it's no use. It's so hot that I'm wondering if we shall be able to stand it here in Dobrunu. You're hot too, aren't you? But you're a man, you can go out for a walk if you like. It's different for me. A lady can't go walking through the fields in her nightdress! "

She laughed and went on talking in this fashion for some minutes, without drawing breath or saying anything that made sense. Dim stared at her face, so pale in the faint light, the sombre eyes, the mouth tense with the restraint she was putting on herself—for plainly the things she was saying had nothing to do with the things she was thinking and feeling at that moment. He did not clearly understand this; he knew only that something was happening. What did Augusta want? Where was she going? Perhaps she had left her room only for the most obvious of reasons. But suppose she were going to meet someone? . . .
" I'll watch her," he thought. He was in a state of delicious perturbation. She had said, " But you're a man," and it was true that he was a man! He stared at her slender neck, and the triangle

of skin exposed by the parted lace, so insistently that Augusta, without ceasing to talk, drew the robe more tightly over her bosom; and he said to himself, " Perhaps it was me she was looking for! " Of course this was nonsense, but still his feeling of dizzy exaltation was suddenly heightened by the memory of the glance she had given him at the dinner-table. Perhaps it was at that moment that she had had the idea of going in search of him. Perhaps that was why she had said, " You're a man "—to encourage him. Yes, to encourage him!

The more he considered this possibility, the more alarmed did he become. " I ought to prove I'm a man by suggesting that we go for a stroll in the garden, where it's cooler," he thought, and found to his dismay that he could not say a word. " I'll wait and perhaps she'll think of it herself." The moments passed, drowned in her babblings. Suddenly, with a sharp, false-sounding laugh, she bade him good night and turned back to the room she shared with Hagibei, at the dark end of the passage. Dim stayed motionless, silent and disconcerted, his eyes fixed on her broad, swaying hips as she departed. Finally he went meekly to his original destination, and then returned to his room and got back into bed. He would have liked to strangle himself, to beat his head against the wall. He bit his clenched fists, furious and despairing at having let slip that golden opportunity. It was so easy now to imagine himself making the proposal, cool and assured, while he offered Augusta his arm; and then the stroll in the garden and out into the fields; and then . . . The picture was wonderfully clear—up to a point . . . Dim groaned and lay panting on his back.

Not until dawn did he fall into a slumber peopled with monstrous dreams. It was midday when he awoke, still heavy with fatigue. Someone had let down the Venetian blind, and a golden, honey-coloured light poured through the slats. The air was filled with the scent of grass and hay. Inside the room the shadows had a russet tint, like a painting by an old master, and the amber-coloured wardrobe and chest of drawers shone mysteriously. Someone was talking outside the house. Dim, still only half awake, lay thinking of his cousins. One thing was certain, he must take Augusta for a walk one evening and do the thing that had so long obsessed him. And if she refused? Well . . . But he had no notion what would happen. There was nothing in his mind but emptiness, an abyss of shadow. " But I'm sure she wants to," he said despairingly to himself.

He got up, bathed his burning face, dressed and went down to the courtyard. He had decided to find Serban and try to make him tell what he had refused to divulge last night. On one side of the courtyard, beneath the glaring sun, stood the motor-cars of Aunt Olga, the Hagibeis and the Romanos, surrounded by a swarm of children. The heat was unbearable. Within the shade of the buildings prostrate dogs lay snapping at the flies, and the plastered wall of the stable was blinding in its brightness. A buzz of insects, bees, wasps and bumble-bees, came from the clusters of wistaria hanging from the eaves. Men were shouting in the distance, from the direction of the mill, and carts were creaking along the road.

Manuel Coziano, Dim's father, was a melancholy, yellow-faced man. That morning he was clad in riding-breeches, boots with spurs and a black alpaca jacket. Standing in the middle of the farmyard with his moustache drooping, a straw hat tilted over his nose, his hands behind his back, belly outthrust, shoulders rounded and chest sunken, he was gazing at a nanny-goat which a peasant held by its halter. Dim went up to them, adopting the formal and dignified manner proper to the owner's son. The peasant did not notice him. He was a sturdily built, red-cheeked man in his forties, and he had his fur cap on his head, having no doubt replaced it after greeting the boyar, his landlord. His feet were bare. His big, gnarled hand kept a firm grip on the halter, at which the goat was tugging.

" Why not buy her, master? " he was saying respectfully. " You bought Nicuta's heifer when she broke her leg, and Cumpanacu's goat when she went barren, and——'

Monsieur Coziano cut him short. " I'm always ready to buy any beast offered by the villagers for feeding the household. But I don't understand why you want to sell this one. What's wrong with her? Is she barren? "

" Why, no, sir, indeed not. You'll be quite safe with her. She'll give you kids and milk as well."

The peasant was gazing at Monsieur Coziano with a look of guileless sincerity, and he seemed to be speaking in good faith. But Dim realised that something was wrong. What the man said might be true, but had he answered the question? Apparently not.

Dim looked at the goat, which was white with a long, narrow muzzle and pink, damp nostrils. She stood chewing a wisp of grass and staring straight in front of her, without either raising her head to look at the two men or lowering it to the ground. Now and then she tugged at the halter, moving her feet sideways and causing her long coat to flutter like the folds of a dress.

" All right, so there's nothing the matter with her. Then why do you want to sell her? She has no disease, she hasn't broken any bones, she isn't barren——"

" Oh no, master, she isn't barren."

" Well, then, why? "

" Well, it's because—well, you see, sir, I need the money."

" Listen, Dobrica, don't waste my time in this heat. I'm ready to buy her from you, but you must tell me why you're so anxious to sell. I want to know the truth."

The man looked at Monsieur Coziano, then at the goat, and then said simply:

" If I kept her it would be for the sake of the milk."

After which he was silent. Coziano asked:

" Well? You've just told me she gives plenty of milk."

" Oh yes, sir, she does. But the trouble is, no one wants to drink it." And in a sudden burst of candour he went on: " It's been like that ever since I found her in the shed with Bizdic. Or, rather, Bizdic was in the shed with her, and he was . . . Well, sir, you know what I mean."

The goat continued impassively to chew the grass. Manuel Coziano sighed.

" All right, I'll buy her." After a further moment of silence he said in a pained voice: " So you won't drink her milk, Dobrica, but you don't mind selling her to the boyar, for him to drink it? "

A smile of subservience and gratification passed over the man's face.

" It's for you to decide what you'll do with her, master. I haven't said you should drink her milk."

" Very well," said Monsieur Coziano, sighing again. " Take her round to the kitchen and come and collect your money."

" Thank you, master." And Dobrica went off, tugging at the goat.

" Come in to luncheon,' said Monsieur Coziano to his son. " Where have you been all the morning? "

" In my room. I—I've been reading," said Dim.

" Can't you think of anything better to do when you're in the country—reading when you ought to be getting exercise out of doors? " grumbled his father, outwardly stern but in fact quite unconcerned. He went on to mutter, as though to himself: " Immoral brutes! These peasants are nothing but animals."

Dim followed him into the house. What the peasant had said had given him a very queer sensation, a sort of physical discomfort but so vague that he could not have described it.

He had no appetite and looked distastefully at the food. It was a country lunch, with tzouica (plum brandy), olives, white cheese, soup with meat-balls, grilled sterlet, mincemeat with cream and finally *baklavas* and *sarailie*, pastries with nuts and honey. But the cheese seemed to have a queer smell, the soup was too greasy and he could not touch even the fish when he saw the grease that exuded from it. The wineleaves enclosing the mince had a metallic taste, the *baklavas* weren't sweet enough. Dim strove to eat while he tried to catch the eyes of Elvira and Augusta; but Elvira did not once look towards his end of the table. Augusta, on the other hand, darted sharp, disquieted glances first at Ghighi, then at Dim and then again at Ghighi; after which she kept her eyes on her plate. Ghighi, who was talking loudly to Monsieur Romano, seemed not to have noticed. The gentlemen at the table were still vehemently debating the subject of war or peace. The morning papers had just arrived.

" The Germans used poison gas at Ypres a month ago," cried Monsieur Coziano, " but they still didn't bring it off."

" Yes, but, my dear fellow——" said Monsieur Hagibei.

" It's no use you talking. You bet me the Russians wouldn't capture Przemysl and you lost."

" Neither of you knows anything about it," said Michel Vorvoreano. " You're both civilians."

Dim's head felt hot and heavy. He'd have to go out that evening to get cool. He'd go for a walk with Augusta; he'd suggest it after dinner. 'I'll meet you under the oaks," or simply, " How about a stroll? " They would go off together, and as soon as they were alone . . .

He raised his eyes, to find that his grandmother was smiling at him, and at once lowered them. Grandmother! A formidable woman! She had had Father with old Coziano, Zoë with

Boniface, Olga with Lascar Lascari . . . Walter had died while he was her lover, and then, when she went abroad . . . In short, Grandmother had once been a woman and marvellous! She had been the mistress of countless men. Dim gazed at the old lady in fascination as she sat listening to Romano, and feeling his gaze upon her she turned to look at him and he bowed his head again.

After coffee and liqueurs, when the company were withdrawing for the siesta, Madame Cléopatre intercepted her grandson on his way to the door and said, reproachful but smiling:

" So now you're ignoring your granny! Why haven't you come to tell me all the things you've been doing at school and how you're getting on? Have you forgotten how you used to want me to come and say good night to you when you were little? I'd sit on the bed and we'd talk until you fell asleep. Don't you remember? Haven't you anything to say? "

" I remember," Dim stammered, and once again had a strange sense of dreaming.

" Come to my room in a quarter of an hour and you can tell me all about everything," said Cleopatra benevolently.

She went out and Dimitri gazed after her, noting that she still moved briskly, old though she was. A quarter of an hour later her maid came to fetch him.

" Master Dimitri, your grandmother's waiting for you."

Dim went along the passage, knocked and entered the room, passing behind the screen which masked the doorway. His grandmother was in bed. The blinds were half drawn, the room bathed in a dusk broken by streaks of light whose colour was like an infusion of camomile. The air smelt of lavender and patchouli. Cleopatra was in bed, with the sheets drawn up to her chin but with her arms outside. She was wearing a long-sleeved night-dress of fine lawn, embroidered with lace at the neck and wrists. She signed to Dim to sit down, and he looked shyly round for a chair.

" Here," she said, and drew back the coverlets a little at the edge of the bed.

Dim sat there and found that he was trembling, although he did not know why.

" Well, haven't you anything to tell me? " Cleopatra murmured.

He stammered something, scarcely knowing what he said. She took his hand.

" Lie down beside me," she said, gently tugging.

Still trembling he lay down. He saw his grandmother's grey hairs very close, the wrinkled face, the sagging cheeks and double chin, the withered neck and the avid dark eyes intently gazing at him. He laid his head on the big lace-embroidered pillow, very cool and pleasantly scented with patchouli, and closed his eyes. But the words which Cleopatra then whispered in his ear, the sudden, swift gesture she allowed herself, caused him to start up. In horror he made a dash for the door, opened it and ran out into the corridor. Regaining his bedroom he stayed motionless. What was happening to him? Where was he? What was wrong? He let himself fall on the bed, fully dressed, with his teeth chattering and shivers passing through his body. Presently he pulled the bedclothes over him, right over his head, and lay shaking with fever.

Late that evening Madame Coziano fetched her husband to his room. The night was clear and hot, but the windows had been closed and the curtains drawn. A lamp was burning on the table, the wick turned low.

" I've put Serban on a couch in Alexandrina's and Romano's room," Madame Coziano said. " I'm afraid it's scarlet fever. There are red spots on his chest and the palms of his hands. And this very high temperature—it must be scarlet fever. The poor child, listen to him! "

With his head turned towards the wall, his face crimson and his eyes glazed, Dim was muttering to himself. For a moment his parents stood listening, and then Madame Coziano exclaimed in utter dismay:

" Manuel, how dreadful! Where did he learn all those horrors? At his age!'

Monsieur Coziano was frowning.

" How should I know where he learnt them? From the village boys, probably. They're all disgustingly immoral. Country life certainly doesn't seem to do him any good.'

" Your mother says she'd like to take him to France next year," said Madame Coziano, still gazing in consternation at her son. Her husband said reflectively:

" I don't know. It might be the best thing. We'll see."

When he recovered Dim seemed to have undergone a transformation. He had become morose and taciturn, secretive and unsociable. " That sort of illness, at the time of puberty, may have far-reaching effects," said the doctor, who recommended a visit to the mountains. If they were proposing to send the boy abroad the best place would be a boarding-school in Switzerland. They asked Dim's grandmother what she thought.

" That's for you to decide. You produced the boy and it's your business to look after him," said Cleopatra, very huffy indeed.

II

Duty

I

Olga, the sister of Manuel Coziano, had married a Monsieur Duca, descended from Gheorghe Duca, the reigning prince of Moldavia at the end of the seventeenth century. This Monsieur Duca was a member of the Conservative Party who had on several occasions held a seat in the Chamber of Deputies and later in the Senate. His marriage to Olga Coziano had led to his becoming a political friend of Boniface Coziano; he was also a friend, and in certain business matters an associate, of Serban Lascari, Olga's cousin, and of Sufana, an oil-magnate married to another of Olga's cousins.

Monsieur Duca's younger brother had passed through the Cadet Officers' College at Potsdam and the Prussian Military Academy. By 1916 he was a colonel in the Roumanian Army. In October or November of that year he was appointed to the command of a brigade composed of a regiment of Frontier Guards and two infantry regiments. His task was to defend the line of mountains around Oituz in the Vrancea region against the advance of the Bavarian alpine troops.

Directly enemy forces began to infiltrate behind the Roumanian lines, however, the three regiments were ordered by brigade headquarters to retreat, which they did from eight o'clock in the evening throughout an autumn night during which an icy rain fell incessantly until it turned into snow. The snow stopped and the rain began again. The heavy downpour pierced the soldiers' capes, dripped from the black and rotting foliage of the forest, streamed down the gnarled trunks of trees and lay in deep puddles and quagmires on the ground.

There was no sound of rifle- or artillery-fire to be heard, nothing but the splash of water and the sighing of the wind in the beeches, and, on the narrow road, the rattle of arms and equipment, and of machine-guns borne on the backs of small mountain horses, accompanied the tread of marching feet. Now and then a man slipped and fell cursing in the mud.

Lieutenant Laurent Sterie, commanding a company of the Frontier Guards, had marched for four hours in the darkness without any sense of fatigue, but with a sense of angry misgiving. Why were they retreating when it seemed to be quite unnecessary? At his right hand was a steep slope flanking the road with a dark floor of rotting leaves above it, and higher still the huge shadow of the forest, its branches stirring now and then with creaks and groans. On his left a sheer descent vanished in the swirling of a grey mist. The ravine was deep at this point, its sides dotted with occasional conifers but more often rocky and bare, with here and there the stark wall of a precipice. There was nothing to be seen ahead, but voices could be heard and the tired footsteps of men and horses plodding steadily on. Sterie could only make out the forms of two or three soldiers, the rest being lost in darkness. " Why did we have to pull out so quickly? " he wondered, and found no answer to the question, either in terms of human or military necessity.

There was a sound of stifled exclamations followed by a brief cry. Someone shouted something—" Watch out! " it sounded like. The murmurs in front grew more audible as the men came to a halt. Sterie was forced to stop, pressed against the haversack of the man in front of him. The soldiers turned to look at one another, their movements rendered sluggish by the kit they carried, rations, ammunition, blankets, waterproof sheet; they appeared monstrous in the darkness, hump-backed and deformed.

" What happened? " asked Sterie.

" Someone's gone over the edge, " one of the men said.

" Who was it? "

Voices ran along the column, and then a man near Sterie said clearly: " Two soldiers have fallen into the ravine, and a horse with two machine-guns."

Someone shouted, " Forward! " and gradually the column broke into movement again, spreading out and becoming less dense as it did so. Sterie moved on with the rest. The rain, running down his neck, was seeping in under the collar of his tunic. He heard a soldier say:

" That must be where they went over."

" No, chum, we've passed it. It was further back, by that pine,"
answered a voice with a Moldavian accent.

" Why are we retreating? " Sterie continued to wonder. " We
aren't beaten, we haven't fired a dozen rounds and we're ordered
to pull out. Why? Has something gone wrong? " Nothing of
note had been reported. A few Bavarian patrols had managed to
sneak over the mountain-crest into the brigade's combat area, but
this, surely, was no reason for a retreat. " The old man must have
his reasons," reflected Sterie. There was no sense in getting
worked up and harassing oneself with questions. The old man
was a good soldier, he knew what he was doing. . . .

Someone caught up with Sterie, moving with difficulty along
the narrow track. Glancing round he saw an officer's forage-
cap.

" What are we up to, sir? "

It was the voice of his second lieutenant, Petru Dumitriu.

" My dear Petrica," Sterie said, using the diminutive form of
the Christian name, " you can see for yourself. We're effecting
a tactical withdrawal."

The boy stumbled. There was no room at this point for two
men to walk abreast. He had to keep behind Sterie, at his right
shoulder, hugging the slope.

" The men are fed up. Why do we have to retreat? "

" The old man knows what he's doing."

" Perhaps he does, but why did he visit the trenches and talk
to the soldiers and all the rest of it if he was simply going to order
a withdrawal? " Dumitriu spoke in a mournful, obstinate voice.
" He made himself popular with the men but now they've no
more use for him. They're angry and grousing like hell."

" Then why aren't you doing something about it? " demanded
Sterie. " If they're getting demoralised why aren't you trying to
steady them? "

" I know my duty, sir," said Dumitriu coldly.

The note of youthful dignity did not cause Sterie to smile. He
pictured young Dumitriu plodding heavily and sullen-faced behind him, his monocle in his breast pocket, soaked to the skin
and spattered from head to foot with mud. The boy came from
the Schwering Cadet School and had served a year with a Pomeranian grenadier regiment. He was a great admirer of Colonel
Duca, the brigade commander, and he would not have spoken as

he had if the men were not in a particularly bad frame of mind.
" But still the C.O. must know what he's doing," Sterie thought.
" There's no better soldier in the Army." Aloud he said: " Listen,
Petrica."

" Yes, sir? "

" You talk about knowing your duty. Our duty is to obey
orders, even when we don't altogether understand them."

Dumitriu slipped again and uttered a grunt; he had fallen
against the rocky wall to the right of the path. He picked himself
up and, still following Sterie, wiped his muddy hand on his
greatcoat.

" At your orders, Lieutenant," he said mechanically.

2

The day broke gloomily with wet flakes of snow falling from a
sullen sky and long trails of grey mist drifting through the valleys,
obscuring the pines. The column of soldiers had come to a halt
on a twisting path. The men were having a meal. Some lay
sleeping in the mud, their rifles clasped to their chests. This was
the rearguard of the brigade; there were two more companies
behind them and then nothing except the mountains and forests
where the enemy was concealed. A party of officers were gathered
on a patch of high ground. They were young and lean, their faces
adorned with the clipped moustaches which were fashionable at
the time, their faces pale with weariness, their high boots and
uniforms smothered in mud and stiffened by the cold. Sterie
was among them. He had a small, hard, bony face with a prominent jaw and cheekbones. He was unshaven and it was a long
time since he had had his hair cut, so that brown wisps escaped
from under his cap. Rubbing his chilled hands together he
stood listening to the stocky lieutenant-colonel, whose face was
flushed with rage.

" Well, gentlemen, now you know. Any officer who lets me

down like this again will be relieved of his command. It's perfectly damnable! No action, not a shot fired, and yet you've contrived to lose at least four machine-guns! Has anyone anything to say?"

The young men were silent, standing stiffly erect as his eyes rested upon them. Sterie blew on his hands to warm them, feeling very depressed. He felt that he wouldn't much care if he were relieved of his command, although it was not he who had lost the machine-guns. The battalion commander went on harshly:

" And I don't want to hear any more excuses about slippery ground and so forth. I don't give a damn. In my battalion we only lose weapons in action, and the men serving them die at their posts. Is that understood?"

" Yes, sir."

The colonel looked disapprovingly at the group and went off followed by the three officers who had accompanied him.

" He's ready to burst into flames, old man Fanica," laughed a subaltern wearing an elegantly cut uniform with red leather gaiters above English hand-made boots. He was very young, with soft, round cheeks.

" It's no time for joking, Apostolesco," Sterie said.

Another subaltern, tall and bony, with a long, curved nose, said as though he had not heard:

" He's furious, all right, but it's because of the withdrawal, not because of the machine-guns. Why the hell should we be retreating? If they'd come down on us last night, while we were on the march, we'd have been helpless. What do you think of it, Laurent? Is this what you'd call Prussian tactics?"

Lieutenant Sterie flushed and replied: " You can't judge an operation until it's completed."

They looked round. Another group of officers was moving up the flank of the hill preceded by a full colonel who bore himself rigidly, carrying a pair of Swedish leather gloves in his left hand, and gesticulating vigorously as he walked. The party of subalterns watched him with unfriendly eyes. They had little liking for the regimental commander, Colonel Vasilache, a staff-officer in the line for the first time who had never yet heard a shot fired in anger. They greatly preferred their battalion commander, Lieut.-Colonel Fanica Visoran, rugged and quick-tempered though he was. Vasilache climbed higher up the hill accompanied by a subaltern carrying his map-case, with several staff-officers following behind. They paused when they reached a plateau of level ground.

Second Lieutenant Apostolesco uttered a sigh.

" What we all need at this moment is a hot bath, a dozen oysters, a bottle of bubbly and a good cigar."

Sterie laughed without being amused, and said, glancing at Apostolesco with a faint envy:

" You blasted civilian! We're fighting a war."

" More's the pity," murmured Apostolesco.

" What do you do in civil life? " asked the long-nosed officer glumly.

" He doesn't do a damned thing," said Sterie. " He's a land-owner, an aristo. He just has a nice cushy time."

Apostolesco laughed, half apologetically.

" No, really—I'm an artist, a painter. That's to say, I hope to be. I'm still studying."

Another young man, with slightly protruding, bright eyes, said:

" I wish you'd paint me a nude to pin up in my dug-out."

" I will if you like," said young Apostolesco.

" She must have black stockings. Absolutely stark except for black stockings and red boots! "

" You seem to worry a lot about girls," said the young man with the long nose, chuckling over this vision.

" If you'd come from Paris, like me, you'd know how much you can miss them," said Apostolesco.

He went on to describe in detail certain brothels he had visited, while the others listened, sniggering and nudging. Sterie turned away in disgust and encountered the gaze of a slender, fair-haired youth with wide, reddened ears and a freckled face.

" What do you think of it, Friedman? "

" Think of what? "

" This retreat," said Sterie, knowing that Friedman was no better informed than himself.

" Perhaps they've got the wind up at brigade."

" Who? The colonel? Don't be an ass! "

" I don't know who, but the whole gang are pretty shaky, if you ask me," said Friedman. " Surely you've noticed. Have a fag? "

" No, thanks, I'm sick of them."

At this moment there was a strident, whistling sound. Something struck the earth with a dull thud, followed by a sharp explosion. The young men started and looked up to the treeless crest of the hill above them, where the regimental commander and his staff were walking up and down. They saw a round, yellow-grey cloud arising at the far end of the plateau. An instant later there was a second explosion, lower down the slope, this time accompanied by a blinding flash of yellow light which turned to red.

From the crest of the hill a shrill cry reached them, almost like that of a woman:

" Oh my God! Oh God! "

A third shell burst in the woods, and there was a crackling sound as broken branches were flung against the surrounding trees. Some artillery observer must have spotted the party of officers on the crest, and an enemy battery was getting the range.

" My God! My God! " cried the same shrill voice. It was that of Colonel Vasilache. His face distorted with terror, he came running down the slope, arms outspread and the tails of his greatcoat flapping behind him. A few more shells burst at irregular intervals on the hillside or amid the trees. The officers of the colonel's escort scattered without undue haste and proceeded to descend the slope, but at a walking pace. Colonel Vasilache, still running, passed close by Sterie and Friedman, sprang on to the road, crossed over and hurried on down, leaping like a hare. The subaltern who was acting as his aide-de-camp hurried after him with the map-case clasped to his breast, crying in a furious, anguished and beseeching voice:

" Colonel! Colonel! Colonel! "

" My God, my God! " the colonel's voice was lost in the distance.

Sterie had doubled up with laughter, but he recovered quickly, becoming more glum and distressed than ever. Friedman muttered under his breath.

" Christ, what an army! That's supposed to be an officer—a colonel! By God, I hope he cops it! "

Orders were now being shouted up and down the column. The soldiers resumed their packs, and picking up their rifles broke into movement, jostling one another and glancing with startled eyes in the direction of their regimental commander, down in the valley, who was crouched with his head in his hands and his cap on the ground beside him. His aide-de-camp was tugging at his arm.

3

The small mountain-ponies, laden with machine-guns, sacks and ammunition-boxes, plodded on with lowered heads, their nostrils steaming. The marching men, red-eyed from lack of sleep, were nearly as heavily loaded. Sterie marched at the head of his company with Second Lieutenant Dumitriu behind him. He was not sleepy but in a state of feverish excitement, his nerves unpleasantly taut. Suddenly he saw the figure he had been looking for standing beside Colonel Visoran and two or three younger officers. There he was, with his pepper-and-salt moustache, his hard face, the flat cheeks seamed with little red veins, his eyes deep-set under Greek warrior-eyebrows and his high beak of a nose.

Colonel Duca was dressed immaculately in a clean, newly pressed uniform and a long greatcoat. He carried no weapon, no revolver belt, but held in his gloved hand a green twig he had broken off in the woods. Friedman left the group surrounding him and came towards Sterie.

" Laurent, you're to halt your company. The colonel wants to speak to you."

Friedman's eyes were shining, and Sterie felt suddenly happy. " Thank God the old man's come at last," he thought. " He'll explain everything."

He passed the order to Dumitriu and Apostolesco and hurried off with Friedman, straightening his belt as he went.

" What does he say? " he asked. " Is he in good form? "

" Calm as ever—we might be on manœuvres," said Friedman with a chuckle.

" Well, naturally. That's the Prussian training."

Sterie had begun to feel positively light-hearted, confident that from now on all would be well. Colonel Duca formally returned his salute and went on talking without raising his voice:

" Therefore, gentlemen, we must take care not to lay ourselves open to a flank attack delivered in wooded country. That is why it has been necessary for this brigade to withdraw to new and carefully studied positions. But the enemy, who is a good soldier and knows his business, will do everything he can to prevent us getting dug in. He'll try to take us in the rear while we're on the move, he'll infiltrate over the ridges, as he has been doing already, and he may try other things which we can't foresee. The essential thing is to cover our rear. A company of Frontier Guards and one of Fusiliers from the Sixteenth Regiment will occupy this position where we are now and will hold it until further orders, without in any circumstances abandoning it. It is a post of honour, and the units most worthy to fill it "—here Colonel Duca gazed about him with a heart-warming smile, filled with benevolence— " are, in my opinion, Lieutenant Sterie's company, which will be reinforced with a machine-gun section under Lieutenant Friedman, and the company of Fusiliers commanded by Lieutenant Stahl. Sterie will be in command of the whole contingent."

Sterie drew himself erect, exclaiming, with his hand to his peak and his face radiant:

" At your orders, Colonel! We'll hold it to the death! "

Colonel Duca smiled and led him aside.

" You quite understand, don't you? You must hang on at all costs. As I said, you will be in the post of honour "—he paused for a moment, looking Sterie in the eyes—" you will have an heroic task to perform. You quite understand? "

" I do, sir! " replied Sterie, trembling with fervour.

" Your force will be disposed as follows," said Duca, and pointing over the ground he gave detailed instructions. Finally he took Sterie's hand and shook it warmly, gazing gravely at him. " I wish you all success. You will report to me tomorrow."

He went off holding himself very erect, stiff-necked, walking with a brisk, supple stride. Visoran, sombre-faced, followed him without saying a word. . . .

Sterie still had not recovered his calm when, an hour later, he settled down in a clump of pines overlooking the road. In a state of intense nervous excitement he had passed on the brigade commander's orders and seen to the disposal of his force. Now he stood smoking a cigarette near the pit where Friedman's machine-gun was installed. The gun-crew of two soldiers were also smoking, lying back in their elbows on a bed of rotting leaves.

" So he hypnotised you too," said Friedman with a chuckle.

Sterie made no reply. He did not like to hear the C.O. talked of in this fashion. But Friedman went on flippantly:

" He said to me "—here he imitated Colonel Duca's aristo-cratic, rather harsh, voice—" ' Lieutenant, you belong to another creed, but you have always shown yourself to be a good Rouman-ian citizen and a worthy officer. Moroever you come of an ex-cellent family. I am sure you will do honour to the name you bear, to your uniform and to the Cross of Michael the Brave '! " He burst out laughing.

" I don't see what's funny in that," said Sterie coldly.

" He's an old tartar, my uncle. He treated me as though I wasn't there," said Gogu Apostolesco.

" What uncle ? " Sterie asked.

" Why, the C.O.—Duca," said Gogu Apostolesco simply, and to the astonishment of his hearers explained that they were related. There were jesting comments, but Sterie merely said:

" He's a fine soldier."

The others said nothing. They were over-wrought and uneasy, suffering from hunger and lack of sleep.

" They still haven't brought those oysters," said Apostolesco. " Wouldn't it be wonderful if we could stop in at Capsa's ? "

" My dear Gogu, don't be a bore," said Lieutenant Stahl.

Sterie looked up inquiringly at this and he explained:

" Gogu and I are old friends. We've been together both in Bucarest and in Paris."

" So you're another of those perishing boyars ? " said Sterie, trying to speak lightly.

Stahl shook his head.

" Not me. I'm just a reporter at the Chamber of Deputies."

" I see," said Sterie, and getting up he strolled off with Second Lieutenant Dumitriu.

Stahl murmured confidentially to Apostolesco: " What about that chap Sterie ? He seems full of military zeal."

" And how! He wants to be a hero. We call him the Man of Duty."

" Army family? "

" Yes—from Pitesti, I think. His grandfather kept a draper's shop, but he turned all his sons into officers. *Des vaches, quoi! Des culottes de peau, des traîneurs de sabres, des abrutis, mon petit!* Look out—he's coming back."

" Apart from which I quite like him," muttered Stahl. " He's quite good-looking—a bit like an actor, but——"

" Anything going on, sir? " asked Apostolesco, speaking loudly to shut him up. " Any sign of the enemy? "

" Not yet. We've simply got to wait. No one's to open fire until they start shooting."

Sterie passed on.

" Now what's he up to—inspecting the positions all over again? " Friedman sat down beside the brown-painted heavy machine-gun. He turned to Stahl and said, laughing: " You heard? We're not to shoot until we hear the pig yelling because we've pulled his tail."

Stahl's expression was one of acute disquiet. His face was pale and his red moustache damp with sweat.

" I'm not going to shoot, anyway," he said in an ill-assured voice.

" What? " exclaimed the others in stupefaction.

" I mean it. I shan't shoot. I can't shoot at a human being. I've shot wounded horses in Transylvania, and I can still picture them."

" For God's sake! " said Apostolesco. " What will you do when we attack? "

" Advance and shout ' Come on, boys! ' at the top of my voice, and that's all," said Stahl with a pallid smile.

The others exchanged glances and Friedman said:

" Listen. You can do what you like, but you'd better not tell Sterie. He'd be quite capable of having you court-martialled."

" Oh, I'll keep quiet. Got a cigarette, Gogu? "

Stahl went off, puffing a cloud of smoke.

" He's mad," said Friedman. " But he's not a bad chap."

" You've never met him in civil life—at Capsa's, for instance. He's tired now. But he's a chap who knows how to live. When he's in form he's wonderful company. Honestly, old boy—I'm sorry; I suppose I ought to say ' sir,' seeing you're my superior officer."

" You can call me ' old boy ' if you like," said Friedman with a faint smile. " While we're here, that is. But if we come out alive you'll find that I'm a stickler for regulations."

Gogu Apostolesco reflected that this was pretty rich, coming from a Jew; but he said no more, for at this moment they heard a distant rifle-shot followed by a flurry of firing.

Gogu lost all sense of time. Half an hour or an hour later he lay in the shelter of a pine-tree listening to the bullets whistling above his head. Now and then there was a thud as one hit a tree-trunk, and occasionally pine-cones and twigs came showering down, causing him to start and tremble while a sweat of terror ran into his eyes and down his spine. He was looking in vain for something to shoot at. In front of him there was nothing but the empty, overgrown valley with the woods beyond, and except for the uninterrupted stream of bullets he might have supposed the whole landscape to be deserted. He had thought several times that he detected a movement and had fired instantly, but he was not sure if he had really seen anything. Straining his eyes he fired a series of random bullets into the undergrowth. How much longer were they to stop here? What were they supposed to be doing? Exploring his ammunition-pouches he found that he had only two rounds left. He looked round and saw amid broken pine-branches, bracken and tree-stumps, the legs of the soldier on his right, the rest of his body hidden by a small hillock. Then on his left he saw two soldiers with big moustaches and drawn, haggard faces making for the crest of the hill, their shoulders hunched amid the ferns. He raised himself on his elbow and shouted:

" You there, what are you doing? "

The men glanced round and then scrambled on more hurriedly, pausing occasionally in the shelter of a tree-trunk. They vanished suddenly from his sight, and Gogu lay flat again. What the devil were they up to? Were they bolting? He suddenly realised that his teeth were chattering with the cold.

Friedman crouched smoking, while his hands trembled slightly. Despite the shooting that was going on his machine-gun was silent. He was awaiting the order to fire, or, failing an order, a sight of the enemy. But the enemy was slow in showing himself, evidently because he was using the undergrowth to get round their flank. Shots sounded in the very heart of the forest, high above him. If they were Bavarian mountain troops they were no doubt following their usual tactic of creeping along the crests of the hills to attack flanks and rear. Good soldiers, as Duca had said. Friedman glanced over his shoulder at the vast, echoing woods. That was the way they might come. And if they did? He looked round for another place where, at a pinch, he might install his gun, and as he did so he saw three soldiers, grey-haired infantry-men, sneaking towards the rear.

" Hey—halt! " he shouted in a clear, high-pitched voice that was almost a squeak.

The men did not even look round. Running with difficulty, they continued to struggle up towards the crest. Friedman was overtaken with fury. Seizing the machine-gun he swung it round, pointing it towards the fugitives.

" Halt or I fire! " he shouted. " Lie down! "

The three men vanished amid the ferns.

" Stand up! " bellowed Friedman, and they rose and stood rigidly to attention.

" Come over here—at the double! "

The men arrived panting and flung themselves into his gun-pit.

" What's the matter with you men? Why are you running away? "

They were pale and exhausted, their nerve shattered.

" No more ammunition, sir, " one of them said, and they showed their empty pouches.

" Didn't you ask your officer for more? "

" There's none left. He could only let us have another eighteen rounds each."

" And you shot them off blind, you bloody fools! "

What was one to do with these fifty-year-old militia men commanded by officers who couldn't bear to shoot at a living creature? And not enough ammunition, on top of everything! Friedman felt sorry for the shivering elderly wretches, but duty was duty.

" Go back to your posts at the double, and try to get more ammunition from the men who still have some. At the double—march! "

He watched them as they set off under cover of the trees. The last of the three was using some skill, darting from one tree to the next. But midway between two tree-trunks he stayed sud-

denly motionless with his arms clasped to his stomach, and then
fell on his side. His legs moved convulsively. He tried to crawl
forward on hands and knees, but his big army boots, scuffling
the ground, moved more and more weakly. Finally he lay still.
Friedman felt a lump rise in his throat and sweat break out all
over his body. He could have wept for terror and despair. " Oh
God, oh God! " he moaned. He flung himself upon the machine-
gun and began to fire at the figures he could now see on the other
side of the valley. After expending half a belt of ammunition he
drew a deep breath, feeling calmer. He fired a few shots into each
clump of bushes, aiming with care.

Sterie was not firing. When the fusillade had begun he had
shouted at the top of his voice:

" Wait for it! Don't shoot yet! "

But the firing had spread through both companies so that in
the clatter his voice could not be heard. He ground his teeth.
What did they think they were shooting at? Where was the
enemy and what was he doing? Sterie had no notion: he could
see nothing. He had sent out scouts on either flank, half of whom
had not returned. The rest had reported that there was nothing
to be seen but that they had heard firing in the woods beyond the
left flank, and down below in the valley, behind the reservists' right
flank. He could not stay there doing nothing. His orders were to
hold the position. But how was it to be done in his present posture,
with both flanks exposed?

He started up quivering as a machine-gun let loose a long
burst of fire that seemed as though it would never end. It must
be Friedman. He must have used up half a belt, but what was he
firing at? Sterie set off at a run, without attempting to keep his
head down. He saw the snipers of his company turn and look at
him and shouted:

" That's it, lads, keep it up! Aim carefully. That's the way! "

Realising that he must not run for fear of panicking the men,
he restrained himself with an effort and fell into a quick walk.
Nevertheless he was breathless when he reached the pit where
for the past two minutes Friedman had been firing short bursts.
The two men of the gun-crew, seeing him upright, cried in
alarm:

" Get down, sir! Get down! "

Friedman also looked round, his face pale, seeming at first not

to recognise his commanding officer. When he saw that it was
Sterie he turned very red.

" Why are you firing? "

" I'm trying—I'm trying to get their snipers," said Friedman
uncertainly.

" What snipers? Where can you see any? " shouted Sterie.

They were interrupted at this moment by the arrival of Stahl,
pale and sweating, who came running through the trees and
finally crouched on the ground behind one. Seeing Sterie he
made a dive for the machine-gun pit. He was in a state of such
agitation that he could only stammer.

" Well, what is it? " demanded Sterie.

Bullets were whistling all round them, cutting small branches
off trees or splintering the rocks.

" My men are deserting! " gasped Stahl. " They've no more
ammunition and they're clearing out."

" Then shoot them! " cried Sterie, getting his revolver out of
its holster.

Stahl's face turned grey. Sterie started to move towards the
right flank. Stahl followed him and gripped him by the arm.

" Sir—— "

Sterie glared at him in a fury.

" Let go my arm or I'll shoot. We'll talk about this later. You
call yourself an officer—my God! "

Stahl was in utter despair, wondering what he would do if
Sterie shot one of the men, and knowing in his heart that he would
shoot Sterie in his turn. He followed him unseeingly staring at
the locks of over-long hair that emerged from beneath his cap.

There was not a man to be seen, nothing but two dead bodies
and a litter of empty cartridge-cases scattered over the pine-
needles. The enemy fire seemed to have died down at that point.
It sounded now in their rear, deep in the forest.

" They're all gone," said Lieutenant Stahl.

Sterie turned furiously upon him.

" And you're supposed to be an officer! You ought to be shot
to set an example! " he said in disgust.

Without lowering his head he went back to where the machine-
gun was still firing short, occasional bursts. He found Second
Lieutenant Dumitriu standing near it and Second Lieutenant
Apostolesco sprawled on his stomach beside Friedman.

" They've begun to show themselves down there," said Friedman. " They haven't spotted me yet but they're shooting in our direction. This chap's been wounded."

One member of the gun-crew was seated on the ground gripping his arm tightly near the wrist, with blood spurting between his fingers, while the other made a touniquet with a strip torn from an army shirt.

" Pull it tight! Blasted, mucking wound—pull it tight for God's sake! " the wounded man grunted.

" They're round behind our left flank, sir," said Dumitriu. He was scowling with the effort to control his nerves, and the struggle made him sound aggressive.

Sterie looked at the others. They were all waiting for him to speak, to order a withdrawal—after he had been ordered to hold the position at all costs. He said loudly: " We're staying here! "

He went on more calmly: " Dumitriu, you will call in the men on your left flank and bring them round to meet the enemy in our rear. Apostolesco, you'll move over to the right wing to occupy the positions deserted by the heroes under this gentleman's command." He glanced contemptuously at Stahl who, crimson-faced, was standing between two pines smoking a cigarette. None of them seemed to notice the tone of his last words. Friedman cried:

" What sort of an idea's that, to keep us here with both flanks exposed! We shall all be killed or captured. Or, rather, you'll be captured, because I shall be the first one to come under fire and I don't propose to stay here twiddling my thumbs! "

" We're only supposed to stay as long as we can defend the position, sir," said Apostolesco. " Well, we can't defend it any longer."

Sterie looked desperately about him.

" No! " he cried. " Our orders are to stay! "

Stahl uttered a sudden groan and collapsed on to a heap of pine-needles. He sat staring at his right foot and took it in both hands as though he were lifting some very weighty object. They saw that a hole had appeared in his boot, a tear some two or three inches long, and almost instantly blood began to pour over the muddied leather. They ran to him and helped him under cover. Friedman fired a burst into the undergrowth directly in front of them. With a metallic clang, vibrant and sonorous, a bullet flattened itself against the inside of the metal protective screen of the machine-gun, leaving a greyish-white scar where the paint had been flaked off.

" Well, what about it, Sterie," said Friedman in an authoritative voice. " What are the orders? For God's sake stop playing the fool. We can't go on like this."

Sterie stammered unwillingly:

" All right. We'd better go."

They jumped out of the pit, pulling the machine-gun carriage and carrying the ammunition-cases. The unwounded soldier and Apostolesco sat Stahl on a rifle and he put his arms round their necks. They followed the only line of retreat, through the forest. Friedman gave a last glance at the dead body of the reservist lying between the third and fourth pine-tree on the right; then, grunting, he dragged the machine-gun up towards the crest of the hill.

4

On the following day the brigade continued its withdrawal, and on the two subsequent days. Thus the mountains were abandoned. On the fifth day they halted on the wooded hills in the region of Putna, and Lieutenant Sterie's company dug trenches and dugouts behind a big forest of beeches. Then they received orders to counter-attack.

Sterie lay waiting on the cold ground at the edge of a trench. He had not seen Colonel Duca again, but he had not ceased to think of him. Women did not interest him, or at least there was no one particular woman he thought of. Nor did he often think of his parents or his brothers. Since he had entered Military High School at the age of twelve and gone on to Officers' College, making a period of ten years, to which had to be added the four years since he had joined the Army—in all these fourteen years he had only seen his family during school holidays or on his short army leaves.

So it was of Colonel Duca that he was thinking at that moment.
From the day Duca had taken command of the brigade of Frontier
Guards and carried out his first inspections, at the Cotroceni
Barracks and on parade-grounds and training fields near Bucarest;
above all from the day when he had delivered his first lecture to
his officers, in front of a blackboard and a staff-map, Sterie had
considered him the finest soldier he had ever met. The tall boyar
of princely descent was more soldierly and more Prussian than
the old King himself, who one day, when he was inspecting officer-
cadets on the rifle-range, had bent down his pale, thin face to see
how far Cadet Laurent Sterie had raised the backsight of his rifle.

Sterie lay on his stomach with his pocket-watch on the ground
beside him. Three minutes to go. After retreating for a week
they were now to launch a counter-attack over the ground they
had abandoned, where the enemy, under cover of the forest,
could observe every move they made. Why had they not dug in
with the forest at their back? Why had they come so far? An
occasional rifle-shot was to be heard, like the crack of the trans-
port-drivers' whips, and from somewhere on their right came a
dull rumble of gun-fire. The ground was frozen. It was a winter's
morning, dark and lowering. Looking along the trench to the
point where it turned, Sterie could see the backs of men wearing
dark green capes. Second Lieutenant Dumitriu came towards
him with his head down, keeping a hand on the walls of the
trench, or on the men's shoulders, to prevent himself from
stumbling. He was flushed and out of breath.

" What is it, Petrica? "

" We're going to have a job getting through all these saplings,
sir. It's not very good country," said Dumitriu, putting his
monocle in his eye.

" Well? " said Sterie, glumly smiling.

" I can let you have a man to maintain contact, I'll give you
Mihalache."

" Fine. Get back to your post and send him along. There's
only two minutes to go."

" At your orders, Lieutenant."

But Dumitriu stayed where he was, his eyes grave, his hand
raised in a salute. For an instant Sterie did not understand what
he wanted. Then he held out his hand.

" Good luck, Petrica. See you when it's over."

The boy hurried off, lurching between the walls of the trench and the bodies of the soldiers pressed against the parapet, and putting his monocle back in his pocket as he ran. Sterie smiled, thinking that he might have said to him, " You have a task of honour to perform " (and here he should have looked him hard in the eyes), " an heroic mission! " And then he was startled at the discovery that he was jesting over serious matters. He was scarcely in his normal frame of mind!

Boom! An artillery salvo thundered from the rear. The shells sped droning overhead, very high, and burst in the forest. Columns of smoke rose between the trees, and branches were flung into the air. A second salvo, also from behind the Roumanian line, was followed by others in an unbroken series. Sterie felt the pit of his stomach quiver with the trembling of the earth as the shells landed. " Well anyway, the gunners are paving the way a bit better this time," he thought with a gloomy satisfaction. For the first time he asked himself, " Supposing I'm killed? Suppose by midday I'm dead! " *Boom—boom—boom—boom.* . . . " But I'll come through, I know I will. Anyway, no point in worrying about it now. One has to do one's duty. That's my job—to die for others, to defend them at the risk of my life." The skin on his scalp seemed to have gone quite dry, and his face was burning, especially his forehead and the wings of his nose. His palms were moist with sweat, and that was bad: he needed to be able to keep a good grip on his revolver. Sterie wiped his hands on a fold of his cape. He had repeated this action perhaps twenty times when the barrage abruptly ceased. Coming simultaneously from three different points the strident note of bugles sounded the attack. Sterie jumped on the parapet, pulled out his revolver and looked round. A long line of soldiers, rifle in hand, were scrambling out of the trenches yelling at the top of their voices. Sterie yelled with them until they had entered the wood, after which there was nothing to be heard but the crackling of timber and stifled cries.

He pressed forward, stumbling over the trunks of fallen trees while small, prickly branches whipped at his cheeks and the thick undergrowth clung to his knees. On his right was his runner and on his left Mihalache, the man sent him by Dumitriu, a sturdy soldier, thick-necked, with a shaven head, the grey tint of his skull showing beneath his cap. In front there was no one to be seen. The first wave had gone ahead two or three minutes earlier

and vanished amid the trees. Sterie began to tire. He was panting. Suddenly he pulled up at the sight of a soldier in a grey
uniform lying on the ground in front of him. His tunic was unbuttoned, all the pockets were turned out and his boots had been
removed. His half-open eyes were deeply sunk in their sockets;
his steel helmet, covered with grey cloth, lay beside his left cheek.
Across both legs, at the level of the knees, there was a deep gash,
red pulp that was almost black, and beneath the legs a pool of
thickening blood with twigs protruding from it. The body
was surrounded by papers and torn photographs. Sterie went
on.

It was a victory. The enemy had withdrawn, leaving behind
dead, wounded and prisoners. In the miry forest clearings soldiers
stood guard over small groups of grey-uniformed men, without
belts or weapons, covered with mud and leaves, who sat waiting
on the ground. Sterie ordered the prisoners to be collected in an
open space surrounded by beeches. The crackle of rifle-fire was
dying away in the distance ahead of them, and soldiers pulling
machine-guns and carrying cases of ammunition were coming
back at the double, red-faced with their exertions.

Sterie sent off runners to bring in the rest of his company,
and then got out his map. In his sense of relief and relaxation he
would have liked to have someone to laugh and talk with. He
looked up at the sky, hoping for no reason to find it blue and
sunny; but it was no more than a smudgy background to the bare
tracery of branches. The German prisoners, looking exhausted,
were talking slowly together, and he tried to understand what
their harsh, foreign voices were saying. Suddenly he heard other
voices coming from behind him, sharp and incisive, and he turned
round. Colonel Duca was approaching, followed by Colonel
Visoran and some junior officers. The colonel was frowning, his
face creased with displeasure. He did not return Sterie's salute.
After listening without comment to his report he went over to
the prisoners, at whom he gazed sternly. The Germans did not
seem to have noticed his arrival. Suddenly, to the general amazement, Duca addressed them in German, speaking with the accent
of a Prussian officer on parade. His voice was like the barking of
a dog.

" *Was ist hier los? Was ist denn das fur eine verdammte Schweine-
rie?* . . . Why the hell are you men slopping about like this?

Party—shun! Dress by the right! *So!* Is there no officer with you?"

"I'm here, sir. *Melde gehorsamst. Oberleutnant von Bernhardi.*"

A young man had risen to his feet, his dapper uniform covered with mud and his shoulder-straps torn.

"Let me congratulate you, mein Herr," said Duca, sarcastic and furious. He turned away and left them, followed by Visoran and the others of his escort, all privately grinning. The prisoners and the soldiers guarding them stood staring in astonishment. Sterie, when he met Friedman that evening, said:

"I didn't know what to think. I simply don't understand it."

"You don't understand it because there's nothing to understand. Either the man's mad or he's a traitor," said Friedman, lighting a cigarette.

"I must ask you not to say things like that in my hearing. Otherwise I shall have to report you."

Friedman smiled brazenly.

"Are you crazy? What do you expect me to think of a man who withdraws his brigade without a fight, who orders it to counter-attack through a forest, and who finally—you'll see!—will make us pull out again without fighting. Either he's mad or else—what I said."

Sterie got up (they were in a dug-out camouflaged with branches).

"I'm going. I can't listen to that kind of talk. Technically it's my duty as an officer to report what you've said. I shan't do so because I'm sure you didn't mean it."

He went off followed by an angry shout from Friedman: "I was talking perfectly seriously and you can go to hell."

That evening they were summoned to Colonel Visoran's headquarters, in a makeshift hut lighted by an oil-lamp standing on the map spread over the table. A new retreat had been ordered. Visoran, his face tense with rage, offered no explanation; he merely passed on the orders and said good night. As they left, walking through the darkness, Friedman took Sterie's arm.

"Well, now what have you got to say?"

"It was a counter-attack to safeguard our withdrawal, that's all," said Sterie without conviction. "What else do you want me to say?"

"My dear old Sterie, there's something wrong about all this."

" Well, it's not your business, or mine. Our job is to do our duty and not worry about things that don't concern us," said Sterie coldly. " It isn't so difficult. Duty, do you understand? Orders have to be carried out, discipline maintained, regulations observed, the honour of the Army safeguarded—and that's the lot! "

5

Colonel Duca's brigade came finally to rest at the foot of the hills, in valleyed fields broken by small escarpments extending to a river, beyond which was the German front line. The Roumanian lines followed the river for a short distance and then curved away from it. Communication-trenches zig-zagged from the front line to the rear, leading to the semi-subterranean company, battalion and regimental headquarters, the intervening spaces being dotted with small hillocks covered by a network of barbed wire on wooden poles. An occasional rifle-shot broke the prevailing silence, in which the wind wailed dismally like an alley-cat.

Sterie was paying a call on Second Lieutenant Dumitriu in his dug-out, accompanied by Friedman, who had left Stahl's infantry company since the latter, having recovered from his wound, had returned to duty. They went down a flight of steps and found Dumitriu stripped to the waist with a soldier pouring hot water over his head and shoulders.

" What are you up to, Petrica—de-lousing? "

Without troubling to stand upright, parade-ground discipline having long since been abandoned, Dumitriu replied as he soaped himself:

" Good evening, sir. I haven't any lice—I've never had any."

He went on washing while Sterie looked about him. The roof of the dug-out was composed of a large piece of corrugated iron which might once have been a shop-window shutter in some small Moldavian town. An oil-lamp hung from a wooden spike driven

into the earthen wall, and Dumitriu's uniform and his revolver
in its leather holster were hanging on similar spikes. There was
a wicker table and chair, an iron stove, a cracked basin, a pot
of water heating on the stove and a portrait of Madame Marie
Ventura, cut out of an illustrated paper, all of which caused
Sterie to remark in a tone of faint envy:

" You've got yourself nicely fixed up." He looked at Friedman.
" How about us having a wash? "

" Help yourself," said Dumitriu, emptying the contents of a
small bottle of eau de Cologne over his head and shoulders. He
sent his orderly for more water and said when he was dressed:
" I'll clear out to make room for you. I want a breath of air. At
your orders, Lieutenant."

He saluted very correctly, which was rather unexpected, and
went out. Sterie laughed.

" Well, well," he said. " He must be the only one who still
behaves like a real officer. The rest of us are like tramps."

Friedman grunted savagely: "To hell with everything military!"

They were alone. The orderly had not yet come back. Sterie,
the senior of the two, sat down on the only chair, leaving
Friedman standing, and stared thoughtfully at the open mouth
of the stove.

" You want to send everything military to hell," he murmured.
" But after all you're only a civilian in uniform. When the war's
over you'll go back to your barrister's chambers, and you'll plead
and win cases, you'll make money and have a comfortable life.
But what's there for me, a career officer? I shall be training recruits and taking courses and examinations to get my battalion
and then my regiment, and going on manœuvres and doing office
jobs. If I'm lucky I'll end up a half-pay general. It's not a life,
it's a bloody bore. But do you know what the real value of it is? "

He glanced up at Friedman who stood leaning against the wall.

" You may think I'm mad, a sort of textbook soldier. Perhaps
you're right. But you see, if I'm like that it's because I want to
be a real soldier. Do you understand? I want to make sense, to
be true to myself, a man all in one piece. Whatever I do I want
to do it well. Doesn't that mean anything to you? I suppose
you're thinking that it all depends on what one does. Well, I
agree. So what am I doing? What's it all for? It's at a time like
this that one can see the point of our profession. That's to say,

of mine. What are we officers for? We risk our lives to protect
our country. The sceptics can laugh. They ought to come here
and see what it's like when we go out on patrol. And why do we
risk our lives? To keep the people at home safe. To stop the
Germans becoming masters of our country. To restore Roumanian Transylvania to the Motherland. It's perfectly plain and
straightforward. You can laugh if you like, but that's how it is."

" I'm not laughing," said Friedman. " You're right."

" Of course I'm right. Do you think I haven't thought about
it? Do you think I haven't asked myself what I'm doing and why?
And I've found the answer. People can say it's crazy; but if I'm
really ready to die for it, it stops being crazy. Nobody dies just
for the sake of craziness."

" You're right," said Friedman again. " The sacrifice is what
counts."

He was thinking that Sterie really was right. People took him
for a fool, a narrow-minded bigot, a stereotyped officer, but in
fact he was a remarkable fellow, a man of character who did his
own thinking.

" You're right, old boy," said Friedman emphatically, and then
turned smiling to the orderly, who had come panting in with his
refilled canvas bucket. " How long's it going to take to warm that
water up? "

6

That same evening, at about the same hour, Serban Lascari, son
of the late Lascar Lascari, was visited by his relative, Colonel
Duca, at the Jassy branch of the bank of which he was vice-
president. He had fled for refuge to Jassy with his wife and his
son Cesar, and had taken possession of two rooms at the top of
the bank building, filling them with the valuable furniture and
rugs they had brought from Bucarest. One room served as a
sitting-room and private office. With his elbows resting on his
rosewood desk, Serban, now aged about fifty, wearing an im-

perial beard in the style of Edward VII, clad in a black coat and
waistcoat drawn tightly over the small rounded stomach also
rendered fashionable by that monarch, with striped trousers and
grey spats, was attentively listening to what his visitor had to
say. There was a faint smile on his lips, crafty but tinged with
indulgence. The colonel was in ordinary field uniform, but his
manner suggested that he regarded this interview as something
quite out of the ordinary.

" The fact that the Germans can manœuvre on interior lines
of communication is enormously to their advantage," he was
saying. " It is perfectly true that the Allies saved Verdun by
bringing us into the war, but now we're beaten."

" Surely," murmured Serban, " it's a little premature to——"

" No, forgive me, we're beaten. I'm a soldier and I know what
I'm talking about. I knew the Germans as friends before I came
to know them as enemies. Believe me, my dear fellow, we've
lost the war. So have the Allies. So what's to become of Roumania? Is she to be handed over to a German military governor? "

" Marghiloman is in Bucarest," said Monsieur Lascari gently.

" Yes, but what about us? "

" Whom do you mean by ' us '? "

" I mean those of us who are descended from the princely
families to whom the Hohenzollern dynasty in Roumania has
always denied all political power and influence. Who else is to
succeed the Hohenzollerns? You surely can't suppose that the
German Kaiser will pardon King Ferdinand? "

" You're aiming high, my friend," said Serban in a tone
that was perhaps admiring. " You certainly aren't wasting any
time."

Colonel Duca shrugged his shoulders.

" I don't consider that I'm aiming too high. Nor should a
Lascari think so either. What were the Lascaris in Byzantium in
1400? And what were the Zollerns in Nuremberg in that same
year? "

" Well, you're right about the Zollerns. But what are you
going to do about Bratiano? " asked Serban Lascari with a
smile.

" He's finished," said Duca. " Like the King and Queen, the
French Mission and all of them. He'll have to make a bolt for
Russia."

A moment of silence followed. Without getting up, with smooth, precise movements, Lascari got a bottle and two glasses out of a drawer.

" *Un doigt d'eau de vie?* "

Interpreting the colonel's impatient grunt as an affirmative he filled the glasses. The colonel said:

" You don't seem particularly delighted."

Lascari considered, stroking his small beard, while the street outside trembled under a passing column of army trucks. In the building everything was quiet. A clock chimed, sounding the quarter. The portrait of Lascar Lascari, wearing the Order of the Crown of Roumania on a red ribbon round his neck, gazed at them from the wall.

" No," said Serban Lascari bluntly, " I wouldn't say that I'd care to follow your example. You asked my opinion. Well, here it is. I do not believe that desertion, if you will forgive my using so crude a word, can ever be a good political platform. It will certainly not make you popular. Apart from that, I think the Germans are going to lose this war. It is obvious that you want more than advice from me, a banker, not interested in politics. I abide by the principles of my father who remained a deputy and a senator until the day he died, although he could have been a minister ten times over. Aren't you drinking? *A la tienne, mon cher, et bonne chance.*"

" You know quite well that I shall need you if I'm successful," said the colonel, his face twitching. He was furious with disappointment. He said bitterly: " You want me to take all the risk! And then some day if I happen to have become Minister for War or Prime Minister or—or even more—you'll come along and offer me the support of your bank and its political customers. That's what it amounts to."

Serban shrugged his shoulders, gently smiling.

" If you succeed, the first to rejoice will be the members of your own family. Whom else should you work with, if not with those who are bound to you by birth, name and so many common interests? "

" All right, I might as well be going. No one will see me leave, will they? " The colonel rose and picked up his cap and greatcoat.

" No," said Serban Lascari, also rising. " You asked me to see you in strict privacy. . . . Listen, Dinu. You'll need money when you've crossed over."

" Of course."

" Well, I'll see to that. Go to Hugo von Rosenfeld at the Deutsche Bank. You know him, I think."

The colonel nodded, buttoning his coat. He looked hard at his cousin and asked:

" How can you send a credit order into enemy territory? "

" We have our methods," said Serban Lascari and smiled benevolently as he opened the door.

" Crooks, the whole lot of you! " said the colonel, laughing with a half-scowl. " We risk our lives and you carry on with your old games."

" That's true," said Serban. " But I never heard of a banker who succeeded to a throne."

The colonel went out, and the woodwork creaked beneath him as he started down the stairs. A smell of dust and dry-rot rose up from the stairway.

" *Bonne chance*," Serban murmured, and then whispered into the darkness : " Have you someone you can trust to help you to . . .? "

" Yes, a junior officer who greatly admires me," said the colonel with a chuckle.

" Well, good luck," said Serban Lascari again, and closed the door.

7

Towards evening the next day Colonel Duca set out to inspect the positions occupied by the regiment of Frontier Guards. The car from brigade headquarters bore him to a shallow depression whence he went on foot accompanied by an aide-de-camp carrying his map-case—a slim, dapper young man. They climbed a gentle slope rutted with wheel-tracks, stamped hard by the heavy boots of infantrymen and dotted with shell-holes filled with ice. The frosty ground crackled beneath their feet. Now and then a rook cawed, but not a shot or a voice was to be heard.

Reaching the lines they entered a narrow communication trench from which there arose in places a hideous stench of excrement. As they moved forward they encountered an increasing number of soldiers, lamentable figures, bearded and caked with mud, who stood rigidly at the salute. There was nothing to be seen overhead but a strip of sky with dark purple clouds. A bitterly cold wind was blowing.

Colonel Vasilache, at the regimental command-post, was evidently disconcerted by the unheralded arrival of his brigade commander. Duca returned his salute in an off-hand manner, gazing at the over-heated stove and then at the roof (the dug-out was protected by six layers of oak logs covered with earth). He frowned and asked dryly:

" How far is this post from the front line? "

Colonel Vasilache's unease increased. He knew Duca had not forgotten his slight attack of hysteria at the beginning of the campaign.

" Two hundred yards, sir."

" Are you sure you're sufficiently protected by barbed wire? "

It was a normal enough question, but Duca had asked it deliberately for the embarrassment of Vasilache, who would, he knew, take it for sarcasm. The latter stiffened and replied coldly:

" There are adequate gaps for the patrols, sir. We aren't as frightened of the Germans as all that."

Duca nodded amiably. " Excellent." Then he went on, in the most casual of voices: " I'll go out and have a look at those gaps, to see if they'll be all right if we decide to attack."

Vasilache exclaimed in sudden alarm: " But, sir, you'll be risking your life! "

Duca glanced at him as though he were about to make some further, biting allusion to his cowardice, but he only said:

" Don't worry. It's getting dark. I shan't be spotted. But I don't want you to come." He spoke the words quite kindly. " You have to take risks enough as it is, in this sector. Detail a man to show me the way—one who knows all about the gaps."

" At your orders, Colonel—certainly," said Vasilache, happy to escape a dangerous incursion into no-man's-land.

He gave the necessary orders. Colonel Duca said to his aide:
" You can stay here too, Armasesco. . . . Has the man come?
Good. Well, good night, gentlemen."

He left the dug-out, with the officers all standing to attention,
and outside regarded a young, sturdily-built man standing stiffly
at the salute.

" Sergeant Mariu Florea, sir, of Number One Company of the
First Regiment of Frontier Guards."

" Good. You can stand easy. Who's in command of your
company? "

" Lieutenant Sterie, sir."

" Ah yes. Well, take me to him and then I'll tell you what I
want. Where's your rifle? "

The young man laughed with a flash of white teeth.

" I don't need one, sir. I've got hand-grenades."

" You've been decorated, I see."

" Yes, sir."

The sergeant was cheerful, glowing and robust. " These sort
aren't bad soldiers either," Colonel Duca reflected, " if they're
properly commanded." He said aloud: " Lead the way, Florea."

They passed along the communication trenches to the front
line, where men pressed back against the trench-walls at the sight
of the tricolour rosette on the colonel's cap and the gold braid on
his sleeves. Here and there look-outs, standing on the fire-steps,
glanced sidelong at the old man as he went by; then they turned
again to face the enemy, stiff with cold, gazing with empty, sombre
eyes over the prospect of shell-ploughed earth, frozen river-bed,
dirty snow, shattered trees and grey hillocks.

The colonel turned up the collar of his greatcoat, shivering
slightly. Most unpleasant weather! And always that wind laden
with dust. . . .

They came to a stop outside the company command-post. A
torn blanket covered with dark stains (a soldier sleeping beneath it
had been caught by a shell-burst) hung over the entrance. A hand
drew it aside. Someone said in a loud, indignant voice:

" Why the devil does this stew stink so much? "

Sterie emerged. Recognising Duca, he blushed to the roots of
his hair, saluted, formally reported his name and rank and then
stood waiting at attention, growing calmer. Duca gazed at him
with a hard, penetrating stare. He was aware that some sort of

confusion was going on in the dug-out, and that a startled eye was observing him through a hole in the blanket.

" I would like you to show me your sector," he said rather distantly. " Please lead the way. Florea, follow me."

Sterie led the colonel on a tour of the company positions, pointing out details as he went, introducing Friedman, the subalterns commanding the platoons and a sergeant who had several times distinguished himself on patrol.

" Good," said Colonel Duca in his dry voice. " Excellent. Well done, Sergeant! That's the way to win the war." He glanced sidelong at Sterie. " Discipline is well maintained in your company, Lieutenant. I see you're a good officer."

" I was your pupil at Officers' College, sir," said Sterie, with a smile in which there was no pleasure but only a sort of embarrassed politeness, awkward and without spontaneity.

Duca darted another swift, considering glance at him; but he could not guess that Sterie was thinking in wry astonishment, " It seems I don't admire him any more. He praises you—' That's the way to win the war! '—but he orders his brigade to retreat when it hasn't been beaten and then he just stays put. *Well done, Colonel! That's the way to win the war!* " . . . Sterie climbed out of the forward trench, passing the look-out crouched behind an earthwork white with frost. The three men moved into no-man's-land, over frozen ground shrouded in the evening mist.

Sergeant Florea led the way towards one of the gaps in the wire. Duca paused and turned to Sterie, smiling.

" What do you think of our military operations so far? " he asked.

" So far as I'm qualified to form an opinion, sir, it is not a high one," said Sterie bluntly. (" Does he expect me to congratulate him? ")

Much to his surprise, Duca's expression seemed to grow less severe. He said in a friendly voice:

" No? Why not? "

" Because we don't attack, sir. We leave the initiative to the enemy and do nothing but retreat."

" Yes, I can't blame you," said Duca thoughtfully. " But you know, against an enemy as capable as this any counter-attack entails grave risks."

Sterie did not reply. He was thinking, " To hell with the risks!

" What is it? " asked Sterie, his heart suddenly thumping. Gogu sat down beside him and said in a low voice:

" He's bolted! "

" What! Who do you mean? " demanded Sterie; but the answer had instantly dawned on him. Gogu said:

" The C.O.! Duca! He's run for it! "

" Run? Where? You mean, gone over to the enemy? *Deserted?* " The words " deserted " and " gone over to the enemy " seemed to Sterie to become meaningless and absurd as he uttered them. But there was no time to think about it. He ran to the other end of the sector and after questioning the men set off with a patrol in the direction from which the firing had come. They hurried down into the valley, finally reaching a point where there was a gap in the wire, about a yard wide, which was normally blocked by a spiked and wired trestle. This had been moved aside, and here they found Sergeant Florea, stretched motionless on the ground. Sterie bent over him. It was too dark to see details. He touched the prostrate body.

" Florea! Florea! "

The man groaned feebly.

" He's still alive. You men pick him up and take him back."

Sterie restored the barrier to its place with the help of Apostolesco, and then followed the men back to the trenches. Sergeant Florea now lay in the command-post, his glazed eyes half closed.

" He's dead, sir," said one of the men. " He got it in the chest. He died while we were bringing him in."

All that evening, all through the night, Sterie sought vainly to understand his own feelings. He did not close his eyes; for that matter, none of the officers was able to sleep. Patrols were doubled. Colonel Vasilache set out for divisional headquarters accompanied by Armasesco, Duca's aide, whom he had had arrested on his own responsibility. Towards morning, while Istrate, Friedman, Gogu Apostolesco and Dumitriu were playing cards, Sterie, who was seated with his hands on his knees staring at nothing, felt someone's eyes upon him. He looked up to encounter the intent gaze of Istrate, who turned his head away. Finally they abandoned the game and returned to the subject of Duca's desertion. Istrate said with a faint smile:

" So honestly, my dear Sterie, you suspected nothing? Not a

At least one knows that one has done something to hi
But there was no point in arguing. Duca was not ask:
However the colonel pursued his questioning, in th
humoured tone.

" And how do you see the outcome of the war?
to win? "

Sterie started. He answered tersely:

" As an officer, sir, the only question I can ask
going to win."

" Quite right! " said Duca. He chuckled and thei
again. " I'm pleased with you. I shall visit your
tomorrow or the day after. The terrain looks favourab
operations. Good night."

" Well, I'm not pleased with you," thought St
anyway, what kind of operations? " But he only said
orders, Colonel. I'll see you as far as Number Two

" No, there's no need. The sergeant will show i
Good night. Sergeant, where are you? "

" Here, sir," replied Sergeant Mariu Florea, a sl
the shadows of no-man's-land.

Colonel Duca moved towards him and they went
Sterie stood watching their departing figures, the on
soldierly, the other more thick-set, heavier in its
They moved without haste across the field, which s
towards the river, and vanished from his sight. Ster
the way he had come, dropped into the trench and m:
towards his company command-post.

Before he had reached it he heard the sound of a d
followed by three more in rapid succession. There was
of silence and then a faint shout. Sterie paused, tryin
mine where the sounds had come from and wonderii
if the colonel had run into trouble. At the same time
scornfully, " A bloody fine officer if he gets himself kill
sheer recklessness! " But such exchanges across no-i
were too commonplace to be worth special attention. F
to his dug-out and sat down to smoke a cigarette on th
outside it.

He had not finished the cigarette when Gogu Apostol
running up, gasping for breath.

" Lieutenant! Lieutenant! "

hint from the way he behaved or from anything he said? You took him as far as the wire and then you left him, and it never occurred to you that he might be on his way over?"

"Don't be a bloody fool," said Sterie.

He had spoken like any innocent man, angrily but calmly, yet he could not be sure that there was not a tremor in his voice, or that he had not turned pale. A sudden terror had assailed him. After a moment it abated, and he thought that it was gone for good.

8

At about ten o'clock the following night Colonel Vasilache stood looking round his regimental command-post to make sure that all the officers and men summoned to attend were present. They were all there—Sterie, Dumitriu, Friedman, Apostolesco, two sergeants and one private.

"Gentlemen, you are ordered to report to divisional head-quarters to testify regarding the desertion of the traitor Duca."

It was with genuine pleasure and in a crisp, military voice that he uttered the word "traitor." Chance had brought him a crushing triumph over a man who for years had been held in admiration by his brother officers; and the puppies who had dared to laugh at him, Vasilache, for a moment of nervous weakness, had now failed in their duty in letting the traitor escape.

"Sterie, you will hand over the command of your company to Dumitriu. You will leave at once for divisional headquarters with Friedman and Apostolesco. You are to report there before midnight. That's all."

"At your orders, Colonel."

They went out into the darkness. Friedman whispered in Sterie's ear: "We're in bad trouble."

Sterie did not reply. He was afraid, chilled with an apprehension impossible to define. He followed Friedman across the

fields, amid the shell-holes, with the others coming behind. " I'm
at fault, I failed in my duty," he was thinking. " I've been relieved of my command. But how was I to know? "

He tugged at Friedman's sleeve.

" Listen," he said, " could I possibly have foreseen it? Honestly? If Vasilache's so clever why didn't he think of it himself?
But who the devil could have expected it? "

Friedman gave a short, dry laugh, stumbling in the darkness.

" You're getting what you deserve, my lad. You should have
studied Army Regulations—' Action to be taken in case of desertion to the Enemy on the part of high-ranking officers.' "

" But there's no such regulation," protested Sterie. And then,
understanding, he said mournfully: " This is no time for
jokes."

" Lieutenant Friedman," said Gogu Apostolesco, " are you
sure you know the way? "

" Yes, of course. Why? Are you afraid we're going over to the
enemy as well? "

" For God's sake shut up! " cried Sterie in exasperation.

" I know the way too. We're all right," said one of the soldiers
calmly.

They had a long way to go, and occasionally they were held up
by patrols who examined their papers by the light of pocket
torches. At length they reached the village school where they
were submitted to a final inspection and required to lay aside their
arms before entering. Friedman was the only one of the officers
with a revolver; the two sergeants and the private had their
bayonets.

" I protest! " exclaimed Friedman. " Why should I give up
my revolver? "

" You're to leave it with me. I'll make a note of your name
and the serial number," said the duty officer.

" Oh, let him have it, don't keep us out here in the cold," said
Sterie impatiently.

The six men were led into a classroom with dingy, peeling walls
covered with pencil scribbles. The floor was dirty, strewn with
straw and discarded papers. A few oil-lamps were burning, but
the earthenware stove was out. A lieutenant entered, a slight
young man, round-cheeked and smooth-haired, wearing clean

boots and tunic and a white collar. He looked coldly at them and consulted a list.

" Lieutenant Sterie, Laurent."

" Here," said Sterie.

" Your papers, please."

" Here they are."

The plump-faced lieutenant took the documents, studied them carefully and then returned them to Sterie.

" Thank you. Kindly leave the room."

Sterie went out. The lieutenant shut the door behind him and again consulted his list.

" Lieutenant Friedman, Aurel."

" Here."

Sterie, outside, found himself confronting a second lieutenant of Gendarmerie who also had a list.

" Lieutenant Sterie? "

" Yes. But why don't you introduce yourself? " said Sterie, flushing.

" You're under arrest," said the subaltern coldly.

Sterie looked swiftly to right and left, like a hunted animal. There were armed guards. The subaltern said:

" This way, please. First door on the right."

Sterie moved slowly. He was tired and dirty, caked with mud. He would have liked a bath, and to sleep in a real bed. He went through the doorway on the right, past a guard with a fixed bayonet. The door was shut behind him and the key turned in the lock. The room was bare and dirty with a malodorous bucket in one corner. A candle burned on the window-ledge, lighting the bars over the window. Sterie sat down on the floor with a sigh, then got up and blew out the candle and lay down again on the bare floor, pulling his coat collar above his ears. He tried to sleep. He was feeling calmer. After all, what could they do to him? They would grill them all to get at the truth, but then they would have to let them go. Anyway, they were no longer in the front line, and that was something.

On the same night, and at the same hour (that is to say, after midnight), a couple of dozen guests were gathered in Serban Lascari's study and bedroom in Jassy, Madame Lascari having draped the bed with a Persian shawl. Round-bellied, bearded gentlemen with neatly parted hair and pince-nez or monocles, and ladies in silk or velvet or nurse's uniform (after the fashion started by Queen Marie, with a veil framing the face and ample skirts designed to conceal Her Majesty's majestic legs), were drinking coffee from British military stores, and cognac from French military stores. There were also two plump elderly generals sitting with their swords between their legs; a few hollow-cheeked Roumanian junior officers on leave from the front (among them Ghighi Duca in the uniform of the Automobile Corps, and the youthful Dimitri Coziano, who had been decorated and given a staff appointment); two French officers, one a colonel and the other a bespectacled captain who in private life ran a bakery; and a Russian major, young and fair-haired, who spoke French like a native. These represented the war; and it was the war which had restricted the menu to two dishes, sardines and canned lobsters, and which caused the building to tremble as the trucks of the Russian army-corps commanded by General Tscherbachev rolled through the streets of the town.

" He's a relation of mine and the brother of *ce cher Prince Duca*," Monsieur Lascari was saying with a glass of cognac in his hand. " But at such a time as this neither Prince Duca nor I can have any feeling except one. If he is caught I shall advocate the death sentence, regardless of all personal considerations."

The older gentlemen nodded approvingly. The younger ones were paying not the slightest heed to the case of Colonel Duca, preferring to gossip with the ladies and murmur compliments and suggestions in their ears—leave was so soon over!

" But isn't he a socialist or an anarchist, or anyway a revolutionary of some kind? " asked the Russian major.

" My dear fellow, he's a boyar! " said Serban Lascari, smiling.

" Well, but with us there are boyars who are in favour of revolution. In fact, it's the fashionable thing in Petrograd,' said the Russian with an unhappy laugh.

" I take it an example will be made? " said the French colonel, turning to the apoplectic and jovial General Cilibia.

" Oh, of course," said the general, " they're bound to shoot one or two of them at least, just to teach the rest a lesson."

Serban Lascari said gravely: " I was talking to Monsieur Bratiano this afternoon. He said positively that an example will be made."

" Why don't you shoot all your revolutionaries? " asked Cilibia, suddenly glaring at the Russian and gesticulating with an amber cigarette-holder held in a white, carefully manicured hand. The latter smiled with an irony in which aristocratic fatalism was mingled with national pride.

" There are too many, General—several times the population of your gallant country. So you see . . ."

And then they all talked about something else.

At daybreak, some little time after Serban Lascari's guests had departed, the officer conducting the preliminary inquiry, the round-cheeked lieutenant, interviewed Friedman. They sat in a room furnished with a safe, a table and two chairs, with another table in the corner where the sergeant keeping the record was seated.

" Did he admire the traitor Duca, or didn't he? " the round-cheeked lieutenant repeated, his manner cold and detached.

" Yes, but we all did," said Friedman. " The fact that Sterie admired him doesn't mean that he was his accomplice. At that rate you could call me his accomplice."

" That is a matter of opinion, Lieutenant. Facts are what we want. It is clear from your testimony that he had a great admiration for Duca. Put that down, Tanasesco.'

" But it's twisting the truth! " cried Friedman.

" You are not the only one to say that he had a great admiration for the traitor Duca. The other depositions confirm it. He has admitted it himself."

" But it doesn't mean anything! Of course he admitted it— why not? "

" Not long ago he was entrusted with the task of covering the retreat of the First Regiment of Frontier Guards," said the lieutenant, calmly. " He was ordered to hold a certain position, with explicit instructions not to abandon it until further orders. Nevertheless he did abandon it."

" You're wrong about that too," said Friedman with a short, nervous laugh. " That was my doing, Lieutenant. I as good as forced him to clear out. We were practically surrounded and being shot at from all sides. We'd simply have been massacred."

" You're saying that now to defend him. You didn't say it at

the time. And why did Duca choose to go over from the sector of
this officer who so greatly admired him? "

" Why, because he *did* admire him. Because he trusted him.
It made things simpler. Surely that's obvious."

" It's not in the least obvious. He might have done so because
he knew Lieutenant Sterie wouldn't try to stop him."

Friedman was momentarily silenced. The lieutenant went
on:

" Don't you see that it all hangs together? That constant retreat, with no military justification . . . And the rearguard was
always the same unit, commanded by an officer who was a fervent
admirer of Duca. The Germans continually harassed the rear of
the brigade from both flanks. How were they able to do it?
Couldn't it be that they were getting advance information of the
brigade's movements from Duca's admirer, acting on Duca's instructions? Then comes Duca's desertion, from the same officer's
sector. One of the look-outs sees him take leave of Duca in front
of the trenches and stand staring after him until he disappears.
A look-out in Number Two Company fires at the deserter, but
this officer doesn't even bother to go and find out what's happening. He goes on back to his dug-out. And then when he hears
the news what does he do? I have here the testimony of a soldier
who was close to him at the time. This is what he says: '. . .
Second Lieutenant Apostolesco said, " He's run for it! " and
Lieutenant Sterie said, " You mean, gone over to the enemy? "
He said this before he knew what direction Duca had run in,
and in doing so he gave himself away. If he had said, ' You must
be mad,' or ' It's impossible,' that might have indicated genuine
astonishment. But he seemed to know instantly what Duca had
done. How did he know? What's your answer to that, Lieutenant? "

" I admit it sounds plausible," said Friedman, " but I don't
believe it. I know Sterie and I'd stake my life on him."

The other did not press the point. He said: " Are you prepared
to sign your deposition? "

" Certainly. I'll stick my neck out," Friedman said.

He was now seriously alarmed for Sterie. He had not expected
anything like this. He read and signed the transcript which
the sergeant handed him. The lieutenant put it in the file and
said:

" If I were you, Lieutenant Friedman, I'd think twice about committing myself. You can go now."

Friedman got to his feet. The round-cheeked lieutenant yawned and stretched himself, while the sergeant arranged his writing materials. Muffled voices were to be heard outside. Friedman had been a law-student before the war, and he perfectly realised the significance of what had been said.

" There's a question I'd like to ask you," he remarked. " What does Sterie have to say about all this ? "

The lieutenant stood up, settling his cap on his head.

" It's not the sort of question we generally answer, but in this case I can tell you that Sterie has admitted all the material facts —everything except his complicity."

" You mean he has said that it was he who gave the order for us to withdraw from that position ? "

" Yes, contrary to your statement," said the other, smiling.

Friedman was badly shaken.

" All the same," he said, " it doesn't call for second sight to see that Sterie's a soldier with a high degree of professional pride, and the last man in the world to admit that anyone else could be responsible for a decision taken when he was in command. Surely that's understandable."

" I don't understand it and I don't believe it. Why should he cover up for anyone else when his life's at stake ? "

" Perhaps he doesn't realise that he's risking his life."

" He'll find out," the lieutenant said. " Well, goodbye. This way, if you don't mind."

9

On the first day Sterie had quite simply answered the questions put to him. So manifestly absurd did the charge against him appear that he had no doubt of his vindication. But on the second day he began to understand where the questions were leading. His interrogator sought to trap him into admissions by reading passages from other depositions, without saying whose they were. Sterie grew apprehensive, lost his head and began to contradict himself.

Between sessions he was confined to the small room with a barred window. He couldn't sleep. Despite his weariness he lay open-eyed with his senses feverishly alert. He did not think clearly, but became, as it were, the passive observer of the ideas and images that teemed in his mind while he relived the sequence of recent events, reshaping the picture as he did so. For instance there was his parting from Duca, who had said:

" You can go back. I'll go on with the sergeant."

But now in a sort of dream Sterie replied: " I'm afraid that's impossible, sir. No one is allowed beyond this point except with my permission or by my orders."

Duca frowned and then broke into a laugh, showing all his teeth.

" Are you refusing me permission? "

" Yes," cried Sterie in his dream, " because you're a traitor! "

Whereupon Colonel Duca got out his revolver. Sterie clutched hastily at his holster, but it took him a couple of seconds to undo the fastening and in that time Duca's weapon was levelled at his chest. Duca was laughing in the most utterly unexpected fashion. It was terrifying. How can a man laugh when he is about to take another man's life?

Sterie came out of this dream with his heart beating in terror, as though he had indeed been confronted by a murderer's revolver.

74

How absurd! He could not have known at that moment that Duca intended to desert, and he had no reason to try to prevent him going on by himself.

Yes, but he might have suspected. He might have felt that there was something wrong. The constant retreats, for no reason, due simply to Duca's lack of confidence in the forces of his own country and his terrified admiration for the Germans. . . . . And then, the sudden question he had asked, as though in passing, " How do you see the outcome of the war? " Sterie should have guessed.

" Yes, I should have guessed," he said, unconsciously speaking the words aloud. But then his thoughts ran on. " No. I couldn't have guessed. I didn't guess."

The fatal mistake had been to let Duca leave the trenches from his sector. Suppose, instead of this:

" Stop, Colonel! You can't go any further.'

Duca, swarthy and hard of face, would have looked disdainfully at him.

" And why not, may I ask? Are you refusing me permission? "

" I must ask you to return to Battalion Command, sir, where a man will be detailed to take you to Number Two Company's sector." It would have been an act of great temerity—to refuse permission to the commanding officer of the brigade, without any precise instructions. There was no rule against going from Number One Company's sector to that of Number Two. The second-line trenches were inter-communicating, as Duca would have known.

" Who has given you an order to this effect, Lieutenant? "

" Colonel Visoran, sir."

" Colonel Visoran is your battalion commander, young man, but I'm in command of the brigade. What's the matter with you? Pull yourself together before I lose all patience! "

" I'm sorry, sir, but I can't let you go beyond this point without express instructions from Colonel Visoran."

" Very well, I'll go and see Visoran. I shall have more to say about this later."

So then Duca marches back along the communication trenches to battalion headquarters, where the plump Colonel Visoran, of the Frontier Guards, bellows at Sterie:

" Are you crazy? Are you trying to get yourself sent to a mad-house to dodge the front? Are you out of your mind? I assure you, Colonel, I never gave any such order. Let me come with you."

" My dear Visoran, there's no need. I want to look over the ground and see how the wire's arranged, and when I get back we'll discuss plans for recapturing the other side of the valley. Goodbye for now."

He would have gone over to the enemy just the same, but everyone would have known at least that Sterie had tried to prevent him from going, and he would not now be under arrest, waiting to appear before a court-martial which might degrade him in rank and even relegate him to a disciplinary unit. . . . Stretched on his bed of straw, he raised himself on one elbow and groaned in his affliction, " Why didn't I do something like that? "

But how could he have gone so far as to invent an order for the purpose of restraining the movements of his brigade commander, the distinguished Colonel Duca, one of the most respected officers in the Army? How could he have questioned his loyalty, and what other grounds had he for trying to restrain him? Who in the world would have suspected Duca? The thing was inconceivable, yet it had happened.

" If I'd known! " groaned Sterie. " If only I'd known!" He went over it again and again, thinking of other courses he might have adopted, conjuring up the wildest possibilities. But it all came to nothing. Things could not have happened differently—except, indeed, that Duca might have chosen to bolt from some other sector. The swine! " Why did you have to pick on me? What harm had I done to you? " he asked Duca in his thoughts; and the colonel laughed and said: " I'm pleased with you, my boy. I'll come and have another look at your sector. The terrain is suitable for certain operations."

" The filthy, lying swine! " Sterie jumped to his feet and paced up and down his prison-cell. " Certain operations! " He wanted to shout aloud in fury because he had not got the man in front of him where he could take him by the throat and break his neck. Finally he came to a stop and lay down again on his bed of straw.

On the evening of the third day an officer of the Gendarmerie entered the cell and ordered Sterie to follow him. He led him

along a series of corridors out of the building. In the courtyard
(Sterie looked towards the gateway, but it was guarded; he looked
at the walls, but they were too high) a car was waiting, an open
car, very dusty. A soldier was seated at the wheel. A gendarme
signed to Sterie to get in, sat down beside him on the sagging
upholstery and produced a pair of handcuffs. Sterie whipped his
hands away.

" What are you doing? What are those for? "

The gendarme looked at him. He was a young man, slight of
figure, with a refined face and a fair moustache, evidently a youth
of good family who had not been brought up the hard way. He
smiled apologetically.

" I'm sorry, sir. I've got to do it.'

" Where are you taking me? " Sterie asked.

" To P——" The young man named a small Moldavian town
not far from the front.

" Why? What goes on in P——? "

" I don't know, sir. Please, may I have your wrists? "

Sterie held out his hands, which after a time grew very cold.
A wind was blowing and the sky on the horizon was the colour of
lead. Long lines of carts driven by soldiers in fur caps passed
them on the road; guns, cars occupied by senior officers, lorries
without tyres, their wheels in rubber wrappings, which made a
hideous noise. In the villages dirty, unhappy-looking children,
fowls that had escaped from their farmyards and half-starved dogs
ran in and out of the traffic on the road. The cold was dry and
piercing and Sterie began to shiver.

They entered the square of a barracks built into a hillside on
the outskirts of the town. Sterie was put in an unlighted room
having no other furniture than a truckle-bed with a straw mattress,
a pillow stuffed with straw and a rough blanket. After a time he
fell into an uneasy sleep, his dreams peopled with the figures of
Colonel Duca, Sergeant Florea, Colonel Visoran, Friedman, Gogu
Apostolesco; and the more unexpected figures of his father and
brothers, his mother, his childhood friends. They were sad and
agonising dreams from which he emerged with a sense of profound
bitterness, only to dream again.

At dawn someone shook him by the shoulder. It was a lieutenant wearing pince-nez, pale-faced, with a long, morose countenance, who introduced himself as Sterie's defender.

" You're to appear before the court-martial at four o'clock this afternoon," he said.

" As soon as that? But it gives you no time to prepare the case! You don't know the facts," exclaimed Sterie in alarm.

" I've studied the dossier," the other said sourly.

" That means you don't know anything. They didn't understand. Let me tell you the whole story."

For two and a half hours Sterie talked, seeking to demonstrate the absurdity of the case against him.

" You know what the Army is. What else could I have done? How could I possibly suspect a man like Duca? How could I?"

His pale-faced advocate made exhaustive notes, asked questions, listened with his head on one side, and stared absently at the ceiling. Finally he nodded, seeming convinced, but still with a gloomy expression.

" What's wrong? Why are you looking so glum?" asked Sterie with an attempt at gaiety. "Anyone would think it was you who were going to be court-martialled, instead of me."

" It's just the way I am," said his defender with a forced laugh.

" Well, but how does it strike you?" Sterie gazed at him in some anxiety. " Am I going to get off? What sort of sentence can they give me?"

The other seemed to hesitate. " We shall have to wait and see."

" You mean you can't even tell me how you think the case will go? And you say you're a barrister in private life!"

The other murmured: " You've given me a complete defence. I'm convinced that you're innocent and that you ought to be acquitted of the charge of knowingly assisting Duca to escape. But I'm not the court. I'm simply a lawyer. You mustn't forget that." He glanced at Sterie and then lowered his eyes. " You must try to trust me. I'll do my best."

He then left, saying that he wanted to study his notes. Sterie was assailed by a momentary spasm of misgiving which he could not account for, but it soon passed. After recapitulating all the reasons which proved him innocent he was so persuaded that nothing terrible could happen that he had even lost the desire to eat. He waited impatiently for the proceedings to begin. The lieutenant had left him some cigarettes and he passed the time smoking and striding up and down the empty room, which smelt strongly of boots.

At length his defender came to fetch him, accompanied by two armed guards. They went along lofty corridors thronged with deep-voiced soldiers and filled with the smells of leather, rifle-grease, sweat and beans. They passed through a room where two soldiers, seated writing at tables, stood up as they entered, and from this they went into a big schoolroom with a map of Roumania on its further wall and school benches piled one on top of the other in a corner. A part of the hall had been cleared exposing the red-brown floor, newly scrubbed and smelling of creosote. Here a long table was installed, with a crucifix standing on it and six empty chairs. There was also a smaller table with a bench. Sterie sat on the bench with his advocate at his side, the guards standing behind. An army magistrate, with the rank of major, entered. He had a cold, solemn manner, bushy eyebrows and a double chin which bulged over the collar of his tunic. They rose and saluted, and he acknowledged the salute without looking at anyone and sat down. A soldier entered, bare-headed and without his belt, carrying yet another small table and a stool. Then the members of the court appeared: a small grey-haired colonel, a plump red-faced lieutenant-colonel, a major with a black mous-tache, a lieutenant and a subaltern in faded uniforms who had evidently come straight from the front.

It was a strange business; Sterie could not believe that it was happening to him. He sat listening while the major read out the indictment in which the words " treason," " traitor," " desertion in the face of the enemy," " assistance rendered to a deserter " and " complicity " constantly recurred; he kept his eyes fixed on the map, on a particular point where the printed paper had been torn away from the canvas backing; but he listened with the utmost attention, seeking to understand. Nevertheless, when his examination began he was overcome with anger and misery. The colonel presiding addressed him in a hostile, peremptory tone, and did not restrain the prosecutor from asking a number of highly offensive questions. Sterie's attempt at protest was harshly dismissed.

" You can sit down," the president said finally. " Bring in the witness Aurel Friedman."

Sterie turned to look hopefully at Friedman, who gave him a

covert nod and thereafter pretended not to see him. But his replies under examination brought him a sharp rebuke.

" You're here as a witness of fact, Lieutenant, not as the defender of the accused."

When he left the witness-stand Friedman gave Sterie a sharp, questioning glance in which there was no hint of levity. Sterie, for his part, was smiling. Despite the evident hostility of the court Friedman had said enough to demonstrate the absurdity of the whole affair. Nor was he less pleased with the testimony of other witnesses, except that of the soldier on look-out who had seen him take leave of Duca and the man who had been on the fire-step when Gogu Apostolesco had brought him the news. These men had started by repeating simply what they had seen and heard, but the prosecutor had cross-examined them in a fashion designed to make it appear that there had been a criminal intention behind all Sterie's actions, simple and natural though they seemed.

" Did the two officers merely exchange salutes, or did they shake hands ? "

" I don't remember."

" Try to remember. Did they shake hands or did they salute ? "

" As for saluting, I don't know. They may have shaken hands but I didn't see them salute."

" Ah. So they shook hands ? "

" That's not true! " shouted Sterie.

" The accused will keep silent or I shall have him removed from the court-room," said the president.

Sterie turned to his advocate and whispered feverishly:

" He never shook hands with junior officers. Anyway it's not usual. Don't they know that? Aren't we all officers? This is rubbish! "

After the examination of witnesses the prosecutor addressed the court, declaring that the traitor Duca had kept the enemy constantly informed of the movements of his brigade, which had retreated with scarcely any fighting. When he had been unable to avoid rearguard skirmishes Duca had entrusted this post to an officer whom he knew to be his fanatical admirer (" as witnesses for the defence have been obliged to admit "), that is to say, to the accused, whom he could rely upon to do what he wanted. The brigade's solitary counter-attack had been launched in thickly wooded country and might have been disastrous in its outcome had not the enemy offered a feeble resistance to the dash and heroism of the Roumanian troops. But the ground recaptured had been abandoned soon afterwards without a struggle. Fearing that he might come under suspicion the traitor had gone over to the enemy with the assistance of the accused, who had stayed behind, no doubt to act as Duca's agent, hoping to take advantage of the good faith of the officers and men of the gallant First Regiment of Frontier Guards. The accused, in short, was guilty of the crime of high treason under—here the prosecutor cited a long list of articles and clauses from the Military Code—for which the penalty was degradation in the presence of his regiment followed by death at the hands of a firing-squad.

" He's mad," thought Sterie. " They're all mad." No doubt the prosecutor felt it his duty to demand the utmost penalty, but could anyone possibly take this rigmarole seriously? Sterie turned in breathless suspense towards his defender as the latter, rising to his feet, removed his pince-nez, wiped them, replaced them on his nose and began to speak in a calm voice. He contended that the entire case brought against the accused was based on no more than supposition, and that it was not sustained by a single material fact, or any positive testimony or evidence. Regarding one of the major charges, that the accused had abandoned a position which he had been ordered to hold to the last, witnesses had testified that it was Lieutenant Friedman, supported by the other officers, who had urged the retreat. The prosecution had here based its charge on Sterie's own statement, in which he accepted full responsibility, and which from a misconceived sense of military honour he had refused to retract. But the defence maintained that the psychological reasons for his refusal were very much more convincing than the machiavellian interpretation placed upon it by the prosecution. . . .

Strangely, as the speech for the defence proceeded, it seemed to Sterie that the argument fell to bits; that it was no more than a string of words like those of the prosecution, words opposed to other words, one lot as true as the other. He scarcely noticed when his defender finished speaking and sat down again at his side. The president said something, but Sterie remained seated motionless on the bench. His advocate nudged him with his elbow, causing him to start. The president repeated his question.

" Accused, have you anything further to say? "

" Stand up," murmured the advocate. Sterie rose and said in an unemotional voice:

" Sir——"

" You must address me as Mr. President."

" Mr. President, I simply did my duty."

" Very well," said the president. " The court will adjourn."

Sterie was taken into the next room and left alone with his defender.

" You're innocent," the young lawyer said. " I think they realise it. Have a cigarette."

" I simply did my duty, nothing but that. Any officer would have done the same," said Sterie. He was feeling terribly tired. " There was only one time when I didn't. That was when I agreed to retreat. It would have been better if I'd stayed where I was and been killed fighting, instead of having to listen while that major called me a traitor in every other sentence, a man without honour or loyalty and all the rest of it. I'd like to know what he'd have done in my place."

The other lit his cigarette for him and he sat smoking in silence. After ten minutes a soldier summoned them and they returned to the court-room. The members of the court entered and everyone stood up. The president read aloud from a sheet of paper. In the light of the charges brought against him, in full consideration of the facts attested to by witnesses and of the arguments put forward by both the prosecution and the defence, and in observance of articles such-and-such, clauses so-and-so, of the Military Code, this court finds the accused, Lieutenant Laurent Sterie, guilty of the crime of high treason, and accordingly condemns him to be publicly degraded in the presence of his regiment and thereafter to suffer the penalty of death by shooting.

The youngest member of the tribune, the second lieutenant, glanced swiftly at Sterie and then looked away. The colonel handed the sheet of paper to the clerk and said:

" Remove the prisoner."

Sterie stood motionless. " They're mad. Or else I'm dreaming. It can't be true! " He was led along the same corridors, filled with soldiers. " I walk past these men, and I'm condemned to death and they aren't. It's queer." He seemed to have become a

different order of being, yet he was a man like any other. It was
very strange.

His defender went with him into his cell and said: " It's
what I was afraid of. They want to make an example. They
don't give a damn whether you're guilty or not. I've already
drafted an appeal to the King. You'll have to sign it. Here's a
pen."

Sterie signed with a shaking hand.

" It's not possible," he said. " They're mad. Anyway I shall
be pardoned, shan't I? "

" We'll do everything we can. You must keep up your courage.
Don't give way."

Sterie nodded, his face haggard. " Anything you say." But
as the other turned to go he gripped him by the arm. " But I
must ask you . . . I must know. . . . Please tell me absolutely
honestly. . . . Do you think I'll get off? "

The young man avoided his eyes.

" How am I to answer that? How can I say? "

Sterie clutched him by both arms and shook him.

" You've got to answer! I asked you at the beginning what
your opinion was, what you personally thought. You knew they
were going to condemn me. You've as good as said so. They
want to make an example. Why should I get off now? "

The other sighed heavily, his face very pale. " You must
keep up your courage."

" But for God's sake tell me! I want to hear it. Have I any
chance of getting off—any chance at all? I want a plain answer—
yes or no. "

" I don't think so," the other said, lowering his eyes.

Sterie abruptly let him go. He went and sat on the bed with
his hands on his knees.

" So there it is," he said in an expressionless voice.

The lawyer was rubbing his arms where Sterie had gripped
them. Sterie said in the same voice: " I can't believe I'm not
dreaming."

" You must keep up your courage. Don't lose heart."

Sterie shrugged his shoulders. The lawyer went out without
saying any more. Sterie jumped up and started after him, but the
door was locked. Terror now clutched him by the heart. There
must be something he could do! But everything had been done,

the appeal had been signed, there was nothing to do but wait. He began to stride up and down the room, and the sentries outside heard the rapid tramp of his boots on the cement. At the end of two hours the guard was changed, two hours later it was changed again, and then again. They all listened.

" Is he still tramping up and down? " the newcomers asked.

" Yes—still."

IO

Sterie was ravenously hungry. He gulped down the contents of the tin bowl that was brought him almost without chewing. The scanty meal allayed his pangs for a little while and then he felt hungry again. He smoked incessantly. Now and then he flung himself on the bed and tried in vain to sleep; then he jumped to his feet and again paced up and down.

Two days later the answer to his appeal arrived. His Majesty had refused to pardon an officer guilty of treachery. The lawyer brought the news. Sterie knew at a glance what it was, but he waited, pale-faced, his eyes dilated with terror, for him to speak the words. Then he uttered a short groan, a sort of gasp, and covered his eyes with his left arm. He moved to the wall and rested his right hand against it. At length he turned to his defender and stammered like a child:

" I'm frightened."

" That won't do. You must be brave."

" I'm afraid I shall scream, or—start struggling and have to be dragged to the shooting-post. I'm afraid of making a fool of myself," whispered Sterie. Tears were running down his cheeks and he wiped them with the back of his hand.

" You must keep calm. You're a man of honour—a man! " the lawyer said. He found the scene agonising, but he could not desert this man whom he knew to be innocent. Sterie said:

" Honour! They'll whip me across the face with my own

epaulettes. You call me a man! Fetch a woman and you'll see that at this moment I'm not even that!"

The other said nothing.

"Why have I got to die?" demanded Sterie, not looking at him. "Why?"

The other kept silent, not knowing what to say.

"To maintain discipline," said Sterie. "An innocent man has to be shot to prevent other men going over to the enemy. God almighty! . . ." He uttered a groan of helpless fury, gritting his teeth, while his hands twisted his cap and beads of sweat rose on his forehead. Sitting on the bed he glared at his defender like a caged animal. "When's it for?"

"Tomorrow at eight o'clock," murmured the lawyer. Sterie stared so fixedly at him that he was alarmed. He asked: "Is there anything you want?" Sterie did not answer. "Well, send a message by the guard if there is."

He went out as quietly as possible, and going to Father Ionesco, the chaplain, asked him to visit the condemned man. The priest was drinking tea and reading a novel with a torn cover. He got up at once, buttoned his grey cassock, put on a round hat to which was pinned the tricolour rosette of an officer, picked up his breviary and with his stole under his arm went and knocked at the door of the cell.

"Who is it?"

"The chaplain, my son—Father Ionesco."

A hideous bellow was the answer. The condemned man roared like an animal, hurling blasphemies and abuse at the priest, the King, the Army, the whole country and himself—all this in a voice so inhumanly distorted that the guards at the door stood rigid, clutching their rifles. The priest waited until Sterie had grown calmer and then said to them:

"Come and fetch me if he asks for me."

This took place early in the evening. At eleven o'clock one of the guards aroused the priest.

"He wants you, Father."

"Very well," said the priest, and looked round for his shoes with a long sigh.

Sterie, seated on the bed, stared hard at him as he entered. Father Ionesco was about forty years old, tall, a little paunchy, with a big, smooth face.

" Good evening, my son," he said, sitting down beside Sterie. Sterie did not move. He asked in a low voice:

" Father, what am I to do? "

" You must pray," said the priest gently.

" I can't. I've tried."

" You must try again, my son. It is in prayer that you will find salvation."

" I can't, Father," said Sterie. " I've tried. I've been trying for hours. Who am I to pray to? "

" To God, my son, the Father of us all."

" But why pray? It seems to me when I try to pray that I'm simply wasting words on air, talking into a void. There's nothing there, nothing anywhere, Father. What am I to do? "

He was utterly weary, his face taut, his eyes glowing and feverish.

" My son, you must pray from the depths of your soul," the priest said. " You must try——"

Sterie cut him short. " What makes you think I'm able to pray? " His voice had grown sharp. The priest sighed.

" We will pray together. Kneel beside me, my son."

Sterie knelt on the stone floor. Father Ionesco draped the stole over his head and began to read a prayer. The words were noble and solemn. But after a minute Sterie thrust the stole aside.

" I'm sorry, Father. I can't go on. I have no faith. We're wasting our time. Tell me what I'm to do."

He was staring at him with an almost demented pity, but when Father Ionesco opened his mouth to speak he interrupted him again,

" Why have I got to die? If God exists why is He making me die? I'm innocent! "

" None of us is innocent, my son," said the priest.

" I *am* innocent. I'm not a traitor! "

" You have committed other sins."

" No! No! I don't deserve to be treated like this. Why are they torturing me? Why am I to be degraded? Simply so that every man at the front will call me a traitor! But why? Do you know anything about the kind of officer I was? Do you? It's grotesque! It's madness, Father! I feel as though I were living in a madhouse, to be judged and killed by madmen. And for no reason, no purpose! I shall end by going mad myself. What am I do to, Father—what am I to do?"

He had got up and was pacing the room again, wringing his hands.

"You are suffering greatly, Lieutenant," said Father Ionesco. "But perhaps you are going to eternal life."

"I don't believe in a future life. Haven't you seen dead soldiers on a battlefield? Do you believe their souls have flown away to heaven? They lie there, they and their souls, and they're just dead. It's no good, Father. I've tried it. It won't work!" He sat down again on the bed and gazed beseechingly at the priest. "What's going to happen to me, Father? What's going to happen?"

The priest talked for some minutes. . . . Suddenly Sterie exploded in a string of oaths and blasphemies. Father Ionesco sought to calm him, but he shouted more and more loudly:

"Don't you see that they've destroyed me? I was ready to die at any time for my country! But now I know what that country is and what it means to be an officer. Die for that lot! I don't need to any more. They're killing me themselves, to suit their own purpose, while the real traitor's laughing his head off somewhere in Germany. A hell of a lot he cares! It's enough to make anyone laugh!"

"I shall pray for you, my son."

"Yes, pray for me," said Sterie, hiding his face in his hands.

When he looked up the priest was gone. Everything was clear to him now. There was nothing in the world but chaos and endless cruelty. Nothing could make life worth living in such a world. You had to be blindfold in order to live in it, a person with fixed beliefs and a closed mind.

Sterie was thirsty. He longed for a glass of good, cool wine. He wanted to eat. And although he did not want a woman he remembered the encounters of other days. He had lost everything, everything there was. The sense of duty done should bring a feeling of pride and joy that helps a man to die; even to die content. But to die as he was doing? "I have been robbed and utterly deprived. I am empty. I am everything that is disgraceful and ignoble, not a man but a cypher, excrement, mere squalid flesh. God, let them come for me quickly, so that I may escape from this filth!"

Then he began to think again of the execution. There were still some hours to go. Not many. He pictured the troops forming a square and the officer who would wrench off his shoulder-straps and whip them across his face. What sort of man would it be? Who would be detailed for the job? Perhaps in the spring he would be carried off by typhus. Sterie pictured the effort he would make in tearing off the straps, the conscientious brutality with which he would use them. Poor devil! Poor blind fool!

Then, as he thought this, he found that he had grown suddenly calm. He noted the fact with amazement, shivering a little. Where did it come from, this calm? He sought to account for it, pacing the room with his head bowed and his hands behind his back.

Perhaps it was due to the word "blind." Had not he, too, been blind? Yes; but now he very clearly understood the law which he had obeyed, the law which had destroyed him. Now everything was explained—the poor fool Duca, the judges, the prosecutor, the defender, the armies bogged down in their trenches from the Black Sea to the North Sea. Now he understood.

He walked with quickening strides until, his mind clear and his spirit cleansed, he stopped abruptly with tears of gratitude in his eyes—tears which he could not have bestowed on any living creature. He recovered from this onset of weeping and in tranquil happiness returned to his meditation. Now and again the face of terror approached him; pictures rose before his eyes —the execution, his own dead body, putrefaction and the endless night of death. But these things grew more and more hazy. He preferred to think of his discovery. " How sad to die now that I know! But after all, it is not important. If I have been able to learn so much, others will do the same."

He flung himself fully dressed on the truckle-bed and fell at once into a strange, transparent slumber through which reality was still to be seen, the cell and the guards outside it, and what had happened and what was going to happen. From this he passed into a deep sleep out of which he awoke as easily as a child, rested and purified. He rose again and paced the room until the door opened and he saw an officer of the Gendarmerie staring at him with a furtive curiosity.

" Is it time? " asked Sterie.

" No. I've come to warn you that it's in an hour. At eight exactly."

" Then why do you disturb me? " said Sterie calmly. " I'm busy. Leave me alone until the time has come."

That night General Cilibia, commanding the division, motored to the field headquarters of Sterie's brigade and sent for Colonel Vasilache. Cilibia, solemn and purple-faced, had black, bushy eyebrows like hog's bristles. He barked at Vasilache:

" Colonel, you will appoint one of your Frontier Guards officers to command the firing-squad."

Vasilache muttered something unintelligible, and Visoran, who had also been summoned, pulled a wry face.

" I'm very afraid, sir," the latter said, " that the men may refuse to fire, and we have no means of compelling them. Ordinarily in cases of insubordination we send the offender into the front line; but all those men have been in the trenches since last autumn."

Cilibia stared hard at him. Visoran's appearance was so perfectly military that he could scarcely be suspected of humanitarian sentiments. The general then turned to the commander of the infantry regiment, who had been following the discussion without saying anything.

" Who was on your left flank when that chap cleared out? "

" Number Six Company, General, commanded by Lieutenant Stahl."

" A German? All right, the Boche can do the job."

" At your orders, General. But I fancy he's French, not German."

" I don't give a damn if he's Chinese. He's to command the firing-squad."

The order was accordingly conveyed to Lieutenant Stahl, standing rigidly to attention in his commanding officer's room. Having delivered it the colonel turned his back on him, hoping to escape a refusal.

" I'm very sorry, sir, but I can't take charge of an execution-squad. I'd rather be shot myself."

The colonel turned sideways to look at him. Stahl's face was deathly white and his ginger moustache was trembling.

" I'll have you court-martialled! " the colonel bellowed.

Stahl did not budge. The colonel considered him uneasily. He had no means of compelling him, and he knew it. He racked his brains for another officer who might take on the job.

" Listen, Boche, if you'll do it I'll give you an extra month's leave."

" I was born in Bucarest, sir," said Stahl, tight-lipped and faintly smiling. " My family are all in Bucarest, in the occupied zone. But no matter where I'd been born I still couldn't do it." He was thinking: " I've done for myself. I can't help it. I don't care." But his heart shrank at the thought of death.

The colonel gazed at him in a cold fury. He was weighing the pros and cons. To have him court-martialled for refusal to obey an order would be to send him, too, before the firing-squad. But there was a danger that it might stir up a considerable rumpus. The case of Sterie was already being talked about. Was it judicious to create two martyrs? It might result in a public scandal, particularly if the Press got hold of it. There were more discreet ways of dealing with Stahl which would also amount to condemning him to death. There were various alternatives, one of which, at least, would be almost bound to succeed.

" All right, you can go," the commander of the regiment said to Stahl, and turned away again.

I I

During the same night, in command-posts all along the sector, lists of officers and men were compiled. Messengers were sent through the trenches to notify all who were listed. In the dawn contingents of officers and men made their way to the town of P——, dragging their feet along the roads or packed into carts. The day dawned grey and cold. Senior officers appeared. The soldiers, after piling arms, were marched to the shooting-range behind the barracks where they were formed up in a square. There were two thousand of them, lousy, exhausted, their eyes

devoid of expression. Heavy clouds passed over the sky. The
fourth side of the square was open, containing nothing but a
solid wooden post stuck in the ground.

Friedman was there; so were Dumitriu, Gogu Apostolesco,
Istrate and Stahl.

Stahl kept his eyes firmly closed. He didn't want to see. Istrate
had had no sleep and his eyes were bloodshot; he had had to
repel an enemy raid during the night. Later he was to say, " What
the hell does it matter if one man dies, more or less? Today it's
him, tomorrow it'll be me, and the day after it'll be your turn.
Why the hell should I care? If only they'd let us have women
at the front. . . ."

Gogu Apostolesco reeked of alcohol. He had received a present
from his parents of a flask of cognac so large that he could scarcely
get it into his pocket, and he had emptied it on the way. Now
he was feeling drowsy and warm and content. He was tempted to
whistle:

> *Non, non, les blondes*
> *Sont trop fecondes;*
> *Non, non, les blondes*
> *Je n'en veux pas!*

Friedman stood waiting. He could not forget Sterie's face
as he had seen it at the court-martial, blankly questioning, with
a smile for him at the end when he went out. A foolish smile in
which confidence was mingled with a vague alarm. " Oh God!
Oh God! " But Friedman showed nothing of what he was
feeling. He was just a junior officer back from the front line,
dirty, unshaven and with big ears, who knew his place and stood
waiting.

A fresh group appeared round the corner of the barracks—an
army magistrate with the rank of colonel, some junior officers and
a chaplain with swollen eyelids who held Sterie by the arm.
Sterie was marching fast, briskly and steadily, swinging his arms.
His face was haggard and he looked the shadow of his former self;
he was newly shaved. He had the absorbed expression of a man
who is paying great attention to what he is doing—someone, for
example, who is counting his own footsteps. Friedman saw him
disengage his arm with a gentle but decided movement from the

priest's grasp and walk alone to the execution-post. The firing-squad, marching behind him, moved towards the centre of the square. An officer marched at their side with a drawn sword, wearing his decorations. Friedman looked at Sterie, who now stood bare-headed with his back to the post; the icy wind was ruffling the hair over his forehead. He was calm but terribly pale. The priest was saying something to him.

" Squad—halt! " shouted the officer in a shrill voice. " Left turn! "

The colonel and the officers accompanying him stood in a group at some distance from the firing-squad. The colonel was stamping his feet to warm them. A lieutenant, the hilt of his sword emerging from a slit in his greatcoat, took up his position in front of the squad, and holding a document in his hand read out the sentence in a rasping, nasal voice. Then he advanced towards Sterie, who stood watching him come. The lieutenant had a most lamentable way of walking, with short steps, like a woman, while the tails of his greatcoat fluttered in the wind. Sterie gently thrust Father Ionesco aside and took off his greatcoat, which he threw on the ground. The lieutenant ripped off his shoulder-straps and brushed them swiftly across his face. Then he threw them on the ground and went to join the colonel. He walked very fast, almost running.

" Oh God! Oh God! " groaned Friedman; but no one heard. After watching two sergeants tie Sterie to the execution-post and bandage his eyes, and the priest move away with his head bowed and his breviary in his hand, Friedman closed his eyes. He heard the command and the sound of the volley—placed in the front rank he could not plug his ears. When he opened his eyes again he saw the body sagging from the post, held by the rope round its waist, the head hanging down. Orders were shouted and the troops moved off, except for a small detachment under an officer which stayed behind to dispose of the body.

Lieutenant Stahl was appointed to command an emergency hospital for typhus cases behind the lines. A week later he had contracted the disease himself and hung between life and death.

In 1921, at the instigation of Lieutenant Laurent Sterie's family, the case was reviewed in the Court of Appeal. The verdict of the court-martial was quashed and the condemned man re-habilitated. His rank and decorations were restored. The family wished to have him buried in a cemetery with a tombstone; but his remains were mingled with those of countless other soldiers, dead of typhus and buried in a common grave. Accordingly, the Sterie family gave up this idea.

III

Augusta, or the Wedding March

I

Late one afternoon in the year 1918 a young couple hurried along a street in Jassy, both seeming preoccupied and anxious to escape notice. A heavy mist lay over the town and the street-lamps were not yet lit. It was a good time for an errand calling for discretion.

The man was a twenty-year-old subaltern, tall and slender as a sapling. His heavy, horizon-blue greatcoat hung loosely about him, and a very high collar kept his small head erect, with its narrow face, hollow cheeks and pointed chin. Ghighi Duca's intimates knew that despite his frail appearance he possessed remarkable health and staying-power. The lady was his cousin, the beautiful, rather plump Augusta Hagibei, who walked with the upper part of her body thrust slightly forward, displaying a wonderfully rounded posterior, and whose head was enveloped in a knitted woollen shawl which covered everything except her eyes and nose, hiding the tense pallor of her face.

The couple turned into a side-street flanked by wooden palings and low walls, and stopped outside a one-storeyed house with thickly curtained windows. On the doorpost was an enamel plaque bearing in large letters the legend:

DOCTOR I. TASSESCO

Gynaecology and Urinary tract

Consultations: 8–10 A.M. *and* 3–5 P.M.

Here they entered, after Ghighi Duca had made sure that no one was looking. He came out again alone a few minutes later and began to walk up and down the street smoking. A long time passed. Now and again Ghighi looked at his watch, put it back in his pocket and nonchalantly went on walking.

Darkness fell and the lights came on. At length the gleam of an oil-lamp showed through the unwashed panes of Dr. Tassesco's front door. A key turned in the lock, the door opened and a woman emerged supporting Augusta, who was walking with evident difficulty. She stood leaning against the wall of the house while she waited for Ghighi to join her. He came up hurriedly, tipped the woman and took Augusta's arm, and they moved off very slowly down the street.

" We must try to go a bit faster," Ghighi murmured. " If I get caught by a patrol we shall both be hauled up before the area commander, and you know what that means."

Augusta pursed her lips and made an effort, but after a minute she gasped: " I can't do it."

" All right," said Ghighi irritably.

He had made little effort to conceal his impatience. Augusta's dark, handsome eyes glanced up at him for a moment.

She said: " It was awful, simply dreadful."

Ghighi did not reply. He started again to go faster, almost dragging his cousin along.

" You simply don't realise how ghastly it was."

He seemed not to have heard.

" All you're thinking about is the wretched patrol! "

" Well, do you want us to be caught? Don't you realise what would happen? "

" I'm feeling too ill—I can't worry about my reputation as much as you're doing," said Augusta. She struggled on for another few yards and then stopped.

" Now what is it? " asked Ghighi.

" I can scarcely stand," said Augusta with a moan.

Seeing her on the point of collapse Ghighi grabbed her swiftly under the arms, breathing the sweet, sickly odour of anaesthetic. Feeling the weight of her limp, sagging body, he thought, " What have I in common with this woman? Why the devil did I let myself in for this? " He had a momentary impulse to leave her there, huddled on the pavement, but he could not treat Augusta like that, and he disliked her the more in consequence. Gradually her body regained its strength. He felt her grow steadier. Presently she raised her pale, white-lipped face to his, and again he caught the smell of anaesthetic.

" I thought I was going to pass out," she said.

She took his arm again, and the rest of the walk to her home was accomplished without incident, except for one moment when they paused as a patrol of bearded Cossacks marched by with a heavy tramp of boots. Augusta was living with her elder sister, Alexandrina Romano, and her brother-in-law, in two very encumbered rooms in the apartment of a high-school master near the Rue Lapusneano. Having brought her safely to the door Ghighi took her hand and bent his head over it. She gazed at him in astonishment.

" Aren't you going to kiss me? "

Ghighi hesitated, then lightly brushed her cold lips smelling of chloroform with his own. But Augusta clung to him and kissed him passionately. He wrenched himself free, saluted and went hurriedly off without looking round.

He stayed away for two days, wondering whether he should say something or simply drop her without any explanation. The second alternative was tempting but dangerous. She might not understand and might come in pursuit of him. It was better to get it over. He called on her towards evening, under a red sky heavy with cloud. A Russian infantry battalion came down the street with long greatcoats reaching almost to the ground. They marched swinging their arms, without weapons, sturdy bearded men in fur caps. One of them shouted something, and the rosy faces brightened and they burst out laughing. Ghighi Duca glanced curiously at them, noting the unbuttoned greatcoats and the absence of belts and side-arms. Where had they come from and where were they going? Whatever they were doing, it was bound to be something strange, unexpected and disturbing.

He found Augusta in an armchair, wearing a négligé. She got up and embraced him, and then sat down again, moving slowly. She was still very pale but had recovered much of her attractiveness.

" We've a whole hour," she said. " Hagibei is at the Ministry and Didina and Romano are out paying calls."

" It's a fine time to be paying calls. Haven't they noticed what's going on in the streets? "

" Why, what is it? "

" What do you think? Revolution, of course. We've got a revolution going on all round us and it looks like being contagious."

" Darling," said Augusta, " have you only come here to talk

politics? In that case I'd sooner be visited by Monsieur Bratiano."

" I've come for a cup of tea," said Ghighi smoothly.

She looked quickly at him.

" What does that mean? What has happened? "

" Nothing. Nothing special. Aren't you going to give me any tea? "

He took off his greatcoat, dropped it over the back of one plush-upholstered armchair and seated himself in another, looking slender and distinguished, with an English cigarette held between the long, bony fingers of a hand adorned with a signet ring. The room with its congestion of miscellaneous furniture was in half-darkness. A silver samovar was hissing on the table, but Augusta did not offer him any tea. She was now watching him closely with eyes that were at once amused and slightly hostile.

" What does all this mean? You don't want to kiss me and you aren't nice. You're cold and unfriendly. What has happened? "

" Nothing." Ghighi smiled and crossed his legs. " Nothing at all. I've simply been taken with a fit of chastity."

" I see. Is it likely to last long? "

" I've no idea. Two or three years perhaps, or even four."
He was looking her straight in the eyes, still smiling.

Augusta also smiled. " Very well then—in that case you might as well go. Go on—clear out! "

Ghighi rose, picked up his cap and took his coat over his arm. He turned towards the door, but as he reached it Augusta rose painfully from her chair and, running after him, took him by the arm.

" No, sit down again. What's the matter? What is it you want? "

" I've told you."

" Don't joke," she said earnestly. " Do you think you and I can afford to play the fool? "

" But I'm not joking." Ghighi sat down again. " I'm not joking in the least. I'm tired of love."

" Ah! " cried Augusta. " You've found another woman! "

" No. I tell you, I'm sick of love. I don't want to have anything more to do with women."

" But why? Why? What's wrong? " asked Augusta in bewilderment.

" It was that business the other day, if you must know. I

didn't like it—the stink of medicine. It just left me feeling I want no more of it. The same thing would be bound to happen sooner or later with another woman—she'd stink of medicine too. Or perhaps she'd die on the operating-table or on the way home. Imagine what would have happened if you'd collapsed in the street. Think of the mess I'd have been in. I tell you, I want no more of it. I've had enough."

"You're absurd," said Augusta with a shaky laugh. "You'll never be able to do without women. You're too young."

"Well, anyway," said Ghighi, "I'll hold out as long as I can."

Augusta uttered a faint moan and went back to her chair. She was frightened now, on the verge of tears. "I don't understand you," she said.

"What don't you understand? It's plain enough."

"You really mean you're leaving me?"

"I've got to. I'm not going to risk that business happening again."

"But it won't happen again, I promise. I swear it!"

He shrugged his shoulders. "You can't be sure. I'd sooner save you the risk, and me too."

She sat with her hands on her knees gazing at him in despair. He got up again and put his arm through the sleeve of his greatcoat.

"I think it would be better for me to go, if you don't mind."

"No, you mustn't! If you go now I shall never speak to you again."

"I shall have to bear it," said Ghighi, getting into the other sleeve.

"Ghighi, are you really giving me up for good?" cried Augusta, trembling with misery, but ready at any instant to launch a furious counter-attack.

"Not only you but all the others—you and your five fellow-members."

"What! You mean to say you're having affairs with—with *five* other women besides me?"

"Not having—*had*. And now it's over. I'm sounding the retreat. I am about to become an ascetic. Anyway, what's so surprising about the others? You've gone on sleeping with your husband while you've been sleeping with me, and probably with other men as well."

" Filthy brute! " shouted Augusta.

" How kind," said Ghighi, buckling his belt. " Well, that's how it is. The moment you escape their clutches they call you names."

" Bastard! Swine! If I were a man I'd kill you! "

" If you were a man," said Ghighi, picking up his cap, " the question would not arise."

2

The First Regiment of Frontier Guards, reorganised, rested, rehabilitated, brought up to strength with thirty new officers and a thousand men, returned to the front line, lost a third of its numbers, and was then transferred to a sector alongside the Russian forces. Lieutenant Friedman was ordered to reconnoitre the position the regiment was to occupy and to make contact with the Russian front-line troops.

A bitterly cold afternoon at the beginning of 1918 found him walking along trenches as wide and deep as valleys. The frozen earth had been trodden flat by soldiers' boots. The firing-steps were deserted, and a scattered and tangled wilderness of wire showed blackly against an ash-coloured sky.

The trenches grew shallower as he went, so that he had to bend down in order not to show his head above the parapet. A great number of soldiers were moving casually about, bearded men in long grey capes with enormous flat fur bonnets pushed on to the back of their heads. All had loud voices. They laughed, smoked cigarettes rolled in newspaper, carted bundles of firewood and cooking-pots, or else sat in groups, gossiping or playing cards. Somewhere a mouth-organ was playing. Friedman went in search of the company commander, bending double to avoid getting a bullet in the head. The Russians, walking erect, gazed at him in astonishment and one or two laughed. " Laugh if you want to," thought Friedman. They were all mad, these Russians, walking upright, nobody on look-out and nobody troubling to ask who he was—he might be a German spy, for all they knew. But he was so exasperated by the laughter that in the end he too went upright. He would have liked to be able to move about as unconcernedly as they did, without so much as glancing towards the enemy, but he could not restrain himself from keeping one eye in the direction whence a bullet might come. In front of the trenches was an expanse of grey, ravaged, shell-pitted earth with huge gaps in the tangle of wire, and beyond this another network of barbed wire, presumably covering the German trenches. Further still were empty fields, ruined buildings and the stumps of trees destroyed by shell-fire. A melancholy, deserted landscape everywhere except in the Russian trenches, filled with the sound of deep, cheerful voices as men played at dice, squatting amid the odour of the galley-pots.

Friedman was feeling tired, depressed and apathetic; any attempt at serious thought seemed to plunge him into a thick-witted drowsiness; but he could feel that something very strange was going on around him. Before he had had time to account for it, a man in a pointed German helmet appeared suddenly in the open space beyond the German wire and began calmly to lay a telephone line. Friedman's first reflex was defensive; he sank his head between his shoulders ready to fling himself flat if enemy bullets started to come across. His second instinctive reaction was to get his pistol out of its holster and fire a shot at the man, who seemed to be taking no notice of anyone. The telephonist promptly jumped back into his trench and disappeared. And Friedman found himself surrounded by a cluster of bearded, fur-bonneted soldiery who abused him in deep, angry voices. At the start they all said the same thing, as though they could only utter a single phrase. Then they began to argue among themselves, pointing at Friedman, who was growing perturbed. In his apathy he had quite forgotten the tales that were being told of revolutionary developments in Petrograd, but now he was dramatically reminded of them. So that was the reason for the strange aspect of life in these trenches! But how was he to explain himself? Knowing no Russian, Friedman found himself virtually a prisoner in the hands of the enraged group surrounding him. Then another man pushed his way through the crowd and began to speak. Friedman caught the word " Roumanian " uttered in a melodious voice but in a tone of the utmost indignation.

" What were you playing at? " the newcomer asked him in his own tongue, while the rest fell silent and listened.

" How do you mean, what was I playing at? " said Friedman, startled at being addressed familiarly in the second person by an ordinary soldier. Even in his steel helmet he was a head shorter than the Russian and had to look up at him.

" Why did you shoot at that German? "

" But there's a war on. They're our enemies."

Friedman had replied mechanically, as he might have done to any soldier. The interpreter translated and the chorus of abuse broke out again, more vehement than ever.

" Listen," said the Russian, threatening Friedman with an enormous, red-haired fist, " you go away, see, or I kill you. We not make war, see? We soldier, German soldier, we not shoot, German not shoot, understand? You shoot, they trust us we not shoot, they think we liars. You not understand? You stupid."

He went on scolding vigorously but with something almost paternal in his manner. Quite at a loss Friedman asked:

" Then why do you stay here? If you aren't fighting why don't you go home? "

When this had been translated the men began to talk together with great seriousness. The interpreter said:

" We stay here till he send for us."

" Who? "

The man laughed slyly. " Someone."

He repeated question and answer in Russian and the others laughed, shrugging their shoulders. One of them muttered something to the interpreter in which Friedman caught the word *spion*, " spy," and the interpreter answered confidently, in a calm, singing voice:

" *Ah, schto, niet, niet, on nie spion, on dourak.* No, he's not a spy, only a fool."

In sudden exasperation Friedman shouted: " I want to see an officer. Where's your company commander? "

The giant again translated, laughing as he did so. The rest were convulsed with laughter, to Friedman's increasing wrath. Between bursts of merriment the interpreter said: " You know what they say? They say not good you go place where officers are. You go back your own place. Not good place where officers are."

Friedman turned abruptly and made off: but by the time he reached the end of the trench he, too, was smiling at the thought of those flushed, hilarious faces. Then the thought occurred to him that he had not seen a single officer—and suddenly he realised where the Russian officers were. . . .

When he arrived back at headquarters he learned that the regiment was not being sent to the front after all, but was to be entrained that evening at the nearest railway-station. And that night a long train wound its way through the hills of Moldavia, loaded with men, horses, rifles, machine-guns, trench-mortars, cases of ammunition, field-kitchens, carts, telephones, signal-lamps, bugles, two dogs and one regimental flag in its leather case.

Friedman travelled with the soldiers in a cattle-truck. The men made a fire on a sheet of metal, and sat round it talking in low, drowsy voices. Friedman rolled himself in a blanket and promptly fell asleep.

He was awakened by the sound of laughter and cries. During the last moments of his slumber he had imagined himself to be in a German trench; he had known that he would have to stay there and that he himself was to blame. He was lost. And suddenly the bearded Russians of the previous day appeared and shouted with laughter, pointing at him. He was the guilty one; they knew it too, and mocked him without mercy. "They're right," thought Friedman in his dream; whereupon he awoke, agitated and bathed in sweat.

The dream had been caused by the fact that the train had stopped at a small station crowded with Russian troops who were surging round the trucks and arguing with the men of the Frontier Guards. Friedman pushed back his blanket and raised himself on one elbow. His men were clustered in the doorway of the truck. Peering between army boots and legs swathed in blue-grey puttees he caught a glimpse of the faces of the men standing on the platform. He got up and saw Russians swarming like ants over the rails and round the station buildings.

Both sides were exchanging cigarettes and packets of tobacco.

" Where are you going—to the front? " a Russian asked.

" We don't know."

" Like us. We don't know, either."

" Don't go, comrades," said a Russian with a strong Moldavian accent. " Don't be fools. Clear out anywhere, go home and divide up the land of the boyars. And if the officers tell you lies, shoot them down like dogs."

Another Russian said something to him and he went on:

" Or go to Jassy and get rid of your King. Chase him out the way we chased out Nicholas. All that lot, they're only worth shooting."

The men stood listening, while Friedman contemplated that wall of silent backs. At any moment one of them might turn round to see if the officer was awake. He lay down again and pulled the blanket over his head.

Similar conversations were going on in the other trucks. A Roumanian whose accent was that of the peasants from beyond the Milcov, perhaps even from the borders of the Olt, cried in a ringing voice:

" Come with us, Ivan! Come on! "

Somewhere near at hand a light tenor voice shouted something in Russian. The Russian with a Moldavian accent said:

" We've got rid of our officers, comrades. We pulled off their shoulder-straps and gave them a kick up the arse for good measure. Now we're going home and we're going to start putting things in order, nicely or with bullets, as the case may be. Don't just stand doing nothing, lads! Don't be such fools! "

" Smooth talkers, aren't you! " muttered one of the frontier guards.

" Meaning you don't believe me, brother? Well, see if you can spot an officer among us. We're five battalions. Show me one single officer, just one! "

The talk went on, noisy and confused. Suddenly the truck gave a jerk, accompanied by a clatter of couplings. Gradually the train began to move.

A voice cried: " Make room for me, lads! Give me a hand! "

It was a firm, youthful voice which Friedman at once recognized as that of Dimitri Coziano, an eighteen-year-old subaltern who had been two months in his company at the front. Friedman heard him climb into the truck as it gathered speed and ask:

" Where's the lieutenant? "

" He's asleep," several men answered.

Coziano's boots came squeaking towards him, and Friedman felt himself shaken. The boy bent over him.

" Lieutenant, please get up. I've got to talk to you."

He was tall, lean and brown, with dark eyes deep-set beneath prominent brows; his uniform collar was too big. He still wore his steel helmet and carried his revolver and map-case attached to his belt, as though he were in the trenches. Friedman rose and they moved to one side, Friedman standing propped against the door of the truck while the other held on to the side to steady himself.

" Well, what is it? "

" The train will be stopping again in five minutes, sir," said Coziano, evidently apprehensive. He glanced round at the men.

" How do you know that? "

" I told Colonel Vasilache what was going on and he gave orders to pull up two miles outside the station. There's going to be trouble, sir, I'm afraid."

Friedman eyed him in some astonishment. Dimitri Coziano had shown himself hitherto to be an unobtrusive young man, conscientious in the performance of his duties but generally quiet and reserved. This display of enterprise was rather unexpected.

The train pulled up in open country. The soldiers were silent, evidently waiting for the officers to turn their backs before they went on talking. Friedman nodded to Coziano and they jumped down on to the track.

" Now tell me what this is all about."

They strolled together through a field. All along the train soldiers were getting out to relieve themselves or to collect firewood.

" Didn't you hear what those Russians were saying, sir? "

" No, I was asleep."

" It wasn't nice. They were trying to persuade our men to shoot us and start a revolution in Jassy. It doesn't look too good. Do you know that the Bolsheviks have taken over in Petrograd? "

" I'd no idea of it. The Bolsheviks—those are the November revolutionaries, aren't they? The ones who overthrew Kerensky."

" Yes, socialists of a sort, but very extreme. The Russian troops are completely disorganised. If they start forming soldiers' councils and march on Petrograd, that will be the finish. We shall have revolution here, too. And all because of that idiot Bratiano, who has lost us the war."

Friedman was silent for a moment, quite taken aback at finding anyone so politically minded in his company. At length he said:

" If it hadn't been Bratiano it would have been someone else. Our politicians are all the same."

" That's true. A gang of crooks and incompetents. The Russians are right. We ought to shoot the lot. Incidentally, I suppose you know that's where the regiment's being taken—to Jassy."

" What? I certainly didn't know that. What are we going to do in Jassy? "

Dimitri Coziano smiled.

" Apparently we're going to relieve the Fourth Cavalry and take over guard duties at the Palace and outside the Government offices. I'd like to have charge of the guard there, I must say. One would be well placed for shooting the lot! "

" Not a bad idea," said Friedman with calm.

Coziano glanced swiftly at him and said with a laugh:

" If I were the colonel I wouldn't put you in charge! "

" To hell with the lot of them," said Friedman. " But what else did you want to say to me? You'd better be quick. They're starting to get back on the train."

" I wanted to ask you to let me talk to the soldiers, to try and calm them down—particularly as there are two men in the company who come from a village where my family owns land."

" You seem to have the makings of a politician," said Friedman. " You ought to try for Parliament when the war's over."

" We have one or two politicians in the family already," said Dimitri.

" Are you related to Boniface Coziano? "

" He's my great-uncle, my grandfather's brother. May I speak to the men? "

" If you want to,' Friedman said.

His momentary cheerfulness had abated. Boniface Coziano— another well-born pirate! He had distinguished himself in the 1888 rising, just as General Avaresco had distinguished himself in 1907. The general was now in command of the Roumanian front-line armies, sending to their death peasants whose brothers he had shot. A sweet business! The Russians were right—the best way was to blow them sky-high and start again. " But we haven't any Bolsheviks," thought Friedman, and climbed back into the truck as Coziano, having fallen the men in, was beginning to address them. He broke off, saluted and waited.

" Carry on," said Friedman and turned to gaze over the countryside, lighting a cigarette. The train began to move again.

" Listen, you men," said young Coziano in a clear, decided voice. " This is the draft of the law for the division of land among the peasants. I'm going to read it to you. And those of you who come from Dobrunu and Reviga, you can talk to the others, because you know me and you know what a big estate my father has. To say nothing of other members of my family—Madame Helène Vorvoreano, Madame Olga Duca, Monsieur Serban Lascari and a great many more. Well, we're being cut down to five hundred *pogones*—two hundred and fifty acres. Do you understand? "

Friedman turned to look at him, more surprised than ever. There was no doubt of it, he would make a first-rate deputy. But Friedman did not trust him. He was bold, intelligent and enterprising; but there was something in him that did not ring true.

" I'm the one who's telling you, and you know you can believe what I say. The soldier who is loyal to his officers and faithful to his military oath will get a better share when the land is distributed. And the man who is decorated will get more still. That's all. You can fall out."

Coziano moved to Friedman's side, mopping his forehead, and murmured: " I'd never be any use in politics. I'm no good at public speaking."

" I don't agree. I thought you argued very well, from your point of view." There was a hint of chilliness in Friedman's voice which the gratified young man failed to perceive.

" To tell you the truth, they aren't all that easy to talk to. The peasants in my part of the country have twice set fire to the Manor, in 1888 and 1907. In 1907 the Army had to use artillery on the village. You can imagine how they feel about us landowners! Well, anyway, they can study the Land Act for themselves. That's one good thing the wretched Bratiano has done, although of course he had no alternative. We've got to adapt ourselves, introduce reforms and so forth, or else we're certain to have a revolution."

Friedman received this with a grunt, feeling that decidedly he was not much taken with this young Coziano. He was only another politician in the making, with no real concern for the men he was seeking to fit into his own pattern by dazzling them with the promise of land-ownership. Thinking over what he had heard, Friedman had a sense of shame. " I shouldn't have let him talk to them," he thought. " I won't do it again." He looked at the peasant faces, young, under-nourished, bony, pallid and hollow-cheeked. The men were murmuring together in low voices, clustered round one of their number who was reading the draft bill aloud, and then they turned to gaze at Second Lieutenant Coziano, dapper and bright-eyed. " You've fooled them. You're just another of the pirates," Friedman thought, and he considered the other officers in his company, Dumitriu, the soldier and nothing else, who had learnt his business at a Prussian military college; and Apostolesco, sceptical and depraved. . . .

Coziano approached him again.

" You know what I've been thinking. After all, Bratiano hasn't done so badly. First the artillery and then distribution of land. In other words, you start by breaking them and then you shut their mouths. It's quite shrewd."

Friedman said nothing, and he went on:

" All the same, the damned fool ought to be shot for getting us into this mess. He's all right for home affairs, but when it comes to foreign policy and war he's no earthly use."

" But who's to shoot him? You say you'd like to. But have you any special reason for hating him? "

" He's incompetent, that's all."

" I don't understand," said Friedman.

Coziano did not answer. The soldiers were talking in under-tones. The train went on its way to Jassy.

3

It was still winter. They had been in Jassy a little less than two months. The First Regiment of Frontier Guards was mounting guard outside Army Headquarters, the Cuza Voda house in the Rue Lapusneano, the Royal Palace, the Military Academy, the Cabinet Offices and the Allied Military Mission.

The sun shone through a blue-tinted, icy mist. Friedman walked through the town under the guidance of Dimitri Coziano, who was talking urgently, without a pause. Friedman listened with half his mind while he watched the crowded street—civilians in goloshes and felt hats half submerged in the flowing tide of officers of all ranks and arms, some in brightly polished jack-boots and new, glittering gold braid, powdered, monocled and immaculate; others in worn uniforms, caps on the back of their heads, with that look of wary alertness which men wear who have come from the front; and beside them, in short skirts, wearing the largest hats that had been seen since 1789, women with too much make-up on their faces, small-mouthed, huge-eyed, who laughed very loudly, talked business, intrigued to get their husbands or lovers jobs behind the lines at the cost of a few tens of thousands of *lei*, and in between calculations darted glances at members of the French General Staff, or at the Russians, who had the handsomest, fastest, noisiest motor-cars in Jassy. Patrols of bearded Kazaks were riding through the streets, scattering pedestrians in their search for Russian soldiers still faithful to the Tsar, who were concentrating in the barracks at Socola.

Friedman had a feeling that he was in a dream. He did not even talk the same language as these people. It was an agonising sensation; he felt madness breathing down his neck. For some months he had been subject to fits of giddiness. The accumulated exhaustion of the years he had spent at the front, and the shock of being buried alive by the blast of a large-calibre shell near

Marasesti, had reduced him to a state of chronic apathy. Occasionally, shaken with grief or despair, he was overtaken by fits of furious, meaningless rage; but for the most part everything left him indifferent.

Young Coziano went on volubly:

". . . and you know what put the idea into their heads? Well, they were for ever arguing, especially Nicou Prodan who never stops talking about what he saw in Petrograd, and about Ulyanov Lenin, the Bolshevik leader, and Leon Trotsky, and their tactics when they came into power—in fact, he nearly drove us all mad. And then one of them, I think it was my cousin, Ghighi Duca, suddenly said, 'My God, if only we had a hundred bayonets! Just a hundred!' So then I said calmly, ' Gentlemen, I'll bring you Bratiano, tied hand and foot, whenever you like, and the rest of his Cabinet, and then you can proclaim the republic.' Sensation! You should have seen their eyes pop. They're nearly all soldiers, company commanders, and when I told them about the frame of mind our men are in, and the kind of man you are, sir, well then they were absolutely carried away. They're all young men, with plenty of guts and energy. All they need is a handful of soldiers they can rely on. As I say, Nicou Prodan is on the side of the Bolsheviks. He edited a review called *Social Progress* before the war. He's a first-rate journalist and——"

" I've heard of him and I've read his articles," said Friedman.

" Good. Then there's Ghighi Duca. In fact, he's the one who had the idea. Nothing scares Ghighi and nothing's sacred to him. He wants to be a big shot, although, of course, what he wants isn't important—we'll decide later how far we can let him go. Then there's Fanica Nicoulesco. He's older than the rest of us— well, Nicou Prodan's pretty old too, he's over thirty; but Fanica's nearly forty. He's a highbrow, a philosopher, in fact he's got a German university degree, I think—anyway he studied philosophy in Germany. He's a chap with brains, a real thinker, and what I admire about him is the objective way he thinks. He's absolutely logical. If he starts at A he goes right through to Z without ever letting himself be sidetracked. It was he who made us see that it all came down to a *coup d'état*."

" Yes," said Friedman in some exasperation, " but do you realise that I still don't understand exactly what you want? " All this aroused his misgivings, attracted though he was by the idea of dethroning the King and overturning the Government.

" The first thing is to get rid of the King and proclaim the Republic and push through the programme of agrarian reform; because, as you know, the thing that matters most to the soldiers is the breaking up of the estates and the distribution of the land. As Fanica Nicoulesco is always saying, if we don't introduce reforms everything will collapse, just as it has in Russia, and the power will pass into the hands of all kinds of riff-raff—workmen, mechanics, God knows what—anyway, proletarians."

" But would that be so terrible? "

Coziano smiled. " Anyway, we're all agreed that the programme will have to be worked out after the Republic has been proclaimed. But I still haven't told you about the others. You need to know about them. There's a friend of mine, Titel Negruzzi, who also had a long spell at the front in the artillery. He's a chap who whoops it up a good deal, but absolutely fearless; nothing much in his head except a few half-baked ideas, but he's a man of action and that's what we need. Then there's . . ."

Friedman stopped listening, letting himself relapse into his habitual state of torpor. What exactly did these people intend? What the soldiers wanted, Russian or Roumanian, was simple enough; they wanted land, a plot of land of their own and the right to cultivate it in peace and get enough to eat. But this gaggle of young hot-heads . . .

They entered a house, left their greatcoats in the hall and went into a room filled with tobacco-smoke where a number of lieutenants and subalterns were all talking at once, with brandy-goblets in their hands. There was a sudden silence. Friedman bowed in salutation, took a seat and looked about him. He found himself contemplating an almost bald lieutenant with a head like a Roman statue, virile, with vigorous, strongly marked features, a firm mouth and intense blue eyes. Which one was he—Nicou Prodan or Fanica Nicoulesco? The talk, as it proceeded, revealed him to be the former. As for Fanica Nicoulesco, he was a non-commissioned officer in training for commissioned rank, with hair turning grey, a swarthy skin, long tufted eyebrows and curious eyes, one brown and the other green. There was also a slim lieutenant with white bony hands, fair hair and moustache and the complexion of a girl. This was Ghighi Duca. Gogu

Apostolesco was there, red-haired and rosy-cheeked; he greeted Friedman warmly, and was plainly overjoyed at being part of a conspiracy. Beside him sat a good-looking, dark-haired young man with a small moustache. He was Second Lieutenant Negruzzi, whom everyone addressed as Titel, and concerning whom Gogu Apostolesco murmured in Friedman's ear that he was not one of the Moldavian Negruzzis but came from a highly respected Vilcean family—" but no connection with the Costake Negruzzis, none whatever." Ghighi Duca greeted Friedman politely; Nicou Prodan reached for his hand and cried:

" You're the man we want! When are we going to start? "

" Whenever you like," said Friedman glumly. The others smiled, filled with admiration. Dimitri Coziano winked at Ghighi Duca.

" It's the only solution," said Nicou Prodan. " *De l'audace, encore de l'audace, et toujours de l'audace.*"

Friedman listened, nodded and answered questions as the discussion got confusedly under way again.

" We've got to re-establish contact with Averesco."

" Then Ghighi will have to go to Bacau, to Army Headquarters."

" We must get Iorga on our side. And what are we to do about the French Military Mission? "

" Who's going to talk to the Socialists? "

" The Socialists won't do a thing, now that your Monsieur Bratiano has murdered Max Wechsler."

" Why do you call him *my* Bratiano? "

" But we ought to go after Frimu or Ghilerev or Bujov. Who says they're under arrest? They can't be! "

" They are. I know it for a fact."

Friedman was putting on a show of alertness and returning prompt, concise replies to the questions addressed to him. He would have sooner been in bed, but his attitude was not wholly feigned. He kept wondering, " What are this lot really after? What's wrong with the whole set-up? " He pondered the matter, but no light dawned in his befogged mind. " I'm too tired," he thought. " The front has finished me."

" I know the officer commanding the Russian armoured cars at Socola," said Ghighi Duca. " He's a revolutionary. If you like I'll bring him along tomorrow."

" Good," said Nicou Prodan. " But where shall we meet?

This house is too public. We're liable to be arrested if we attract too much notice."

"There's a lady I know," said Titel Negruzzi. "One of my admirers."

The others laughed.

"Has she any family or neighbours?" asked Nicou Prodan.

"The other people in the house are all in hospital, down with Spanish 'flu. She's on her own. She's very charming, I promise you. A rare nature, capable of any sacrifice."

"We don't want women mixed up in this business," said Ghighi Duca.

"I'll vouch for her. I'm risking my neck too," said Titel Negruzzi. "Are you getting the wind up?"

Ghighi Duca flushed scarlet. "You chaps from the front are intolerable, the side you put on. You seem to think you're the only ones with any guts."

Prodan laughed. "You'll have to go to the front yourself, if you want to be taken seriously. At least we've proved ourselves."

"I intend to go," said Ghighi Duca with scorn.

Fanica Nicoulesco said: "Yes, but not yet—not until after the revolution. Until then we must stick together. The immediate problem is to dispose of the King, Bratiano and company. We've got to be methodical. When we've settled that business we can decide upon our next step."

"I still don't want women around. Conspiracies always get blown because of women."

"All right, but in that case where are we to meet?" asked Nicou Prodan.

"I don't know," said Ghighi Duca. "We shall have to think."

"We're to sit and think, and in the meantime go on meeting here until we get rumbled!" cried Titel Negruzzi. "I've said I'm ready to go bail for this lady—don't you understand what I mean? I can hardly put it more plainly."

Ghighi Duca looked at him with a grin. "You're so confident of her devotion?"

"I must ask you not to make insinuations regarding a lady whom you don't even know," Titel said loftily.

"What's her name?" asked Fanica Nicoulesco.

"Madame Hagibei."

" But she's my cousin! " cried Gogu Apostolesco. " And Ghighi's and Dim Coziano's! Well, that settles it. She'd scarcely be likely to send three near and dear relations to the firing-squad! "

This produced a burst of laughter. Nicou Prodan said:

" That seems to answer your objection, Duca. Presumably you know the lady, if she's your cousin."

" I certainly know her," said Ghighi Duca. " It's a reason in itself for mistrusting her."

" Oh, come off it! " cried Gogu, still chuckling at his own joke. " You can't really be afraid she'd give you and me and Dim away."

Ghighi Duca made no reply. He could not explain why he feared Augusta; and surely, in any case, she would not send ten men to their death simply because one of them had treated her badly.

Friedman had paid no attention to these last exchanges. He was still asking himself, " Why is it that these people are all wrong? Where am I going wrong? " He rose mechanically when the others started putting on their greatcoats, made his adieus and left the house. Coziano hurried after him, in a highly exalted state of mind.

" Well, what do you think? It's the right thing to do, isn't it? Don't you think it's right? "

Friedman reflected in dismay, " At the front he never opened his mouth, but now that it's a matter of politics he can't stop talking." And young Coziano babbled on:

" What did you think of them? Do you like them? You're keen on the idea, aren't you? It's all settled, isn't it?—we're going ahead! "

4

The next day Dim Coziano led Friedman along a side-street not far from the Rue Lapusneano to a door with stained-glass panes under an iron portico. It was here that Madame Augusta Hagibei lived. Titel Negruzzi had shown him the house during the morning.

They were not the first arrivals. Titel Negruzzi was already there, looking very much at home, and Gogu Apostolesco, a little drunk, and two others whose names Friedman did not remember. Nicou Prodan arrived a minute later and was followed by Fanica Nicoulesco. The smoke of cigarettes grew thick in the room. The alluring Madame Hagibei, smiling with a gleam of white teeth, offered them tea and small, tasteless cakes. Titel Negruzzi said:

" My love, haven't you anything stronger than this? "

Augusta fetched cognac and tumblers.

" I'm sorry I haven't any brandy-goblets," she said demurely. " You'll have to make do with these."

She went round with the bottle. Friedman, who had been examining his surroundings, caught the scent of expensive French perfume and looked at her for the first time. He watched her as she moved among this party of men, with lowered eyes and an air of unassailable virtue, and he noted the intent glance which Gogu Apostolesco directed at her admirably shaped behind. The two young men whose names he did not remember were no less spellbound. But Augusta seemed unconscious of all this. She smiled fondly at Titel as he patted her in passing, and went on to serve Fanica Nicoulesco, who stared hard at her with a faint, gangsterish smile at the corners of his mouth. Even Nicou Prodan was in a state of some excitement, discoursing more than usual:

" . . . the thing we mustn't do is what Robespierre did when they brought him the order for the arrest of his enemies in the

Convention. You remember? He picked up his pen to sign, dipped it in the ink, wrote ' Rob . . .' and then paused, saying that he wanted time to think. That was what took him to the guillotine, my friends! We don't need to think, we have to *act*! " He banged his fist on the table, and Madame Hagibei mopped up the little pool of spilt brandy with an indulgent smile.

Fanica Nicoulesco was also anxious to shine. " Who said anything else? " he asked sarcastically. " All the same, I fancy Lenin and the rest of your Bolsheviks did a bit of thinking before they acted."

" That isn't what I meant," said Nicou Prodan.

" I'm sorry. I seem to have misunderstood you."

" What I meant," said Nicou Prodan, glaring at him, " is that when you've decided on a plan of action you shouldn't waste any more time arguing—you should carry it out! "

Fanica Nicoulesco gazed blandly at him, and he flushed and was silent. Madame Hagibei exchanged a glance with Nicoulesco, and Titel noticed it and frowned. At this moment Ghighi Duca entered, accompanied by a Russian officer in his middle twenties, a heavy-featured bespectacled young man with fair hair plastered carefully down on his head. His manner was polite and calm; he had red lips with a slight pout.

" I should like to introduce Lieutenant-Major Goloubenko," said Ghighi Duca, glancing sideways at Augusta. She had not offered him her hand, nor did she once look at him throughout the evening.

Nicou Prodan went excitedly up to Goloubenko. " You've been told all about it, haven't you? What do you think of our plan? "

The Russian smiled amiably and began to ask questions. His French was very different from that of the young Roumanian boyars, Ghighi, Titel and Gogu Apostolesco, who had all been brought up by French governesses; he spoke it like a man who has learned it at school, slowly and carefully, and with a soft, plummy Russian accent which sounded strange in a language whose characteristic ring is tonic, rapid and sonorous. He asked:

" What have you done to arouse the masses? "

The others looked at one another. Nicou Prodan replied after a moment of silence:

" We're going to draw up a manifesto for circulation in Jassy.

Your armoured cars can also distribute them in the various barracks."

" I see. And how are you going to win over the Army? "

Dimitri Coziano answered: " We shall proclaim the distribution of land and the immediate cessation of hostilities."

" But we can't do that! " cried Titel Negruzzi. " Do you mean that we're to give up Transylvania? "

" That's not important for the present," said Ghighi Duca. "Transylvania will have to wait. The first thing is to gain power."

Fanica Nicoulesco said: " But we can't disregard a national aspiration."

Augusta maintained an enigmatic smile. Nicou Prodan began to shout, and Ghighi Duca also grew heated. The Russian continued to smile amiably. Raising a hand for silence he said:

" It seems to me, gentlemen, that you are not altogether in agreement. How do you prose to carry out your coup? "

They then turned to Friedman, who, emerging from his customary torpor, outlined his plan of action in a cool, casual voice. His company, on guard duty at the Palace, was to arrest the King: after which Friedman himself, revolver in hand, would compel the monarch to sign an Act of Abdication in favour of a Directorate composed of men appointed by the conspirators. At the same time another company, commanded by one of his friends, would arrest the Government and the members of the Allied Military Mission. A third company would occupy the Central Post Office and telegraph exchange, and a detachment would go to the railwaymen at Nicolina and prevail upon them to stop all trains.

" That's my plan," said Friedman.

The Russian looked hard at him and asked a number of questions regarding the timing of the operation. He also mentioned the possibility, by no means negligible, of some minister or general being absent and so escaping arrest.

" And what action will you take? " Nicou Prodan asked him.

Goloubenko replied with the utmost seriousness: " I can let you have two machine-guns for each company, and of course I shall liquidate General Shtcherbachev and his staff."

His listeners were dumbfounded. The verb " to liquidate " was one generally used in connection with banking or commercial

matters—in short, an accounting term. They did not know precisely what meaning Goloubenko attached to it; but since his
general intention was obvious they hesitated to ask for any further
definition. The Russian went on:

" The essential thing is to frustrate a counter-offensive by
Avaresco's army. Petrograd is still threatened by reactionary
forces. What will the Social-Democrat party be doing? What
about the railway-workers' union? Are you in touch with
them? "

" He's right," said Nicou Prodan, turning to the rest. " He
knows his business."

Ghighi Duca was delighted by this. " I hope you're grateful
to me for bringing him along," he said cheerfully, for the moment
forgetting his discomfort at seeing Augusta again. But Titel
Negruzzi shouted, with a coarse vehemence that was unusual in
him:

" Oh, for Christ's sake, do we have to worry about all that
sort of thing? No offence, Lieutenant, but you're raising a lot
of unnecessary complications. The thing is to go ahead—get
cracking! "

Goloubenko started to point out what the consequences might
be if the coup were insufficiently prepared but Titel shouted
him down. It was all a lot of tripe! At the front there was only
one thing you thought about—forward, lads!—get at them!—
let them have it in the guts! . . . He then sat smirking, highly
pleased with himself, while the two youngest officers applauded
and Fanica Nicoulesco laughed loudly. Nicou Prodan broke
into a furious protest. Meanwhile Ghighi Duca was gazing
apprehensively at Augusta, who had now adopted a madonna-
like attitude, with her hands clasped on her knees, her head
lowered and her long lashes shading her warm-tinted cheeks. . . .

The argument continued into the small hours. They decided
to appoint representatives to make contact with socialist circles in
Jassy, or with what remained of them after the latest wave of
arrests. Titel Negruzzi was vehemently opposed to this, and the
two second lieutenants and Fanica Nicoulesco said that they
didn't want to be led up the garden by those types.

Finally they went out into the icy night, separating into groups
of two or three. Ghighi stayed to the last, hoping for a word with
Augusta. He was uneasy and perturbed, anxious to know what

was going on in her mind. But Augusta, after taking leave of the others, sat down again in an armchair without looking at him, and Titel Negruzzi, who was apparently staying, firmly brought him his greatcoat.

Ghighi was irritated. He said a curt good night to Titel who responded with jesting good humour, while Augusta stayed motionless and faintly smiling, as though to say, " I care nothing for any of you. I'll sleep with whom I like and treat you as I please."

Ghighi strode down the street muttering furiously under his breath. Why the devil did she have to grin about it? Who cared who she slept with? . . . A senior officer returning late from the gaming-tables glared with disapproval at this lieutenant who went about talking to himself and failing to salute his superiors.

Friedman and Goloubenko, meanwhile, were walking together towards the Socola Barracks.

" I don't know what it is that leaves me feeling so dissatisfied with these discussions," said Friedman, not knowing, either, what it was that had suddenly moved him to speak. " We've nearly all been at the front. We've seen human beings robbed of all dignity, everything that gives a meaning to life. We want something different, a better, cleaner world. We used to think that a cause was sanctified by the sacrifices it inspired. But we've seen so many soldiers, so many peasants, killed for a cause which wasn't theirs. Literally murdered. Hundreds of thousands of men murdered. . . ."

" Millions," said Goloubenko gently.

" But why—why? What's it all for? Who gains anything by all the slaughter? Why should I have been robbed of my health, both in body and soul? I want to destroy that world. So I've joined forces with the men you've just met. But I scarcely know why I'm doing it. I don't even understand myself. Everything seems to me horrible and meaningless—grotesque. I had a friend who was shot without having committed any crime, simply to make an example, and what made it so hideously ironical was that he was a believer in the established order of things, a man with a particularly strong sense of duty. You see how fantastic it all is? It amazes me that he didn't go mad before they led him out to execution. I'm surprised I haven't gone mad myself."

" And yet," said Goloubenko, smiling at him, " it's all clear enough—the meaning of this war, the people who profit by it, the people who are in favour of it, and why. You've seen what goes on. Surely you don't need to be told about the profits made by the big industrial corporations, heavy industry in particular; or about the problem of world markets?"

Speaking calmly and lucidly, like a university professor, he went on to outline Lenin's theory of imperialism. Friedman, who knew nothing of Marxist doctrine, listened in silence, asking an occasional question. Goloubenko went on to talk of the theory of class-war, rapidly describing the development of capitalist society and the growth of socialism.

"It's extraordinarily interesting," muttered Friedman. "It's all new to me."

"It's hardly what you can expect to be taught in universities subsidised by bourgeois governments," said Goloubenko, smiling.

The political implications of this remark were lost on Friedman. The Russian spoke with a kind of modest simplicity, seeming to apologise for the recital of facts so self-evident and universally known; and in doing so rid his words of anything that might have rendered them suspect. He added with a light laugh:

"After all, what do you suppose the monopoly-capitalists are after?"

He talked of things that no newspaper ever mentioned—anyway, none that Friedman had seen. It was all unanswerably logical, and Friedman's dumbfounded excitement increased. He wanted to know much more. For several hours they walked up and down outside the barracks housing General Shtcherbachev's staff and an armoured-car company. A row of cars stood in the barrack-square covered by tarpaulins, long, angular vehicles with a small turret at the rear.

"All this is unique in history," murmured Friedman, staring at the ground, while the sentry at the barrack-gates, standing with fixed bayonet, watched them as they strolled.

"This time it will become a world revolution," said Goloubenko calmly. And he went on to reveal that it was for this that he had come to Jassy—to help spread the world revolution which was to achieve socialism and universal peace.

"Do you now understand? I believe that even your little group may come in useful. Any revolution, no matter what starts it off, is bound to become socialist in the end, because in this age nothing else is possible. It's a great pity your socialists didn't seize power in the spring of last year, when the revolution broke out in Petrograd. But that is understandable; the most powerful section of the proletariat in your country was under German occupation, and the socialists here aren't sufficiently ruthless. Your Max Wechsler paid for his indecision with his life. It's sad that he did not survive to lead the revolution, but the work must go on."

" I can't feel that my friends are the right people to do it," said Friedman.

" They seem to be mostly aristocrats and adventurers. As for Prodan, he's a man who thinks emotionally, not an intellectual revolutionary. I don't know what that woman was doing there. Women are out of place in this sort of business. A good many of your friends seem very anxious to sleep with her, if they haven't done so already, which is obviously rather beside the point."

" Don't you think we may end by achieving nothing? " said Friedman. " And even that things may turn out very unpleasantly for us? "

" Well, obviously you can't plan a revolutionary *coup d'état* without running risks. But that mustn't deter us from going on with the work. Countless attempts of this sort have to be made all over the world. Many are bound to fail, but the rest will lead to socialism and the new age."

" Yes, of course, of course. . . . We've got to go on."

Friedman was beginning to feel as though he had known this matter-of-fact, self-confident young man all his life. Unconsciously he was beginning to think in the Russian's own terms—" obviously," " evidently," " of course." Everything was beginning to seem self-evident.

As they were about to separate, he asked: " Have you any French or German books? "

The other looked at him and then said: " Yes, I have one. Wait here a minute."

Friedman stood waiting on the empty pavement, contemplating the shrouded rows of armoured cars on the barrack-square, bathed in the glare of powerful arc-lights. The sentry at the gate said something in Russian, and he replied:

" He's coming back."

He pointed towards the figure in the flat cap and long, flapping greatcoat now striding briskly towards the far side of the square. The sentry said something in a louder voice, and signed to Friedman to cross to the opposite pavement. He did so, and presently Goloubenko returned with the book.

" If anyone asks, we've been discussing French literature," he said with a chuckle. " Racine, perhaps—or Molière."

Friedman was smiling as he turned away, feeling his heart grow suddenly light. He felt very wide awake as he walked back to his quarters, turning the night's talk over in his mind. He stopped under a lamp to look at the book—" K. Marx et F. Engels: *Le Manifeste Communiste*. Paris, les Editions Sociales 1905." Back in his room he sat reading until dawn. His orderly called him at seven. He was on guard-duty that day at the Military College, where the King and his suite were in residence.

5

They continued to meet at Augusta Hagibei's house, and the tone of the debates grew increasingly heated. Titel Negruzzi, Nicou Prodan and Ghighi Duca were several times on the verge of dropping out altogether, but the others managed to smooth them down. One night, as the last of her guests was leaving, Augusta murmured to Titel Negruzzi:

" You go too, Titel. I'm not feeling very well. I've got a headache."

She avoided his eyes. Titel, seeing a covert smile on the lips of Fanica Nicoulesco, waited in the street outside hidden behind a tree. After a couple of minutes he heard the rapid tread of a soldier's boots and knew at once who it was: Fanica Nicoulesco was the only one of them who was not an officer, and who wore a police-helmet instead of a cap. Titel was about to spring on him, but then drew back. What could he do to Nicoulesco? What right had he? He watched him tap on the window and disappear into the house, and then he went off down the street clenching his fists. The blasted whore! If she was through with him, why couldn't she have the decency to say so? Why double-cross him in this fashion? He felt bitterly humiliated. The next night he did not address a word to Augusta, but he could not refrain from quarrelling openly with Fanica Nicoulesco who, looking particularly pleased with himself, took issue with him over some quite unimportant point. Titel refused to give way or to abate his truculence. There was a heavy silence, and some of them rose to leave. The whole thing seemed to be breaking up. But Goloubenko said good-humouredly:

" No matter, gentlemen. . . . Let us leave that question till tomorrow and go on to the next."

This saved the situation for the time being; but they still had not established contact with the socialists or appointed a representative to visit General Averesco's headquarters; nor had the membership of the proposed revolutionary Directorate yet been agreed. Fanica Nicoulesco had demanded his own inclusion.

" On what grounds, Monsieur? " Nicou Prodan asked sardonically. " As a doctor of philosophy or as a temporary sergeant-major? "

" As the author of the plan," answered Fanica Nicoulesco, disregarding the sarcasm.

They seemed to be getting nowhere, despite the urging of Nicou Prodan who said despairingly at every meeting:

" Gentlemen, we have no time to waste."

Friedman said one night as he and Goloubenko walked back to their quarters: " How would it be if we announced at the next meeting that we intended to go into action at midnight? If we confronted them with a *fait accompli* and forced them to follow us? "

" Or to scuttle like rabbits! In any case there aren't enough of us. You and I might find ourselves alone. The movement has got to be on the largest possible scale, embracing all the troops in Jassy and extending eventually to the front. The social and historical conditions are less favourable here than in Russia. It calls for a great deal of patience."

After another of these fruitless meetings Friedman said: " Don't you get the impression that they aren't really serious and that we're bound to fail? "

" Certainly they aren't all I had hoped for," said Goloubenko

with a wry laugh. " As for succeeding, at the moment I'm thinking of another plan. I'll tell you about it if it seems to offer any
chance of success. The trouble is that I don't know Roumanian.
I'd give half my life to be able to speak your language at this
moment."

They went on talking till one in the morning and then separated.
Entering his barracks Friedman made straight for the long,
single-storeyed building where he shared a room with another
officer. He was walking fast with his eyes to the ground, thinking
over his talk with Goloubenko. The sentry saluted him as he
entered the building, clicking his heels on the stone flags.

He opened the door of his room and then stood petrified. Two
officers of Gendarmerie were seated on his bed. They rose promptly
as he entered and the door was slammed behind him. Friedman
swung round to confront a third gendarme who had been seated
on a chair beside the door. All three covered him with their
revolvers.

" Put your hands up, Lieutenant! Are you armed? "

Friedman did not reply. They searched him and took away his
revolver. One of the officers said:

" You're coming with us. Don't make any trouble or you'll
be shot."

He was marched out of the room with two of them holding him
by the arms while the third followed behind. As they emerged
into the open they heard the sound of rifle-shots from the barracks where General Shtcherbachev's staff were housed. This
was followed by a long burst of machine-gun fire and a few
isolated shots. Then there was a very short burst, as though
some machine-gunner had been hit just as he pressed the trigger.

Friedman uttered a groan and tried to struggle free, but his
arms were savagely gripped. The man behind said:

" Any more of that and I'll shoot."

At about three o'clock that morning a military magistrate, bearded
and skinny, looking like a priest in uniform, was driven to the
residence of Monsieur Bratiano, the Prime Minister. The house
was guarded by a detachment of the First Regiment of Frontier
Guards. The colonel-magistrate, a brief-case under his arm, was
led by a sleepy secretary through a series of darkened rooms into a
library lighted by a green-shaded lamp on the writing-table. The

Prime Minister, in a morning coat, was lying on a leather sofa with a rug over his legs. He was a handsome man, sallow-skinned, with a thin, straight nose, very black hair and beard, and magnificent eyes, big and dark with long lashes. He had been Prime Minister of Roumania for a long time and all-powerful in the country for even longer. The brother-in-law and lover of the Queen, who could do what she liked with King Ferdinand, and related to the richest people in the land, Bratiano was the leader of a highly influential clique and possessed a large political following.

" At your command, Excellency! " said the colonel, clicking his heels.

" Good evening," said Monsieur Bratiano in a tired voice. " Take a seat, Colonel, and tell me your news."

He did not offer his hand. The colonel sat down in an armchair, produced some notes from his brief-case and proceeded to report on the situation.

". . . proving that the information sent me by your Excellency was entirely correct. The first two confessed under the threat of excution coupled with proof that I already knew everything. They gave way, and so did two of the others when I confronted them with the first two. I may add that General Shtcherbachev has himself attended to the execution of the traitors in his command."

" Were there many? "

" I can't say, but certainly there are a great many dead. They fought to defend themselves."

" And ours? What age are they? "

" Most of them are under twenty-one, Excellency. But this does not exonerate them or absolve them from paying the penalty."

For some moments Bratiano's handsome eyes contemplated the colonel in silence. Then, with a limp movement of his hand, he said indolently:

" You can stuff them up their mother's arse."

The colonel gave an embarrassed laugh. " Ha-ha! . . . I should like to draw your Excellency's attention to the case of the traitor Friedman, whom our country has honoured, despite his foreign extraction, with high military distinctions, and in whom she showed her trust by appointing him to His Majesty's personal guard. Despite these marks of signal favour he has joined in a conspiracy directed against the King and the Government. It is a particularly bad case."

He was silent. The Prime Minister continued to gaze thoughtfully at him. Finally the colonel rose. It made him uneasy to be stared at like that. He bowed and said:

" Has your Excellency any further need of me? "

" No, thank you."

The colonel clicked his heels and saluted, and receiving no acknowledgement withdrew as rapidly as possible. He got into his car and was driven back to his quarters. It was late and he was feeling horribly tired.

All the conspirators were put under lock and key that night except the Russians, who were dead, having first killed three of General Shtcherbachev's staff-officers. The next day the First Regiment of Frontier Guards was entrained at Nicolina railway-station and sent back to the front, whither the arrested officers followed them within a few hours. Orders were given that they were to be granted no leave until the cessation of hostilities and the demobilisation of their respective regiments. Friedman was transferred to a regiment of the line. The written order to this effect was followed by certain verbal instructions.

6

The train which bore Friedman to the front, under the escort of a sergeant and two gendarmes, was not heated and all its windows were broken. The passengers for the most part travelled standing, packed so tightly together that they had scarcely room to turn. There were civilians wrapped in fur-collared overcoats, with fur caps and army boots, peasants in rags and soldiers with all their equipment. Friedman stood in the corridor, with his escort on either side of him, listening to the groaning of axles, the snores, belches and coughing of slumberers, the voices of those who could not sleep because they were clinging to the steps or the buffers, and, in the compartment behind him, the low voices of a party of Russian soldiers seated amid piles of kit with their rifles between their knees. The train was travelling slowly, as though it had no precise destination. There was nothing to be seen except when one of the Russians lit a cigarette, its red glow in the darkness affording a glimpse of a wrinkled, bearded face.

" The number of them there are! " Friedman thought in his half-sleep. " A hundred and fifty millions! He was right in saying that they are the fly-wheel of the machine. When the fly-wheel starts to rotate it takes everything with it."

He was thinking of Goloubenko, still unable to realise that he was dead. The gendarmes at Jassy had told him what had happened at Shtcherbachev's headquarters, and the thought brought a lump to Friedman's throat. He wanted to weep for Goloubenko, and this in itself tormented him because his eyes remained dry. He could not weep. He remembered him very well. Standing there in the darkness, shaken by the clatter of the wheels, he could picture him vividly, his smoothly shaved face, his kindly, reserved smile and his thoughtful gaze behind steel-rimmed spectacles. He heard his voice slowly enunciating French with a Russian accent, and again the lump rose. This plot had failed. But the Revolution would succeed. It was inevitable. It was *obvious*.

The Russians in the compartment were still talking, and one of the gendarmes murmured to the sergeant:

" They're going to Pascani."

" Can you understand what they're saying? "

" A little."

" It's still a long way to Pascani," said the sergeant with a sigh.

They were silent again, listening to the monotonous clack-clacking of this train that seemed to be heading for nowhere. Friedman tried to face the fact that he was going to die. " No way of escape. That's how they dealt with Max Wechsler. It's idiotic to hope for a way out." But hope persisted. If they really wanted him dead they could have tried and shot him for treason, as they had done Sterie. It was not hard to find reasons for hope.

He thought of Sterie, and of that dark morning in the icy wind. Who could want to go on living in such a world, with people like that? But still the longing was there—" I *must* live! I must see the Revolution and the coming of socialism. I must be there to see!"

The train was travelling even more slowly, stopping at every station, sometimes for as long as an hour. Friedman wondered whether he could escape through the window; but it was narrow and obstructed by a pile of baggage. Anyway they'd grab him by the legs. He cleared his throat and said:

"Sergeant."

"Sir?" said the sergeant, half asleep.

"What would you do if I jumped out through the window?"

"You mustn't do that, sir," said the sergeant, starting upright.

"But supposing I did?"

"Well, but where would you go?"

"Never mind about that. What would you do?"

"Our orders are to shoot, sir," the sergeant said.

Friedman was silent. A sob rose in his chest. "I'm going to die." It was obvious. He thought of the reservist who had been killed through his order; and of all the others—Sterie, the soldier Fotache, who had been his runner, Goloubenko . . . Suddenly he began to talk, without logic or sequence, the words pouring out as the thoughts teemed in his head. He talked of men and the respect which was their due, the love of one's fellows, and the mocking of humanity, the degradation of mankind. . . . He talked almost without knowing that he did so until suddenly he was conscious of the sergeant's voice in his ear, sharp with dismay:

"You mustn't go on like that, sir!"

But still he could not stop. The sergeant shook him by the shoulder.

"Lieutenant, be quiet! You mustn't talk like that!"

He checked himself at last. The two other men were stiff and silent, seeming scarcely to breathe. Friedman laughed weakly in the darkness.

"What will happen to me if I don't keep quiet?"

"Well, you see, sir," said the sergeant gently, "I've got orders to report everything you say and do. Perhaps they won't be so hard on you if you don't talk."

Friedman was silent. He wanted to go on talking so that the soldiers and peasants, everyone in the coach who was wake, should hear what he had to say. He seemed to have been struck dumb,

but then he thought—why not? Why should he not say what he
pleased now that he had given up hope—the ray of hope with
which they sought to trick him? . . . *Sell your soul and perhaps
we'll give you a chance. Keep quiet and perhaps we'll let you off.
Dance to our tune, play the fool, and perhaps we'll let you live!*
And then, when it suited them, he'd get a bullet in the head. . . .
Friedman drew himself to his full height, stiffened his backbone,
and with his head back and his eyes closed began talking again.
He continued loudly despite the sergeant's horrified efforts to
check him. There was complete silence in the coach.

He talked until exhaustion overcame him, and then, as he
started to doze, he was assailed with questions. He replied
scarcely knowing what he said, without considering his words,
simply expressing as best he could the thoughts that were in his
mind. An hour or more passed before they would leave him in
peace. Those strangers, in the darkness of the corridor, men
without faces, must all be thinking over what they had heard,
and asking, " Who are we? What is being done to us? "

The train pulled up in a station filled with the murmurs of an
impatient crowd. Under the dim platform lights Friedman could
see a surging of fur caps, capes and rifles. One of the two gendarmes pushed his way to the end of the coach, and a moment
later his voice rose from the platform, shouting in a mimicry of
the official tone:

" Pasca-ani! Pasca-ani! "

" Pascani already? " the sergeant asked sleepily.

" Let's move into the compartment," the other gendarme said.
" It isn't Pascani. Ghita's doing it to get the Russians out."

" By God, that's a good one! The cunning devil! "

The sergeant led the way chuckling into the compartment
vacated by the Russians and Friedman apathetically followed,
dropping heavily on to the seat. He knew he should keep awake,
alert for any chance to escape, but his exhaustion was too great.
His time at the front had shattered his nerves. He fell asleep
with a sense of anguish, to be presently awakened by a blow on
the head. He shivered and opened his eyes. A huge, burly figure
had thrust its way into the compartment and one of the gendarmes
was whispering:

" Wake up, Ghita—we're rumbled! "

The Russians were back, with their equipment. One of them

began to throw everything else out of the window, while the others
laid about them, shouting furiously in Russian. The Roumanians
fought to defend themselves. Friedman got a punch on the ear
and another on the back of the head which knocked his cap over
his eyes. After a good deal of scuffling they managed to get out
into the corridor. The Russians settled themselves again in the
compartment and one of them burst out laughing.

The two gendarmes were silent. The sergeant said glumly:
" Blast you, Ghita! That was a hell of a good idea! "

A thought came to Friedman as he rubbed his bruises. Perhaps
those great bears of men might save him. They would surely do
so if they understood what was happening; they were all armed.
The trouble was that he knew no Russian and could scarcely hope
to explain the situation by gestures in the darkness. He could
only wait for the light.

But it was still not daybreak when the train reached Pascani.
The Russians came crowding out, crushing the Roumanians
against the sides of the corridor, and said in a stern, half-mocking
voice: " *Vo ti: sdesi Pascani*—you see, this is really it! "

Friedman was tempted to shout the only words of Russian he
knew, *Tovarisci, svoboda*—but it would convey nothing to them—
a Roumanian officer in a battered cap absurdly shouting two dis-
connected words. It was no use. He could only wait and desperately hope that in the place where he was being taken he would
be allowed some degree of freedom—enough to give him a chance
to bolt for it, run anywhere and start his life again, his real work
in the world. . . .

But the colonel commanding the regiment kept Friedman under
guard in a building near his headquarters. He kept him there for
two days, until he had found the man he wanted. During this
time Friedman lay smoking and pondering. He was thinking
over the things he had learnt. Everything was now clear to him,
the past and the future as well. He closed his eyes and smiled.
" It will be all right," he said to himself. He remembered that a
Rabbi who used to visit his parents when he was young had told
him that he must always say, " It will all come right. . . ." " But
not for me," he thought, lying bathed in sweat at the thought of
death. " It won't come right for me. It will come right for the
others, and that's what matters. I'd do it over again if I had the
chance. I'd take the same course, but I wouldn't let myself be

caught. I'd see to it that I wasn't betrayed by any gang of play-boys. But it will all come right! "

He was got out of bed in the early morning by a sergeant-major in a steel helmet who carried a rifle. Friedman had not been asleep. He looked hard at the man and the colour drained from his face.

" There's somewhere we've got to go, sir," said the sergeant with a calm, vacuous grin.

Friedman jumped up. He had not had his clothes off for five days. He buttoned his tunic with a shaking hand and put on his greatcoat. He would have liked to put on his cap as well, but seeing its battered state he left it where it was.

" I'm ready," he said.

He encountered soldiers who stood aside to let him pass. He did not know that there was a faint smile on his face. He walked erect along the communication trench leading to the third line, and emerged from it into a field, behind a low ridge. The sky was blue and cloudless, and birds were flying overhead. The damp earth was putting on a coat of short, thick grass, like a green veil. The air was light. " How beautiful! " thought Friedman, and suddenly the tears ran down his cheeks. " How beautiful! " a voice sobbed in his breast. He walked slowly, hearing the heavy footsteps of his escort. He wanted to sing with joy and grief. He knew the tune of the " International " but not the words; he had heard Russian soldiers singing it. He began to hum it in a choking voice. And suddenly he turned to face the man following a few paces behind him with his rifle at the ready. He went to meet him, humming with his mouth closed, with the tears streaming down his cheeks and with such a look in his eyes that the sergeant-major lost his head, turned pale and fired instinctively. Friedman heard the report but felt nothing. A warmth pervaded his whole body. He saw the stalks of grass pointing to the sky and lost consciousness before he touched the ground. The sergeant turned him over with his rifle-barrel, saw his glazing eyes and put a bullet in his head to make sure. His name, following instructions, had already been entered on the regimental roll, together with the words " killed in battle," and the date.

Ghighi Duca was severely wounded in the spring and for two

months hung between life and death. He suffered intense pain
and was given a great deal of morphia.

In the autumn he reappeared in Jassy, permanently discharged
from the Army. One evening he went to the theatre to see the
great success of the season, " The Wedding March " by Henri
Bataille, with Maria Ventura, Tony Balandra and the young
Manolesco. The public was much the same as ever—powdered
officers with gleaming boots and braid, ladies in tailored suits of
military cloth, bright-lipped, bright-eyed and loudly laughing.
Ghighi, his cheeks hollow, with dark patches under his eyes and
the skin drawn tight over his temples, entered the foyer and came
face to face with Augusta Hagibei. She was in mourning. He was
so taken aback that he greeted her instinctively, and she answered
with a forced smile.

" What has happened? " asked Ghighi. " Have you lost a
relative? "

" Haven't you heard? Hagibei is dead. So is Alexandrina's
husband, although she recovered. Spanish 'flu."

Ghighi smiled faintly.

" So now you're a free woman! "

She said nothing but lowered her eyes and glanced swiftly at
him. Ghighi said in a low voice:

" Tell me. It was you, wasn't it, who gave us away? "

" I don't know what you're talking about."

" Don't be a fool, I know it was you. But it didn't work. We've
all survived, except that wretched Jew."

Augusta had turned pale but her eyes were gleaming. She
smiled.

" It seems," she said, " that you very nearly died."

" If you aren't careful," said Ghighi between his teeth, " I'll
give you a clout that'll knock your brains out. You slut! You
whore! By God, I'd like to beat you to death! "

Augusta grew paler still, but still she smiled.

" You nearly died! " she whispered. " You nearly died! "

Perhaps Ghighi would indeed have hit her. But at this moment
the bell rang for the rising of the curtain and people ran to take
their seats. The lights went down and the play began.

IV

The Lettuces

I

During the nineteenth century there lived in Transylvania, in the county of the Three Estates, a family of the squirearchy bearing the name of Debreczy. Its origins are obscure, nor is it known at what period a King of Hungary or a Prince Palatine of Transylvania tapped with the flat of his sword on the shoulder of one of its members and conferred upon him the Order of Chivalry.

The family saw fit to abandon the Church of Rome soon after 1600, and in the course of the ensuing decades more than one Debreczy bore arms in defence of their new sour-faced mistress, the Reformed Church. In the second half of the seventeenth century, when the Rakoczy prince, Francis II, rebelled against the House of Austria, the Debreczys invited all the Hungarians and Szeklers on their estates to mount their horses and follow them to war in the cause of religion, liberty and loot. Rakoczy learned to value those olive-skinned Szekler captains; and one evening, being under the roof of one of their number, he drank his host's health from a goblet of Bohemian crystal with floral decorations. This goblet, preserved in an iron casket eaten by rust, was handed down from father to son and is today in the possession of the latest descendant of the Debreczy family.

When later, in the course of a famous Diet of Hungarian landed gentry, Maria Theresa of Hapsburg, Empress of the Holy Roman Empire, Queen of Bohemia and King of Hungary, Archduchess and Duchess of Austria, Carniola, Styria, Corinthia and other regions, called upon her Magyar subjects for aid and protection, the assembled magnates unsheathed their glittering Turkish sabres and gallantly proclaimed the Latin slogan: " *Vitam et sanguinem pro rege nostro Maria Theresia!* " A Debreczy in the retinue of one of the Transylvanian nobles also drew his sword and in consequence rode the length and breadth of Silesia, Bavaria, the Palatinate and Württemberg. In the course of his extensive campaigning he discovered that all smoke issuing from the mouths of cannon, whether French, Prussian or Austrian, had the same smell of powder, and that the same stench of death arose from every battlefield, irrespective of whether the corpses were French, Prussian or Austrian, clad in uniforms of white, blue or green. But he also noted that the riches discovered in private coffers, or in sacked churches, had no smell at all. After a good many years he returned to his ancestral hearth, bought vast tracts of land, and never failed to baptise his daughters and those of his relatives with the name of the " King " of Hungary, Maria Theresa. The particular fondness of the Debreczy family for this name, borne by so many of its womenfolk, dates from this time.

Nevertheless the family remained obscure, scarcely known except in the district where they lived and where they were notable only for their tallness of stature. They were proud of their ancient lineage and connection with so many noble houses, in particular that of the Barons of Apor, who had refused to accept any other title, having inherited the one they bore, they said, from one of King Arpad's generals (but in fact the name probably came from an ordinary soldier who served under the Anjou dynasty).

There was a Colonel Debreczy, commander of a cavalry regiment, who died without issue; then came two old maids, Maria Theresa and Caroline Françoise Josepha, and their younger brother, Karoly von Debreczy.

Caroline Françoise Josepha and Maria Theresa were in the habit of taking their small brother on outings in a barouche with silver-studded harness, drawn by two handsome horses with roses on their blinkers. In this elegant conveyance the three would set off to visit their relatives in the great houses of the neighbourhood, where the ladies drank tea, smoked thin cigars and for hours on end discussed such burning questions as whether the Bathory family was more ancient and illustrious than the Bethlens, and whether there was any more truly aristocratic family in the whole county than those of Apor and Debreczy. They all agreed that the Barons Fay de Uramhaza had been unheard of, not merely in the days of King Steven but even under the Anjou Dynasty.

When these topics were exhausted the conversation would sometimes take a loftier turn. Maria Theresa, for example, was given to asserting that no true Hungarian aristocrat could tolerate injustice and lack of generosity, while Caroline Françoise Josepha maintained that a nobleman must be prepared to give his life for those weaker than himself, that he must never lie or commit any base action and that the best example was that of their ancestor who had devoted his entire life to the service of his King, Maria Theresa of Hapsburg-Lorraine, and had died in harness: to which, however, Maria Theresa would reply that one must look elsewhere for the best of all examples, namely to that ancestor who at the dictate of his conscience had renounced Catholicism and turned to the Reformed Church, well knowing the persecution he must thereby incur. Long arguments would ensue to which Karoly von Debreczy, a ten-year-old boy, listened wide-eyed, not suspecting that his sisters were slightly mad.

Finally the ladies would return to their manor-house, there to be greeted by moustached and high-booted peasants awaiting them in the courtyard, whose fathers and forefathers had warred and looted for the Evangelical Church at the command of the Debreczy fathers and forefathers. All would remove their caps when the ladies appeared.

"What do you want?" Maria Theresa (or perhaps Caroline Françoise Josepha) would ask, her arm on the edge of the barouche, a stuffed bird in her hat and a glint of folly in her eyes.

"Excellency, the winter has been hard and I badly need a sack of corn. I humbly beseech your Worship to lend me one."

"A noble does not lend," Maria Theresa (or Caroline Françoise Josepha) would reply. "Antal, give this man two sacks of corn. And you, what do you want?"

"I too have come to ask for the loan of a sack of corn, Excellency, for alas——"

"A nobleman does not demean himself by lending. He only gives. Antal, see to it that this man, too, receives two sacks of corn."

The peasants would then depart, mumbling their thanks and bowing to the ground, and some such conversation as the following would take place among them:

"Indeed, Pista," (or Sandor or Janos) "it would be a wonderful thing if all lords were like ours."

To which Pista (or Sandor or Janos), after spitting and medi-

tating, and grunting beneath the weight of the sack he carried,
would reply:

" And if they were, what would happen? "

" Why, they would all be saints! "

" They would all be beggars, you poor fool! "

The Debreczys were not wholly beggared when Karoly von
Debreczy went to do his military service at Szegedin, in the
Twelfth Regiment of Maria Theresa Hussars. An elderly sergeant, having occasion to rebuke Private Debreczy, did so in
crude and even offensive terms. Private Debreczy, who was a
head taller than any other man in the squadron, replied promptly
and with violence. Under a flood of abuse such as can, it seems,
only be encompassed by the noble languages of Hungary and
Spain, he drew his sabre, whirled it in the air and slashed it down
the sergeant's face. He had slightly checked the blow at the last
moment because, nettled though he was, he did not want to kill
the man. The sergeant's skull escaped shattering, but he spent
six months in hospital, while Karoly von Debreczy went before a
court-martial. His colonel passed a word to the judges, explaining
that the young man had been subjected to an affront such as no
Hungarian of any condition could be expected to endure, still
less one of noble stock. Accordingly he was treated with as much
leniency as the case permitted, being sentenced to five years'
confinement in one of his Majesty's fortresses.

When Karoly was released—handsome and slender, with a
long, fair moustache and a romantic pallor due to the years he
had passed in a dungeon infested by rats—his sisters no longer
possessed either house or land. Nothing remained to them but
their clothes, their barouche and the horses which had taken them
to visit their Apor cousins. After the fashion of their ancestors
a thousand years earlier, while they still possessed horses and a
home on wheels they felt themselves to be free of all shackles and
all obligations; any place was good that provided pasture, and
there they could stay.

But Karoly being a man, had to learn a calling. He attended
the University of Vienna, became an engineer, and got a job with
one of the new oil-companies. It was the period, between 1880
and 1900, when wells were sunk all over the foothills of the
Carpathians. The engineer Debreczy worked first in the Galician
oil-fields, and here he came to be looked at askance, it being

murmured that he was a socialist, a thing unheard of in a Debreczy. He was no longer invited to drawing-rooms and his aristocratic friends ceased to address him by the familiar " tu." He fought two duels. His employers then transferred him to Roumania, where they held concessions, and here, while travelling by train, he made the acquaintance of a Mademoiselle Sofia Lascari. He fell violently in love with her, and after a courtship as brief as it was stormy eloped with her to Transylvania. The young lady's family never forgave her this aberration with a foreigner who was not merely non-Orthodox but not even a Catholic, and who, moreover, no longer possessed an acre of land.

Karoly von Debreczy died not long afterwards and his widow had to turn to her parents for charity. Her mother, Davida Lascari, was ready to take her back, but Lascar Lascari, her father, made one condition: he would have nothing to do with the child born of the marriage. Thus it came about that Maria Theresa, the daughter of Karoly von Debreczy and Sofia Lascari, was brought up by her two aunts, Maria Theresa and Caroline Françoise Josepha, who smoked cigars, read Russian novels and talked of the noble and chivalrous spirit of their ancestors. As for her mother, Lascar Lascari, who became increasingly pre-occupied with money as his death drew nearer, married her off to a certain Monsieur Sufana, a negligible person who had become a millionaire overnight when oil was discovered under his land. She was never allowed to see her daughter again.

After the Great War and the collapse of the Dual Monarchy, her aunts having died in the meantime, Maria Theresa married a captain in the Roumanian Army, a young officer with every prospect of a distinguished career, had not his life been disrupted in consequence of a few words exchanged at an evening party given by Madame Vorvoreano.

2

The event occurred in early summer in the year 1925, in a small
garrison town not far from the frontier, on an evening when the
poplars and willows, rising above the roof-tops, were silhouetted
against a cloudless, deep-blue sky.

Madame Vorvoreano lived in a two-storeyed house, with thick
walls of cut stone and brick, which dominated the modest, crumbling, creeper-covered dwellings around it. The house had a
wrought-iron balcony and a *porte cochère* in the pillars of which
were niches large enough to accommodate a man, as indeed they
had done in former times, when they were occupied by Albanian
guards with daggers and pistols in their belts. That evening all
the windows were ablaze with light. Cars containing the town's
notabilities drove in a steady stream into the courtyard, while
young officers rode up on horseback, punctiliously saluting their
superiors, among them the general commanding the garrison,
and house-servants and troopers occupied themselves with tying
up the horses or walking them to cool round an old walnut-tree
in the middle of the yard. From the house across the street—the
only other two-storeyed building, which bore on its façade the
legend " Grand Union Hotel "—the town's five prostitutes,
lamentable, underfed and over-painted creatures, were peeping
round the window-curtains to admire the brilliance of the company.

A certain Lieutenant Tortoreano, arriving that morning from
the frontier, where he commanded an outpost, had begged one
of the general's aides, Lieutenant Spahiu, to take him to the party.

" Surely you can smuggle me in, old boy. I can't tell you how
much I need a change from those blasted Bulgarian peasants, and
the *comitadjis* and the Danube frogs. I simply must have a sniff
of civilisation, even if it's only for a few hours."

Lieutenant Spahiu, in long trousers strapped under gleaming, spurred boots, with gold braid, white gloves and an immaculate tie, considered his friend before replying. Lieutenant Tortoreano was wearing dusty boots and an army tunic of faded linen, marked with dark patches under the armpits. He had no sword. Spahiu would have to lend him one of his own uniforms and find him a sword and suitable boots and spurs, which was not easy.

" I'll take you if you'll stand champagne for dinner," he said, after thought.

Tortoreano, a tall, bony young man with a small snub nose and round grey eyes, rather too close together, laughed a little sourly; but he was so anxious to go that he replied, " All right, it's a deal."

This was before lunch. At eight o'clock that evening the young men, in full rig and highly pleased with themselves, marched stiffly together down the street running from the Mosque to the Danube. Soldiers saluted them as they passed, Turkish vendors of peanuts and popcorn offered their wares, gipsy-women pursued them with flowers at exorbitant prices; but the two officers, stern of countenance, their heads held high, walked imperturbably on, brushing aside these rowdy importunities. Plump, respectable citizens of the town, strolling with their wives and daughters along the poplar avenue bordering the river, responded deferentially to their cool and distant greetings, reflecting that—who could say?—they might one day honour them by asking for the hand of one of their daughters in marriage. The young ladies, also aware of the possibility, blushed and smiled with expressive flutterings of their eyes.

Having reached Madame Vorvoreano's house the young men paused. It occurred to Lieutenant Spahiu that they were perhaps a little early and that it might be easier to introduce an uninvited guest at a later hour. Moreover the champagne had put ideas into his head. Taking Lieutenant Tortoreano by the arm he said:

" How would it be if we first paid a visit over the way? "

The other turned and considered the Grand Union Hotel. He grinned.

" Fine! We'll dance all the better for it."

They went towards the hotel, dragging their sabres and clinking their spurs as they marched up the steps. But the door was locked. They knocked on its dirty glass pane, so begrimed that nothing was to be seen through it, and went on hammering until a skinny woman appeared, clad in a wrapper of dingy grey and carrying an oil-lamp in her hand.

" What's going on? " demanded Lieutenant Tortoreano. " Why's the door locked? "

" Doctor's orders," said the woman glumly. " He paid us an official visit this afternoon and decided to close the place."

" Too bad," said Tortoreano. " Well, old boy, we'd better not hang about here."

They paused for a time on the pavement, recovering their spirits in the soft, caressing air of the summer night. A warm breeze was blowing from the Dobrudja across the Danube, over lakes and canals, reed-covered plains and numberless marshes, bearing with it an odour of swamps and mud, stagnant water and rank grass. Stars were beginning to glitter in the sky. A carriage passed, drawn by two English thoroughbreds with blankets on their backs, and pulled up at the *porte cochère* of the Vorvoreano house. An officer got out, a broad-faced man of medium height, very stiff in his bearing, with a monocle gleaming beneath the peak of his cap, and extended a white-gloved hand to the lady who accompanied him. She was slender and tall, clad in a pink satin ball-dress with very ample skirts, and with a fringed shawl of very pale-pink silk, almost white, covering her fair hair. The two lieutenants saluted, clicking their heels. The officer returned the salute with extreme gravity and offered the lady his arm. They went into the house, and Tortoreano whistled under his breath.

" Did you see her? That chap's a lucky sod. By God, I'd like to have a woman like that with me at the frontier! "

" She's not for you, my boy," said Spahiu. " The general has his eye on her, but Petrica's as jealous as hell. He'd be quite capable of fighting a duel even with the general if he thought there was any funny business."

The soldier on the driver's seat of the carriage was tugging at the reins, having difficulty in keeping the two grey horses under control.

" Look at them," murmured Tortoreano. " By God, I'd like to have a pair like that! "

" The things you'd like to have," said Spahiu, grinning.

" You wait, old boy. You wait a few years. You'll see! "

Spahiu took no notice of the words, but he was destined to recall them some twenty years later when he ran into General

Tortoreano at divisional headquarters, somewhere between the Dnieper and the Don. For the present he merely thought to himself that it was late to be standing there on the pavement, and taking his friend by the arm he led him through the courtyard into Madame Vorvoreano's house, and walked with him up the wide staircase with its crimson carpet, above which hung a full-length portrait of a certain Preda Coziano Serdar, wearing the big fur hat of the boyars and a caftan lined with sable, with his hand resting on the hilt of the dagger thrust in his dove-grey silk sash. Madame Vorvoreano, standing beside her brother, Serban Lascari, who was on a visit to her at her country home, was receiving her guests at the head of the stairs. She wore a black gown which, in the prevailing fashion, did not quite reach the floor. Her hands, already withered, bore no other adornment than a single large emerald, dark like a crystal ball filled with some alarming poison. Her hair was grey and the folds of flesh hung loose beneath her ageing face, where no expression was to be read but one of polite but profound and incurable boredom. She was giving this party for precise reasons known only to herself and her brother, Serban. The latter, a stockily built man whose beard was beginning to turn grey, was in full evening dress and wearing his decorations; his hands clasped on his round paunch lent him a look at once crafty and good-humoured.

" What a mob! What a mob! " he muttered, watching the girls as they glided in the arms of the officers over the newly polished floor of the salon, dancing the Boston, which was then in fashion, and the tango, whose vogue was only just beginning. There were also a few civilians present, in tightly fitting tail-coats and over-high collars—the prefect, the mayor, the chief magistrate and one or two younger officials. " What a mob! Surely, my dear Helène, this place must drive you mad."

" I've been just as bored in Paris. I don't see that it makes any difference," Madame Vorvoreano murmured, and then smiled kindly at a young couple mounting the stairs who bowed as they greeted her. " So here you are at last," she said in a quite motherly voice. " They've started dancing without you."

The couple passed on, and Monsieur Lascari said:

" How can you possibly pretend there's no difference between Paris and this village? "

" It's all the same to me. I'm ill, Serban."

Serban Lascari turned to look at her, startled and suddenly observant. Her face was drawn and sallow, with heavy black circles under the eyes, and her skin was like parchment. What sort of illness was it—of the body or the soul?

General Ipsilanti, the divisional Chief of Staff, a lanky man buttoned into his tunic as though it were a corset, came up to them with his monocle in his eye.

"A most delightful occasion," he said, bowing. "*Je vous remercie infiniment. . . . Je suis ravi!*"

Madame Vorvoreano smiled.

"You see how kind I am to you? Cilibia thinks I've given this ball in his honour, but the truth is that I arranged it for you, so that you can dance with the lady of your dreams."

And as though by chance she glanced towards a young woman whose head was covered with ringlets of soft fair hair like that of a boy. She was tall and graceful, with a delicate, straight nose, a rounded, exquisitely moulded forehead, and brown eyes that at moments laughed and sparkled and at other times were dark and intense. Altogether she looked enchanting in her rose-pink satin dress.

"Who's that beauty?" asked Serban Lascari, while General Ipsilanti, grateful and delighted, kissed Madame Vorvoreano's hand before moving in the direction of the lady.

"She's the wife of the captain over there, the stiff, square-headed man with a monocle," said Madame Vorvoreano, pointing to him where he sat at a small table playing cards with the mayor, the chief magistrate and the town's medical officer. The captain was a man of about thirty with constantly knitted eyebrows, who seemed not to know how to smile. The steady gaze of his blue eyes was not easy to meet. He was playing with intent concentration, seemingly unaware of what was going on around him.

"He's a Captain Dumitriu, and she—do you know who she is? She's Sofia's daughter by her first marriage."

"Good heavens, let me look at her!" said Serban Lascari, and turned to study her more closely. "*Ça, par exemple!* I'd never have guessed it. I must say she's remarkable, a most lovely creature. But she doesn't take after—she's not at all like——"

"She takes after her father's side," murmured Madame Vorvoreano. "She has never even hinted at the relationship between us. Perhaps she doesn't know about it. Anyway, it isn't for me to say anything, and I think it would be better if you didn't rush up and greet her as your darling niece."

Serban Lascari nodded with understanding and turned towards General Cilibia, the commander of the garrison. His face a mottled crimson, his thick neck bulging over the collar of his tunic, his enormous stomach dotted with buttons and decorations, the general was moving towards them on short bow-legs.

"Chère Madame, what an unforgettable evening! Let me offer you this flower." He wheezed as he spoke, being asthmatic, and held out a rose to Madame Vorvoreano. "Monsieur Lascari, your sister is the most attractive woman in the world. I have known her since 1907, since the days when—well—and ever since I have been her faithful adorer."

"If that is really true," said Madame Vorvoreano, "I'm sure you will grant the favour I mean to ask you in the course of this evening, which has been organised in your honour and so that you may not be too bored in our little town. Will you promise not to refuse me?"

"Most certainly, dear lady. But tell me at once what it is, because I'm infernally thirsty and I long for a glass of wine."

"Well, it's this. My nephew, Cesar, Serban's son, is a trooper in the Sixteenth Hussars. I want you to send him home and not go on making the poor boy's life a misery with military service."

General Cilibia gave a fat chuckle. "All these preliminaries for the merest trifle. Of course it shall be done. Hey—Prince!"

General Ipsilanti, who was now talking to Madame Dumitriu, swung round.

"Prince, would you mind coming here a moment? . . . I hope, dear lady, you will excuse him. . . . Prince, I want you to arrange for Trooper Lascari, of the Sixteenth, to be released from service and sent home—back to his toiling parents, simple tillers of the soil who badly need his help!"

General Cilibia concluded with a burst of laughter. The long, lean Prince Ipsilanti glanced from Madame Vorvoreano to Serban Lascari, nodded his head, smiling, and started to withdraw. But Cilibia caught him by the sleeve, and pointing to his monocle said:

"You know, my dear chap, if you were to put another monocle in your other end you'd make a wonderful telescope!"

He laughed at this happy thought till he nearly choked. Prince

Ipsilanti drew himself stiffly upright. He gulped and said, clicking his heels:

" General, if you looked through the back lens you'd always see the enemy through the front one."

This soldierly reply drew from Cilibia a positive bellow of delight. Ipsilanti bowed stiffly and went off to invite Madame Dumitriu to dance. Cilibia recovered his breath, called for wine and said:

" I must say, I like that animal! But I beg your pardon, he's probably a relation. You members of the aristocracy are all related."

" It isn't so in the case of the general," said Madame Vorvoreano indulgently.

" Well, he's an animal, but I like him. He was under me in 1913, during the advance into Bulgaria. I got despatches from the Government every day—'Advance to be stopped. Displeasing to the Great Powers. Austria-Hungary has protested to the King.' So I called my officers together and I said to them: ' Gentlemen, those bum-crawling ministers want us to stop. But we're going ahead. To horse, gentlemen, and—forward! ' And who was the one who went furthest? It was Colonel Prince Ipsilanti, madame! A stout fellow, and I don't mind saying it. An animal, but a stout fellow. May I please have another glass of wine? "

General Prince Ipsilanti, meanwhile, was waltzing with Madame Dumitriu and murmuring as he gazed at her:

" I never dreamed I should find anyone like you in this dreadful little town. The first time I set eyes on you—do you remember? "

" No," said Madame Dumitriu, with the most charming and indifferent of smiles.

" I was riding along the road by the Danube, and you were out with your children, and the nurse was following behind you pushing the baby in its pram."

" Ah, yes, the nurse."

" You know what I thought? I said to myself, ' Who on earth can those children belong to? ' That German governess is really remarkable! "

They were circling round the centre of the salon, beneath a bronze chandelier in which the candles had been replaced by electric bulbs.

" Later on I saw you out riding with Petrica, and then I

realised . . . I give you my word, I've very seldom seen a woman ride as well as you."

" I used to be a bareback rider in a circus," said Madame Dumitriu with a perfectly straight face, and continued gravely to dance with the fold of her pink skirt held in her left hand. The general stared at her in bewilderment, and then laughed uncertainly.

" You're pulling my leg, eh? But I know you're a great lady— a relation of the Lascaris, if I'm not mistaken? "

She smiled without answering, and gracefully inclined her head towards his shoulder to avoid the smell of wine on his breath.

" You know, I'd very much like to see you again," Ipsilanti said.

The gipsy orchestra led by the celebrated Cascarachi, famous throughout the region of the Danube basin, had just finished playing the waltz.

" I have no doubt Madame Vorvoreano will be receiving again," said Madame Dumitriu coolly.

" Yes, but before then," the Prince murmured, kissing her hand. She smiled, this time more amiably, and said:

" My household takes up all my time. When the children are older I hope to be able to go out more, and then it will be delightful to see you again."

" But when will that be? "

" Oh, when they're quite big," said Madame Dumitriu, laughing. " Let us say, in five or ten years."

Driving home with her husband, Madame Dumitriu let the silk shawl slip back from her shoulder. The breeze was blowing more strongly across the Danube and the sky was flecked with cloud, but to her the night seemed very warm.

" Did you win or lose? " she asked.

" I won," said Captain Dumitriu. There was a silence, while the horses' hooves clopped on the cobbles and the rubber-tyred wheels made a muffled sound; then he took his wife's hand and pressed it to his lips.

" Oh, it's gone! " exclaimed Madame Dumitriu, turning suddenly. The precious shawl had been caught by the wind and carried away into the darkness.

" We'll go back and look for it. Hey—Georghita! "

The driver reined his horses, but Madame Dumitriu said lightly: " It's not worth the trouble. Perhaps some needy person will find it."

" Very well, my darling—but I must warn you that it may be some time before I can buy you another." Captain Dumitriu gazed devotedly at her, and took her hand in both his own. " I've been thinking that I might apply for a transfer—to another garrison or even another regiment."

Madame Dumitriu did not instantly reply. After a moment she said in a voice that she strove to make non-committal:

" But why? You're doing very well here. You're well thought of. You get on well with your senior officers."

" All the same, I'm going to put in for a transfer," Dumitriu said in a lower voice. " Do you really mind? "

She pressed her head against his shoulder. " No, my darling. I think, perhaps, it would be the best thing to do."

He put his arm round her and drew her close. With the roughness of the gold braid against her cheek she said with a sigh:

" How happy we are! "

" Yes," said Captain Dumitriu, knitting his eyebrows above the monocle.

The next morning he called on General Ipsilanti and announced, standing stiffly to attention, that he wished to apply for a transfer to some other garrison or some other branch of the service. He looked steadily at his superior with those blue eyes whose gaze was not easy to meet. The general's face fell and he fiddled with the papers on his desk.

" H'm. . . . Well, of course . . . All right, I'll see what I can arrange."

Outside the window was a strip of waste-land where garbage was dumped, and beyond this a long grey windowless wall, the barracks of the Frontier Guards. The wavering notes of a bugle, badly blown, were coming from some place where a party of recruits were having a lesson from a bugler-instructor. . . . Then the instructor himself played the call—" Forward, forward, the Tenth Regiment."

General Ipsilanti rang up the colonel commanding the regiment posted on the Bulgarian frontier.

" Colonel, I don't think you've yet had a replacement for that

officer—what was his name?—the one killed by the *comitadjis* . . .
Yes, that's the chap. . . . Well, I'm sending you Captain Dumitriu,
from divisional headquarters. . . . Exactly—it's time he saw a
little frontier service, ha-ha! . . . Quite so, quite so. . . ."

3

The sky was an incandescent blue. The trees, thin-leaved
acacias, were covered with a fine dust blown in from the steppe.
The grass seemed to turn browner as one watched it.

The village streets, at the approach of midday, were deserted.
But suddenly there were shouts and a sound of running footsteps
—a mad dog was being chased. The peasants hunted it with
stones and the creature fled howling like the damned. It was
knocked on the head and ceased to howl. Then there was silence
again.

Towards evening ox-carts appeared with Bulgarian peasants of
forbidding aspect. A Turkish peasant-woman walked down the
street in a black veil. Tartar women were gathered round the
well at the cross-roads, clad in wide trousers of pink or mauve,
ample garments which attracted the gaze of the unhappy sentry
on duty at the gate of company headquarters.

The platoons which had been on field-exercise came back from
the training-ground. The men's tunics were soaked in sweat, their
faces puffy, their eyes red and their open mouths parched with
thirst. Those who had the task of carrying the water-cooled
machine-guns and ammunition-cases on their backs looked
crushed beneath their loads. The officers seemed no less distressed
than the men. They too had dust-caked faces and uniforms damp
with sweat; but they were mounted, and the slow-walking
horses seemed to recover strength as they approached the stables.

Captain Dumitriu had put his monocle in his breast pocket,
because the glass was constantly getting fogged. He dismounted
in the middle of the barrack-yard, gave orders for the night to the

frontier-patrols, and walked across the yard to where a soldier
was pouring water from a bucket over the bare torso of Lieutenant
Tortoreano.

" Don't you want a shower too, sir? " the lieutenant asked.

But the captain was too tired. He pushed open a whitewashed
wooden gate, and passing through a vegetable garden, where the
limp, withering leaves of tomatoes, aubergines and lettuces were
grey with dust, entered a low peasant house with a thatched roof.
Behind him he could still hear the talk and laughter of the soldiers,
the stamping of their boots and the click of rifle-bolts as they
unloaded their weapons.

Madame Dumitriu was seated in a folding chair by the open
window, looking out over the huge expanse of yellowish earth,
the sparse grass scattered with cattle-dung, without a tree,
without a shrub.

" Admiring the view? " her husband asked.

" Yes, I like it," she said and continued to gaze at the great
drifts of purple cloud in the distance, hanging low over the steppe.
The captain went into the bedroom to change. Their dwelling
consisted of three rooms, the bedroom, the children's nursery and
a living-room, all with clay floors, small-paned windows and
hangings of local cloth upon the walls. The Bulgarian whose
house it was had been reduced to a single room, and his sons
lodged with relatives. The children's nurse did the housework,
looked after the children and quarrelled with the captain's orderly.
Madame Dumitriu passed the time reading in her canvas chair,
or going for walks. The captain spent his days, and often his
nights, in the company offices or on the frontier with the patrols.

He came out of the bedroom washed, scented with eau de
Cologne and wearing a white jacket. He was tired and very
hungry.

" Is dinner ready? "

" Eva! " called Madame Dumitriu.

The nurse's head appeared round the door and then vanished.
A few minutes later she returned to lay the table, assisted by the
orderly in slippers of khaki cloth, a white jacket and an apron.
The oil-lamp was lighted, and a swarm of flies, midges and
mosquitoes at once began to buzz round it, to fall later with
singed wings into the dishes, where their bodies floated on the
oil and vinegar of the tomato-dressing.

" These tomatoes are positively warm," said Captain Dumitriu after beginning to eat. There was a silence. He sipped from his glass. " The water's tepid too." Then he stopped eating and said: " Nothing seems to taste of anything."

He gazed for some moments at his wife.

" You mustn't be sorry you married me. We shan't be here for ever."

" But I like it here," she said. " Truly I do. This is real country—real people—like Tolstoy's stories of the Caucasus. We're together and we don't have to worry about other people."

He kissed her hand. They stayed there for a long time, seated at the table with their hands clasped facing the dishes they had scarcely touched, the salad with its drowning insects, the jug of brackish water looking yellow in the light of the oil-lamp. The captain made another attempt to eat.

" These tomatoes really aren't edible," he said. " They're all squashy. What's wrong with them? "

" They haven't had enough rain—it's the drought."

" I'll send a party of soldiers tomorrow to spend the day watering them and the lettuces. There's precious little else for them to do in this desert. Shall we go outside? It's dark but the sky's wonderfully clear."

He gave her his arm and they went into the garden. Then he came back and fetched her chair and another for himself. He lit a cigar and again took her hand in his, a long, slender hand with tapering fingers. It was a gesture that had become habitual with him. Thus they continued to sit in the darkness, without speaking, beneath the purple vault of glittering stars. The stones were hot on the ground, the earth dry, the air torrid. Dogs were howling at the far end of the village. Men were stirring in the yard, a night patrol was getting ready to leave. Suddenly they heard the hoarse, angry voice of Lieutenant Tortoreano.

" Hey! Who's that? Come here! "

There followed some moments of talk, and then the sharp, echoing sound of a slap on the face. A voice grunted:

" Don't hit me, Lieutenant! "

" By God, I'll hit you! " Tortoreano's shout was accompanied by further blows. " You filthy swine! "

Madame Dumitriu had started up, her slim fingers tightly gripping her husband's broad, stubby hand.

" What's he doing that for? " she asked sharply, getting to her feet. " He's abominable! "

The captain rose and went into the yard, where he found Tortoreano still slapping the face of a soldier who stood rigidly to attention, trembling violently and staggering at every blow, for the lieutenant was standing well back and using the full length of his arm.

" Lieutenant Tortoreano," said the captain coldly, and the other stopped at the sight of the white-jacketed figure emerging from the shadows, the glowing cigar-end and the monocle gleaming in the starlight. " Will you be good enough to come with me for a moment."

Captain Dumitriu led the way towards the company offices. A warrant-officer was seated in one room, bent over a table with a pen in his hand, his back to the rack of rifles along the wall. Entering his own room, the captain turned up the wick of the oil-lamp and then looked at his subordinate. Tortoreano was sweating profusely, his eyes uneasy. His face was flushed and his big hands were red.

" Lieutenant Tortoreano, I forbid you to strike the men. This is the third time I have had to speak to you about it. I shall not do so again, but I warn you, I shall take disciplinary measures."

" I beg to state, sir, that the man was relieving himself against the wall of company headquarters, on the pretext that it was dark, instead of going round to the back of the building like everyone else," said Tortoreano, whose breath reeked like the tap-room of an inn.

" And you consider that a reason for hitting him? The men are peasants, what else can you expect of them? " The captain went on in a tone of contempt: " You've been drinking, Lieutenant, and when you've had too much you disgrace the uniform you wear. You will be confined to your quarters, when off duty, for a week. Provided you keep the door locked you can get as drunk as you like."

" I have the honour to inform you, sir, that in every unit I have served in it has been the normal thing to beat the soldiers when necessary," replied Tortoreano, flushing more than ever.

" That may be so, but it is forbidden in any unit under my command. Good night."

Tortoreano clicked his heels. " At your orders, Captain."

But outside he muttered to himself: " By God, you won't command many units, you bloody square-headed German sod! "

Back in the garden the captain found his wife walking up and down past the rows of lettuces. She ran to meet him.

" What was it all about? "

" Nothing. The man's a clod. But you mustn't worry about these things."

They sat down again and he lit another cigar. After a pause he said in a low voice:

" That's how it is, you see, if you marry a soldier."

" I didn't marry a soldier," Madame Dumitriu said. " I married you."

That night Madame Dumitriu could not sleep. She lay awake after midnight listening to the calm, steady breathing of her husband at her side, broken now and then by a slight snore. Outside the room the silence seemed to be unending. Even the ceaseless stridency of the cicadas did not make itself apparent as a sound but seemed rather to be a part of the stillness. Occasionally there was the sound of marching boots in the street as one of the patrols returned from the frontier, and then the silence fell again, a burning emptiness peopled only by the whispering drone of the crickets. From their bed Madame Dumitriu could see the open window, a square outline against a sky filled with stars.

From somewhere in the distance there came the sound of a shot, followed by another, also very far away.

Then there was a steady crackle of fire. A green star soared into the glittering sky and burst into three other stars which fell softly, melting into the night. A sharp detonation followed by the rumbling of an explosion broke in upon the fusillade of rifle-fire. Another explosion followed, and then suddenly there was nothing more to be heard. But this lull lasted only for a short time. A confusion of sounds broke out, shouts and the tread of heavy boots running across the yard. Someone hammered on the door.

" Captain! Captain! "

" Petrica, you're wanted," said Madame Dumitriu, shaking her husband. He jumped out of bed without a word and dressed hurriedly in the darkness. Pulling on his boots with a grunt he ran out and asked sharply:

" What's the matter? "

The man who had called him said something which she could not hear, and both men hurried off, their voices sinking into the vague tumult that now filled the night. Nearer at hand there were sounds of movement and footsteps, and then a string of orders.

" Fall in! Party, 'shun! Left turn! By the left—march! "

The boots went marching along the street.

A new sound came from the yard, like that of cartwheels. Then everything grew calm. There were still soldiers talking, but in quieter tones, and over the countryside the sound of the crickets rose again like a scarcely perceptible vibration. Madame Dumitriu went out in her dressing-gown and found the nurse and the orderly standing together in the doorway.

" Have the children woken up, Eva? "

" No, madame, they're still asleep."

" What has happened, Vasilly? "

The soldier, barefoot, with his shirt unbuttoned, muttered:

" It's the *comitadjis*, they've attacked Post Sixteen again."

" And—the captain has gone there? " asked Madame Dumitriu with a slight hesitation in her voice.

" Of course, madame. The whole company's gone. But they won't get them. They make a raid and then they bolt. No hope of catching them on a moonless night like this. They always choose their time."

Madame Dumitriu said no more but for a long time stood listening. Presently there was a burst of firing and another rocket rose, breaking into three stars. The firing died away and again there was silence.

" Jesus and the Holy Virgin defend us! " moaned the nurse, crossing herself.

" Probably only some chap getting the wind up and shooting in the air," the soldier said in a low voice.

Madame Dumitriu stayed with them for a while, but then sent them back to bed and went and sat in her chair by the lettuces, withering in the heat of the night. She sat anxiously waiting, straining for every sound. An hour passed, and in the east, beyond the waste-lands, a pale mist seemed to rise, flooding the sky.

Voices and the tramp of boots sounded in the street, and men and horses entered the yard. Madame Dumitriu went to the gate, hoping to hear her husband's voice or at least to learn what had happened. But there was no sign of him yet. Soldiers were talking in the yard. A voice ordered:

" Put them over there in a row. Hey, you, go to the store and get something to cover them with."

Two men were talking together near the fence.

" Who is it? Florea Ion? "

" Yes, poor devil. He's over there. You can go and look if you like."

" You don't mean they really cut them off? "

" Go and see for yourself. They cut a ring round the mouth and the lips just come away. It's like a death's head—a red mess with white teeth in the middle. You'd think he was laughing! "

" You're pulling my leg. "

" I tell you, go and look."

Nothing more was said; but a minute later the voice that had ordered a man to fetch coverings shouted in a tone of authority:

" That's enough staring. There's nothing to see. Put back that blanket and mind your own business. Get moving! Corporal Motancea, you'd better post a couple of sentries to stop these fools gawking at the bodies. Well, perhaps at least it'll teach you all a lesson. You'll know enough to keep awake next time, you bloody recruits! "

Madame Dumitriu shivered and went back to her chair by the lettuces.

A long time later, when it was quite light, she again heard the sound of boots accompanied by the creak of small gun-carriages and, at last, her husband's voice. She ran to meet him as he came through the gate. He did not look at her but said sombrely:

" Why aren't you in bed? "

" Petrica, I want to know what has happened! "

" Nothing important—a *comitadji* raid, that's all. Set the alarm for eight o'clock."

He lay on the bed without undressing, and his breathing at once became deep and steady. She lay down beside him. He reached out and placed his hand on her breast, and thus lay sleeping, muttering inarticulate words.

4

Madame Dumitriu also slept, worn out after the wakeful night.
She had hideous and terrifying dreams in which she constantly
told herself, " It's nothing—I'm dreaming—it isn't true." She
heard the voice of the soldier, Florea Ion, speaking to her with a
lipless mouth, confronting her with a gaping red void beneath his
nose, the hideous grin of white teeth like those in a skull. She
said to herself, " I'm dreaming. It didn't happen. It's all a
dream." In a half-waking moment she thought, " There's no
such man as the soldier Florea Ion. I heard his name in my
dream." She was conscious of the ringing of the alarm clock and
of her husband getting up and changing his clothes without
making a sound. She knew that in a minute he would leave the
room and, still only half awake, she wanted to ask him what had
really happened; but then she slipped back into sleep and did
not reawaken until after midday. Her head was heavy. The air
was hot and the wind was loaded with fine dust from the plain.
Men were talking quietly in the yard, and in the vegetable garden
fifteen Bulgarian peasants clad in home-woven garments of
coarse brown cloth were carrying water from the well in buckets
and watering-cans. A perspiring soldier with a rifle and bayonet
was leaning against the fence, looking half stupefied by the heat.
The peasants were also sweating, but despite the large beads of
perspiration on their temples and foreheads they did not pause in
their business of fetching water and emptying the buckets round
the roots of the tomato-plants and the aubergines, and into the
little gulleys separating the rows of lettuces. Those with watering-
cans sprinkled the leaves, which glistened with silver drops.

Madame Dumitriu stood gazing at the peasants. They were
men in the prime of life, settled men, no longer young. One had a
big moustache and grey eyebrows. Another was red-cheeked with
a face round as an apple and dark, round eyes; for an instant he

put down his bucket, took off his hat and passed the sleeve of his jacket over his shaven, blue-tinted head which shone like a metal ball. His appearance was so quaint, he looked so respectable, that Madame Dumitriu was tempted to laugh: but there was a gleam of apprehension in the round eyes which for an instant made her think of the terror of death. She stayed for a little while watching them as they worked. There was one man of imposing stature, tall and broad-shouldered, with a deep voice, who looked as though he could not be more than thirty-five. She was almost ashamed that he should be watering her garden. Such a man should be at liberty, master of his hearth and home.

When Captain Dumitriu came in and sat down at the luncheon-table, drawn with fatigue and with knitted brows, she asked:

" Petrica, why are those men watering the vegetables? "

" I thought they might as well have something to do."

" But why are they here? "

" They're under arrest—pending investigation."

The captain was eating his salad with a good appetite. The tomatoes were fresh and cool.

" They certainly haven't anything to do with the *comitadjis*," he went on. " Those fellows nip cross the frontier at night and get back as quick as they can. But the police and the Gendarmerie want to show their zeal, so they've planted this lot on me. I have to interrogate them and write a report."

" But what did happen last night? "

" The usual thing," grunted the captain. " They attacked the frontier-post at Staro-Selo and killed the soldiers manning it— all of them."

" How many were there? "

" Eight. But I don't know why you should be so interested. It's entirely an army matter."

" I heard the soldiers bringing them back. I heard them talking last night."

He raised his head and looked at her.

" What exactly did you hear? "

" What had been done to them."

" H'm . . . yes," muttered Captain Dumitriu. " They mutilate the corpses . . . and sometimes not only corpses. . . ."

" But why? Why do they do it? " demanded Madame Dumitriu, gazing at him wide-eyed.

He shrugged his shoulders and said: " Because the Bulgarian Government is claiming the southern part of the Dobrudja, and our Government, which captured it from them in 1913, refuses to return it."

" And that's why men are tortured? "

" My dear, it's what they all do—it's quite normal in the Balkans. Ten years ago, when I was a second lieutenant just out of military school, I fought in the Bulgarian campaign. We attacked their forces on the flank, which wasn't properly guarded. They weren't expecting an attack. We took them by surprise, just as they had attacked their former allies, the Serbs and the Greeks, by surprise, after the whole lot of them had attacked the Turks, also by surprise." Captain Dumitriu gazed at his wife through his monocle.

They were silent for a moment while Vasilly, the orderly, cleared the table. The captain lit a cigar. His wife sat thinking, her head with its blonde ringlets inclined to one side. She asked at length:

" And these peasants—are you making them work for us for nothing? "

The captain removed the cigar from his mouth and flushed slightly.

" We'll pay them," he said.

Then he had to hurry away; officers from the Gendarmerie and the Security Police were awaiting him. Madame Dumitriu went into the garden again. The Bulgarians were grouped under a lean-to shed, sheltering from the intense heat. Some lay sleeping on the ground while the flies walked over their faces. Madame Dumitriu seated herself on a stool beneath a bunch of brightly coloured pimentoes, yellow, orange and red, that hung from the roof. The little man was sitting near her, the one with frightened eyes, and also the tall, handsome man. The little one addressed the big one as " Bre Dimitr," and the big one addressed the little one as " Bre Petko." They were talking in undertones, the little man speaking rapidly and insistently while the other answered calmly in his deep voice. Presently they fell silent while they rolled cigarettes, and Madame Dumitriu asked:

" Have you had anything to eat? "

The big man looked at her without replying, and then looked away. The little man said: " Nothing, madame." He pro-

nounced the word "madame" with a marked Bulgarian accent.
The men seated nearby glanced in their direction, but indifferently,
as though it were not a matter that concerned them.

Madame Dumitriu went into the house and ordered the nurse
and Vasilly to cut slices of bread and cheese. She herself took
them out to the Bulgarians. The little man, Petko, said:

"Thank you, madame, but you need not have troubled. We
shall soon be going home."

But he looked anxiously at her as he said it, with round, dark
eyes containing both hope and apprehension, as though he were
breathlessly awaiting her reply.

"It was no trouble," said Madame Dumitriu. "You must have
something to eat before you leave."

The little man smiled faintly in relief. The big man, Dimitr,
bowed his head and said: "I kiss your hand. May God return
your kindness."

"My husband will pay you for today's work," said Madame
Dumitriu, and at this they were all speechless with astonishment.
Dimitr broke the silence.

"He must not, madame. In any case, we had nothing else to
do."

He gazed steadily and very gently at her. He was a man who
breathed strength, with a powerful neck and a countenance of great
dignity, deeply weather-worn and generally immobile. The
words he had spoken, coming from him, acquired an especial
weight. They meant: "You are a good woman. We would
prefer to work for you for nothing, so that you may have your
due and we shall have earned the food you have brought us."
But Madame Dumitriu shook her head.

"That makes no difference, Dimitr. When I come to visit
you at Staro-Salo it will be your turn to give me bread and
cheese."

"You will be welcome, madame," said several of the other men
who had been listening.

"And so I must pay you for the work you are doing today. It
would be wrong otherwise," she said kindly but firmly; and they
nodded their heads, murmuring, "Very well."

Petko wiped his mouth, shook away the crumbs clinging to
his hand, and got to his feet.

"All right, then—at least we must work. We'll show you how

we work in our village." He turned to the others. " Come on,
all of you. Come on! "

By evening the lettuces seemed to have been restored to life,
the earth was dark with moisture and the tomatoes glowed with
renewed colour. The Bulgarians had cleared a fresh patch of
soil, dug it and raked it smooth. With no sign of haste, moving
steadily back and forth, they had got through an astonishing
amount of work. As evening fell they seated themselves in a
circle near the house. At intervals a soldier came to the gate,
shone a lantern on the sheet of paper in his hand, and called out a
name.

Madame Dumitriu came out of the house with her bag, meaning
to pay what she owed. She had intended to start with Petko, but
the soldier had just called him out into the yard, so she started
with Dimitr instead. The others listened intently, not always
understanding, for they did not all speak Roumanian. As the
business of settling accounts neared its end Petko returned and
with a low groan squatted down against the wall. Dimitr put a
question to him in Bulgarian, and he answered briefly, in a woe-
begone voice.

" What were you saying to him? " asked Madame Dumitriu.

" I asked him if he'd been beaten."

After a pause Madame Dimitriu said:

" And—have they beaten him? "

" Of course. Why not? They've beaten us all," replied Dimitr
with a short, mirthless laugh. " But he's not as tough as the rest
of us."

" Why should they beat us, madame? " asked Petko, who was
sitting in the shadow, huddled against the wall like a small, round
sack. " Why should we be beaten? We haven't done anything.
In the old days we were part of Bulgaria, and we paid our taxes
and did our military service. Now we're part of Roumania, and
we pay our taxes and do our military service. When I was a boy
at school I sang songs for Ferdinand of Bulgaria and I was taught
that the Roumanians were bad people. Now when our children
go to school they sing songs for Ferdinand of Roumania and they're
taught that it's the Bulgarians who are bad. What do they want
with us? " He seemed to be on the verge of tears, and he ended
with a sigh: " For us, it makes no difference which side we're on."

" The bread is always bitter," said Dimitr in his deep voice.

One of the other men said: " The *comitadjis* are Macedonians, they don't come from the Dobrudja."

Madame Dumitriu was unable to speak. Her heart was beating violently. She wanted to run away, to hear no more, to forget what she had heard. " They've beaten us all," Dimitr had said, as though it went without saying. No doubt it seemed equally natural to them that they should be brought there between fixed bayonets, and put to watering the garden of the officer commanding the Frontier Guards. It was natural that they should be beaten, natural that the frontiers should be changed beneath their feet, moved this way or that to the accompaniment of national anthems and history-books.

She got up. She had to leave for fear of bursting into tears and hearing them say, " We're the ones who get beaten, and she's the one who weeps," or else, " She'd do better to speak to her husband and make him give an order for us not to be beaten any more." She was ashamed, consumed with shame; she wanted to sink into the earth, to die, to cease to exist. She said in a trembling voice:

" Good night. You're good people. . . . Good night to you all."

" Good night," they replied amicably, or if not amicably at least without anger. She had done them no harm.

She sat in the living-room with the lamp unlit waiting for her husband. Now and then she heard the murmuring of the Bulgarians and saw the glow of a match in the darkness. But for the most part there was silence. They were talking very little. They were worried—not seriously frightened, but worried.

Suddenly the gate in the fence was violently slammed. There was a sound of heavy boots and a harsh voice shouted:

" You two here! And you two across the yard. You're not to let them come within less than ten feet of you. If they try to come any nearer, shoot at once! "

It was the voice of Lieutenant Tortoreano. Then Captain Dumitriu spoke:

" Go and have your dinner, Lieutenant, and afterwards wait for me in the office."

His voice sounded remote, without emotion, as though it came from another world. He entered the house.

" You're here, are you? But why haven't you lit the lamp? "

Then he said without any change of tone: " But never mind—
it's better like this."

" Don't you want anything to eat? " she asked.

" I'm not hungry."

He sat down on a chair that creaked. Everything was quiet
outside. The Bulgarians kept silent, with sentries mounting
guard over them. Madame Dumitriu got up and called to the
nurse:

" Eva, tell Vasilly to lay the table for the captain and light
the lamp."

By the yellow light of the oil-lamp she was able to examine
her husband. His face was pale, with a greyish tinge, and he tried
to avoid her eyes. He sat down at the table and made an effort to
eat, with his head bowed over his plate. But he gave it up almost
at once and thrust the plate aside.

" Petrica, what's wrong? "

" Nothing. You'd better go to bed. I've got some work
to do."

But he did not move from the table. The orderly cleared away
and withdrew. Madame Dumitriu got up presently and went into
the bedroom, leaving her husband still sitting there, staring in
front of him with his eyebrows knitted and his lips pursed. . . .

After an hour or two she sat up in bed. There was still a light
in the next room. She put on a dressing-gown and slippers and
softly opened the door. Her husband had not moved. He was
sitting with his elbows on the table, his clenched fists pressed to
the sides of his head, staring unseeingly at the lamp. He had laid
his monocle on the table. Gnats and midges were buzzing round
the lamp, fluttering and falling as they touched its glowing
chimney. Outside the cicadas were shrilling, and dogs were
barking in the distance. Taking care to make no sound, Madame
Dumitriu went and sat in her usual place. Her husband glanced
at her with a look of great distress. Still with his hands pressed
to his head he turned towards her, forcing a smile that was like a
grimace. It was as though he had some terrible confession to
make, of a crime or a shameful disease. . . . He said after a pause:

" I've had orders to shoot them all."

She stared at him and gasped: " What did you say? "

" I'm to have them marched under escort to the wood that
stretches along the frontier, and there our men will be given the

order to shoot. It's intended as a reprisal, a warning to the *comitadjis*."

" No," said his wife in a low voice. " No, you mustn't do it."

" I know I mustn't. I'm an officer, not an executioner." The captain was silent for a moment and then said: " But an officer has to obey orders."

" Petrica——"

" Please! Don't say anything. I know. I've got to think."

He continued to stare at the lamp with its cloud of dazzled insects. Faint sounds came from outside as one of the Bulgarians rose, went to relieve himself against the fence and then returned to stretch himself on the earth with a sigh. Once more there was only the buzz of hypnotised midges round the lamp.

5

Early next morning the office telephone rang, and the duty-telephonist hurried to fetch the captain.

" The colonel's on the line, sir."

Captain Dumitriu, bathed and scented with eau de Cologne, wearing an immaculately white tunic, with his monocle screwed in his eye and a cigar between his teeth, went into the office, locked the door and took up the receiver.

" Captain Dumitriu speaking. At your orders, Colonel."

" Well, what's the news, Captain? Has my order been carried out? " demanded a harsh, staccato voice.

" I have the honour to state, sir, that I expect a written order," said the captain calmly. He knew perfectly well that an order such as this could not be given in writing. The telephone spluttered furiously.

" Have you gone off your head? The order's to be carried out instantly and you're to come and report to me in person. Instantly, do you understand? I expect you here before midday."

" I have the honour to inquire whether you wish to see me before or after the execution of the order."

" Afterwards, of course."

" I have the honour to repeat that I await a written order," said Captain Dumitriu, speaking with extreme deliberation.

There was a click as the colonel hung up. Captain Dumitriu unlocked the door and went out to watch the drilling of a platoon on a nearby patch of waste-land.

His wife had opened the door of their house at the same moment, and then stood rigid in the doorway. The Bulgarians had resumed their task of watering the lettuces. In a shaking voice she bade them good morning, and several greeted her in reply.

" Who told you to go on watering the garden? " she asked. She could not bring herself to look at them, fearing lest she should lose all self-control and say things she had no right to say, or be led into committing some act of wild folly. She was trembling with horror and indignation at the thought that although they were to be shot they had been ordered back to work. How could God permit such things?

" No one told us. We did not want to sit here idle," the tall Dimitr said gravely, and she could have wept. His words and eyes were saying, " We're honest men. We only ask that others should not harm us, and we will behave well on our side. Perhaps you mean to bring us more food, and so we are working to deserve it."

Petko came towards her, small and plump, but with cheeks that had lost their bright colour and were now grey. He asked timidly: " You don't know if—if they are going to keep us here? "

" They won't be keeping you much longer," she said, not looking at him.

He was silent for a moment and then stammered: " But—but what are they going to do to us? "

Madame Dumitriu made a superhuman effort and looked him in the eyes. " They're going to let you go home, of course."

" I don't think so," said Petko, with a full bucket in each hand. " I don't believe it. You don't know how the officers shouted at us last night, or how they beat us."

" But, Petko, I promise you! They'll send you back to Staro-Selo," said Madame Dumitriu. He looked at her with widening eyes. How could he fail to guess? He would realise the truth in another instant. Madame Dumitriu said with all the calm she could command: " I hope, after you're released, that some of you

will come back from time to time to attend to my garden for me.
I'll pay you by the day."

"Yes, we'll come," said Petko. "We'll certainly come. . . .
But why do they put armed men to guard us if they mean to let
us go?"

She turned very pale, but still contrived to laugh.

"That's what soldiers are like," she said. And she added
gravely: "They're angry because the *comitadjis* killed their
comrades."

"Ah," said Petko and went off with his buckets. A moment
later she saw him talking in undertones with the others, who had
gathered round him, looking uneasy but listening with close
attention to what he said. Dimitr, a head taller than any of them,
saw her still standing in the doorway and gave her a questioning
glance. Then Madame Dumitriu could bear it no longer. She
ran back into the house, locked herself in the bedroom, and lay
quivering on the bed.

6

At a little before midday a dusty motor-car arrived, and from it
emerged the colonel commanding the regiment and a tall, lean
general. Entering the company offices they ordered the sergeant
on duty to go at once in search of Captain Dumitriu, who was
still out watching the platoon at exercise. The captain arrived in
due course, not having hurried unduly, and stood rigidly at the
salute as he had seen it done on ceremonial occasions in Schwerin,
at the march past of the Pomeranian Grenadiers, the regiment
which Wilhelm II of Hohenzollern, Emperor of Germany and
King of Prussia, had placed under the patronage of Carol I of
Hohenzollern, formerly Prince Regnant of the United Princi-
palities of Moldavia and Wallachia, and later King of Roumania.

General Ipsilanti, lordly and icy in his demeanour, listened
in silence to the captain's report and then asked:

" Petrica, what's your objection to this order the colonel has given you? You said you wanted it in writing."

" Yes, sir."

" Well, now I personally am giving you the order. I take it you aren't going to ask me to put it in writing? "

Captain Dumitriu was still standing to attention, but with his body tensed like that of a man ready to spring upon his adversary, or to take flight. There was an intimidating light in his clear, cold blue eyes.

" I have the honour to state, sir, that I expect a written order," he replied in an impersonal voice.

The colonel started up, ready to explode. General Ipsilanti smiled smoothly and said: " Would you mind leaving us, Colonel? I want to talk to him." He waited for the door to close and went on: " Listen, my dear boy. Do you realise that you're wrecking your career? "

Dumitriu stayed motionless and silent.

" You're an outstanding officer, intelligent and well educated, which is not often the case in our army, I'm sorry to say. You've been through Military Academy and you're on the list for promotion. One of these days you'll command a regiment, and if there's a war you may get a division or even an army-corps. With your German training I can see you becoming Chief of the General Staff by the time you're my age."

Captain Dumitriu's jaws tightened.

" Your wife has influential connections—the Lascaris have the *entrée* to the Queen. Which means that . . ." The general paused, but Captain Dumitriu remained obstinately silent. " Well, anyway," the general said, " all we're asking of you is— how shall I put it—a little——"

" A trifling crime," said Captain Dumitriu calmly.

At the back of General Ipsilanti's mind was the calculation that if the captain did what was asked of him he would be in a position to break his career if he chose, since an officer guilty of such an act would be in no position to defend himself; and on the other hand, if he refused to obey orders . . .

" You can call it what you like," he said, " but you must realise that if you refuse to carry out this order you will never get a command in the Roumanian Army, not even of a regiment. You will grow old as a junior officer, although you're fitted for far better

things. You'll be passed over in favour of every half-wit in the
officers corps and you'll end up one of the thousand or two
thousand half-pay lieutenant-colonels, when you might have had
a brilliant career. Well? "

Captain Dumitriu continued to stand motionless, his forehead
shining with sweat.

" I'll give you until this afternoon to think it over. Meanwhile
it's time for lunch. Is there anywhere in these parts where we can
get a reasonable meal? "

" May I invite you and the colonel to lunch, sir? My wife will
be delighted," said the captain, white to the lips.

" And I shall be charmed to accept," said the general, beaming.
He gave the captain a fatherly tap on the shoulder. " You'll think
it over carefully, won't you? I'm sure you'll come to the right
decision."

" I shall try to do so," said Captain Dumitriu.

7

General Prince Ipsilanti sat at the end of the table at the right
hand of Madame Dumitriu in his admirably cut uniform, his
monocle gleaming beneath a greying eyebrow, distinguished
to his finger-tips.

" Thank you," he said affably. " May I help myself to some
more of this delicious salad? "

" There wouldn't have been any salad," said Madame Dumitriu,
" the drought was killing everything—there wouldn't have been
any salad if the Bulgarian peasants in the yard hadn't watered
my lettuces."

The general stopped eating, put down his fork and stared at
her. The colonel choked and coughed. There was an unhappy
silence while the orderly served coffee.

" Vasilly, have you given the Bulgarians something to eat? "
asked Madame Dumitriu.

" Yes, madame."

The general said with an acid smile: " I gather that you're taking great care of them. Perhaps you have a particular sympathy for the Bulgarians? "

" I have sympathy for everyone who's in trouble."

" You should also think of our own soldiers," said the general gravely. " The ones who were killed."

" Is anything being done to help their families? " asked Madame Dumitriu.

Her face was very pale and her eyes red. The general no longer found her to his liking. Indeed, his only feeling for her was one of hostility, the seed of which had been implanted during those few moments at Madame Vorvoreano's ball, and which had now grown into a solid and considered distaste.

" That, my dear lady, is a matter for the Government. It is not your concern."

" But you said that I should think of our soldiers," said Madame Dumitriu. " I assure you, I do. But I'm no less concerned for people the Government doesn't worry about. I mean the peasants outside."

The general was decidedly ruffled. No one had ventured to talk back to him since he was four. He uttered a short, vicious laugh.

" Let me assure you that the Government is giving them its closest attention. Very much so! "

The colonel joined in his laughter, and so, without much gaiety, did the two junior staff-officers present at the table, Lieutenant Spahiu and another. Captain Dumitriu remained unsmiling. As for his wife, she smiled in bitterness, anguish and contempt.

" Yes, indeed, they're giving them their very best attention— oh, most decidedly! Thank you, dear lady, for a most pleasant luncheon. And when are you coming to see us at headquarters? . . . Captain, I expect you in ten minutes. . . . I'm relying on you, madame, to make him see reason. He's very obstinate at times."

The general bowed. Madame Dumitriu bowed in return, politely smiling, but without offering him her hand. After briefly hesitating the general clicked his heels and went stiffly out. The colonel, not seeing what had occurred, held out his hand and stood thus for several seconds, after which he blushed violently, clicked his heels in his turn, and followed his commander. The two younger officers were treated in the same way, and Lieutenant Spahiu muttered when he got outside:

" The bitch! She thinks she can get away with anything because she comes from a family of aristos—and Hungarian at that! "

Encountering Lieutenant Tortoreano in the yard he led him away and talked to him for several minutes, then gave him a push with his hands on his shoulders.

" Don't be a fool! Go and tell the general you want to make a confidential report. Old Telescope's absolutely livid. He's hating the captain's guts. Go on! You can't miss."

" All right, I see what you mean, you don't have to shove me," said Tortoreano. He went towards the offices, knocked and entered, clicking his heels. . . .

Meanwhile Madame Dumitriu, in her living-room, was standing with her hands pressed to her mouth.

" What is it? " her husband asked.

" I shouldn't have done it. I shouldn't have behaved like that. I should have swallowed everything, been sweet and feminine, and perhaps I could have saved them," she said in a low voice.

Captain Dumitriu shrugged his shoulders.

" He isn't responsible. The decision must have come from the Cabinet. The Minister for War probably telephoned the order to Cilibia, Cilibia to Telescope, and Telescope to the colonel—all by word of mouth."

" But what are you going to do, Petrica—what can you do? " she cried in horror, and seized his arm as she saw that he was about to leave the room. He gently disengaged her fingers from his sleeve and raised them to his lips. Then he said with a pale smile:

" If I could save them by sacrificing my own life I would do it to make you proud of me. But, you see, it would make no difference."

" Petrica! " she cried, but now he turned away.

He crossed the yard without bestowing a glance on the Bulgarian peasants as they sat by the wall eating bread and cheese and onions. He walked steadily on, stiffly erect in his white tunic, his monocle in his eye, punctiliously returning the salute of the sentries. Arriving at the door of his office he tried to open it and found that it was locked. The sound of voices came from inside. He stood waiting. After a little while the door opened and

Lieutenant Tortoreano emerged, broadly grinning, and saluted him with a cheerful amiability that was wholly out of place. The general and the colonel were in the room, the general on his feet and the colonel standing to attention. General Ipsilanti considered Captain Dumitriu as he entered, looking down at him from his greater height, and said dryly:

"Captain, I must request you to ask your wife to adopt a different attitude towards the enemies of our country, and also towards your superior officers."

"I have the honour to reply," said Captain Dumitriu, standing to attention, "that my wife is not borne on the strength of the division and cannot, therefore, accept orders from the divisional commander."

The general started and said even more coldly:

"But she can talk to you about the orders you receive from your superiors, and persuade you to oppose them?"

Captain Dumitriu now realised what Tortoreano had been doing there. He must have questioned the sentries on duty in the yard; perhaps he had even eavesdropped at their open window. The captain was tempted to laugh; all this seemed to him so shabby, so shameful and at the same time so grotesque. He replied almost cheerfully:

"I have the honour to inform you, sir, that I do not discuss my orders with anyone. I obey them."

A gleam of surprised satisfaction appeared in the general's eye. So the fellow was giving away! Henceforth he would be able to despise him and humiliate him with casual reminders. And perhaps—who could tell?—perhaps she, too, would come to see reason.

"So we're beginning to understand one another at last! I'm very glad. That's splendid. Now tell me, how do you intend to— er—deal with the matter? You'd better report to me by telephone when it's over and follow it up with a written report. You know the sort of thing—attempted escape on the part of the prisoners while being moved under escort, assisted by a surprise attack by *comitadjis*—but I leave the details to you, my dear fellow."

"If you please, General, I must first have a written order."

The general started and then bellowed:

"By God, you're sticking to it, are you? I'll teach you to make a fool of me! Colonel, this officer is to be relieved of his command. He can be replaced temporarily by the young man who was in here just now, the lieutenant. Send for him and order him to carry out the removal of the prisoners, on foot and under escort, to the village of Staro-Selo. As for you, Captain, you will hold yourself at the disposal of divisional headquarters. You will receive instructions in due course. Dismiss! "

Captain Dumitriu again saluted as he might have done the Emperor of Germany and King of Prussia on the parade-ground at Schwerin, turned on his heel and went out. Crossing the yard he passed lieutenants Spahiu and Tortoreano, who paused in their conversation to observe him with a gleam of triumphant mockery in their eyes. He walked through the vegetable-garden, where the Bulgarians were again at work, and went into his house.

His wife was awaiting him, and he was shocked by her expression. He told her briefly what had happened, and now it was she who took him by the hand. They stood with their fingers intertwined listening to the Bulgarian voices outside. These were lower than before and seemed more agitated. For the next hour or two everything was quiet, but late in the afternoon, as the sun was beginning to sink over the bare, calcined plain, there was a sudden shouting of orders in the yard. Tortoreano's voice was to be heard. A car started and there was a sound of horses' hooves. Lieutenant Tortoreano, who must have been standing at the gate separating the yard from the garden, shouted almost in their ears:

" Hey, you Bulgarians, get in line! March! We're taking you home."

Madame Dumitriu made a single movement and then was still, listening to a voice which at first she did not recognise.

" Mister officer, you mustn't take us away! You mustn't kill us! "

The words were uttered in a long-drawn cry, so humble and beseeching, so heartrending, that Madame Dumitriu felt a wave of agony and terror pass through her body. It was the voice of the small, plump Petko, whose cheeks only the day before had been round and red. That cry from the depths of his being sounded like the lament of the earth itself, of all nature, all life.

" Don't take us away. . . . Don't kill us. . . ."

Another man shouted in a harsh, defiant voice:

" We've done no harm. It isn't right! "

Petko continued to beg for mercy, and behind her drawn window-curtains Madame Dumitriu put her hands to her ears.

" For Christ's sake stop your wailing! " shouted Tortoreano. " Nobody's going to kill you. You're the ones who kill our soldiers, you pack of animals. Get moving! Come on! "

" We have children," Petko moaned.

" Jump to it, or do you want your head bashed in? For God's sake stand up! " The wretched Petko must have sunk to his knees. Dimitr's deep voice said something in Bulgarian, in a tone of encouragement and gentle reproof.

Madame Dumitriu ran to the door giving on to the garden. Lieutenant Tortoreano, who was supervising the peasants as they filed out into the yard, pretended not to see her. She stood in the doorway. The men had ashen faces and walked vague-eyed, as though in a dream. One was swaying on his feet. Petko was scarcely moving at all, his round, black eyes darting in terror from left to right, searching for a way of escape. Seeing her he cried:

" Lady, help us! They're taking us away! They're going to kill us all! "

Dimitr was walking at his side, his cheeks covered with a stiff, black growth of beard. He gave Madame Dumitriu a single, anguished glance, and driving the points of her finger-nails into her palms she summoned all the strength she possessed. She must not fail them now. She said lightly, almost gaily:

" What is it, Petko? I don't like to see you all going away like this. I haven't paid you for today's work."

Tortoreano snapped: " No one is allowed to speak to them, madame."

" They're going to kill us," wailed Petko as he shuffled past.

" You're absurd," she said. " Why should anyone want to kill you? You've done nothing wrong. At present I mayn't speak to you, but when you're released and back in your village I hope that one of you, perhaps Petko, will come and collect the money I owe you. And then we'll arrange for you to look after my garden."

" We'll come—I'll come! " cried Petko with a wild fervour, and he moved on more briskly, seeming now to do so of his own accord, rather than in response to the soldier who was prodding him with a rifle-butt. Dimitr again looked at Madame Dumitriu. directing at her a long, anxious glance in which there was a hint of questioning still tinged with fear. But he walked out holding himself well erect, with a certain stiffness in his powerful head and shoulders. The soldiers followed, shutting the gate behind them.

Madame Dumitriu turned back into the room and sat trembling in her chair. Her husband had not moved. In the deepening obscurity she could not see his face.

Darkness fell. The nurse laid the table, and Vasilly brought in the dishes: but Captain and Madame Dumitriu could eat nothing. They sat facing one another without speaking, while the midges whirled round the lamp. At last they heard the sound of the soldiers returning.

"Party—halt!" shouted Lieutenant Tortoreano. Boots thudded in the yard, further orders were given and there was a rattle of rifle-bolts. After a time silence fell again.

Madame Dumitriu said in an uncertain voice:

" Perhaps nothing happened. . . ."

Her husband did not reply. Possibly he was thinking of his wrecked career, and the small and squalid business which their life must now become.

" Vasilly," called Madame Dumitriu.

" Yes, madame."

" Go and find out what has happened."

She had spoken in a very low voice. The young man left the room without looking at her.

He did not come back for a long time. Finally she went out to the porch and found him standing there alone.

"What are you doing? Did you go? What did they tell you? "

Vasilly looked at her with sombre eyes, then looked away and murmured:

" They killed them all. They shot them. They were supposed to be trying to escape."

She went back into the living-room without saying anything and sat down again at the table. She sat staring at some object in front of her, not knowing what it was. Suddenly she réalised that it was the salad-bowl with its pile of crisp, green lettuce-leaves on which the oil and water shone softly, like beads of sweat, or like tears.

" Vasilly! " she cried, and the man came running in, startled by the sudden outrage in her voice. " Take this away. Take it away at once! "

He picked up the bowl and hurriedly withdrew. Madame Dumitriu sank forward over the table. Her husband reached out a hand and mechanically stroked her hair while she wept as though her heart would break.

8

On the following morning Captain Dumitriu reported in person at divisional headquarters to General Cilibia. He was covered with dust, having ridden the whole way, and his face was still damp with perspiration when he entered the general's office. The general was seated with his back to a wall on which hung photographs of the King and Queen and, somewhat lower, that of Marshal Avaresco, whose small beard and helmet made one think of a white mouse with its head in a nutshell. The room was cool, with a smell of leather, old documents and paintwork. General Cilibia's face turned a deeper crimson, and his thick neck bulged over the stiff collar as he glared at the officer standing rigidly before him. Captain Dumitriu stayed silent, seeming not to turn a hair beneath that intent regard, and at length Cilibia said abruptly:

" Captain, at first sight you give the impression of being a man of sense."

Captain Dumitriu remained impassive. After considering him for another moment the general unexpectedly asked:

" Is your wife a communist? "

Dumitriu's rigid posture was unchanged; only his voice betrayed his astonishment.

" I beg your pardon, sir? "

" Are you deaf, Captain, or are you pretending to be stupid? You heard what I said. Is your wife a Bolshevik? "

" No, sir, she is not."

" Young man, if you're not pretending to be a fool it means that you really are one. Where did you first meet her? In Budapest, wasn't it, in 1919? I have reason to know, since you were in my division. Well, and wasn't there a revolution in Hungary? How do you know what sort of people she'd been mixing with—communists, socialists, Jews—eh? "

" General, my wife is not a communist," repeated the captain who was beginning to grow angry.

" Then blast and damn it all, why did she have to take the side of those peasants? I have here two confidential reports——"

" Which means that there are two swine in my company," said Captain Dumitriu coolly.

The general rose to his feet, crimson and enormous, and bellowed:

" I will ask you to moderate your language. In the first place, it's no longer your company. And secondly, what I would call a swine is an officer who marries a woman of enemy nationality and refuses to carry out an order coming directly from the Government, so that the Minister of War is bound to learn that there has been a case of insubordination in the Cilibia Division, *my* division! I'll make you pay for that, young man. There'll be an appropriate entry on your dossier. You'll be shifted from one garrison to another, you'll be harried from pillar to post with scarcely time to get your belongings packed. I'll see to it that you serve under commanding officers who'll make your life a hell. I'll break you, do you hear? You'll retire with the rank of captain, like any warrant-officer who has managed to scrape a commission. Now clear out! "

He sat down again, breathless, with his moustache ruffled and perspiration running down his temples. Captain Dumitriu, pale to the lips, was still standing rigidly to attention; but now he got the monocle out of his breast-pocket, fixed it in his eye, and simply said:

" At your orders, General. I am Captain Dumitriu of the Tenth Regiment of Frontier Guards. I have the honour to inform you that I hold myself at the disposal of the division."

Cilibia was still gasping for breath.

" You're transferred to the Nineteenth Infantry Regiment," he said with an effort. " Good day."

Captain Dumitriu saluted, and after leaving the room made

for the stables at the back of the barracks, since this was the
one place where at that hour he could hope to be alone. His
horse, not yet unsaddled, was tied up in the shade, and he went to
it and patted its neck. It looked at him with big, dark eyes and
snorted. The captain pressed his forehead against the saddle and
closed his eyes; then, still with lowered lids, he groped with one
hand for the side-pocket of his tunic. Officers were under orders
to go armed in the vicinity of the frontier, and he carried an
automatic pistol whose weight and outline he could feel against
his hip.

The horse champed its fodder. The air was hot and scented
with hay. There was no sound except the faint creak of the saddle-
girth and an occasional rumble in the horse's belly. Captain
Dumitriu set his teeth and tightly screwed up his eyes to prevent
himself from bursting into tears. If he shot himself what would
become of his wife and children? . . . Finally he unhitched his
horse, led it out of the stable, mounted and rode at a walk to
the barracks gate. He rode bowed forward in the saddle, and
to anyone seeing him he must have looked like a man mortally
ill.

The next day Army Transport removed the captain's few
pieces of furniture and his wife's and children's belongings. He
followed with his family in their carriage, reflecting, as he held
his wife's hand, that now the carriage and horses would have to
be sold. He played absent-mindedly with the children, seated
on the nurse's lap. The nurse, too, would have to be got rid of.

Arriving back at the town they had left, Madame Dumitriu
changed into a white dress and went to call upon Madame Vorvoreano, the one person to whom she felt able to turn. She was
not immediately shown into a room, but had to stand waiting
at the foot of the stairs. Finally a manservant came down and
announced that Madame was now ready to receive her.

Hollow-cheeked and clad as usual in black, Madame Vorvoreano
was sitting in an armchair. She did not rise to greet her visitor
but merely signed with a yellow and withered blue-veined hand
for her to be seated.

" What can I do for you? " she asked, looking slightly embarrassed.

Madame Dumitriu was still red-eyed with weeping.

" I have come to you," she said, " because, after all, I feel nearer to you than to anyone else in this town."

Madame Vorvoreano's lips writhed in a faint grimace, as though she had encountered an unpleasant smell.

" I like that ' after all.' I find it charming," she said in a tone that caused Madame Dumitriu even greater distress at the thought that she had offended her. " And why, may I ask, do you consider me the person nearest to you? "

" Why—because you're my mother's sister."

" Hadn't you realised that before? Or are you now condescending to acknowledge the relationship simply because you're in trouble? "

" It isn't for my own sake, it's for people who are even worse off than I am," said Madame Dumitriu. She went on to tell the story, talking with such earnestness that at the end there were tears in her eyes. " It's a crime! " she cried. " Those men's names must be cleared. Their widows and children must be looked after. The Government must be told the truth, and the Press too. The men who are guilty must be punished."

Madame Vorvoreano stared at her in silence and suddenly began to laugh. The act of laughing caused her acute pain.

" You've made me hurt myself," she said with a little groan, pressing her hand to her side. " But, for heaven's sake, what kind of world do you think you're living in? You say that the guilty men should be punished. Whom do you mean—General Ipsilanti, the brother of Bubi Ipsilanti, who has so many influential friends? You must be mad. And do you really imagine that the Government or the Press will take notice of anything you say—a foreigner, coming from the country most hated by Roumanians, and in any case suspected of communist sympathies? What were you doing at the frontier, if you didn't go there to spy? That is what people would say—everyone except me, of course, because I know your limitations. Try to have some sense! What do those peasants or their families matter to you? The men were Bulgarian nationalists, or else communists, which is worse. You'd do far better to worry about your own problems. You and your husband will have to make yourselves very inconspicuous if you're to go on living in our society; you'll be wise not to show yourselves too much in public. You snubbed General Ipsilanti when he was disposed to be friendly, you've ignored your relationship with me, and on top of that your husband, under your influence, has chosen to become a pro-Bulgarian or pro-communist or whatever it may be. Really you're an impossible pair! If you've enough to live on, your husband should resign his commission and you should go and hide in some out-of-the-way place where nobody knows you. Failing that, you must just make yourselves as small as you can. That's the best advice I can give you—although I really don't know why I bother."

" But those men are dead." stammered Madame Dumitriu. " They were shot! And they were innocent."

Madame Vorvoreano uttered another short laugh, showing her yellow teeth.

" I'm dying too," she said. " You'll die some day. Why worry about people like that? "

V

The Pleasures of Youth

I

Serban Romano was a young man of staid and serious disposition, which perhaps explains why he was fascinated by his cousin, Ghighi Duca. He returned from Germany in 1928 with an engineer's diploma and the intention of going back there to study philosophy. In Bucarest he heard of nothing but Ghighi Duca—Ghighi's Rolls, his ties, his hats, his women, his jokes and his escapades. But Ghighi had little time to spare for his family, which made it difficult for a well-conducted, rather retiring young man like Serban Romano to meet him.

However, one evening Serban visited a night-club with Elvira Vorvoreano, who was recently divorced, and Prince Bubi Ipsilanti, who at the time was paying court to her. Scarcely had they taken their seats than Elvira cried:

" Why, there's Ghighi! "

She waved. Ghighi nodded coolly and then ignored them. He was sitting with an Englishman whose close friend everyone knew him to be. They had become acquainted during Ghighi's last visit to England, but he had not introduced him to anyone. The Englishman was a man of about thirty, of medium height, with a long head, a high-coloured complexion, grey eyes and large hands covered with brown flecks. Like Ghighi he wore a dinner-jacket, but Ghighi looked the more distinguished of the two. He was tall, very slender, and fair-haired with a narrow, triangular face. Two deep folds running from his cheekbones to the corners of his mouth, and deep shadows under his eyes, gave him an unhealthy, slightly disquieting, appearance. Yet everyone knew that he played tennis, shot, hunted, drove his own car and could pilot an aeroplane—in short that he was a vigorous, sporting type who enjoyed perfect health.

Serban was struck by his jerky habit of speech, his excitable laugh, and the haste with which he devoured his food, as though anxious to be done with it as quickly as possible. He had to devote most of his attention to Elvira and Bubi Ipsilanti, but now and then he glanced in Ghighi's direction, and Elvira, who was doing the same thing, said as she caught him at it:

" Ghighi has changed, don't you think? He's not looking well."

They went on to talk of other things while they sat drinking and watching the couples on the dance floor, until suddenly a sharp sound—it was that of a face being slapped—caused everyone to turn and stare at Ghighi's table. Ghighi was still seated, but the Englishman had risen swaying to his feet, his cheek reddening with the imprint of Ghighi's hand. He snatched up a bottle, evidently meaning to use it as a weapon, but it slipped out of his grasp as he swung it back and struck the head of a woman sitting behind him, who uttered a sharp cry. The Englishman looked slowly round, first at the woman and then at her escort, who had jumped up and was making a rush at him. He warded off a blow and floored his attacker with a punch on the jaw. Several other men joined in the fray with bottles and siphons, and Ghighi picked up a chair and went to his friend's assistance. The women screamed hysterically, waiters struggled to separate the combatants, bottles flew in all directions and Bubi Ipsilanti got up so hurriedly that he overturned the table, saying with a gasp:

" Take cover or we shall all be laid out! "

Laughing nervously the three of them crouched behind the table, which Bubi and Serban held in place by its legs. The battle proceeded. Peering round their rampart Serban saw that Ghighi and the Englishman had picked up a man by his arms and legs and were preparing to fling him on top of a confused mass of black jackets and crumpled shirt-fronts. Ghighi was green in the face, the Englishman crimson, dishevelled and hilarious. Serban drew back his head. The commotion went on for several minutes more and then a calm descended. Serban peeped out again. No one was left except Ghighi, stretched on his back in the middle of the dance-floor, and the Englishman, who was systematically jumping on him. Although the waiters and the proprietor begged him to stop, the young man, suffused of face, sweating and breathless, continued to jump up and down on Ghighi's body with a methodical and stubborn ferocity. When finally he had had enough of it he picked Ghighi up, slung him over his shoulder and bore him off to the lavatory.

" Let's get out of here," said Bubi Ipsilanti to Elvira and Serban. He beckoned to the head waiter, and said as that function-ary approached: " I'll settle up tomorrow. We're in a hurry." And outside he said to Elvira: " All it needs now is for us to be hauled in as witnesses! "

" Oh, rubbish," said Elvira. " The police can't do much to Ghighi."

" No, but just the thought of seeing our names on one of their filthy bits of paper makes me sick. And even Ghighi's bound to get into trouble if he goes round with types like that."

" What a savage he is, that Englishman," said Elvira, with a tremor in her voice. She had evidently taken a fancy to him.

" Yes, that's how the English built their Empire. That's how they've always gone on, from Elizabeth's time to the Boer War. It's a pity about Ghighi, who's not a bad sort really. There's a lot of good in him. But he's only getting what he deserves. He's a roughneck too," said Prince Bubi with unexpected venom.

2

Serban returned to Germany in October and was back in Bucarest in December, just before Christmas. He had seen nothing more of Ghighi Duca.

Late one afternoon in the week after Christmas he found him-self in the Rue Cimpineano. It was nearly dark and the weather was cold. He wanted a drink and looked around him. There were bars and restaurants all down the street and a line of cars parked beside the kerb. Through the café windows he could see people sitting at tables, women with worn furs and platinum-blonde hair, garishly made-up, middle-aged men with drooping mous-taches and young men with tie-pins and hats from Clark or Mossant.

Serban pushed open the nearest door, above which was the

sign: " Express Bar. V. Tassopol." There was a glass tank with
a few goldfish in the window. He went up three steps into a room
with blue plush banquettes round the walls, a piano in one corner,
two tables and, beyond them, a bar. The walls were decorated
with large photographs of film-stars—Mae West, Mary Pickford,
Ramon Novarro, Douglas Fairbanks, Elissa Landi.

Vasilache Tassopol was in the habit of receiving his customers
with a smiling reserve, a man of affable dignity with a large
stomach and a jacket of questionable whiteness. Two mixed
couples were seated on stools at the bar, but Serban paid no
attention to these because he had seen Ghighi Duca lolling on
the banquette with a bottle of whisky and a siphon. He was
wearing a dark grey suit, a starched collar and a black-and-white
tie. He looked impassively at Serban, who went up to him shyly
smiling.

" Well, Serbanica, how goes it? " said Ghighi, without rising
or taking his hands out of his pockets. " Sit down. How are you?
You've filled out. How old are you now? "

" I'm twenty-five."

" Vasilache, bring us another glass. . . . You're five years
younger than me—just the length of the war. How's Aunt
Alexandrina? "

" She's quite well."

" And Aunt Helene Vorvoreano? Incidentally, I think I saw
you one night with Elvira."

" Aunt Helene isn't at all well. Her skin's yellow and she's
got terribly thin. The doctors are surprised that it's taking so
long."

" Yes, cancer goes quicker as a rule. And what about Elvira?
Who's she sleeping with these days? "

" I don't know."

" Discreet, eh? Quite right. And what are you doing, Serbanica? Never mind about the others, tell me about yourself.
Will you have some Scotch? "

" Thanks—on the rocks."

" Oho, an expert! You've been learning things abroad, I see.
Well, and what are you doing? "

" I've done my engineering course and now I'm reading
philosophy."

" Splendid. Here's to you, Serbanica! May you become a

great man and an illustrious philosopher, if the thing's still possible in this country."

" Why shouldn't it be? "

" My dear boy, in Roumania? "

" But why not? "

" Serbanica, don't be a fathead. The French and English don't even know that Roumania exists, and as for the Americans—but don't let's talk about them. You're too much of a Moldo-Walla-chian, my lad—small country, small problems, limited interests —nothing to be done except drink whisky and later on clean up the family cellar."

" I don't agree," said Serban earnestly. " In the year One of the Christian Era, Judea was nothing but a small, impoverished and despised Christian colony. The Jews were only known for their unpleasant smell and their barbarous superstitions. And yet that's where the new order of thinking came from that revolution-ised the culture of the Western world. Do you think that Weimar in Goethe's time was anything like New York? And what about Dutch painting, or Norwegian literature? Come to that, I might mention Icelandic literature. Do you know anything about it? "

" Not a thing. All I know about the Icelanders is that they're well stocked with ice."

" They have a remarkably rich literature, and yet there are not much more than a hundred thousand of them."

" And mostly snowmen at that," said Ghighi Duca. " All right, Serbanica, you win. And so what? For instance, what do you expect me to do?—revolutionise the world?—write? I've no talent."

Serban stared into his glass and did not answer. Ghighi re-peated suddenly, in an altered tone:

" Seriously, what do you think I should do? "

" That's something only you can decide."

It was now quite dark outside. Tassopol made a move to switch on more lights.

" Leave it the way it is, Vasilache," said Ghighi. " Too much light bothers my eyes." He went on, speaking in a low voice: " I wish you'd tell me. Should I go into politics—make lying speeches to half-wits and spend my days in the Chamber, from ten in the morning till midnight, to end up a provincial governor or a minister by the time I'm forty, or perhaps not until I'm fifty?

Fancy being a minister! Ministers bow and scrape to me as it is, although I'm completely useless, just because I'm descended from the great Voivode Duca. To hell with ministers. So what am I to do? Become a man of science? It's too difficult and too late."

" It's never too late," said Serban. " Schliemann revolutionised archeology although he didn't take it up till he was over forty. Nothing that you're saying makes sense. You're still young enough to learn anything you like."

They emptied their glasses.

" Listen, Serbanica, I'll tell you the truth. How many great men have come from very wealthy families? You can skip the politicians and generals. Politics in these days aren't what they were in the time of Pitt, and war isn't what it was in the days of Condé. Give me a few instances of rich men who have really amounted to something—I mean, really rich."

" Byron was a lord."

" Yes, but cleaned out. Try another."

" Goethe."

" He wasn't an aristo, and he wasn't as rich as all that. Who else? Tolstoi? A unique case. Any more? "

" There's a German, Thomas Mann, and a Frenchman, Marcel Proust. They're both highly thought of."

" Never heard of them. What are they—musicians? Never mind those sort of people. When it comes to rich Germans, think of von Bucqoy, who owns mines in Silesia. Or if you want members of the great French families—the name Proust stinks of the bourgeoisie—there's the Prince de Courtenay or the Duc d'Otrante. And have any of them ever done anything? It's a darned sight easier to throw parties, travel, cruise, hunt, gamble, drink and fornicate. Look, suppose I made up my mind I was going to study something—anatomy, for example——"

" I've thought of someone else," said Serban. " De Broglie. In fact there are two or three of them, all scientists."

" But all exceptions, dear boy. Suppose, for instance, I settle down to study anatomy. Someone drops in to see me, so I have to stop. He goes away and I start again. It begins to be tiring —much pleasanter to ring up a wench and arrange to do a little anatomy at first hand. The next day I've arranged to go hunting, so I try again the day after. It's tough. I take along a bottle to keep me company, and after the second glass, mixed the way I like it, which is pretty stiff, I sink into a state of beatific euphoria, all the nervous tension gone. I feel wonderful, I've no ambition left. And so on. Of course I'm an idiot, a worthless clod, but I'm simply illustrating what amounts to a scientific law. People like us—good family, money and all the rest of it—never do anything worth while. Have some more whisky."

" No, thank you."

" Well I will, thank you. Your health, Serbanica. I wish you success. . . . Vasilache, you can switch on now."

The lights flooded harshly over the shoddy stucco of the walls, the soiled antimacassars, the scratched paintwork of the chairs. Serban found the place dingy and unpleasant. As for Ghighi, his face was pale and his eyes dull. He murmured abstractedly:

" Other kinds of men, ones without money, they've got all sorts of things—ideals—values. . . . But me, I'm simply bored. And tired. And anyway there's something wrong with me. I don't feel well."

He looked anything but well, and Serban was alarmed by the sudden change that had come over him.

" Should I try to get a doctor? " he said.

" No, stay where you are and don't fuss," said Ghighi, with beads of perspiration on his brow.

At this moment the door opened and two young men came noisily in. Serban recognised them as friends of Ghighi: Titel Negruzzi, his bowler hat on the back of his head, wearing a black overcoat with an astrakhan collar, and Dodel Dodesco, one of a great boyar family descended from the Ban of Oltenia, which Lady Raven, in her travel reminiscences, called the Ban Dodescolo. Dodel Dodesco was small and puny with a large, shiny, hooked nose, a thin moustache and lips that were always moist. He wore a black coat lined with mink, with a blue-gleaming beaver collar. Both young men were in high spirits.

" Ghighi, this is wonderful! How are you, dear boy? How are you, my blessing? How are you, my poppet? " They made a chant of it as they came up the steps.

" I saw your car," said Titel. " It was neatly parked midway between two shops, so we didn't know where to start looking for you. Why, it's Serbanica! Serbanica, how are you? "

Ghighi got up and vanished past the end of the bar.

" Vasilache, let's have some more glasses and plenty of ice! " shouted Titel Negruzzi.

Dodel Dodesco was looking round the room. " She's not bad, that girl over there. Does anyone know her? "

They all turned to stare at her. She was a fair-haired girl with blue eyes, clad in a cheap coat and talking and laughing with two young men with over-long hair.

" She's a sweetie," said Titel Negruzzi, screwing in his monocle to study her better. " What happened to Ghighi? Has he fallen down the loo? "

" I'd like to have her," said Dodel Dodesco.

" Dodel, you revolt me," said Titel. " The minute you set eyes on anything in skirts you start dribbling. ' I want to have her!' Calm down, can't you? Don't be so bloody randy."

Dodel took no notice but continued to stare fixedly at the girl. Titel examined her again.

" She makes one think of a Madonna by a Rhenish master. She's certainly a dish, but she'll be terrible by the time she's forty."

" I'm not interested in her at the age of forty. I'm interested in her now, at the age of eighteen."

Ghighi reappeared and said, grinning, " So you've started in on my bottle! " He looked completely transformed, rejuvenated, his eyes shining. He called for another bottle and said: " I'll play you something. You shall see, Serbanica, what a great artist is perishing in me—*qualis artifex pereo!* "

He sat down at the piano and began to vamp a rumba. Dodel asked the blonde girl to dance. Titel stayed drinking with Serban Romano.

" Your health, Herr Doktor! And how are things going? "

" Quite well. This is a dismal joint."

" It's dismal everywhere. But after one has lived through a war nothing's dismal. Anyway, what are you grousing about? We're in the middle of a boom, everyone's got plenty of money and everyone's having fun. What more do you want? "

" Do you call this having fun? "

" Can you think of a better way? I can't. If you hear of one, I hope you'll tell me. Have some of this tipple. No? Well I think I'll try it. It may turn out to be good for me."

Dodel Dodesco stayed for some time with the girl, the two

long-haired young men having departed after a brief conversation with Vasilache. But presently, while the others were discussing the merits of the various drinks that were brought to them, he came back to their table and sat down, looking gloomy.

" Back so soon? " said Titel Negruzzi. " But I suppose you've got it all fixed. The boy's a flyer! "

" Go to hell," grunted Dodesco.

They were still there at eleven, with the barman bringing them salted nuts, salami, and further supplies of liquor. Serban Romano said with a sigh:

" Ghighi, I'm worried about you."

" Shut up," said Ghighi.

" I'm not just being morbid, but it upsets me to see all your talents and energies going to waste. You really ought to do something."

" Shut up, I tell you. It's too late, Serbanica. For God's sake go jump in a lake and leave me alone."

Serban was not put out by this. He was filled with benevolence, ready to help anyone. His eye fell on the blonde. She was alone now, sitting with her hands clasped on the table, staring into space and smiling and nodding her head. Serban went over and sat down beside her.

" What are you doing here? " he asked.

She did not answer but continued to smile gently with her head on one side.

" You aren't doing too well, by the look of it," said Serban. " Don't you want to go home? "

She nodded.

" Well, come on, I'll take you, " said Serban, putting his hand on her arm.

" Monsieur Serbanica," murmured Vasilache, amiable but concerned, " there's something you should know."

" What is it? "

" Let me have a word in your ear."

They moved away from the girl.

" She's sick, Monsieur Serbanica. You'll catch it if you aren't careful."

" All right, so she's sick. So what? I don't want to touch her. Why the hell doesn't she get herself treated? "

" She's sick and everyone knows it, so she can't earn anything and can't afford treatment. They're even trying to turn her out of the hotel where she lives. She's a bit . . ." Vasilache tapped his temple. The girl did indeed look a bit mad.

"Well, thanks for telling me. Come along, my dear. So-long, chaps—I'll be back soon."

"Hey, wait!" cried Dodel Dodesco. "Hasn't Vasilache told you?"

"Yes, he has."

"But are you crazy?"

Serban went out with the girl and then paused for a moment. A scurry of snow was falling. The pavements were deserted and cars were moving slowly, their drivers able to see scarcely a yard ahead. Serban hailed a taxi. The girl got in and pressed herself against him. They drove on a circuitous route which took them past the royal palace, and pulled up in a side street at a glass porch with the single word "HOTEL" on a luminous sign above it. Snow beat about their ears as they got out. The houses in the street were shabby and disreputable in aspect. It was astonishing to find a slum like this in the very heart of the town.

The night-porter, a small, threadbare, elderly man, looked at the girl and said:

"So you're back, are you? Well, you can clear out. You've no business to bring men here. Clear out, do you hear me? It's not allowed, monsieur. You can't go up with her."

"Why not," asked Serban, "if I'm ready to pay for the room?"

"I tell you, it's not allowed."

"I'm asking you why not."

"Because it isn't, that's all. It's none of your business."

Serban held out a note. The little man promptly changed his tone and said confidentially:

"She's behind with her rent."

"How much?"

The porter consulted a book and told him the amount.

"Here you are," said Serban, laying the money on the counter. "How much is a week in advance?"

He paid two weeks in advance and in addition gave the girl some money.

"This is to pay the doctor. You've got to get yourself treated. If you need anything else tell Vasilache. He'll let me know."

The girl smiled coyly, putting her head on one side. "Aren't you coming up? " she asked, and Serban shivered. Was she really mad?

" No, my dear, I'm not coming up. Some other time."

He went out to the taxi, which he had kept waiting.

" I thought you wouldn't be coming," said the driver as he opened the door.

Although he had been more or less drunk when he left the bar, Serban was quite sober when he re-entered it, melancholy and depressed. He found his friends more exuberant than ever.

" Why, it's Serbanica returned to the fold! Come to my arms, my wandering boy! " shouted Titel Negruzzi in the high height of intoxication, and Dodel Dodesco spluttered with laughter and added obscene variations which caused Ghighi Duca to slap him on the back of the head—" You're perfectly foul."

Dodel was annoyed. " If you want to fight do it with that bloody Englishman who jumps on you! "

" Don't you d-dare say a word against him! " shouted Ghighi, stammering slightly. " In the first place he's my friend. In the second place he's a good chap—a fool and a savage if you like, but not the kind of filth you are. You follow me, I hope ? If you don't like it you'd better clear off before I knock your teeth down your throat. That's all. And what did you get up to, Serbanica? "

" Nothing. I was bored. Isn't there anything left to drink? "

" Forgive me, gentlemen "—said Vasilache in his smooth, unctuous voice—" your Highness—I'm afraid I shall have to— you see . . ."

" I get it," said Ghighi Duca. " We're being thrown out, chums. Nothing more to be done with this poor devil. Madame Vasilache's waiting for him behind the door with a broom-handle. We'll go to Scheherazade."

3

A squall of wind came whirling down the Rue Cimpineano as though it were a funnel and the hard-frozen snowflakes whipped into their faces.

" The wind's gone mad," said Titel. " Listen how it's wailing. It ought to be locked up. What are the police thinking of? They let it run loose in the streets like a dog howling at the moon. There's no law and order in this country. Ghighi, where's your car? "

" Watch it," said Dodel Dodesco. " There's Ghighi, behaving like a true gent—nipping into his car without a word. If we don't look out he'll leave us here to freeze."

They piled into the car, slammed the doors and sat shivering. Dodel shouted: " What are we waiting for? "

" She won't start," said Ghighi. " Frozen stiff, and no wonder. She was built in a country where the temperature never falls below zero."

" Try giving her a little brandy."

" You try getting out and pushing. Go on, all of you—get out and shove—there's a bit of a slope."

" Anything to oblige," said Titel Negruzzi, still in high spirits.

They got out. Serban and Dodel Dodesco used their weight, but Titel only made a pretence of pushing. After travelling a few yards the car started abruptly. Titel staggered, Serban fell on his hands and knees and Dodel sprawled full-length, hitting his nose hard on the kerb. He got up rubbing it, while the others ran after the car.

" Hey, Ghighi, wait for us! "

The Rolls slowed and waited. They got in again and Titel and Serban uproariously described what had happened. Dodel, seated in front beside Ghighi, said nothing.

" What's wrong with you? " asked Ghighi, glancing at him.

Then he exclaimed: " By God, look at his nose! Have you seen Dodel's nose? "

The others craned forward to examine Dodel's profile as he turned towards Ghighi. His long nose, which thickened slightly at the end, was now even larger than usual. It was beginning to swell remarkably, and in a fashion that quite transformed Dodel, who was no beauty at the best of times. The others were convulsed with mirth.

" What's so bloody funny? " Dodel asked, not much put out. " Do you think you're all pin-up boys? "

They slowed at a large building with a neon sign outside and turned in under a vault of grey concrete.

" A filthy entrance," said Ghighi. " You'd think you were in Sing-Sing. Have you noticed the hideous buildings they're putting up in Bucarest these days? A squalid town, Monsieur Serbanica."

" Have you any idea what London was like in the days of Shakespeare and Bacon? " Serban asked acidly.

" Shakespeare? And who might he be, Monsieur Serbanica? " said Ghighi, and pushed through the door leading to the bar.

They went down into a large basement, and up a flight of stairs to the circle of loges on a higher level which flanked the room. The dance-floor of unpolished glass was lighted from below. The loges were in semi-darkness, the walls brightly painted. The pillars supporting the gallery were of imitation mahogany, as was the bar-counter at the end of the room, behind which was a glittering array of bottles, all shapes and sizes. The air was thick with tobacco-smoke. The women were clad in lamé dresses, the men in dinner-jackets, the musicians in red tail-coats. They took possession of a loge and shouted for champagne.

" The filthy row that band's making," said Ghighi Duca, as though his nerves were suddenly on edge.

" What's the matter with you, toothache or something? " asked Titel. Ghighi did not answer and he did not pursue the matter, being carried away by another burst of laughter at the sight of Dodel's enormously swollen nose. " It's like a sausage, my poor old Dodel! A blood-sausage, I give you my word! "

Dodel was not to be ruffled. He was studying the women on the dance-floor.

Ghighi seemed plunged in gloom. He put a hand abruptly on Serban's arm. "You mustn't think I don't take anything seriously. I'm really damned serious. You don't believe me? Well, you're a fool. I'm much more serious than you think. Sometimes, when I've had a good night's sleep and my nerves are relaxed, I catch a glimpse of things you'd never dream of. I understand the way the world works, the laws of nature and society, even the human soul. I ought to write it all down, think about it, reason it out. But it's such bloody hard work. Drinking's so much pleasanter and easier. . . . So you see, old boy, it's no use, there's absolutely nothing to be done. . . ." He sat staring abstractedly at the tablecloth.

"Here's the champagne!" cried Titel happily. "Your health, my children, *et vive la vie!* Dodel, what is it now?"

"Pepita Pinelli's going to dance," said Dodel, intently surveying the dance-floor, which was beginning to clear.

The lights went out, leaving a single spotlight directed at the red plush curtain whence Pepita Pinelli suddenly appeared. She was an oval-faced, tight-skinned brunette with large dark eyes spaced widely apart, black hair with a blue tinge and, in general, the look of a malevolent reptile. She wore a black sheath dress with flowing skirts, on which sequins glittered like the snake-skin of the sorceress in a fairy-tale. This was in the days when the dancer Argentina was the rage of Paris. The orchestra played a tango and Pepita began to swirl round the floor in the circle of the spotlight.

"She's really a Roumanian, and her name isn't Pepita or Pinelli," said Titel Negruzzi.

Dodel was gazing avidly at her from behind his huge, obscene nose.

"Do you want to have her?" asked Titel with a grin.

"Yes, and I'm going to, what's more."

Serban was not listening. He was covertly observing Ghighi, who was looking suddenly old and tired, his face grey and flabby, his eyes dull. Serban poured him some more to drink, and they raised their glasses together. For a little while Ghighi seemed to revive, but then he relapsed again. There was a burst of clapping as Pepita's dancing-partner entered, clad in tight black silk trousers and a white shirt, with a red sash round his waist. He, too, was dark-skinned and slender, with a little moustache like that of Douglas Fairbanks in *The Son of Zorro*. The pair performed a dance which the audience fondly supposed to be Spanish. There was more applause and then the lights went up.

"I'm going to ask her," said Dodel laconically, and went off down the stairs. Titel sat watching him, with his elbows on the balustrade.

"Is he really so virile?" asked Serban. "He seems incapable of thinking about anything except women—more like a stallion than a man." He laughed in his placid fashion.

"He's a degenerate," said Titel. "You've only got to look at him. They've all got huge noses and no chin in that family. Complete idiots into the bargain."

"As a description of degeneracy that's a masterpiece," said Serban, chuckling.

Ghighi got up abruptly, looking very pale, and went out. Titel glanced swiftly round at him and then turned back to Serban.

"Have some more champagne, Serbanica. To your health, dear boy, and may all your dreams come true."

After ten minutes Ghighi reappeared, again looking rejuvenated, his eyes bright. Titel by this time was very drunk.

"Feeling all right now, Ghighi? That's fine. Come and sit here, I want to talk to you. We see each other practically every day but nowadays we never talk about anything serious. . . . You, Serbanica"—he tapped him on the arm—"do you know what the 'Leopard Chamber' was? But of course you don't. You don't know what friends Ghighi and I used to be in those days, and how much I admired him. He's always been a hero to me, ever since we were kids. I've never stopped liking him, even when we quarrelled over a bitch of a woman who—I say, I'm sorry, Serbanica. She's a relation of yours."

"Who do you mean?" asked Serban.

"No one. He's talking tripe," said Ghighi. "We've never quarrelled."

"What's become of her? Is she still alive?" asked Titel.

"I hope she's dead, the slut."

Titel then lost track of the conversation. He had turned to watch the dancers.

"By God, he's dancing with Pepita, him and his nose! Ghighi, tell Serbanica about what Dodel did in England."

Ghighi burst out laughing, looking youthful and radiating charm—so, at least, did Serban see him at that moment.

"Dodel and I were in England together last year," he said. "Some people invited me to spend a week at their country place for the hunting. I left Dodel at our hotel and I begged him to try and behave, so as not to cover us with shame. He swore that he would. Well, when I got back I found our suite half empty—all the armchairs and settees were gone. I asked Dodel what had happened, and he looked blank and said, ' I don't know. They just came and took them away.' Then the hotel sent up its bill —so much for the room and meals, and so much for repairs to the furniture. I don't remember how much it came to, but it was a hell of a lot. It seems that while I'd been away Dodel had amused himself by practising standing jumps from one armchair to another. He's quite mad."

"Not mad, just half-witted," said Titel. "Here he comes now."

Dodel came bounding up the steps.

"Ghighi," he said breathlessly, "let me have the key to your car."

"What for?"

"I've dated her up. She's leaving by herself and we're meeting at a hotel. Let's have the key."

"You'll have to get a cab, and good luck to you," said Ghighi with a chuckle.

"Don't be a swine. Give me the key."

"Not bloody likely. You'd better hurry if you don't want to keep her waiting."

Dodel glanced at him over that bruised and swollen nose, its purple tinge like the gizzard of a newly killed fowl, and hurried off muttering.

The others laughed and forgot about him. Not until some time later did Titel notice that something odd was taking place.

"What on earth was that fool talking about? The lady's still here. Do you see? She's dancing with Carlo."

"So she is!" exclaimed Serban.

It was now very late. Most of the loges were empty, and there were only two or three couples on the floor.

Ghighi Duca said nothing. He had had another relapse, and

sat there dull-eyed and hollow-faced, looking to Serban like a debauched elderly man. Titel was still wondering about Dodel when the hero reappeared, trembling with cold and fury, and returned to his place at the table.

" Don't say she's stood you up," said Titel cheerfully. " Well, what a wicked shame! Her courage failed her, I suppose. You're a pretty ghastly sight, my poor Dodel."

Dodel filled a glass, emptied it and refilled it again. He was white with rage.

" I'll kill her! " he exploded. " The damned, blasted trollop! I'll beat her up! I'll rip her clothes to shreds! "

Pepita and Carlo were still circling the floor, and as they passed below them he flung his glass at the girl, soaking her neck and shoulders. She uttered a cry, looked up and took to her heels. At the same moment Ghighi, who seemed unconscious of what was going on, rose and left the loge.

" Two blasted hours I sat waiting in the hall of that bloody hotel. The bitch was just stringing me along. I'll teach her to get funny with me! "

" Better take it easy," said Titel. " It looks as though Carlo wants to have a word with you."

Dodel sprang up and leaned over the balustrade. Carlo, shouting furiously, was struggling with several waiters who were trying to restrain him from coming up on to the balcony. He fought his way through and started up the stairs. Dodel cried frantically:

" Stop him! Don't let him get at me! He's stronger than I am."

He was terrified, and Titel Nebruzzi was almost helpless with laughter.

" Why should we bother? He hasn't done us any harm, nor has she. You do your own scrapping."

" No, please—for God's sake!—he's coming! Where's Ghighi? Why isn't he here? "

Serban was feeling acutely uncomfortable at the thought of getting involved in a public brawl. And what would Titel do? He was capable of anything, of fighting or of bolting. Dodel seemed now on the verge of tears.

Fortunately the waiters caught Carlo just in time and dragged him out of sight. The lights began to go down.

" You see what it is to be a wealthy and esteemed customer? "
said Titel. " The manager knows you're a boyar. You can spit
in all their faces and they won't say a word. It's okay as long as
you can pay. Cheer up, Dodel! You'll find another woman,
you're so attractive. Come on, both of you."

" But what's happened to Ghighi? " asked Serban.

" I don't know, he was here just now. He went to the gents,
I suppose. I hope he hasn't left without paying. I haven't got a
bean."

They went down to the cloakroom and retrieved their overcoats, telling the waiter that Prince Duca would pay.

" You don't happen to know where he is? " asked Titel. " You
haven't seen him? "

" No, I haven't seen him," said the waiter, in the tone of irritated disquiet that is used towards customers who want to go
without paying. The other waiters were leaving.

" I hope he's all right," Titel said.

He led the way to the men's outside lavatory with Serban
following behind him.

Ghighi was there, stretched full-length on the black and yellow
tiles, spattered with melted snow, mud and urine. Water was
flowing uninterruptedly in the urinal, which smelt of ammonia
and disinfectant, filth and cigarette ends.

Ghighi lay like the dead, his face white and shrunken, the whites
of his eyes showing beneath the half-closed lids. His pockets
had been turned out, his waistcoat was unbuttoned and his
trousers pulled up to his knees.

" He isn't dead," said Titel, " but he'll kill himself if he goes
on doping like this."

" Dope? Is that it? What does he take? " asked Serban,
horrified.

" Cocaine, the bloody fool. It'll do for him one of these days.
Whisky and champagne and three or four shots of coke all in
one evening—how can he possibly stand it? And now someone's
robbed him. He had a gold cigarette-case, the poor sap. How
are we going to pay? "

" I've got some money on me," said Serban.

" Well, that's lucky. Let's have it, and I'll settle up while you
ring for a doctor."

They took Ghighi home and left him in the doctor's hands, and then they parted.

Serban never saw Ghighi Duca again. Whenever he thought of him he recalled the picture of that lean body stretched on the damp, stinking tiles. Nor did he again enter the Express Bar and he went only once to the hotel where he had taken the blonde.

" She went away to the country," said the porter, without looking at him.

" Where ? "

" I don't know, sir."

Serban offered him a tip, but he really didn't know. The girl had simply packed her shabby belongings and gone away.

A year or so later Serban ran into Dimitri Coziano, his cousin and Ghighi's, on the train between Vienna and Salzburg.

" Why, Dim! Where are you going ? "

" To Geneva, the League of Nations. I'm on the Roumanian delegation."

" Congratulations—you're turning into a statesman ! "

" Come off it, Serbanica. I'm just a very minor official."

" But I know what you're like. You'll be head of the delegation one of these days."

" Time will show. What do you think of Titulesco ? " asked Dim, smiling. " But never mind. Have you heard the news ? "

" What news ? "

" Ghighi Duca has just died. He was found dead in his car outside his house."

There was a moment of silence. The train was travelling through a countryside of fruit-trees in blossom, under a clear blue sky dotted with small clouds.

" He had great possibilities," said Dim Coziano, " but he never did any good at anything. A lion in an ass's skin. . . . Well, now he's dead, and that's the end of it."

VI

Royal Flush

I

In the course of an evening party at the home of Monsieur and Madame Scarlat, during the summer of 1931, four of the guests left earlier than the rest. Monsieur Scarlat was clad in conventional evening dress, but there was something about him—his handsome, somewhat flabby face, his velvet-dark eyes, his black moustache—which made it seem as though he had only just exchanged his caftan of damask silk, his cashmir sash and his slippers for European attire. His wife, twenty years younger than he, looked exhausted by the effort she had been called upon to make at the party, which was one of the first she had given since her marriage. They accompanied the departing guests on to the steps of the house, and here paused to exchange a few last words, a group of men in tail-coats and women in long evening gowns, standing in a cluster outside the big open doorway under the light shed by two lanterns in wrought-iron frames.

"Alexandra always gets migraine just when I'm enjoying myself," said Cesar Lascari, in jesting apology.

"If you go too, Elvira, the whole evening will fall flat," said Monsieur Scarlat. "Can't I persuade you to stay?"

"My dear, I told you, I promised Lili Mavromihali I'd call on her this evening. I couldn't resist coming here first, but I mustn't fail her altogether." Elvira Vorvoreano drew her cloak about her bare shoulders, kissed Madame Scarlat, patted her cheek, and offered her hand for the master of the house to kiss. "Good night, Scarlat."

"Have you got your car here?" asked Cesar Lascari. "If not I'll drive you home."

"Manolica's taking me. Hadn't you noticed him? Are you so distracted by Alexandra's migraine?" said Elvira in a voice that was more acid than jesting.

Cesar Lascari laughed amiably, while Alexandra, his wife,

closed her eyes, scarcely able to stay on her feet. She kissed
Madame Scarlat and then Elvira, who murmured something with
her lips to her ear which caused her to smile wanly.

" Try it. You'll find it works wonders," whispered Elvira.

" I couldn't," said Alexandra with the same forced smile.

" Don't be a goose. Try it and you'll see."

Meanwhile Cesar Lascari and Manolica Giurgea-Roscano were
taking leave of one another. Cesar, invariably good-humoured,
with a light, easy laugh, had a well-fed look. A bank-director and
wealthy at the age of thirty-one, he had recently married for love
his cousin Alexandra Sufano, who brought as her dowry a substantial part of her millionaire father's oil-shares. As for Giurgea-
Roscano, he was dry, thin, stiff and wore a monocle. He had a
manner of speaking peculiar to himself, self-pleased and assertive,
with nasal intonations and distorted vowels. So much did he
resemble a tailor's dummy that it was surprising to discover that
he knew how to smile.

" Which doesn't mean that I've become quite unapproachable,"
Cesar Lascari was saying to him. " My time's pretty taken up with
Sandra, of course, but whenever I've five minutes to spare——"

He broke off with a laugh. Giurgea-Roscano, repressed as
ever, said without any change of expression:

" I think you should try to spare a little time for my wife.
I personally cannot——" He gazed at Cesar with eyes that were
disconcerting in their sheer lack of expression. Cesar coughed and
smiled politely. Giurgea-Romano persisted: " No, I beg you to
believe me. It's so long since . . . Yes, Elvira, take my arm. . . .
She's a wonderful woman, I wouldn't want to you to think otherwise; but you see it's been so long. . . ."

He made a gesture with his hand, as though to signify that all
was over, and then went down the steps with Elvira on his arm.
The door of his car slammed and it left the courtyard. Cesar's
car followed.

Alexandra Lascari leaned her head against her husband's
shoulder. " Do you think Elvira's having an affair with Manolica? " said Cesar. " It looks like it to me."

Alexandra did not reply.

" What a spitfire that woman is! Did you see how furious she
was when I pretended not to notice Manolica trailing at her heels?
A real vixen! "

With her nose buried in her husband's shoulder Alexandra murmured in a muffled voice:

" She's furious at getting old."

" What, darling? I didn't catch."

" Don't shout, I've got a dreadful headache. I said, Elvira's furious because she knows she's getting old."

" Oh, I see. How old is she, exactly? Let's see—she's ten years older than me, which makes her forty or forty-one. Good lord! " exclaimed Cesar in astonishment. " She doesn't look it."

" Men never notice anything," murmured Alexandra. " It's obvious enough."

Cesar was silent while he thought this over. Talking with some difficulty Alexandra asked:

" What was Giurgea-Roscano saying to you? "

Instantly on his guard, Cesar replied with careful casualness:

" Oh, nothing important."

" He said somebody was wonderful."

" His wife. He's in love with his wife, you see—like I am with mine," said Lascari fondly, kissing her hair. . . .

Elvira meanwhile was sitting silent in the back of Giurgea-Roscano's car while from time to time he glanced covertly at her. Elvira's profile was of a classic purity. Her face with its delicate, slightly curved nose, full lips and green eyes was at present framed in a pearly white head-scarf which she had bought in Venice, and the light sheen of the material enhanced the brown tint in her skin and the redness of her mouth. Giurgea-Roscano badly wanted to know what she was thinking, so that he might find something to say and perhaps make tactful advances, but he had no notion what was going on behind that narrow, stubborn forehead. As they drove along the Calea Victoriei she kept her head turned to the window, gazing with an air of cold dislike at the couples coming out of the theatres. He concluded that she was simply in a bad mood, no more. But the truth was that Elvira detested everyone she saw. She hated the town, the country, the whole world, and particularly at this hour, when the streets were filled with carefree people, women in summer dresses, men in shantung suits and panamas. New cars swished past, the café terraces were crowded, rubber-tyred fiacres rolled silently over the tarmac. The night was scented and serene, and there was gaiety in a thousand houses in the centre of the town. The Legations were holding receptions. Evening garden parties were very much in fashion that year.

It all meant nothing to Elvira. " My money, my name, my social position . . ." Here in Bucarest her fortune looked quite respectable, but in the larger world of London, for example, it would be no more than a modest competence, and in Paris it would be ignored. As for her name, who was there, outside the frontiers of Roumania, who had ever heard of Lascar Lascari? In any case, he was only her grandfather. Her father had been a retired army officer, and her husband, whom she had divorced, was negligible. The same applied to all her friends and relations, a miscellaneous string of nobodies. And even if they had been people of importance—important in this absurd little country!— what had they to offer her? At the best protective friendship, patronising kindness, a diamond in exchange for a brief love-affair. This was all she had to show for the forty years of her life; for this she had so many times stripped the clothes from her body, often with indifference, sometimes with acute distaste. She had wasted her time. She had wasted her life. In a little while she would be an ageing woman of no interest to anyone; very soon, next year perhaps; and finally a rotting corpse. It was only a few years since her mother, Helène Vorvoreano, had died; and Elvira thought of her as she had lain amid the chrysanthemums surrounding her coffin, waxen-faced and with closed eyes, looking younger than in life but her expression profoundly sad; and now transformed into shreds of decomposing flesh, bones crumbling to dust. Presently it would be her turn. Her body that was still beautiful, her face that could still look young, these too would wither and decay. And in the meantime there was nothing but endless mediocrity.

Tight-lipped she sat contemplating the throng in the Calea Victoriei, well-dressed people with their stomachs well lined, on their way from the theatre to the restaurant or the cabaret, to the conjugal bed or the brothel—all unconscious of her existence, living their lives without a thought for her increasing age, her shrivelling, her death.

An open car went slowly by, driven by a bare-headed man with reddish fair hair and an English-style moustache. Thick lips, the receding chin of a degenerate, slightly protruding eyes, an authoritative, insolent expression, at once brutal and sensual—it was not hard to recognise his gracious Majesty, King Carol of Roumania. A man of about thirty-five sat beside him, dark-haired and with the same kind of moustache, since this was the fashion. The King was studying the crowd on the pavements, that is to say, the women, whom he examined with a cool and greedy effrontery. He noticed Elvira, her big green eyes shining in the dark face thrown into relief by the white scarf, her fur cape and necklace of brilliants. The man at his side also looked at her, and then the cars separated.

" His Majesty in search of prey," murmured Giurgea-Roscano.

" What? " she asked, although she understood perfectly. " What do you mean? "

" He's on the look-out for a tart. He spots them on the pavement and invites them into his car."

" He's not interested in—better-class women? "

" It's not easy for them to get near him. The *camerilla*'s always on guard. Ionel Protopopiu, the man you saw sitting beside him, sticks to him like a leech. He's the one who holds the keys—nobody can get to the King except through him. Through him or through the Queen."

The Queen, it went without saying, was not the King's wife, who lived separated from him with her family in Athens, but his mother, Queen Marie.

" What were you saying just now? " asked Elvira, to change the subject.

" I wasn't saying anything. I was wondering what was in your mind."

Elvira scarcely heard. She was thinking, " The King is separated from his wife. He has had mistresses and has one now, but not one of them has been able to hold him. The woman who could do so would be the real Queen of Roumania. . . ." Her hand descended in a sudden, unconsidered gesture on Giurgea-Roscano's leg, just above the knee, and she thrust her fingernails into it through the thin stuff of his trouser. Giurgea-Roscano started in astonishment and let fall his monocle. But instead of exclaiming or seeking to release her grasp he concluded that the long-sought moment had come, and with a hand on her thigh and his other arm about her shoulders he sought to embrace her. Elvira promptly slapped his face, causing him to stare in openmouthed amazement.

" May I ask what you think you're doing? " she inquired coldly.

Flushed and indignant, Giurgea-Roscano spluttered:

" Are you out of your mind? You made the first move, and then——"

" I made the first move? When? "

He told her and she burst out laughing. With parted lips she was irresistible.

" I'm sorry. I didn't mean to." Her laughter ceased abruptly. " Do you know Ionel Protopopiu? "

" Yes—why? Do you want to slap his face too? "

" I just wondered," murmured Elvira. She then looked him straight in the eyes and asked in a formal voice: " Would you care to have tea with me tomorrow? "

In Giurgea-Roscano's experience such a look could only mean one thing, but he was afraid to jump to hasty conclusions. He replied no less formally:

" I shall be delighted. You know how much I enjoy seeing you."

She smiled at him, slowly lowering her long lashes. Then she turned her head away and went on staring at the street. The smile faded, giving place to a look of tense determination which so hardened her face that she looked ten years older. But Giurgea-Roscano, seeing nothing but her profile, was now in a state of hopeful excitement that he scarcely knew how to contain. . . .

On an afternoon a fortnight later Giurgea-Roscano sat up in Elvira's bed, propped himself against the pillow with the bed-clothes round his chest, and lit a cigarette. The frilled embroid-ered pillow-case made him look more dried-up than ever, and the light of the bedside lamp threw his wrinkles into relief. A limp lock of hair hung cross his forehead. Over the other pillow flowed the dark tresses of Elvira, who had just repaired her make-up and now lay smiling, with one smooth arm beneath her head. She was casually questioning him about the King.

" He dropped Zizi Lambrino while he was in Paris, you know that as well as I do. Now he picks up tarts in the Calea Victoriei or has singers and actresses brought to the Palace. I used to think he was one of those types who stick to the same woman for life, but I've got to admit that he's matured. He's not such a fool after all."

Giurgea-Roscano blew a cloud of smoke into the room to mingle with the scent of Soir de Montmartre, patchouli, sandalwood and, embracing all others, the scent of Elvira herself, a smell of brunette, tangy and untamed.

" It seems that his latest mistress is a woman called Lupesco, the wife of an army officer nobody has ever heard of."

Elvira gazed thoughtfully out of the window. She did not shrug her shoulders as Giurgea-Roscano had done, but she told herself that this Madame Lupesco could be no serious obstacle where she was concerned. A shopkeeper's daughter perhaps, or the daughter of some minor official; a commonplace Bucarest woman who had never set foot in Paris and knew nothing of high society in London or Madrid—the sort that Helene Mavromihali or Betsy Ipsilanti, or even Marthe Bibesco, would never receive in their drawing-rooms, although God knew they collected some queer customers, artists and suchlike. Yes, at all costs she must conquer the King—and she was sure that it could be done.

It *must* be done! . . . A time must come when that flower of the nobility, Prince Dimitri Stirvey, who at present did not even know of her existence, would be honoured to do her service; when Messieurs Maniu, Nicolae Iorga, Bratiano and the rest of their tribe would bow with deference over her hand while she glanced indifferently at their bald heads; when really rich and exclusive circles in London and Paris, to whom even the King's fortune was trifling, would accept her as one of themselves as she entered on his Majesty's arm. She *must* suceed! Otherwise there was nothing for her but an obscure ageing into boredom and despair, the bridge-party, the latest novel, the endless country summers, squalid adventures with chauffeurs and valets, the loneliness of luxury hotels. . . . She shivered and pulled the bedclothes round her neck.

" Are you cold? " asked Giurgea-Roscano.

She did not answer.

" It isn't cold. In fact, it's rather warm."

Elvira still was silent. She was considering the best means of approach to the King. He was well protected, surrounded by a small circle of people jealous of their privileges. It would be difficult enough even to get to Ionel Protopopiu, his secretary and general factotum. This was something that would have to be accomplished by stages, of which Giurgea-Roscano was merely the first. . . .

Having disposed of his cigarette, Giurgea-Roscano turned to her and took her in his arms. Dismissing her train of thought Elvira responded promptly and with passion. Passion was one of the first requisites of success. It was necessary that at each stage a man should think, " What a woman! ", until finally the King himself thought, " What a woman! " Unreal though the passion might be, it must be simulated with such energy and ardour that every fool of a man would be deceived. And in the event Giurgea-Roscano, breathless and overwhelmed, did say to himself, " What a woman! My God, what a woman."

2

A week later Elvira paid a visit to her cousin, Alexandra Lascari. Cesar and Alexandra were living in the family mansion in the Rue Culmea Veche during the absence of old Serban Lascari, who was abroad. Elvira and Alexandra sat drinking tea with a number of other callers. The curtains were half drawn; a golden light fell slantwise across the carpet, retrieving part of a faded gilt armchair and a round-fronted cabinet from the surrounding shadow.

" Papa Serbanica simply won't let me have this house done up," said Alexandra. " It smells of damp and it's so old-fashioned that one can hardly breathe. When I invite people in I'm half inclined to offer them camomile tea, just to be in keeping. But he won't hear of any change. He's stuffy beyond words. He insists on keeping the portraits of his ancestors on the walls, with their beards and their caftans, and he won't be parted from his horribly uncomfortable furniture."

" Well, after all, it's his house," said Madame Mavromihali, who was a friend of Serban Lascari. She was a plump person with a shaved neck, short hair and rounded shoulders, who sat dangling a small sunshade on her knee and rattling her bracelet. " I must say I think these old houses have a charm of their own, and they're wonderful for parties. I mean you really can't give parties in a five-room flat on the fourth floor. But you take Bubi Ipsilanti's house, with ten or fifteen reception-rooms—that's what I call a real house! "

" Twenty," corrected Madame Ipsilanti, who was seated beside her, with a faint smile.

" Twenty houses? "

" Twenty reception-rooms. You said fifteen. But there are twenty."

There was a touch of condescension in her voice which irritated Madame Mavromihali, who said acidly:

" My dear, of course—twenty reception-rooms, furnished with twenty suites of imitation French furniture, all Louis Seize or Empire. Your father-in-law might at least have settled for Louis Quinze, seeing that he only bought imitations."

Madame Ipsilanti continued to smile with the same serene indifference. " If the house is furnished in different styles, my dear, it's only because the effect would be really rather monotonous if it were Louis Quinze from top to bottom."

" But then, you never give parties," said Madame Mavromihali. " Bubi spends so much of his life playing cards."

Alexandra Lascari was growing slightly apprehensive. Prince Bubi Ipsilanti had become a sort of uncrowned king of the gambling dens of Bucarest, to his wife's extreme annoyance, and the matter was best not referred to. She accordingly changed the subject.

" They don't give parties at the Palace either. The Queen receives at the home of Madame Theodoru-Costaki, and the King doesn't receive at all."

" Yes, he does, but only personal friends," said Monsieur Scarlat, who was seated on a couch upholstered with Aubusson tapestry. By his very manner of sitting he contrived to give this article of furniture, designed in a period of strict etiquette, rigid manners and formal costume, the look of a Turkish divan. The company smiled.

" What's more, he's extremely mean," said Colonel Misu

Vorvoreano, Elvira's brother. " Have you heard the story of him and Lenutza Cascarache? "

Lenutza Cascarache was a cabaret singer. The company had not heard the story, so the colonel related how the King, having sent for the lady, gave her a hundred lei when he dismissed her. He mimicked Lenutza's hoarse voice and gipsy accent: " ' You call that a king? When you plough a girl the way he did me the least you can do is pay her. A hundred lei! I spit on it, and on his little king's moustache! ' "

The ladies laughed. Elvira, who had taken little interest in the story, became suddenly intent.

" And Madame Lupesco, is she still with him? " she asked casually.

" I've seen the Lupesco," said Madame Ipsilanti. " I was with Bubi in a bar she goes to. Bubi does go out with me sometimes"—and here she glanced at Madame Mavromihali—"he doesn't spend all his nights gambling. It seems that the Lupesco often goes to this place, the Monte Cristo, but always with a bodyguard."

" Does her body really need so much guarding? "

" Well, it's the King's property," said Madame Ipsilanti.

" Yes, but is she really beautiful? " asked Madame Mavromihali.

" She's not bad. *Bien en chair, vous savez*—a good, well-shaped red-head. Her legs are a bit . . ." Here Madame Ipsilanti paused, remembering in time that Alexandra's legs were a little on the thick side. ". . . Well, they could be better. But apart from that she's quite good-looking, not bad at all."

" But what else has she got? " asked Elvira, disdainfully. " Nothing but a body? "

" Do you really think the King cares about anything else? You evidently don't know him! "

" He's supposed to be an intelligent and highly cultivated man," said Elvira.

She regretted the words the moment she had uttered them, for Helene Mavromihali gave her a quick, scrutinising glance before she could turn away her head. " No matter," Elvira thought. " She can't hurt me. Anyway, she's too stupid to guess." She went on to talk about other things.

3

The next evening Elvira walked down the stairs leading to the basement of the Monte Cristo, while a commissionaire in braided uniform closed the door behind her. Lamps of modernistic design on chromium holders flung splashes of amber light on the walls. The dance-band was something to be felt rather than heard. Elvira, escorted by Giurgea-Roscano, had a remote smile on her lips, alluring and mysterious. From the age of eighteen she had experimented with different kinds of smile, studying their effect; and for circumstances such as these she had devised one, directed at no particular person but addressed to the world at large, which was particularly effective in causing the beholder to look twice at this striking, dark-haired woman with green eyes. She wore a deep red, almost purple evening gown, the sleeves slit from shoulder to wrist, with a diamond parure in her hair and on her finger a ruby that was almost black. She walked down the stairs lifting her skirts in a gesture as graceful as it was needless, since in the prevailing fashion they did not reach the ground. She had not taken the arm of Giurgea-Roscano, who followed stiff and sallow-faced behind her, looking more than ever like a croupier in a casino. When they were halfway down the stairs the door to the bar abruptly opened. A gentleman in evening dress thrust it back and stood holding it to allow a party of two ladies and three gentlemen to pass. Elvira raised her long eyelashes and at once lowered them again, contriving, with an effort, to preserve that serene, mysterious smile. The first of the ladies to emerge was Madame Lupesco, white and pink, wearing a slender gold chain on her left ankle. A fair-haired young woman came after her and the gentlemen followed. The one who had opened the door was Ionel Protopopiu, vigorous, plump and groomed to the last hair. The party, laughing and talking, started up the stairs, and suddenly Madame Lupesco looked up and noticed the couple descending—the slender dark woman in a wine-red dress, and the sere, insignificant-looking man. As they drew near to one another Elvira raised her eyes and without ceasing to smile examined the other woman from head to foot. Madame Lupesco sensed something indefinable, a sort of frightening intensity, in the green eyes, and responded to it with a look of faintly perturbed astonishment. She turned to glance at the couple after they had passed, and saw that the gentlemen of her escort were nodding to the man.

" Ionel," she said.

Ionel darted forward, while the other gentlemen smiled among themselves. " What a woman! " one of them said, and then coughed, realising that Madame Lupesco must have heard, and pretended to be talking about something else. It was not merely tactless but highly imprudent to admire any other woman in the presence of Madame Lupesco.

" Ionel, who were those people? I saw you nod to them."

" I only know the man," said Ionel Protopopiu, as though in apology. " He's Giurgea-Roscano, a lawyer. He goes everywhere, quite the social figure—a complete stuffed-shirt."

" The woman's good-looking," said Madame Lupesco, and then forgot about her.

Meanwhile Giurgea-Roscano was murmuring, " Did you see her? That was Madame Lupesco."

" That woman? I didn't notice," said Elvira.

4

On an evening some weeks later Titel Negruzzi left Madame Lupesco's apartment to dine with Elvira. It happened as follows.

After leaving the Jockey Club, where he had been playing chemin de fer, Titel Negruzzi had dropped in on Madame Lupesco hoping for a game of poker to make a change. Titel was now aged about thirty. He had obtained a sinecure on the staff of one of the big credit banks. No one ever saw him in his office and very few people saw him in their homes. He passed his time in drinking-places, restaurants and clubs, whence he returned very late to his bachelor flat, generally in the early dawn, and slept the restless sleep of the whisky-drinker. He went out at lunch-time and only went back to the flat in the evening, to change into a dinner-jacket or tail-coat, according to what his programme was. Thanks to his name (he was not one of the Moldavian Negruzzis, the collaterals of Constantine Negruzzi, but came of a Wallachian family related to the Ipsilantis, the Lascaris and the Cozianos), his good looks and his invariable good humour, he was received everywhere.

Madame Lupesco was wearing an indoor gown of black velvet trimmed with ermine.

" You look like a queen," said Titel, bowing over her hand. And he added as he straightened himself: " Which is, after all, only natural."

" Be quiet, flatterer! " said Madame Lupesco, tapping him on the shoulder. " Do you know Monsieur Gherson and Monsieur Corfiotu? I know you know Ionel. . . . Monsieur Lascari— Monsieur Vasilesco-Rimnic—Monsieur Negruzzi."

Titel shook hands with Monsieur Gherson, a large industrialist, with Monsieur Corfiotu, who owned a factory in Bucarest, with Ionel Protopopiu, Cesar Lascari and Monsieur Vasilesco-Rimnic, the latter a member of the Government. Gherson, short and bald with a fringe of grey hair, had the wrinkled face of an elderly monkey. He seemed to be saying, " Don't think you can fool me. I know you're all for sale. Let's get down to discussing the price."

He and Corfiotu were at the time competing for a Government contract for field-guns. The Supreme Commander of the Army was the King. So now Monsieur Gherson and Monsieur Corfiotu were calling on Madame Lupesco. Both had sent her flowers. Both were consuming whisky and caviar sandwiches, and hoping to play poker.

Cesar Lascari was a director of the bank which would furnish credits for the import of raw materials to whichever of the rival concerns secured the contract. Monsieur Vasilesco-Rimnic was the Minister of Finance, and it was he who would sign the document authorising the expenditure. Ionel Protopopiu was the King's secretary, his confidant and man-of-all-work. As for Titel

Negruzzi, who had arrived without knowing what was going on, he understood at once that he was expected to play the part of the casual visitor whose presence would give the gathering a fortuitous, friendly and innocent appearance.

Vasilesco-Rimnic, plump, with sagging cheeks and violet pouches under his eyes, protested bluffly: " Really, you know, I don't play poker."

" You don't play games of chance? And yet you go in for politics," said Monsieur Gherson with a melancholy smile.

" Do you dare to suggest that politics is a game of chance? "

" There's no question of chance if one calculates correctly," said Monsieur Corfiotu, in a small, colourless voice.

Gherson laughed good-humouredly. " But you need to be able to calculate."

" It's really a matter of knowing how to bluff," said Titel Negruzzi, who had swiftly downed two glasses of whisky.

" What do you say to that, Corfiotu? " asked Gherson.

Corfiotu had the look of a man who has just bitten into a lemon.

" In politics the great thing is to know what cards your opponent holds," said Vasilesco-Rimnic.

" One can generally manage to find out," murmured Corfiotu.

Madame Lupesco was playing ecarté with Ionel Protopopiu. Gherson was the first to leave the others and approach their table.

" May we not be allowed to join in, madame? "

" At écarté? "

" Will you be long? Why don't we play a more sociable game? "

" Poker? " said Madame Lupesco negligently.

Ionel Protopopiu and Titel Negruzzi sat down on a sofa to chat. Leaning his head against its upholstered back Titel gazed slowly about him, his eyes half closed. Drowsiness was overcoming him; he had had too much to drink. To keep himself awake he made a methodical examination of the room. Oriental carpets, from Tebriz and Chiraz, and a big one from Hamadan, old and dull red, which put one in mind of the curled slippers of odalisques and the bare feet of enuchs; old chests of walnut and darkened oak, with carvings of foliage and plump *putti*, from Florence or Rome; a *vargueno* with twisted legs, covered with worn red velvet and Cordovan leather. " Not bad, not bad for a little Bucarest trollop," Titel reflected. " She's learnt to furnish a house like a lady. One might expect chromium fixings and lamé curtains, and a four-poster bed and a cocktail-bar, like in an American film. Where did she learn good taste? Certainly not from the King. Ah, but there's where she falls down. Ikons on the walls. Good ones, certainly, very lavish and splendid, and probably really old. But ikons! They spoil everything."

" Are you bored? " asked Ionel Protopopiu.

" Me? "

" I thought you wanted to play? "

" Me play poker with old man Gherson and Corfiotu? Do you think I'm a Rothschild? No, dear boy, I don't belong in this party. I'm just part of the setting. Anyway I shan't be staying long because I'm dining at Elvira Vorvoreano's. Do you know her? "

" No," said Ionel Protopopiu without interest. The name meant nothing to him.

" You don't? Well, of course, you were away so long in Paris. She's the daughter of Helene Vorvoreano, who was the sister of Serban Lascari, Cesar's father. She's Cesar's and Alexandra's cousin, and also the cousin of young Serban Romano and of Serban and Augusta Hagibei. I'm surprised you haven't met her. She married that half-wit Ipsilanti—you know, the one who's called Telescope. But she divorced him and for a time she was Niki Mavromihali's mistress. At present she's going round with another half-wit—Giurgea-Roscano."

" Giurgea-Roscano? " said Ionel Protopopiu, suddenly aroused. " A very dark woman with green eyes, smothered in jewels? "

" Smothered is right. She has the finest jewels in Bucarest, apart from the Queen's pearls and the Brancoveano emeralds and the Ghica emeralds. I don't know, of course, what you might find in the Gherson or the Corfiotu coffers, but with a very few exceptions the Vorvoreano jewels are the best in the country."

" And you're dining with her this evening? You must introduce me some time," said Ionel Protopopiu.

" I'd better tell you a bit more about her first. She may not be your type," said Titel, good-natured as ever.

A footman entered and murmured something to Ionel. He

got up promptly and left the room, to return a moment later and go over to Madame Lupesco.

" Princess, you're wanted on the telephone."

She looked up at him, and he nodded and smiled. Madame Lupesco laid her cards face down on the table.

" Please excuse me. I'll be back in a minute. Titel, will you play for me? "

" Of course," said Titel. He sat down in her place, picked up the hand and said: " Where have we got to? "

" I've opened with two," said Monsieur Gherson, pointing to two gold pieces on the green cloth.

Titel took six gold pieces from the heap at his side and put them on the table in front of him. Monsieur Corfiotu made it twelve. Titel raised the bet another eighteen. Two of the players stayed in but Vasilesco-Rimnic dropped out.

" Straight to the ace," said Titel.

Gherson laid a straight to the queen on the table and Corfiotu had three aces. Gherson smiled faintly as he looked at Titel's cards, of which four were spades.

" Very nearly a royal straight flush," he said.

" I've no doubt if Madame Lupesco had been sitting here it *would* have been a royal straight flush," said Titel, who was still finding it hard to keep awake.

" It's your deal, Monsieur Negruzzi," said Vasilesco-Rimnic.

When Madame Lupesco returned, a quarter of an hour later, Titel was smoking a cigar and looking decidedly pleased with himself.

" I never thought you'd turn out to be such beginners," he was saying with a chuckle. " From now on I shall only play with industrial tycoons. I see a rosy future ahead of me."

" We aren't as bad as all that," said Gherson good-humouredly. " We're simply out of luck. His Excellency has been having the luck. Look at his winnings."

" They're nothing to mine," said Titel, who had indeed amassed such a pile of notes and gold coins that he was having difficulty in finding room for them.

" So you've been doing well? " said Madame Lupesco.

Titel gazed at her in ostentatious admiration.

" How wonderfully beautiful you look! You're dazzling—like the flowers in this room! I can guess who was on the telephone

—*quelqu'un qui vous aime.* I can hear it in your voice and see it in your eyes."

He had risen as he spoke, and mechanically, with the movement of an habitual card-player, was picking up the money. Madame Lupesco said with a tight smile:

"Let's share it, Titel, like good partners."

Titel blinked and with a glance took in the scene—Gherson, like an elderly, sad-faced monkey; Corfiotu, silent and abstracted; the minister, flushed with success, contemplating his pile of notes and pieces of gold. How refined, he thought, to grease people's palms by letting them win your money at cards!

"Dear lady," he said, "they were your cards and your luck. I was merely the agent. There can be no question of my sharing your winnings."

Madame Lupesco's face relaxed. She said sweetly:

"No—fifty-fifty, like old friends."

"*Jamais de la vie,*" said Titel. "I wouldn't dream of it."

He stood firm during the minute of amiable argument which ensued, and when Madame Lupesco gracefully yielded took his leave. She rewarded him with the warmest of smiles. Had he accepted his share of the winnings, amounting to several hundred thousand lei, she would never have received him again. Gherson shook his hand with an air of paternal benevolence, as though to say, "You're a clever young devil. You'll go far. I like the sort of monkey that knows how to skip lightly from one branch to another." Corfiotu, preoccupied with his business problem, shook his hand without looking at him. Vasilesco-Rimnic, still intoxicated with his winnings, clapped him on the shoulder and said sonorously, "Young man . . ." He seemed to be about to make a speech, but checked himself abruptly and concluded, "Good night, young man!"

Cesar Lascari was getting quietly drunk in a corner. He took solemn leave of Titel, who laughed and said to Ionel Protopopiu as they left the room together:

"Anyone can see Cesar's on duty. You do at least manage to look as though you were enjoying yourself."

"That's enough of that," said Ionel, smiling. "By the way, you won't forget, will you? You'll introduce me?"

When he returned to the drawing-room Madame Lupesco asked:

" Why didn't Titel stay? Where's he off to? "

" A dinner engagement, I gather."

" Who's he dining with? "

" I've no idea," said Ionel Protopopiu.

5

Since separating from her husband Elvira had lived in an apartment in one of the new concrete blocks that were going up in Bucarest at that time. Titel Negruzzi entered the narrow entrance hall, floored with black and white tiles, and ignoring the porter, who asked whom he wished to see, pressed the button of the lift.

In the lobby of the apartment he gave his hat to the maid and looked about him with a quick glance that took in everything— the pieces of old Biedermeier furniture of honey-coloured wood, the massive hall-stand adorned with bronze and marquetry, the Venetian mirror and the topaz-coloured chandelier. On his way to the salon he passed through a sitting-room containing several armchairs upholstered in dove-grey silk and a cabinet of *bois des iles* on which stood a Sèvres lamp decorated with delicate Poitevin brushwork. Through the open double-door he could see Giurgea-Roscano, Nicolas Prodan, the journalist, and Bubi Ipsilanti . . . no women guests, apparently. The mistress of the house came smiling to greet him, her hand extended.

" You should have come to see me long before this, Monsieur Negruzzi," she said, and turned to lead the way into the salon.

Titel followed, scarcely believing his eyes. Elvira's long, bare neck—she wore her hair short, in the current fashion—rose above the collar of a suit of midnight-blue voile pyjamas which clung so tightly to her slender body as to make it apparent that she was wearing nothing else. Titel mechanically greeted his fellow-guests while his good breeding struggled against an over-mastering desire to stare. The other men were talking with a forced and feverish liveliness, not venturing to let their eyes dwell on Elvira's breasts, their nipples out-thrust against the gauzy material. Torn between physical excitement and the need to restrain it, they were doing their best to behave in a sophisticated and seemly fashion. This state of tension continued throughout dinner, over which Elvira presided with the utmost poise and good manners, as though everything were entirely normal. The man-servant who waited on them did not fill the glasses too often, and the brandy, at the conclusion of the meal, went round only once. In short, the gentlemen were not allowed the pretext of drink for letting themselves get out of hand. Everything passed off with extreme propriety.

"I tell you, dear boy, she might just as well have been stark," said Titel the next day in the bar of the Salon Rouge, tapping Ionel Protopopiu on the knee. "But she handled the whole thing so well that we all had to behave as though there was nothing out of the way. What's more, she'd chosen us pretty cunningly—she knew just who she was inviting. Giurgea-Roscano was appalled but lost in admiration, simply bowled over. They were all thrilled at being invited to the most original dinner-party in Bucarest. My God, what a woman! Come right down to it, she treated us the way you treat a horse when you want to make it rear—you dig in your spurs and rein it in at the same time. But you've got to know how to ride or it'll have you off. No doubt about it, she's terrific."

"I gather that you reared," said Ionel, chuckling.

"We all reared, but we didn't throw her," said Titel. And he repeated, staring into his glass: "Absolutely terrific!"

"And has she really got such a good body?" asked Ionel, his eyes gleaming.

"Like a girl's!" Titel went on to describe it in detail.

Ionel Protopopiu was silent for some moments and then asked, "Do you think she's easy?" which caused Titel to stare fixedly at him. Slightly embarrassed, although he scarcely knew why, he went on: "I mean, she sounds like it, from what you say. And besides, if she's sleeping with that fool——"

"Easy? I tell you, old boy, she's a terror. She'll sleep with you or me or anyone if she feels like it; and if she doesn't you can't buy her for a million. She's a woman who does exactly what she wants."

"And what does she want, exactly?"

Titel shrugged his shoulders. " How should I know? "

" I'd very much like to meet her," said Protopopiu after a further pause.

" I mean to have a go at her myself first. If it doesn't come off I'll introduce you."

" Too kind! " said Ionel, grinning. " So you consider me a dangerous rival? "

6

Elvira's plan of campaign envisaged two channels of approach to the King, either to be pursued if the other failed. They were Ionel Protopopiu and the Queen Mother. At present she was pursuing both, with a remorseless energy which had its roots in the acute distress she had suffered at the time of her mother's death.

After Helene Vorvoreano died Elvira had lived in retirement for some months, brooding over her life and contemplating the dire prospect of having nothing more to show for it than her mother. She had been plunged in a misery of frustration, alone in that empty house which she soon sold, thinking, " I'm still young, still beautiful, still myself," but seeing no way of escape from her obsession of failure and oblivion. Now, at last, she had discovered a purpose in life, and she embarked indefatigably upon a round of visits and parties, reducing the luckless Giurgea-Roscano to exhaustion as she laid particular seige to Madame Theodoru-Costaki, the daughter of a palace-marshal and one of Queen Marie's ladies-in-waiting. This campaign was developed in three stages. To begin with she called on her uncle, Serban Lascari, on a day when she knew Madame Theodoru-Costaki would be there. She was especially attentive to the grey-haired, kindly and not over-intelligent old lady, entertaining her with the latest gossip, and praising in fulsome terms the charm and elegance and perfect taste of her receptions and at-homes. Madame

Theodoru-Costaki, although perfectly aware that Elvira, who had already visited her, was angling for another invitation, was gratified by the flattery, and since she had no reason for refusing her she invited her to a musical evening the following Thursday.

This occasion represented a further step in the campaign. Elvira was distant with the other guests, keeping constantly at Madame Theodoru-Costaki's side, and in particular she was careful not to indulge in too much conversation with any of the gentlemen present. The old lady-in-waiting, charmed by this new recruit, invited her a second and a third time. " I didn't know her well enough, I hadn't learnt to value her as she deserves," she thought. No one could hold anything against Elvira, for at this time her private life had given rise to no scandal. The tale of the pyjamas, which was later to become the talk of Bucarest, was still only circulating among the gentlemen. One afternoon when Elvira was about to leave her house Madame Theodoru-Costaki murmured:

" I want you to keep the evening after tomorrow free. I'm counting on you. The Queen Mother will be coming at about eleven."

Elvira said nothing but kissed the old lady warmly on both cheeks, causing her to reflect fondly: " Such a dear child! So natural and impulsive! . . ."

The royal visit interrupted the performance of a piece by Francoeur for flute and piano. Suddenly both instruments were silent. The flautist stood gazing towards the doorway of the salon and the pianist swung round on his stool. Those of the company who were seated rose to their feet. A car had drawn up at the entrance to the house, disgorging several police officers who took up positions on either side of the doorway, inviting the passers-by to use the other pavement. A second car drew up and three ladies got out. A third car arrived with three more ladies.

Followed by her five ladies-in-waiting the Queen mounted the steps, to be received at their head by Madame Theodoru-Costaki, who, after making a rather awkward bob, and walking on her left a few feet away from her, led her through the rooms in which the guests were assembled to a small drawing-room. The company formed up in two lines as they passed, the gentlemen bowing and the ladies making deep curtseys. Tall, with her figure tending to stoutness, her bosom swelling beneath its low décolletée, her slightly curved nose held high, the Queen, in a mauve silk gown, with a lamé stole lined with mink over her shoulders, walked slowly through the rooms, gazing indifferently about her with violet eyes.

In the small drawing-room a high-backed armchair was awaiting her Majesty, surrounded by a circle of lesser chairs. The Queen sat down, let her stole slip from her shoulders, and glanced round at her ladies, who at this signal also took their seats. Getting a ball of wool and needles out of her bag, her Majesty began to knit, chatting with the ladies as she did so. She spoke sometimes in English and sometimes in French, with a slight English accent. She had come from a concert where she had heard Honegger's *Pacific 231*.

" But I must say, when it comes to listening to railway-trains, I'd sooner do it at a station," she said, waving an over-large, almost masculine hand.

Madame Theodoru-Costaki, active and smiling, was busily seeking out guests suitable for presentation. She presented women for the most part, but also a few men, among them the young flautist, Valentin Mavromihali, who had just returned from a visit to India. It was important to find people who might amuse her Majesty. The chosen bowed low in the case of the gentlemen, curtseyed deeply in the case of the ladies, and then behaved as naturally as they could, standing in respectful attitudes, replying to the Queen but never volunteering a remark of their own. The Queen, after smiling graciously, would turn back to her ladies. Madame Theodoru-Costaki would then bring forward a new candidate and the one who had been dismissed would retire backwards from the room. It was like a slow-motion ballet.

Elvira sat waiting, tense and resolute, gathering all her wits and energies for her own turn. When at long last Madame Theodoru-Costaki came beaming in her direction, she rose at once and followed her. Being ushered into the presence she made a deep and flowing curtsey, thinking as she did so of her great-grandmother, Sophia von Bodman, who had made her wear gloves at table when she came to stay in the holidays and had taught her the rules of etiquette. She thought of her presentations at Schönbrunn and the Hofburg, and of the approving smile which she had won from the youthful Imperial Chamberlain, Graf Hoyos.

At Stuttgart, at Munich and at Dresden her curtseys, always perfectly executed, had won the admiration of neurotic elderly duchesses. " Thank you, Grandmamma," she thought. . . . The thing was, not to hold one's skirts in one's finger-tips, in school-girl-fashion, but to let one's slender arms in their long gloves lie gracefully along their broad lateral folds, the hands relaxed and half open, the bust inclined slightly forward, the head up and face offered to view, with a faint smile and deep, intent eyes; a reverence both solemn and languid, grave and appealing. Elvira bent one knee to the ground in a rustle and swirl of stiff yellow skirts. The Queen signed to her to take a seat beside her, and the ladies-in-waiting exchanged glances. The Vorvoreano was having an astonishing success that evening! How had she managed it?

" *Que vous êtes belle, chère madame!* " said the Queen. " Like a Tanagra statuette. You have a Byzantine type of beauty such as one does not often see in Europe."

" In your Majesty's presence all other beauty is eclipsed," said Elvira, and she laughed, her lips red and her teeth gleaming.

The Queen examined her critically and with evident approval. She seemed to be considering.

" I'm glad to have met you. I should like to see you again."

Elvira's heart beat faster. She caught her breath and murmured with glowing eyes: " I shall not soon forget the day when I was presented to a great Queen, the mother of a great king."

She had turned the phrase well—a great Queen, the mother of a great king. The Queen looked inquiringly at her.

" So you think my son is a great king? " she said, half flattered and half in irony.

" He has everything to enable him to become a great king," said Elvira, "—his family, his mother, his exceptional intelligence. I believe he will come to rank as one of the greatest statesmen in Europe, particularly if he surrounds himself with people who will serve him truly."

" People who will serve him truly. . . ." The Queen looked still more closely at her and said: " And women who will love him clear-sightedly."

Elvira stayed motionless, gazing with devoted eyes.

" They must always let themselves be guided by your Majesty's advice," she said in a low voice so that the ladies-in-waiting should not hear.

The Queen smiled and repeated: "I hope to see you again, *chère madame.*"

Elvira slipped from her chair, bent her knee, causing her skirts to billow, and smiled in ecstatic veneration. The Queen bowed her head slightly and turned to her ladies.

"How charming she is," she said as Elvira withdrew, her head held high amid the curious and envious regards.

Victory! It was victory! Clearly the Queen was looking for a mistress for her son who would be her adherent, and through whom she could control him. She detested Madame Lupesco. She was ready to thrust Elvira into his arms. As to what happened afterwards, Elvira would do as she thought fit, serving her own interests and those of no one else. But first she must get there. The Queen had attempted before now to act as a procuress for her son, but had failed, no one knew why. "I don't care, I'll bring it off!" thought Elvira behind her fan.

Two or three weeks later the King, seated in his study, looked through the proposed list of guests for a forthcoming luncheon-party, while Ionel Protopopiu stood at his side.

"Elvira Vorvoreano? Who the devil's she?"

"Her Majesty the Queen wants to invite her."

"Damn her Majesty!" said the King. "She's trying to saddle me with another of her trollops. I've got plenty of my own, and I'm not going to have my mother arranging my life for me. I don't want to meet this piece." He struck Elvira's name off the list, and then asked, glancing up with his protruding eyes: "Do you know her? What's she like?"

"I haven't met her. She's a good-looker by all accounts," said Ionel Protopopiu in a non-committal voice.

"She can go and lose herself," said the King, and passed on to other business.

A fortnight later the Queen tried again. She mentioned Elvira to her son, but his forbidding expression made her realise that it would be rash to persist. Ionel Protopopiu, needless to say, did not refer to the matter. He feared the King as a possible rival for Elvira's favours, just as Titel Negruzzi feared him. But Titel ended by giving up when it became clear that Elvira had no intention of having an affair with him; and one day after losing heavily at cards he asked Ionel for the loan of a large sum which he did not propose to repay. The next day he introduced him to Elvira.

By the beginning of the autumn Elvira was the mistress of both Giurgea-Roscano and Ionel Protopopiu. She talked to Ionel about the King as often as she dared, asking about the things he did, the most trivial details of his daily life. These questions invariably caused Ionel a pang of jealousy, and it cost him an effort to answer them. He could not bring himself to admit that Elvira was only interested in the King, although this was perfectly apparent. He was the only one who guessed it, but he affected not to see.

It dawned upon Elvira, as the summer passed, that some obstacle was being put in her way at the Palace. She could no longer hope for anything from the Queen. Ionel was her only means of approach, and his lack of enthusiasm was manifest. So one afternoon she telephoned him.

" I'd rather you didn't come this evening. I've a dreadful headache."

During the next two days she did not answer his phone-calls and ignored the agitated notes he sent her. Ionel made inquiries and found that he would be able to meet her at Serban Lascari's. He got himself invited, and murmured at the first opportunity:

" Why ? "

" I've lost interest," said Elvira coolly, and moved away to mingle with the other guests; but Ionel pursued her, begging to be allowed to see her in private, and finally, with a show of reluctance, she agreed.

He came to her apartment, went on his knees to her, and at last was allowed to take her in his arms and carry her to her bed. He was intoxicated with relief and rapture, ready to put up with anything. Elvira had made her plan. She would be kind to him for a week or two, then break it off again, and thus continue to torment him until she had reduced him to a state so abject that he would do whatever she wanted. A half-promise, a smile, and he would agree to anything. But she had to break him first.

7

On an evening in September Elvira sat alone in her apartment struggling to read a novel, the work of a man called Proust, a friend of the Bibesco princes, which was having a great success in Paris. She was finding it dreadfully dull. Finally she put the book down and sat thinking. The last stage of her battle was in progress. For ten days she had denied herself to Ionel, and had gone nowhere and seen no one in order to avoid meeting him. She was running the risk, as she knew, of a definite rupture, which would mean the ruin of all her plans. But she had had enough experience of men to know that the reverse was more probable.

Ionel, as it happened, was at that moment in tête-à-tête with Madame Lupesco. They were chatting, the lady stretched on a couch while he sat in an armchair beside her.

"I'm tired, Ionel," Madame Lupesco was saying. "I don't know what's wrong with me. Perhaps it's the weather. I seem to be aching all over. I've got twinges in my leg."

She raised a long, muscular leg with a fine gold chain round the ankle. Ionel gazed at it absently, having no interest in Madame Lupesco's legs. At the time, indeed, he was not interested in anything. He hadn't slept, he was harassed and despondent. "What has she got against me?" he was asking himself while he stared unseeingly at Madame Lupesco's firm, round calf. "What more does she want? I've offered to get a divorce and marry her, but she doesn't seem to care. What does she *really* want?" In his heart he knew perfectly well what Elvira wanted, but he was struggling desperately not to admit it.

"I wish you'd rub it a little," said Madame Lupesco.

Ionel started and said, "What?"

"I asked you to rub my leg."

"Your leg?"

She burst out laughing.

" Why, what's the matter with you? My leg needs massaging, that's all. Sit down here on the couch and rub it for me." She drew up her skirt above her knee. Ionel sat on the couch, taking care not to come in contact with her, and gazing at her in a startled fashion began to massage the leg, holding it at arm's length. Madame Lupesco uttered little, exaggerated murmurs of pleasure.

" That's it—that's better. . . . A bit higher up, above the knee. . . . Oh, that's wonderful! "

Ionel had flushed crimson, finding the task excessively embarrassing. However, he went conscientiously on with it until Madame Lupesco said rather tersely: " That'll do for now."

She pulled down her skirt and he returned to his armchair. There was a brief silence.

" Well, say something. Tell me the latest scandal," said Madame Lupesco, with a note of exasperation in her voice.

But her good humour gradually returned as she reflected that the poor boy had been taken by surprise and was evidently timid. He would have to be educated by stages. . . .

Ionel had not at the time fully appreciated the momentousness of the occasion. To be invited by the King's mistress to massage her leg! In due course the significance of this dawned upon him, and when, a few days later, Elvira consented to see him, he remarked as he sat in an armchair in the light of the Sèvres lamps:

" Do you know what I'm threatened with now? The Lupesco! "

He described what had happened, and how, since then, Madame Lupesco had taken every opportunity of getting him alone in order to tell him about the state of her soul and to hint—in the most guarded terms, certainly—at her dissatisfaction with the King.

" I suppose it might mean something to me if I weren't so madly in love with you," said Ionel, kissing his mistress's cool, brown hand.

Elvira gave no sign of being flattered or gratified by this declaration. She was reflecting that Ionel, besides having so far been no use to her, was now in danger of harming himself. The thought alarmed her. She had never meant him to fall in love with her to the extent of losing his head. He went on:

" Anyway I'm a friend of the King. I can't go cuckolding him."

This attempt to appear high-minded irritated Elvira. She said coldly: " Which of you has the greater influence over the King, you or Madame Lupesco? "

He looked rather startled. " But they're two different things. We operate in different spheres."

" Don't be silly. Do you realise the risk you'll be running if you sleep with her? "

" There's no question of my sleeping with her. You're the only woman I'm interested in."

" Idiot! If you sleep with her you'll be ruined with the King if he finds out. And if you refuse she may try to ruin you to get her own back."

" But what can they do to me? It would only mean that I should have to retire to private life. Who cares about that? I don't give a damn provided I've got you."

He half rose, reaching out his arms, but she pushed him back. Did the poor fool understand nothing? Must she say to him bluntly, in plain language: " Monsieur Protopopiu, I want you to arrange matters so that I can sleep with the King "?

" Go home, Ionel. I'm tired tonight. I'm not feeling well."

He looked anxiously at her.

" Are you upset about something? Are you angry with me? "

" When I'm cross with you I'll let you know," she said in a half-mocking, half-weary voice, giving him her hand. He tried to kiss her lips, but she refused.

" Not now. Good night."

When he had departed, wondering in despair what he had done to ruffle her, Elvira went into her bedroom and sat down at a rosewood writing-desk. Holding the pen with both hands she wrote:

Madame,

You may be unaware of the fact that the whole town has heard of the very special interest you take in Monsieur Protopopiu, and is commenting upon it in the way you would expect. You may also be ignorant of the reason for his indifference, which is giving rise to no less amusement. Monsieur Protopopiu's coldness towards yourself is due to

his unhappy love for Madame Elvira Vorvoreano. Only a
very few people know of this, among them the writer of these
lines.

Adding no more, she put the note in an envelope, sealed it and
addressed it to Madame Helene Lupesco, at the address Titel
Negruzzi had given her. It was from Titel that she had learned
that the head of the Post Office was Madame Lupesco's protégé,
and not that of Ionel Protopopiu or the King.

She sat rigidly for another minute, overtaken by a slight nervous
tremor. What she was doing was rash and dangerous. But she
had to chance her luck.

8

Ionel was again keeping Madame Lupesco company. Guests
were expected, but they were not due for another hour. Through
the wrought-iron grill which separated the room from the salon
the dinner-table could be seen, decorated with big Capodimonte
vases filled with freshly cut flowers.

" Come closer," said Madame Lupesco.

Ionel drew his chair towards hers, looking thoroughly uncomfortable.

" My rheumatism's bothering me again. Rub my leg," said
Madame Lupesco.

But this time she said it without languorous undertones, with
a cool little laugh, looking him in the eyes. Ionel was far from
happy. In the past few days he had noticed a change in her manner
which he had reported to Elvira, who had merely shrugged her
shoulders.

" I told you it was dangerous. Whether you give way or turn
her down you'll probably end by losing your job with the King.
And I warn you, Ionel, I shan't be interested in an obscure
Monsieur Protopopiu. You're very charming, my dear, but you've

no name, no standing and no money worth mentioning. You'd better watch out."

Madame Lupesco's leg was warm and supple, and in other circumstances Ionel might have enjoyed himself; but now his mind was furiously engaged in considering his possible courses of action, which were not many. Suppose, for instance, he were to go to the King and tell him that his mistress was making advances to him? Within an hour the Lupesco would have persuaded his Majesty that she was his alone, and that Ionel was raving mad.

" Harder," said Madame Lupesco with perfect calm.

Ionel toiled away, his flace flushed and a little damp. All things considered, it would probably be best to sleep with the woman and make what use he could of her. The affair might simply run a brief and normal course. Or they might get caught, in which case she would doubtless find some way of getting round the King, whereas he would be done for; but at least while it lasted he might turn her influence with the King to his own advantage. . . . Having decided upon this course Ionel massaged with a greater vigour, moving his hands higher up Madame Lupesco's thigh. He did so quite cold-bloodedly, and indeed with a sense of slight unreality, since she was no longer the alluring lady of a few days before, but had become so queerly distant. And suddenly she exclaimed in a voice that cut like a whip:

" May I ask what you're doing? Do you want me to ring the bell? "

Ionel withdrew his hands; but she did not let him go.

" I simply asked you to massage me. I don't expect you to lose your head."

She might have been addressing a servant, and this altered tone added greatly to Ionel's dismay. He returned submissively to his task, and after a few moments of silence Madame Lupesco said:

" I'm told that Elvira Vorvoreano is still quite attractive, in spite of being over forty."

Ionel raised thunderstruck eyes to gaze at her, and she went on:

" From what I gather, she's very much a woman with an eye to the main chance, a scheming, spiteful creature. At one time she was living quite openly with that fool Giurgea-Roscano, but

I understand that now . . . Why, what's the matter? Why have you suddenly stopped? Is something wrong? "

" So that's it," Ionel was thinking. " She's heard about Elvira and she's furiously jealous. So now she'll try to get the King to kick me out. She's capable of anything." He went on massaging, but at the sound of the King's voice in the ante-room he stopped abruptly and returned to his armchair.

" Don't you want to go on? " asked Madame Lupesco with mockery; but realising that Ionel Protopopiu was too thoroughly scared to fall into this trap, she pulled her skirt down over her knees.

The King, after saying a few words to the manservant as he took off his overcoat, entered the room and at once perceived, from the unnatural silence of its two occupants, that something had occurred. Ionel Protopopiu rose and bowed. The King kissed Madame Lupesco's hand and said:

" Only the two of you? What's happening? Why are you both so silent? "

Madame Lupesco laughed, but before she could speak Ionel forestalled her by saying:

" Madame has been teasing me because I've lost my head over a woman."

" What woman? "

Keeping the initiative at all costs, Ionel replied: " It's Madame Vorvoreano—Elvira Vorvoreano—the ex-wife of old ' Telescope ' Ipsilanti."

The King looked hard and suspiciously at him.

" I thought you said you didn't know her? "

" Your Majesty has an astonishing memory. You've only seen her name once, on a list of guests," said Ionel, smiling.

" I remember everything, as you ought to know. Why didn't you tell me you knew her? "

" I met her later, sire."

" Really? " said the King, still suspicious and ready to fly into a rage.

" Shortly after your Majesty asked me who she was."

The King said no more; but Ionel was well aware that this was not the end of the matter, although it was not mentioned again that evening.

Late that night he rang up Elvira and asked to be allowed to come to her. He arrived in a state of extreme agitation and told her what had happened.

" Well, there you are," said Elvira. " So she set a trap for you to make the King jealous. She's just playing with you. You managed to get out of it this time, but she'll think of something else. You're done for, my poor Ionel."

" It's no use scolding me. Tell me what I ought to do," said Ionel in despair.

He was sitting on a stool in front of her, with his hands hanging between his knees, his tie crooked and his eyes haggard. Elvira, in a yellow taffeta house-gown, embroidered with lace at the neck and sleeves, was seated in an armchair dangling a Louis-Quinze slipper from one foot. Suddenly making up her mind, she got up and took him by the hand.

" Let's go into the other room," she murmured, " and not worry about those people any more. Let's just think of ourselves." She put her arms round his neck, raising her face to his with her eyes closed.

In bed two hours later, with Ionel relaxed and in a heaven of happiness, they returned to the matter of Madame Lupesco.

" You were right to try and make people think you were still having an affair with Giurgea-Roscano," said Ionel. " But there's no point in it now. Everybody knows about us."

Elvira was tempted to laugh. Her liaison with Giurgea-Roscano had never been broken off, nor had she any intention of dropping him for anyone except the King—certainly not for Ionel, in connection with whom he might come in useful as a last card up her sleeve.

" Darling, none of that's important," she said. " You've got to be thinking about how you're to get out of this mess. I've told you before—I'm very fond of you, but I don't want to ruin you, or to be involved with someone who has been ruined."

" Yes," murmured Ionel, breathing the acrid scent of her body. He had scarcely heard. He said again, " Yes."

" There's only one way. You'll have to get the Lupesco away from the King."

" There's no hope of that except by finding a substitute," said Ionel, " and I don't see who . . ."

" Why not me? " said Elvira softly. " I'd do it. I'd do it for your sake—because I love you."

" You! " exclaimed Ionel, raising himself on his elbow.

" Yes, my darling. I'd do even that for you," said Elvira firmly, and drew him to her.

Confronted by this proof of her love, and others which followed, the dumbfounded Ionel was finally persuaded that his truest interests would be furthered by Elvira's becoming the King's mistress. However, in the course of that tumultuous night, which left him exhausted, blissful and despairing, second thoughts occurred to him.

" My darling, how can I let you degrade yourself? Why don't we go away together? We'll live abroad and leave all this filth behind."

" No, Ionel," said Elvira firmly. " Exile, ruin, poverty—I can't bear the thought of them. I'd rather die."

Ionel was still very much at sea. He continued to raise objections but finally gave way, heart overflowing, body limp, no longer able to think clearly, or to do anything but acquiesce while he listened to the long and careful instructions which Elvira proceeded to give him.

Bathed and shaved, wearing a suit of English cloth cut by Pyle in Paris, Ionel went next day into the King's study to report for orders. His Majesty was seated at his desk with a puffy face and accusing eyes.

" You and the Vorvoreano woman," he barked. " So you're at it too, are you? You've started to have secrets from me? "

His manner was aggressive. With a sinking heart, but knowing exactly what he had to say—Elvira had thought of everything— Ionel prepared to play for desperate stakes.

" I assure you, sire, I didn't mean to hide anything from you. I had no idea that your Majesty would be interested. I've simply been caught, the way we all are sooner or later. I've fallen madly in love. I shall probably have to get a divorce, because I can't live without her."

He forced himself to smile while the King glared suspiciously at him; and suddenly he realised that he was beginning to loathe his master, the thick mouth, the insolent eyes and ginger moustache, the face sodden with over-indulgence. He wanted to hit that face, particularly when, his manner changing, the King asked with a slight leer:

" How did you get that way? "

Ionel continued to smile. " I couldn't help myself. She's the most wonderful woman in the world."

" You sound like an infatuated schoolboy," said the King, now grinning.

" If you were in my place, sire," said Ionel, speaking with a most convincing fervour, " I think you would understand."

He was lost to all sense of shame and dignity, but with a corresponding gain in eloquence he went on to describe Elvira, her talents as a mistress, in terms which were both lyrical and crudely precise. The King had become thoughtful.

" Honestly? She's really like that? "

" I can't tell you! " cried Ionel, and turning paler he added further details of the utmost intimacy. The King, whose sense of decency in such matters had vanished long ago, sat staring at his secretary with a new expression, a light dawning in his eyes. He laughed uncertainly, seeming on the verge of speech but doubtful of what to say.

" Now that I have told you all about it, sire, won't you allow me to present her? She's one of your Majesty's most ardent admirers. She's always asking me about you. I'm sure you would enjoy meeting her."

" Well, it's not a bad idea," said his Majesty with a relieved and gratified chuckle. Restored to the utmost good humour he rose and clapped Ionel on the shoulder. " My dear boy, it's very nice of you. You know how fond of you I am. I shall be delighted to meet her."

Ionel knew him well enough to know that at this moment he was on better terms with the King than he had ever been; indeed, that he had become the most influential man in the country. To his astonishment, he was delighted. Nothing around him was changed—the furnishing of the room, the light, the crowds streaming along the Calea Victoriei. Nothing was changed, outside or within himself—and nothing bore witness to his irreparable dishonour. . . .

A few days later he arranged with the King to bring Elvira to him late at night, to avoid the watchful eyes of Madame Lupesco. There would be no one in the Palace but the equerry on duty, the usual contingent of the royal bodyguard, a few footmen and the King's valet. Ionel himself fixed the exact hour and the way Elvira was to enter the Palace, even deciding that she should be clad in mourning, with a black veil over her head. The King was charmed by this detail.

" I'll tear it to shreds," he said happily.

Ionel gulped and pretended not to hear. " After all, I'm the one she loves," he reflected, but drew no great consolation from the thought.

The King was in a mounting fever of excitement as the moment approached. On the evening of the rendezvous he dispatched his business with so much haste, cancelling an audience, that he found himself at a loose end three hours before the time. Ionel had left him and was to return in due course with Elvira; and he had no means of knowing that the wretched man was at that moment in her bed, trying to convince himself that he was the one she truly loved. His Majesty sent for champagne, and after drinking several glasses paced nervously up and down the room. Finally he exclaimed aloud:

" This is more than flesh and blood can stand! "

He ordered his car and went downstairs.

" I shall be back in half an hour," he said to the footman who helped him on with his overcoat.

A sentry opened the wrought-iron gates and the car left the Palace by a side entrance.

9

Among the thousands of prostitutes who walked the Bucarest pavements there was one who was widely acquainted with the young gentlemen of good family, the officers, journalists and business touts who passed their evenings in the night-spots on the Calea Victoriei. She was nicknamed the Crow. Tall and very thin, she wore her black hair in a schoolboy crop which had the effect of increasing the severity of her narrow face with its high cheekbones and hollow cheeks. Her mouth quivered in a look of constant suffering, even when the Crow was not thinking of anything un-pleasant—when she had been handsomely paid for a half-hour in an hotel bedroom, for example, or had just had a sniff of cocaine. Her dark eyes might shine with a darker brilliance under the ridge of her thick eyebrows, but still the look of suffering remained. The Crow was to be had for very little money and she never lacked clients—provincials, travelling salesmen, society rakes with peculiar tastes, and now and then a visiting diplomat who wanted to sample the erotic refinements of Bucarest, even at the risk of catching something.

That night the Crow was gambling away the last of her money at the Cercle des Commerçants, a small dive on the top floor above the Alhambra restaurant. Having put her shirt on the red, and lost, she picked up her imitation snake-skin bag and pushed her way through the crowd of players, who did not trouble to move aside. No one took the slightest notice of her.

" Going already? " grunted the porter, whose name was Gogu.

" I haven't a bean left. I'm strapped."

He looked at her dull-eyed, with no particular expression. " I've got some money."

" Well, let me have a couple of hundred."

Gogu grinned. " The trouble is, I can't get away just now. Afterwards, if you like, when we're closed."

" Hell, I want the money now. What's wrong with this place? "

She looked round his small office, seeking for a dark corner.

" No good. The boss might come in. Come back after we're closed. I'll give you two hundred then."

The Crow passed two men on her way downstairs but although she smiled at them they ignored her. A third man clicked his tongue but wagged his chin in sign of refusal. Three drunks appeared, one of whom pinched her bottom as he passed, and she paused for a moment to shout abuse at him.

After half an hour on the pavement of the Calea Victoriei she found a customer who took her to his hotel and let her go at about half past ten. She stood hesitating for a moment outside the hotel, wondering whether to go back to the Cercle des Com-merçants. But there was still some time to go before it closed, and she was not sure that she wanted to. She had no particular ob-jection to Gogu, the porter, but now that she had a little money in her pocket she might as well reserve his offer for some future occasion.

She hailed a taxi and drove to a large building in the Rue Blanari, where she rang a bell on the third floor, standing well under the light so that she could be seen through the Judas window. A woman in a black dress let her in.

The Crow sat down at a baccarat table and in a quarter of an hour had lost her half-hour's earnings. She got up and looked about her. The hostess, going round the tables followed by a girl with a tray of coffee and wine, paused as she saw her.

" Not playing any more? "

" Your customers have cleaned me out, Madame Zina," said the Crow in a sweet-sour voice.

Madame Zina said sharply: " I've told you before not to talk like that. You're all my guests, my personal friends. There are no customers."

" And what about the *cagnotte*? "

" You surely don't expect me to pay for the drinks and everything out of my own pocket? "

" You know you make plenty out of it, so why pretend you don't? "

Madame Zina was indignant. " I'm an officer's widow and I live on my husband's pension. I'm not going to be insulted by a common prostitute. You'd better hold your tongue or you'll get your face slapped, and then I'll send for the police."

She had spoken in a low voice so as not to attract the notice of her guests. The Crow murmured: " It'd be more sensible if you gave me a louis. I'm strapped." She put the coin in her bag and turned towards the door. " When I land a really rich customer I'll bring him along here."

She went out again and did the round of the streets near the Calea Victoriei, for some time without any luck. But then a hoarse voice called:

" Hey, you—come here! "

Looking round she saw a long, black car with a gleaming radiator. The door was open and the driver was beckoning to her to get in. It was the King. She had had dealings with him before. She got in obediently, knowing that she was still out of luck, for his Majesty was a bad payer. The door slammed and the car drove rapidly to the Calea Victoriei.

IO

Elvira felt that she was in a dream. Victory was within her grasp. It was inconceivable that she should not please the King. She would know just how to stir his senses and arouse his desires without quite satisfying them—all her weapons were in readiness. She was feeling wonderfully relaxed, although also a little fatigued after the several hours she had spent in Ionel's arms. Perhaps she would have been wiser not to indulge him, the better to conserve all her freshness and vigour; but she had been terrified lest in his agitated state he might commit some unpredictable folly which would ruin everything. However, as to herself she was not much troubled; she would know how to rise to the occasion. . . .

A car with drawn curtains bore them in silence to the Palace, where the side door was promptly opened. A man in livery led them without speaking along low-ceilinged passages to a lift, and finally showed them into a curtained room containing a few blue-upholstered armchairs and a small, low table standing on an Ispahan carpet. The walls were oak-lined, and a large painting of red flowers in a vase, attributed to the " velvet " Brueghel, hung facing the window. Ionel sat her down and said in French to the footman:

" Is his Majesty ready to receive us ? "

" Not at present," the man replied.

Ionel looked at him in some surprise. " He's not waiting for us? What's he doing? "

" His Majesty is busy. He has visitors."

" Who ? "

" Colonel Gabriel Marinesco and a lady."

" I see. Thank you. Let me know when he's ready to receive us."

Ionel was very much astonished, but a sudden hope was mingled with his perplexities. Perhaps the whole thing would have to be postponed. Perhaps, after all, nothing would ever come of it. But he reflected that this was absurd. Marinesco, the Chief of Police and the King's close associate in all kinds of shady transactions, must simply have called on some matter of urgent business. The woman was very likely a police-informer.

Elvira, who had not heard this exchange, was thinking meanwhile that the King might be persuaded to have her appointed lady-in-waiting to the Queen Mother, thus conferring upon her a recognized status. Her next task would be to get him to divorce his wife, Queen Helena; and so, by gradual degrees . . .

Perfect quiet reigned in the room. . . . She would rid herself of Ionel as quickly as possible: perhaps a diplomatic post somewhere abroad. . . . Giurgea-Roscano could be silenced by threats. What mattered was to establish a firm hold over the King, and for this every stratagem must be used, simple, subtle, harsh, tender; every device known to honest women and to harlots, provided only that it were unexpected: she knew and would use them all. . . . The Lupesco must be disposed of with the utmost promptness by any means that offered—if necessary by spells. . . .

The minutes passed and it was like a dream. Time had ceased to matter. At any moment the King might enter, or perhaps he would send for her, and then——

" What the devil's he doing? " muttered Ionel.

" Who? " asked Elvira in the husky voice, warm and languorous, which she had rehearsed for the occasion.

" The King, of course. He's with Marinesco and a woman. I can't think what's going on."

" A woman? What sort of woman? " Elvira sat up abruptly, her voice and manner transformed.

Ionel told her what little he knew and she cried:

" Idiot! Go at once and find out. Go on! "

She sprang to her feet and pushed him out of the room, filled with an irrational terror that the King might have sent someone who had not known where to look for her, and that the delay might irritate him and ruin everything. She was out of all patience with this fool who could not even arrange an appointment without a hitch.

Ionel presently returned grinning. The woman, it seemed, was a common prostitute known to everyone in Bucarest, the lowest kind of street-walker.

" He sometimes likes to amuse himself with the riff-raff," he said, and was amazed when she smacked his face. " What was that for? It isn't my fault."

She was tempted in her fury and frustration to tell him precisely what she thought of him, but she controlled herself and sat down again, staring at the pattern of the carpet. What was to be done now? She was frightened. Had the King been in bed with the woman? If he had, what was the best line to take? There seemed to be nothing for it but to proceed according to plan. But her self-confidence was badly shaken. A sweat of anguish broke out over her body, and the thought occurred to her that her sweat had a strong smell which might not please his Majesty. . . .

The time dragged past—half an hour, an hour. . . . Elvira's face had become one of utter weariness, her skin sallow, her eyes dull. Ionel Protopopiu tried once or twice to talk to her, only to meet with a fury of abuse. He lay back in an armchair smoking, feeling far from depressed. Hope had returned to him.

I I

While the King was getting dressed the Crow had sat wondering whether she dared. Finally she had said:

" You'll give me a bit extra, won't you? I lost all my money gambling tonight."

They were in a bachelor flat on the tenth floor of a building in the centre of the town. There was a private entrance with its own lift. The King frowned. He hated giving anything away. To change the subject he asked, seating himself in an armchair and lighting a cigarette:

" Where were you playing? "

" Well, first at the Cercle des Commerçants—you know, over the Alhambra. They cleaned me out. So then I got some more money and went along to Madame Zina's, and in no time I was cleaned out again."

" Who's Madame Zina ? "

" You may not know her. You can't expect to know all the dives in Bucarest."

" Zina . . . she runs a gambling-place, does she ? " The King knitted his eyebrows in an effort to remember.

" Well, it certainly isn't a girls' school," said the Crow. " Go on, give us a bit extra. I'm strapped."

But his Majesty was not listening. He was ransacking his very capacious memory.

" What's the name of this place ? "

" It's name ? It's just called ' Zina's place.' But it isn't the sort that puts up a sign over the door."

" In fact, an illicit gaming-house. All the same, I ought to know about it. Look, I need you. Put on your skirt and come along," said the King, stirred suddenly to action.

He drove the Crow to the Palace and bustled her into his study, steering her past guards and flunkeys who had seen too much to be surprised at anything. Leaving her standing in the middle of the room, as he did everyone, he sat down at his desk and got a typewritten list out of a drawer.

" What's this woman's full name ? "

" Madame Zinaida Bugesco."

" Address ? "

The Crow told him. After a careful study of the list the King dialled a private telephone number.

" Colonel, I want you to come here at once. . . . Yes, at once. . . ." His face flushed with rage, he put down the receiver and sat tapping on the desk, paying no attention to the Crow. The Chief of Police arrived in a very short time and clicked his heels, darting a rapid glance at the woman still standing in the middle of the room.

" At your Majesty's service ! "

" What the hell does this mean, Marinesco ? You're supposed to keep track of everything that goes on in Bucarest. You don't seem to be doing it."

" I don't understand, sire."

" I'm talking about a Madame Zinaida Bugesco, who's running a clip-joint that isn't on the list. I take it you don't know about it—or am I to assume that you've been making your own arrangements on the side ? "

·After some further talk the King called for champagne. The Crow would have welcomed a drink but was too terrified to ask. She stood listening while Colonel Marinesco bellowed into the telephone:

" You blasted ullage, what the hell do you do with yourself all day? It's your business to know all the joints, every last one. Off you go and bring the woman into headquarters. What? I don't give a damn if you're in bed. Get cracking! "

The colonel put down the receiver, straightened himself and said with calm:

" The matter will be dealt with at once, your Majesty."

" It will, will it? Don't forget that I'm the one who gives the orders. How long has this woman been holding out on us? Have you any idea? Well, damned well find out—and ring me up as soon as you've got it settled."

The colonel saluted. The King dismissed him with a wave of his hand, at the same time indicating that he could take the Crow with him. " Give her a hundred," he said, and turned his back on them.

Half an hour later Madame Zina was shown into the colonel's office.

" So you've been playing the fool with us, have you? " said the colonel. " No sign on the door, no registration and not a single contribution to the Police Welfare Fund. You've been holding out, eh? There isn't a single dive in this town that doesn't pay its share. The ones that try to dodge get closed down. You'll pay a year's arrears, and from now on you'll report to me once a month. That's all. Now clear out."

The King took the colonel's phone-call in the small drawing-room where he had had Elvira Vorvoreano brought to him. Elvira was in process of telling him in a warm, smiling, modest but voluptuous voice how it had always been her dearest dream to be personally acquainted with his Majesty. The buzz of the telephone cut her short in mid-sentence.

" Well? " said the King.

The voice of the Chief of Police came over the line—to Elvira a series of unintelligible squeakings.

" All right—but I don't like it. See that you keep on your toes another time. Good night."

The King then turned back to listen to Elvira, but his thoughts were elsewhere.

The monthly contributions paid by all the dives and clip-joints in the town went into the royal coffers, by way of the Chief of Police. His Majesty did not permit the slightest irregularity in the collection of his revenues. This business had upset him, and he did not pay much attention to what Elvira was saying. His ardours had moreover been diminished by his encounter with the Crow, and in any case he was disappointed in Elvira. He preferred big, fleshy women.

Elvira sensed what was happening, and the effect was to make her nervous, over-effusive and maladroit. When eventually the meeting reached its predestined climax a sad comedy ensued, their embrace being as much marred by Elvira's excessive show of passion as by the King's lack of interest. At the end he seemed more out of sorts than ever, even irritated. He replied to her only in monosyllables and made it clear that he wished her to withdraw.

Elvira went out like a person in a trance, walked past Ionel Protopopiu without seeing him, took her seat beside him in the car and did not say a word. Arriving at her house she got out and said:

"Thank you. Good night."

He asked if he might come up with her.

"No," she said decidedly, without raising her voice, and left him standing on the pavement.

She had a bath and then sat down in an armchair. She was exhausted, burnt out, done for. She flung herself dry-eyed on the rug, and lay writhing and biting her clenched fists, uttering strange little animal cries.

VII

*The Method of Leonardo
da Vinci*

I

Davida Lascari, née Coziano, gave her first-born son the name
of Alexander, after his father, the only member of the family who
inspired her with neither shame nor disgust. One of her daughters
married a Monsieur Romano, a magistrate in his forties, at the
age of seventeen. Thanks to the Lascari family connection with
the Liberal Party, this Monsieur Romano had a rapid and brilliant
career, and he was on the verge of being appointed to the High
Court of Appeal when the country entered the war in 1916. With
his wife he accompanied the Army and the Government in their
withdrawal to Moldavia, and here died of Spanish influenza. His
widow never re-married, and thus his son, Serban Romano, when
he came of age, entered into the sole inheritance of a large fortune.

From 1930 to 1935 Serban Romano lived alone in an old house
in the Rue C. A. Rosetti. He was a quiet, serious, rather reserved
young man of medium height, neither handsome nor ugly. His
parents had wanted him to become an engineer, and he had spent
four years in Charlottenburg, where he gained his diploma.
Having done so he elected to follow the course in philosophy
conducted by Professor Hartmann. Thereafter, instead of returning to his own country to get a job with one of the big industrial concerns, he went to Frieburg and for two semesters attended
the lectures of Professor Heidegger, travelling during his vacations
in Germany, Austria and the Low Countries, but otherwise doing
nothing worthy of note. He spent two successive springs in
Bucarest, attending lectures by the illustrious Fanica Nicoulesco,
who occupied the Chair of Metaphysics at the University. At the
conclusion of the second series he introduced himself and asked
the professor a number of questions of no particular importance.
The interview took place in a small lecture-room situated behind
the Odobesco Amphitheatre. The professor answered perfunc-
torily, without showing much interest. But suddenly he looked

up and gazed intently at Serban with his rather disconcerting eyes, one of which was brown and the other green. Fanica Nicoulesco had almost white hair and a very dark skin suggestive of gipsy descent. His contrasting eyes and mephistophelean eyebrows, shaped like a circumflex accent, gave him the look of a wooden image with an opal and an agate inserted in the eye-sockets.

" Did you say your name is Romano? Are you a relation of Madame Augusta Hagibei? "

" She was my aunt. She died last year."

The professor continued to examine Serban without giving any indication of why the name of his family should have aroused his interest.

" And you're reading philosophy? "

" Simply for my own satisfaction. I'm not thinking of an academic career. I'm a qualified engineer, but I think philosophy is the most important of all subjects."

" It's a view that does you honour. But why, precisely, have you come to Bucarest to study it? "

" Simply on your account, sir. Because I think you have something to offer which cannot be found in any other university. Of all the professors I have studied under you seem to me to be by far the most interesting, although you have never published anything."

" You've been studying in Germany—Heidegger, I suppose, and Hartmann and Klager."

" Hartmann," said Serban, in his composed fashion, " is nothing but a philosophy professor who deals in professor's philosophy."

" That's an amusing way of putting it, but it isn't original."

" If I hadn't been sure you would recognise the saying I shouldn't have used it," said Serban, smiling.

The lecture-room was almost empty. Most of the students who had stayed behind to talk to the professor had drifted out, wearied by the length of this conversation. Only two well-dressed young women were left, seated together in a corner. The professor let them wait. He motioned to Serban to sit down and did so himself.

" What about Heidegger and Klager? "

" I haven't studied under Klager. Heidegger has a remarkable literary talent, which is by no means unimportant in a philosopher or a man of science, but I don't find him interesting as a man, and I consider that his teaching is unsound. A philosophy of nihilism can only end in religion or mysticism; he shows a lack of logic in not going the whole way. The solution of the problem, as he conceives it, does not lie in culture—how does one translate the German word *Bildung*? I think that only a basic certainty can save us from the limbo of nothingness. I mean certainty in the most absolute sense. A culture can never be anything but an edifice built with perishable materials on a foundation which needs to be constantly reinforced, and by the activity of humanity as a whole, not that of any one man. Limbo lies ready to engulf every one of us, and *Bildung*—culture, education, philosophical formation, whatever you like—cannot finally relieve the doubts and terrors that are at the root of human existence. . . . We must, we *must*, have a certainty."

" Who must? All of us? "

" Yes, all of us. That is to say, each separate one of us."

" And without this certainty you think we cannot live? "

Serban replied simply and modestly, in his quiet, pleasant voice:

" Well, I don't see how we can. It's very difficult."

Professor Nicoulesco laughed outright.

" And do you possess such a certainty? "

" No, but I'm looking for it. That is how I'm trying to justify my existence." Serban smiled as though in apology. " I did not mean to talk about myself, but you put the question to me. I'm working in purely theoretical terms."

The professor tapped on the old wooden desk scarred by the penknives of generations of students. He gazed thoughtfully at this aspiring young man.

" Tell me—if you're looking for a certainty why aren't you a Marxist? "

Serban frowned in slight embarrassment and said:

" I think that what attracts me in Marxism is its logical consistency. But Marxism does not allow us to separate our thinking from revolutionary activity."

" Aha! " murmured the professor, in a tone which seemed to say, " So you've realised that, have you? "

" And you see," said Serban, with a hint of private misgiving or embarrassment, " I think independent theoretical work is of value."

" Yes," said the professor, and again considered him for some moments before holding out his hand. " You interest me. Come and see me again and we'll go on talking. I shall look forward to it.

In the course of that spring Serban Romano paid Professor Nicoulesco a number of visits in the small bungalow where he lived. One entered it by way of a verandah where visitors left their raincoats and goloshes. The ceiling was very low, and the whitewashed walls were hung with tapestries from Oltenita, woven in blue and green with patterns of foliage and stylised birds. It was an idyllic, patriarchal abode. In summer meals were served out of doors under an arbour of wistaria and virgin vine.

The work of the house was done by a grey-haired woman in an apron, apparently a relation of the professor, who would appear silently with a tray of preserves and as silently withdraw. A bronze bust of Fanica Nicoulesco stood by the door of the room where he was accustomed to receive his guests, and there were a number of portraits of him on the walls, in oil, gouache, crayon and charcoal, and engraved on wood and copper—always the same curious eyes, with the same mephisophelean brows beneath a huge forehead.

In the course of one of these visits a conversation of particular consequence took place between them. Serban Romano was wearing a light-grey suit with a tie of even paler grey, and the mere sight of his immaculately white shirt conveyed a sense of coolness. He sat with his legs crossed, reserved, calm, correct as ever, with his elbows at his sides and his hands motionless, in one of the armchairs in the professor's library.

" So far," he said, " I have come here simply for the pleasure of listening to you and enjoying the brilliance of your intellect. But today I want to talk to you about something which is of great importance to me, and to ask your advice."

Professor Nicoulesco sat waiting with his elbows on his desk. Serban asked leave to smoke, and getting an expensive cigar out of a crocodile-skin case nicked the end with a gold cigar-cutter. The professor watched this procedure with an amused smile, although there was a certain intentness in his expression. Unconscious of this, Serban lit his cigar, blew a cloud of smoke and proceeded:

" I have been thinking that in order to organise such knowledge as I have acquired, and more especially to integrate the principles of the different kinds of knowledge . . . Mark you, this is only an experiment. You mustn't laugh at me. I'm not so foolish as to think I shall succeed. . . ."

" But you do think it, nevertheless."

He blushed like a girl.

" Well, it seems to me that if one is to discover any solid basis, even a single fixed point, in our knowledge of the universe and of ourselves, something more than exceptional power and capacity for thought is needed. There must be a method and an approach which will enable us to grasp the essence of different branches of knowledge and different philosophical disciplines, and relate their essential content to human knowledge and understanding as a whole. The problem is to find the best method."

The professor was no longer smiling. He merely blinked his eyes.

" I think I may have found the answer in a small work by an unimportant French poet who is no more than a second-rate thinker. Although he wrote it when he was quite young, it is the only one of his works which seems to me to have any lasting quality. He talks about the method of Leonardo da Vinci."

" I happen to know the book you mean," said the professor, without any show of approval or otherwise.

" You know it? " Serban's eyes lit up and he leaned forward in his chair. " Then as you know he believed that Leonardo had managed to achieve a sort of generalised intellectual standpoint from which, by a process of analysis and discrimination, he could arrive at the understanding, and the practice, of any scientific discipline or any form of art."

" Has anyone except Leonardo ever attempted anything of the kind? " the professor asked seriously.

" No, but the prospect is—it's intoxicating! *If* it's true, and *if* it's possible, it has got to be tried! "

Serban's eyes were shining and his face was flushed. The professor remained impassive.

" You say it has got to be tried. But for what purpose? What do you hope to find? "

" An ultimate truth! " cried Serban Romano.

Fanica Nicoulesco looked out of the window. Two women in light summer frocks and big hats were passing the house. He got up and closed the shutters, so that now Serban could see nothing of him but the gleam of his eyes and that great expanse of forehead.

" I want to read everything that Leonardo has left us," said Serban. " I may find no more than a hint, a pointer—but perhaps I shall unearth the whole secret! "

" The manuscript of the Notebooks is in the library of the British Museum, the Arendal bequest," murmured the professor, still displaying no great interest. " Or anyway a large part of it is there. There is more in Paris, I think, or at the Vatican. But you'll find it easier to use the facsimile edition, transcribed by Ulrico Hoepffi and published in Milan in 1895 or thereabouts— anyway, round the turn of the century."

" Can I buy a copy? "

" I don't think so, but you'll find it in any big library. I saw it in the Staatsbibliothek in Munich, when I was a student."

" Then I'll go to Munich. Which means that this must be my farewell visit."

" You mean to say you're going at once? "

" As soon as possible. It may take me a day or two to get my visa renewed."

The professor rose and came and sat down beside him, putting a hand on his shoulder.

" Listen, dear boy," he said in a tone of blunt familiarity. " I'm going to tell you something important—the most important thing anyone can tell you."

Serban had started slightly at hearing himself addressed as " dear boy " and in the second person. Professor Nicoulesco went on to talk in a somewhat strange manner, flippant and almost coarse.

" I liked you when I first saw you. I liked you in your stiff collar and your tie-pin and your London suit, talking about the search for truth. But you mustn't be angry if I say that it's only now that I'm disposed to take you seriously—and I'm still wondering whether you're really purposeful and single-minded enough to deserve it."

" Why shouldn't I be purposeful? "

" Because young men like you know nothing about the meaning of poverty and hunger and the struggle to get somewhere. You're too accommodating and too soft, too comfortable and easy-going to persevere, really persevere, in the study of difficult matters like philosophy, science and art. What generally happens is that people of your kind pay people of my kind to do these things for them. I'm afraid you will never have the tenacity of my Macedonian students, the sons of peasants and workers who come here and starve while they study to become professors or officers or doctors or lawyers—in short, for the honour of serving people like you. That's what I mean by purposeful."

" But are they purposeful in the search for knowledge, or simply in their ambition to get somewhere? "

" That's beside the point. It doesn't matter what the purpose is. The thing is to have one and stick to it."

" Even if it is an ignoble purpose? " said Serban.

There was a moment of silence.

" You're an odd case," said the professor, " and perhaps genuine. I think you'll turn into a man, perhaps even a great man. Anyway, I don't want to leave you groping. Life's too short." He went to his bookshelves, and without having to search for it in the half-darkness found the volume he wanted. " Read this. Do what it says, and one of the three truths it contains, the third, will be revealed to you."

" What are the others? "

" I'll tell you that some other time."

" Well, what is the third truth? " asked Serban with the book in his hand.

" The third truth is that *nothing is impossible*," said the professor, smiling.

Serban went into the next room in order to study the title-page by the light of day. He read: *Exercitorum Spiritualium Sancti Ignati de Loyola, editio princeps qualis in lucem prodiit, Romae MDLVII apud Autonium Bladum.*

" It is an essay that will teach you to forge your will and your mind into weapons of steel that may be destroyed but cannot be defeated," said the professor. " That little book saved the Church of Rome and perhaps all Europe—indeed, perhaps civilisation itself. The men who tempered their will-power by the exercises it prescribes became missionaries in China, Japan, Tibet, Africa and the two Americas; they founded the State of Paraguay, and controlled and directed it; they were the all-powerful counsellors of the Hapsburg dynasty, of Philip II of Spain and of Louis XIV; they became so formidable that all governments were afraid of

them and even the popes became their enemies, a fact which seems
to me of some significance."

After this eulogy of the Society of Jesus he was silent for a
moment. Then he took the book from Serban and laid his hand
on it.

" When you have read it and followed its instructions, put it
there." He thrust it into the hip-pocket of his trousers as though
it were a pistol. " Forget about Jesus Christ and all such
trivialities, and you will accomplish whatever you set out to
do."

Pulling the book out of his pocket again, he handed it back to
Serban, who took it with some hesitation.

" But doesn't the practice of these exercises imply at least
some acceptance of the dogma that gave rise to them? With my
scientific training I would find it difficult to——"

" You don't believe in God? "

Serban shrugged his shoulders, looking uncomfortable.

" I believe in scientific fact. Do you yourself believe in God? "

The professor uttered a small, dry laugh, that of a man confined
within his own, solitary cell.

" I'm not sure. . . . I'm *afraid* God exists. His existence would
be a terrifying thing from many points of view."

" Perhaps it would," said Serban Romano calmly. " But for
the strictly logical mind, informed by works of historical criticism,
the question no longer arises. And where the exact sciences are
concerned you know what Laplace said—' God? It is an hypothesis that can have no bearing on our calculations.' "

Fanica Nicoulesco nodded.

" That would be wonderful, if true. Well, my dear boy, *bon
voyage* and good luck. Be sure to come and see me when you're
next in Bucarest. There was a favour I was going to ask you, but
I won't do so now."

" Please tell me what it is."

" There'd be no point, as you're going away. We'll leave it till
you come back."

" But you can at least tell me."

" I don't want to delay your departure."

Serban persisted, and after a further display of reluctance the
professor confessed that he was most anxious to meet his family
and see something of the social world in which he moved.

" But they couldn't be more dull! " exclaimed Serban in genuine astonishment.

" Perhaps they would seem more interesting to a bookworm like myself than to anyone who knows them as well as you do. You must remember," said Fanica Nicoulesco with an embarrassed laugh, as though he were confessing to a shameful malady, " that I've spent my whole life among books."

Serban said that he would speak to his mother. A few days later the covers were removed from the furniture in the ground-floor rooms of their house, carpets were beaten, vases and candelabra dusted. And on the eve of his departure Serban gave a party to which were invited both friends of his own age and a number of older persons, among them his great-uncle, Serban Lascari, Elvira Vorvoreano, Alexandra Sufana, Constantine Lascari, Titel Negruzzi, Prince Constantine Commeniu, General Ipsilanti (who was then paying court to Serban's mother), and finally—deferentially introduced to everyone by Serban— Professor Fanica Nicoulesco, who so favourably impressed the company that General Ipsilanti was quite jealous.

" For heaven's sake, Aristitza, who's that moth-eaten peda-gogue? Who invited him? Where does he come from? "

" He's one of Serban's professors, a highly distinguished man who may some day become a member of the Government. So do, please, be civil to him."

" Anyone would think I wanted to bite him. Do you imagine I never open a book, just because I'm a soldier? You may not realise it, but I was passionately keen on philosophy when I was young."

" Just what Victor Hugo said when he wrote *The Merchant of Venice*," said Serban's mother.

The general in his monocle darted a swift glance at her, sus-pecting that his leg was being pulled but not quite knowing how, and found it prudent to change the subject.

Meanwhile Titel Negruzzi, his face a fiery red, was gripping Serban by the arm and saying loudly:

" Take it from me, Serbanica, I'm the only person, the only blessed one, capable of understanding that scoundrel Nicoulesco. *Erstens und überhaupt*, as the Germans say—first and foremost I understand him because I understand what he's talking about, because I did two semesters at Tub—Tub——"

" Tübingen," said Serban composedly.

" That's it—Tübingen. How did you guess? You're getting quite bright. Tübingen, Bonn, Halle, Freiburg, I've been to all the places, I don't remember how many but I've got them all written down in my diary. So when it comes to philosophy, dear boy, you've only got to consult me. And I don't mind telling you that Fanica, he's quite a chap. The women go mad about him. One poisoned herself, another burnt herself alive, another went into a loony-bin and another swallowed a broomstick like Madame be Brinvilliers—you remember? You don't? Do you mean to say you've never read the writings of old Ma Sévigné? What the hell do they teach you at Charlottenburg? In my time——"

" Titel, you're plastered. Charlottenburg is where one goes to study engineering. And your time, as you call it, is only three years ago. But I'd like to know if there's any truth in those stories about women. You're so tight that you're bound to be exaggerating."

" What, me? *Mein lieber Schwann, du hast keine Ahnung!* You've no idea. And I suppose you think I'm exaggerating when I say that he's the confidential adviser of someone whose name I prefer not to mention. Well, I don't see why I shouldn't mention it—I mean, the King. On top of which he's a friend of Malaxa and his circle and the most influential of all the right-wing journalists. Do you mean to say you didn't know? "

" I don't read the right-wing Press."

" You prefer the left-wing, I suppose," said Titel Negruzzi, looking for more champagne.

" No. I don't read any kind of Press."

Serban turned away, having had enough of Titel. He looked at Professor Nicoulesco, who was standing with his mother, listening to her chatter with the most amiable of smiles. Had he a copy of the *Exercices* of Ignatius de Loyola in his pocket? *Keep it with you and you will accomplish whatever you set out to do.* Once again Serban was conscious of the vague feeling of unease which had assailed him at the sight of all the portraits of the professor hanging on the walls of his study. Suddenly he felt slightly sick. " I've had too much to drink," he thought.

2

Three elderly men seated at separate tables were immersed in the study of Greek manuscripts copied in Byzantium in the fourth century. A very thin, very pale young man was reading a musical score by Roland de Lassus and making notes in an exercise-book. A library-attendant in a grey smock was approaching with four heavy volumes.

Serban Romano sat bowed over a large in-folio opened at a sheet of sketches, among them a complicated geometrical design, a drawing of a tree with all its roots and leaves, and at the bottom a human arm, laid open to display the muscles in meticulous detail. Across the top of the sheet the artist had written an inscription in a small, angular, almost Gothic script, which was reversed and aligned from right to left. Serban picked up the mirror which he used to check the deciphered texts and read: " Oh, seeker after the nature of things, I do not praise you for discovering what Nature is accustomed to produce by herself; but you may rejoice if you understand the meaning of the things your own mind conceives."

Serban, whose head was aching after hours of sustained concentration, laid down the mirror and rubbed his smarting eyes. He stayed for a moment with them closed, breathing slowly and deeply; but the air of the library was dusty and smelt of decay.

What good was he doing? He knew now that the method of Leonardo da Vinci had been lost at the moment when its author had ceased to breathe. He had learned to know and love that unique being in the way in which one may love a mountain or a sea or a law of thermodynamics. Leonardo was a man whose mind had encompassed all natural phenomena, seeing through trees, rivers and living creatures to the physico-mathematical structure of the universe; he had invented engines of peace and

war, had painted on plaster and on canvas, sculptured marble and
cast bronze, had used the pen and the brush, as well with his left
hand as with his right, and had seen all things without illusion,
as though from a far, high place; like Nature herself, he had
taken a childlike pleasure in concealing his purposes behind an
enigmatic veil which might only with great difficulty be drawn
aside. " Nature contains countless meanings that have yet to be
discovered," Leonardo had written on a page of his notebook.
It was true; and the universe at this moment harboured within
itself the principles of the integration of all knowledge. Yes, but
the method—the method . . .

The method must be revised and adapted to the huge mass of
knowledge acquired since Leonardo's day. . . . Serban reopened
his eyes. The sun was shining outside. He closed the book, got
up and went silently out into the Ludwigstrasse, where he paused
for a moment, dazzled by the brilliance of the day. Cars and blue-
and-white trams glittered between rows of buildings copied from
the most handsome edifices of Rome and Florence. The library
was the Medici Palace; beyond it were the Farnese and the Pitti
palaces, and further still the Loggia dei Lanzi, and at the end of
the street a triumphal arch copied from the Arc du Carrousel in
Paris. Nothing was genuine except the double row of magnificent
poplars along the Leopoldstrasse, beyond the arch, and the
baroque towers, with their green cupolas, of the Theatinerkirche.
Serban was feeling dissatisfied with himself, jaded and over-
stimulated. He went to the fencing-school in the Theresienstrasse,
exercised for an hour, took a cold shower and then went to the
Faculty building to join the study-circle of Professor Herbstblom,
professor ordinarius of the history of philosophy. On his way there
he fished a sheaf of typewritten sheets out of his pocket bearing
the title *Dynamische Begriffe und dynamische Begriffsbildung bei
Jakob Boehme*—The Dynamic Concepts and Dynamic Formation
of Concepts of Jacob Boehme. He reached the lecture-room only
just in time, and the twenty students already assembled turned to
look at him. Harnischfeger, the albino, raised a hand in greeting:
his irises were pink like those of a rabbit, and he squinted and
had difficulty with his speech. The professor entered and asked
Herr Romano if he had prepared his thesis.

" Yes, sir."

" Then please read it to us."

Serban read his essay aloud, and when he had done so Harnisch-feger raised a hand for permission to speak.

" The reader has made intelligent use of our previous discussion," he said, " but he seems to have no new contributon to offer."

" Because I don't trust the original text," said Serban, rather ruffled.

Professor Herbstblom opened his eyes wide. Harnischfeger turned towards Serban, stiffly moving his whole body, and looked at him with interest.

" Why don't you trust the text? " the professor asked.

" Because it affords no criteria whereby the validity of the argument may be judged," said Serban. " How can I trust it when I have no means of verifying its premises? "

Outside the poplars rustled in the depressing breath of the *föhn*. Herbstblom was smiling. He had an ugly face that looked as though it had been punched into shape.

" What interests us in any system of philosophy is not its intrinsic truth but the beauty of its construction," he said.

Harnischfeger raised his hand again.

" One might add that even our friend here cannot utter a sentence that does not imply a metaphysical background, a series of premises which cannot be discussed separately and whose validity can only be assessed in relation to one another. If the premises are coherent in this sense we may either accept or reject them as a whole. But without them we cannot pursue any train of thought, even about the most everyday matters."

The other students murmured approval, and two girls in Tyrolean costume uttered little cries of rapture. Serban was about to reply, but Harnischfeger went on:

" Moreover that argument undermines any general philosophical system seeking to embrace reality as a whole. In our contact with the world we are bound to have recourse to a mythology. Mathematics, for example, are merely a more lucid part of the mythology of the twentieth century in Europe."

" But that's turning the world into a nightmare! " cried Serban. " How can one live in a world like that? "

" Philosophically speaking we can't escape from it," said the albino, serenely smiling.

Serban was silent, his face pale. The professor called for other views and a general discussion followed, gravitating round the sombre and confused theodicy of Jacob Boehme.

At the close Harnischfeger waited for Serban and said with a smile:

" Are you coming this evening? We shall all be there. We can go on talking then."

Serban nodded and went his way.

That evening, in the little restaurant Zur Hopfenperle, he was again made angry. Harnischfeger was there, Heinrich von Brederode, Rinaldo Fischer, Nita Ghita and a German whom Serban had not met before.

Serban had made the acquaintance of Heinrich von Brederode at the fencing-school. He was a short, slightly built young man with a hook-nose that was a little askew. Upon discovering that Serban was Roumanian he had told him that he was a cousin of Dietrich von Rabestein, whose mother's maiden-name had been Racovitza. One of Serban's great-uncles had married a Mademoiselle Racovitza. In consequence of this young Brederode had invited Serban to his parents' house in Swabia and Serban had invited him to Bucarest. Heinrich, a quiet, soberly conducted young man, was studying philosophy and the early Semitic languages.

Rinaldo Fischer, large, burly and fair-haired, was the son of a Leipzig advocate. He had happened to be sitting beside Serban one night at a concert, and after looking him over for some time had asked him tentatively what he thought of the performance. This had led to a general conversation about music which they continued over a drink in a café, and since then they had become the best of friends. Through Rinaldo, Serban had met a taciturn Englishman who was, it seemed, a painter, and who was one of the party that evening. Rinaldo also dabbled in painting, although he was reading law. He wrote poems and preferred Rinaldo to his baptismal name, which was Reinhold.

The German newcomer was bony, heavily built and red-faced, clad in a grey flannel suit, with close-cropped fair hair. He and Brederode called each other by their first names, Heinz and Ulrich, and addressed each other as " du," which meant that the stranger, too, must be of noble lineage, the descendant of some former captain of mercenaries.

As for Nita Ghita, he was a Roumanian with a Bucarest theology degree and a studentship in philosophy at Munich. The son of a prosperous farmer in the region of Constanza, he had been attending universities for six or seven years. His parents no longer sent him any money and he had contracted tuberculosis. He generally wore a little jacket buttoned up to his neck, like a theology-student. He had met Serban in the lecture-room and since then had scarcely left his side. Serban stood him a meal as often as he could, and Nita Ghita accepted this as a matter of course, being too unversed in the ways of the world to be surprised by the frequency of his invitations.

At the end of the meal Heinrich von Brederode's friend, the blond and rubicund Ulrich, called for the monumental glass beaker which, together with hunting horns and some silver goblets, adorned the chimney-piece in the restaurant. He had it filled with beer and emptied it at a draught. The Englishman did the same. Harnischfeger smiled, observing them with his pink cross-eyes, but did not break off his discussion with Brederode and Rinaldo.

" The hypothesis of a discontinuous structure of matter is absurd," he said. " Suppose the particles of matter to be like this——" He arranged some breadcrumbs on the beer-stained tablecloth. " How do you envisage their movement? You aren't going to tell me that it's a matter of contact and elasticity? "

Brederode stared at the crumbs, twisting the end of his nose. He picked one up and put it in another place.

" By the suppression of a particle at one point, its passage through nothingness and its reappearance at another point."

The albino sat thinking. " Yes, that would be the extreme of movement."

Nita Ghita said: " What you say to some extent conforms to Christian dogma, except that it presupposes a ceaseless process of creation and destruction in Nature, whereas according to the dogma there is only one act of creation and one of destruction— ' When the Angel shall stand with one foot on the land and one foot on the sea, and shall cry in a loud voice that the time is come. . . .' "

Brederode listened patiently. Rinaldo raised his glass to Nita Ghita.

" Splendid! So it seems that between the philosophical implications of micro-physics and the Revelation of St. John the

Divine there is a link which none of us suspected. Congratulations, my dear fellow. *Heil!* "

" That's enough of *heil*," said Brederode, without raising his voice.

" What do you mean? " asked Rinaldo.

" Yesterday Harnischfeger quoted Bergson in the study-circle, and old Herbstblom made a face and said, ' Bergson, as you know, is a Jew.' That was all. He simply washed out Bergson."

" I had never imagined that a metaphysical argument could be answered with an ethnological one," said Harnischfeger with a good-humoured laugh.

" It makes one sick! " said Brederode, banging his glass on the table.

" Old Herbstblom's a Nazi, didn't you know? " said Rinaldo. He turned, grinning, to the Englishman. " The best solution would be for Bavaria to become a British colony, wouldn't it, Jimmy? "

Jimmy, who had also had a good deal to drink, nodded and said placidly, " I daresay that's what'll happen in the end." He then lit his pipe and took no further part in the discussion.

In any case, it was at this point that Serban began to grow heated.

" You're all being too damned flippant," he said. " It is your German philosophers, since Schopenhauer, who are responsible for the fact that in these days nobody believes in anything at all. The four of us here have followed Muller's course on Nietzsche and discussed the *Umwertung aller Werte*, the revaluation of all values. No one attempted to oppose that lunatic and unworkable system of morality."

" Unworkable like any other moral philosophy," murmured the albino.

Ulrich, drinking again out of the glass tankard, said ponderously: " A philosophy for heroes and aristocrats."

Serban's cheeks were flaming. " But it isn't just a question of the lack of moral principles, although that's a disaster in itself. It's a matter of the lack of a *philosophia prima* of knowledge, dealing with the generalised forms of being—existence as such. What are we given except foggy and chaotic images? Heidegger? He hangs back at the last moment and won't accept the logic of his own position. Husserl? What are we to think of a man who

reduces all the achievements of the human mind, the broad conclusions and abstract principles which we have painfully arrived
at in two thousand years, to a mere string of psychological anec-
dotes? I'm not criticising them on philosophical grounds but
simply from the standpoint of the ordinary man who as an in-
dividual, as a member of a family and as a citizen, has need of a
metaphysics of being, a theory of knowledge and a code of ethics."

" And of aesthetics," said Rinaldo Fischer.

" Are we no longer capable of producing these? Because it's
no good pretending that the moral philosophy of Martin Heidegger
is any use to the citizen or the father of a family. The philosophers
hover on the edge of mysticism without having any more than a
bookish knowledge of what it means, and on the edge of religion
without being able to accept its fundamental dogmas with faith.
The more positive thinkers, such as Wittgenstein, impose strict
limitations on their thinking and, in effect, abandon the privilege
of being men; that is to say, of dominating the universe through
reason. Where are we to find the answer we need? "

Ulrich said with a challenging smile:

" Why not in Nietzsche? "

" But can one live according to Nietzsche's scheme of morals? "
demanded Serban hotly, but still with the courtesy of his good
breeding.

" If one is cast in the role of a master, a *Herrenmensch*," Ulrich
said.

They were all growing heated. Brederode and Harnischfeger
were rendered uncomfortable by what Serban had said, perceiving
in it an element of truth, something genuinely compelling. Rinaldo
Fischer grinned sardonically: to him it was all too ingenuous.
The Englishman was simply bored. As for Nita Ghita, he was
irritated by this elegant and wealthy young man who claimed to
be searching for the truth when the truth was self-evident, staring
him in the face. But it was people of another kind who saw it,
those with faith and fire in the bellies!

" I don't accept any kind of philosophy that applies to some
people and not to others," said Serban. " Are you claiming that
truth is not universal? "

Ulrich laughed offensively. " I'm afraid we're talking different
languages. Of course, one can't expect everyone to possess an
aristocratic mind."

Serban sat up straight and stared at him. " Shall I tell you what that word aristocratic means to me? It means magnanimity pursued to the utmost limit."

"I take a different view of aristocracy," said Ulrich coolly. " Perhaps I'm prejudiced, but they're ancient prejudices, handed down in my family for generations."

Serban was stung by the sarcasm but made no retort. Heinrich von Brederode came to his rescue, saying in German:

"*Red' kein Quatsch, Ulrich, der ist auch vom Adel*—he's an aristocrat too."

" Roumanian aristocracy!" said Ulrich, shrugging his shoulders.

" It's a damned sight better than the German aristocracy," said Serban, boiling over, although he was half inclined to laugh at the unphilosophical turn the argument had taken.

But Ulrich took this very seriously indeed.

" If you were German you would have to answer to me for that insult."

" He doesn't have to be German! " cried Brederode. " Go it, lads! This is splendid! "

" I'm entirely at your disposal," said Serban, reverting to his customary quiet manner.

" I'll second you," said Brederode, draining his glass. " I'll find the other second as well—don't worry, Serban."

" Are they going to fight? " asked the albino turning to Rinaldo Fischer.

" You needn't be alarmed," said Fischer with a hint of envy in his voice. " It won't be dangerous."

The party broke up, all in a highly excited state. Serban left with Nita Ghita.

" You're being silly," said Nita, taking him by the arm. " You know I like you. That's why I'm saying it. All this is childish. Why did you have too——"

" It was a matter of—of keeping face," said Serban awkwardly.

" Do you really think you can preserve our national prestige in that way? I like you, and that's why I hate to see you going adrift like you are. I think you're one of the rare specimens of your breed who ought to be on our side."

" What side is that? "

" Ours, of course. Don't pretend you don't know. But nobody's going to invite you. It's for you to ask to be received."

Serban was irritated. " And supposing I don't ask? "

Nita Ghita shrugged his shoulders. " Between us and the outsider," he said loftily, " there is a great gulf fixed."

" Well! " exclaimed Serban. " I asked you to dine with me. I hadn't realised that you were doing me an honour in accepting."

They both laughed.

" Those aristocratic attitudes don't mean anything to us," Nita said. " Either you're one of us, and we're all comrades and equals, or else you're outside and couldn't matter less."

" You'd better tell me more," said Serban, still half annoyed but prepared to listen.

" I think you're worth saving. There's stuff in you. You've the makings of a man, and we only want real men. You must realise that you can do nothing by yourself. You've got to be part of an order, a movement, a bigger thing than you are. I was thinking as I listened to you just now, ' He's looking for Truth, and the Truth was found two thousand years ago! ' "

" What truth? "

Nita Ghita raised a thin hand. " ' I am the Way, the Truth and the Light,' said the Lord! "

" What! Is that what it's all about? You want me to turn Christian? "

" You're one already, by the grace of baptism," said Nita emphatically. " But you're pursuing all kinds of heresies, driven by a devilish pride. You should seek the real truth. The Holy Fathers found it long before you, and they were thinkers on a far higher plane."

Serban hesitated before replying. " I find it difficult to accept the dogmas of the Church," he said a little reluctantly. " I'm trained in positive thinking. Don't forget that I'm a mathematician and an engineer."

" That has nothing to do with it. You've only got to look about you. All Europe is in process of renewal—it is taking on a new and younger face. And we Roumanians are in a state of profound upheaval. We're on the verge of conferring a stupendous revelation upon the world! "

" What revelation? " asked Serban in amazement.

Hollow-cheeked and long-haired, his breath smelling of cheap tobacco, Nita Ghita leaned towards him.

" We are the chosen people—the God-bringers! " he cried.

Serban stared. " The God-bringers! What on earth do you mean? And why should one race be the God-bringers more than another? Why particularly the Roumanians? "

" The ways of God are inscrutable. You overlook the dimension of depth in Roumanian culture. It is an active force which may be said to possess the attributes of Boehme's bottomless Abyss. The resurgence of our country under the sign of the Cross will infallibly take place before 1950. It will be a *total renewal* of the country—religious, political, social and racial."

" But not economic? "

" Yes, economic as well."

" I'd like you to explain a little more fully."

Nita's further exposition was far from clear. Apart from racial renewal, by the expulsion or extermination of the Jews, and social renewal by the liquidation of the Bolsheviks, it did not seem that his revelation had much to offer. Serban finally said in disappointment:

" My dear fellow, all this sounds remarkably like the German National Socialist creed, as preached by Rosenberg."

" A great thinker, it's a pity he's a heretic," said Nita; and unconscious of Serban's dismay he asked abruptly: " Do you know Professor Fanica Nicoulesco? "

Serban wondered afterwards why he should have answered this question with a half-truth. " I've attended his lectures," was all he said.

" He's a very remarkable man. You should try to get to know him personally. He can explain everything."

" He hasn't produced any serious work, nothing but journalism."

" What does that matter? His real teaching is verbal. There's no one like him. He's unique! "

(" Shades of Leonardo! " Serban thought to himself. " Is this another unique being—this word-spinner in Bucarest? ")

" Well, this is my house," he said, without offering Nita Ghita his hand. " If I were a Christian I might be tempted to point out that you talk about exterminating the Jews in the same breath as you talk about the Cross. You talk of vengeance in the name of a Man who was all love, mercy and forgiveness. I don't hold myself competent to expound Christian doctrine, but as a mathematician

I may say that I am unable to follow your reasoning, which seems
to me to be a kind of philosophical delirium."

" You'll be sorry for that piece of boyar insolence! " cried Nita
Ghita in a voice that echoed down the empty street. " We shall
meet again! "

Serban went unhappily to bed. The *föhn* was shaking the
windows. During the night the weather broke at last and the rain
that so long had been threatening began to fall. At eight the next
morning Heinrich von Brederode knocked on Serban's door and
got him hastily out of bed and into a taxi. They drove to a *salle
d'armes* with a linoleum-covered floor dusted with talc. Foils and
sabres arranged in trophies glittered on the walls. Serban took
no notice of these but concentrated his attention upon the fair-
haired young men who shook him by the hand, stiffly bowing
and clicking their heels.

" Pappenheim . . . Ravensburg . . . Callas. . . ."

To which he replied no less formally:

" Romano . . . Romano . . . Romano. . . ."

Heinz was solemnly intoning, " Graf von Pappenheim . . .
Baron von Ravensburg . . . Graf Callas . . ." and a string of other
names which two centuries before had stood for all Germany,
but now signified nothing whatever. Serban offered his hand to
Ulrich, who laughed in his face and ignored it. He let himself be
got ready. They took off his jacket, wrapped a thick bandage
round his neck, and rigged him up with an enormous mask and
chest-protector and gauntlets reaching to his elbows. In spite of
this, when, rapier in hand, he found himself facing Ulrich, he
had a sense of extraordinary physical lightness, as though he were
moving in a dream. " Well, we must go through with it. We must
try to rise to the occasion and not be laughed at," he thought,
without quite knowing what he meant by " we."

The order was given to begin—" *Meine Herren* . . . *zur Mensur*
. . . *los!* "—and Ulrich's rapier whistled through the air. Serban
parried at the last moment in quart—clang—cling-clang—cling-
clang—he riposted in quart, lunged and made a touch. To his
great surprise he saw blood flowing from Ulrich's cheek.

" Stop! "

Graf Callas separated them, congratulating both as he did so.
They took off their gloves and everyone shook hands, first the two
antagonists, then the antagonists with the seconds and then

the seconds with one another, while the blood of the duellists (Serban had been touched without noticing it) dripped on to the floor.

A young man in a white smock manifested himself, a medical student who was there to stitch them up. Wincing with the sting of surgical spirit Serban said, "If you don't mind, the finest thread you've got." He had no wish to carry a scar. But Ulrich demanded the coarsest thread and cursed as the operation was performed.

Heinrich von Brederode was delighted with the whole affair. "Splendid, splendid! Now let's all go and have plenty of beer!"

3

Parting from his new friends after much beer-drinking Serban wandered at random through the streets, smiling benevolently upon the passers-by. He strolled under the blossoming chestnuts in the gardens of the former royal palace, past tables at which girls in summer frocks and youths in leather shorts sat eating ices. Outside the Feldherrnhalle he paused, wondering whether to go to the Carlton or the Luitpold Café.

As he crossed the Karlsplatz he saw an American car outside the Hotel Regina with a Roumanian number-plate. Roumanians in Munich? He turned into the hotel, and entering the restaurant sought to guess the nationality of three people seated at one of the tables. The cut of the men's clothes suggested that they were either Roumanian or Italian—certainly not English. He went up to them swaying slightly, his body held stiffly, his eyes a little over-bright, with a large cross of sticking-plaster adorning his cheek.

"May I be allowed to join you for a minute? I can't tell you how glad I am to see you. I've no one to talk to. The only other Roumanian I know in this town, as I discovered last night, is quite different from me. I really am delighted to see you. Perhaps

I can be useful to you in some way. My name's Romano—Serban
Romano."

He bowed, but lost his balance in doing so and nearly fell.
One of the two men of the party put out a hand and steered him
to a chair while they all laughed. The other man, aged about
thirty, was looking hard at him. He murmured something to the
first man, who was older and olive-skinned, his general aspect
resembling that of a Pasha in the thousand-and-one nights dis-
guised as a gentleman. The young woman seated opposite the
Pasha was gazing at Serban with a friendly curiosity. She was
fair-haired and slender, clad in a tight-fitting grey tweed suit
with a long skirt and walking-shoes, and her manner conveyed
an impression of energy and forthrightness. She laughed undis-
guisedly, as though she and Serban were old friends.

" You look as though you'd been in an accident," she said.

" It's only that I've come from a *Biermorgen*, a morning beer-
party," said Serban, blushing.

" I didn't mean that, but——" she pointed to her cheek.

" Oh, I see," said Serban in embarrassment. " I cut myself.
I pushed my head through a window-pane and——"

" Look, Serban," said the younger man, " are you so tight
that you can't recognise your relations? I shall have to write to
Bucarest and tell them the kind of life you're leading."

Serban now realised that he was George Lecca, a distant cousin.
" Of course I knew you," he said, flushing more deeply amid the
general laughter.

" Well, I want to hear what you've been up to and how you got
yourself in this state," said George Lecca, and introduced the
others: " Monsieur and Madame Scarlat."

Serban, half rising, extended a rather limp hand. Madame
Scarlat, who was obviously twenty years younger than her husband, smiled as though she were particularly glad to meet him and
pressed his hand with unexpected warmth.

" Well, what's been happening? " asked George Lecca.

" I told you. I—I shoved my head through a window——"

" That won't wash, dear boy—I know too many Germans.
Are you really trying to collect duelling-scars? ·Such vanity!
It's the last thing I'd expect of a character like you. What's
the real story? I suppose you quarrelled with someone over a
girl? "

Madame Scarlat gave Serban a quick glance, and he said hastily:

" No, honestly, nothing like that. It's just that I got into an argument last night at dinner and——"

" Well, never mind," said Madame Scarlat. " You're no one to preach, George. Look at the scar on your own forehead. Isn't it true that you made yourself the talk of Madrid by being the first foreign diplomat to go in for bull-fighting since the time of Philip II? "

" Oh, that was just tact, conforming to local custom," said Lecca, embarrassed but also gratified.

" Well, I expect that's what Monsieur Romano was doing."

" All right, Valentine, you win. Serban, won't you show us the town? We're going on to Switzerland tonight. The Scarlats are on their way to Paris and I've got to get back to Madrid. What is there for us to see? "

" But everything, it's a wonderful town. In fact, life's wonderful altogether," cried Serban, and really meant it at that moment.

" The change that has come over him," said George Lecca. " I hardly recognise this young Romano. Well, come on—let's go."

Serban was filled with an unaccountable happiness. He waited, scarcely noticing, while Scarlat and Lecca paid their bill and gave their orders at the hotel desk, and then, taking Valentine Scarlat by the arm, led them off to the English Garden. The park with its noble trees, its lawns and its rides, seemed that day to be enriched with a special beauty as it shone beneath a bright sky in which an armada of clouds sailed slowly past, gold-tinted by the afternoon sun—a rich and turbulent sky, like that in old pictures of battle.

But presently, as they strolled by the lake watching the swans, there was a mutter of thunder over the beeches and the rain came down. The clouds merged and then scattered, disclosing through the curtain of rainfall a pale, china-blue sky, and a rainbow appeared to add a final touch to a scene as majestic and dramatic as a *concerto grosso* by Handel. The party ran for shelter beneath a tree. When the storm was over they walked back into the town.

Captivated by the charm of the day, Serban had talked without ceasing, and later he could not remember a word that he had said. He only knew that he had returned with the others to the Hotel

Regina, that George Lecca had embraced him, that Monsieur
Scarlat had shaken his hand with a nonchalant, protective air, and
that Madame Scarlat had smiled intimately at him, in kindness and
gratitude, and had turned to wave as the car drove away. Still in
a dream of happiness Serban drifted through the town and finally
came to earth in the Hopfenperle, where he found Brederode and
Ulrich, the latter with his face heavily plastered. He sat drinking
with them until the place closed—and to hell with the method of
Leonardo! He would have to begin all over again, and it was
going to be damned difficult. But first he must have a pause to
get his breath.

Some time after midnight, and again in his cups, he returned
to the house where he lived, entering by the *porte cochère.* A wide,
vaulted entrance-way led to the courtyard, with a door on the
right leading to the stairs. As a rule when he came in late Serban
had to press the minute-button, but tonight the lights were on.

He stood on the step of the door leading to the stairs, gazing
benevolently over the crowd of men assembled under the vault.
They were a curiously miscellaneous lot, all ages, shapes and
sizes, with felt hats, bowlers and cloth caps, but at one in the
shabbiness of their clothes. Serban blinked and said in Roumanian:

" You don't look very well, you people. You look like ghosts.
Were you waiting for me? "

One of them muttered in broad Bavarian, " He's soused," and
turned his back on him.

" You don't want to talk to me? " said Serban. " Well, never
mind." He pushed open the door and moving towards the stairs
exclaimed, " Why, there are more of them! "

There were indeed. Men were seated on the stairs or leaning
against the walls, pale-faced, with a look of despair in their eyes.
They gazed apathetically at him as he pushed his way past. His
rooms, in the Pension Wilhelmina, were on the second floor. But
the queue went higher still.

Serban woke the next morning with a severe hangover. He said
to the proprietress of the pension:

" Frau Bergmann, what was going on last night? What was
that crowd doing on the stairs? "

" They were waiting to apply for the job of dental-mechanic

The dentist on the fourth floor put an advertisement in the paper."

" But good heavens, are there that many dental-mechanics in this town? "

Frau Bergmann smiled faintly.

" Of course not. They hadn't any qualifications, they were just men out of work—decent, respectable men, Herr Romano."

" But why were they there at that time? It was about two in the morning."

" I know. The advertisement said to call between eight and nine. But it's a matter of getting there first, you see. Life's hard in these days for anyone who's out of a job." She sighed and then said: " Perhaps Hitler . . . He has promised to find jobs for every one. We're a hard-working people, we Germans—but what can anyone do when there's no work to be had? "

" But Hitler——" Serban began. He was going to say that Hitler had no economic policy, had never written a word on the subject, and that the stuff he talked didn't make sense.

" Yes, Hitler . . ." repeated Frau Bergmann dreamily. " Perhaps he'll do something. There's no one else." And she went off, walking with slow, short steps, like a half-starved old grey mouse.

A few days later, as Serban was walking along the Ludwigstrasse, he found the crowd suddenly thickening around him. Everyone seemed to be moving in the same direction, and he had to walk faster to keep pace. But after going a little further he was brought to a stop by the solid mass of bodies on the pavement, beyond which he could see a row of uniformed figures shouting furiously as they linked arms to form a cordon. A party of young men in black and brown uniforms came marching down the street, and after them, closely escorted by a half-circle of blond, pink-cheeked fanatics, there stumbled a wide-eyed man with a bruised and bloody face, his hair dishevelled and his clothes torn.

Voices in the crowd were shouting, " *Haut ihn z'samm' den Saujud!*—Beat him up, the Jewish bastard! " Serban stared in appalled fascination at the terrified figure, while a blue-eyed man at his side cried: " That's the way! That's the spirit, lads! " Others in the crowd glanced covertly at the speaker and slipped away without saying anything. Serban asked what the Jew had done, but no one knew.

After this Serban gave up regular attendance at Herbstblom's study-circle. There seemed to be no one to whom he could talk freely. One day he opened his heart to his fencing-master, old Van Knapen, who with his moustache, black bushy eyebrows and long hair looked like an Italian conjuror. The old man knew a little Roumanian.

" *Siguro, siguro che*, great misery," he said. " Great disaster, Monsieur Romano. This Germany is unhappy country. Ah, if I could go back to Roumania, so beautiful, so peaceful! My father made there the Cirque Sidoli, and I was young apprentice. Such happiness! "

" When was that? "

" In 1907. Roumanians, so friendly, such nice country. But in 1907 nice everywhere, all Europe. I go to Italy with no passport, only a few moneys in my pocket. Now is all over— finished—done for. . . . Take your foil, Monsieur Romano. *En garde!* "

Serban spent an occasional evening with Brederode and Ulrich. Like all Germans of good family they despised Adolf Hitler and considered that it was not at all the thing, thoroughly vulgar in fact, to go beating up Jews in the street. Ulrich said:

" In any case there are decent Jews. Well, take Horst Frank, for instance, who has a Jewish grandmother. He's a bit dark-skinned, certainly, but he's practically like one of us."

Serban had also given up going to the Hopfenperle. One sultry afternoon, being unable to stand the atmosphere of the library, where he was still peering over the notebooks of Leonardo, he wandered out into the streets. A dense crowd was gathered at a crossing, making it impossible to pass. Serban waited, listening to a deep distant murmur of voices and wondering where it came from. No one around him said anything. The people were craning their necks, trying to see past the black caps of the police cordon. Then a sound of tumultuous cheering came from the direction of the Leopoldstrasse and Serban found himself suddenly surrounded by a forest of outstretched arms. A man in shorts held up his child as though it were a sacrificial offering while he shouted his head off, his face distorted with a rapture that resembled frenzy. Serban caught a glimpse of Adolf Hitler, clad in a raincoat, standing bare-headed in an open car. He thought him singularly unattractive, with a dull, banal ugliness. The car passed out of sight and the crowd gradually dispersed in an atmosphere of spent emotion, as though at the end of a football-match.

During that autumn Serban passed nearly all his time at the library; but the big in-folios of Leonardo's notebooks could no longer satisfy him. And one afternoon he went back to the study-circle and took a seat on one of the benches, silent and out of sorts.

Heinrich von Brederode was defending his thesis on " The Concept of the Abyss " in Jakob Boehme, while Herbstblom, presiding, beamed benevolently over the intellectual acrobatics of his disciples. There were, however, a number of students present who did not join in the discussion except when called upon to do so. They were young people in modest circumstances, destined to become schoolteachers and, if they were lucky, heads of schools. It was from this group that a slight flurry arose.

Harnischfeger read a paper on " Neo-positivist logic, its relation to mysticism, and their reciprocal delimitation." He concluded by saying that the Boehme philosophy afforded no basis for empirical examination. It was a closed system, outside logic and of a different order, perfectly valid, but only in terms of itself.

He bent over his notes and Serban said loudly:

" So we aren't interested in the application of the system or its relation to reality—in other words, in its truth? "

" What precisely *is* reality? " asked the albino in a suave, sarcastic voice.

Brederode, smiling like a fencing-virtuoso secure behind his flourishes, added: " And what is truth? "

This was when the contretemps occurred. From the row of " non-speakers," as they were called, a round-headed young man with shabby clothes and large red hands got to his feet. He said with a deliberate simplicity in which there was an undertone of irony:

" Truth is the image of reality in our minds, an image capable of being verified in practice; and reality is the infinity of matter in space and time, comprising an infinite number of facts, *all of which can be known*."

Herbstblom looked hard at him and asked coldly: " Why do you find it necessary to tell us this? "

" Because it appears to me that there are persons present who

are unaware of the nature of truth and reality," said the young
man in a voice of mock-innocence.

Was he trying to lecture his own professor? Herbstblom began
to grow annoyed.

" You're simply a dogmatist," he said, " a man of blind faith."

" In a study-circle devoted to the doctrines of Boehme the word
' dogmatism ' seems to acquire a rather special philosophical
flavour. In any event, it is a word dear to the hearts of idealists,
who never cease to fling it in the faces of materialists."

" Do you happen to be a Marxist? " asked Herbstblom, looking
shrewd.

" I'm trying to deserve the title. I believe that historical and
dialectical materialism provides the solution to most of the
problems of our time."

Harnischfeger smiled in a superior fashion while Brederode
shrugged his shoulders. Herbstblom felt a certain tension in the
air.

" If this gentleman is a Marxist we have nothing to say to him.
We are here to talk philosophy. Let us return to the subject of
our discussion."

" The subject was—Truth and Reality, do they exist and what
do they consist of? " said the interrupter, grinning.

" Herr Wegener! " exclaimed Herbstblom. " If you will allow
me to say so, in this seminar I am the person who decides what
shall be discussed. The subject is—The relationship between
Logic and Mysticism and their reciprocal delimitation."

The proceedings ended without further interruption; but when
the session broke up Heinrich von Brederode and Harnischfeger
were amazed to see Serban Romano leave the lecture-room with
his hand on Wegener's shoulder. They exchanged glances. These
Balkan types were really extraordinary!

Serban and Gaspard Wegener sat sharing a meal in Serban's
room. After two hours of impassioned controversy they seemed to
have come to the end of their arguments. Serban refilled the
glasses and said unhappily:

" But still, it does mean revolutionary activity."

Wegener looked at him. " Are you rich? "

The blunt question was the more disconcerting in that it clearly
implied that this was at the root of Serban's dilemma, and he was

at a loss to find a straightforward answer proving that it was not. Was he quite sure that it was not?

He attempted to change the subject, but Wegener would not let it go. He said with a reassuring smile:

" A man capable of serious thought need not let his attitude be determined by his place in the economic scheme of things. He should be able to overcome his class-prejudice."

Avoiding his friendly gaze Serban got up and fetched another bottle of wine.

He could not come to terms with Wegener either, much as he would have liked him for a friend. He was a young man of courage and intelligence, gentle, widely informed, and with a solid mathematical training. " But it's a system of philosophy, not politics, that I'm looking for," Serban told himself.

Their last meeting occurred late one evening in the lecture-room. They left together, and the door with its air-compressor closed behind them as they went down the long, tiled passage. At the foot of the main stairway there was a bronze copy of Polycletus's spearman, seeming to stand on guard beside a marble plaque bearing the names of students and members of the Faculty who had fallen in the 1914 war, a long list. Here they paused, while the cupola over the hall seemed to float above their heads in a violet light and the marble stairs flowed down towards them like a petrified waterfall. Serban could find nothing to say, and Wegener had been increasingly taciturn during the past few days. As they moved towards the door he said abruptly:

" A true man of our time can only be a communist, part of the tide of history."

Serban coughed in slight embarrassment, and with displeasure at himself. They left the building, and as they paused again on the pavement in the gathering dusk Wegener turned towards him. There was distress in his eyes, the desire to say something important, weighty, perhaps unpalatable. But he was allowed no time to do so. A group of students was assembled near the doorway, and one of them exclaimed:

" Here he is! "

Serban found himself suddenly surrounded by youths in black mackintoshes with hats pulled over their eyes, among them Ulrich. The flow of pedestrians passed unheeding along the pavement, cars swept by along the street. " What do you want? "

Serban asked; but it was not him they had been waiting for. One of the gang stepped up to Wegener and said in a calmly ferocious voice:

" Well, and how goes the revolution? "

" It's going very well," said Wegener no less calmly.

" Filthy sod! " said the youth, and swung a fist at his jaw.

Wegener side-stepped and returned the blow, causing him to stagger back. Ulrich got a rubber truncheon out of his pocket and shouted:

" Let him have it, lads! "

More truncheons appeared. Serban was thrust aside and doubled up by an elbow in his midriff. He drew back a pace, but although his first instinct was to go to Wegener's assistance he did not do so. Instead he retreated further still, turned and made off rapidly, scarcely thinking what he did. He heard shouts at his back and the sound of running feet. Wegener passed by him, his body bent double, with blood running down his face. His attackers followed, panting and cursing in Bavarian dialect. At this moment a lorry loaded with factory workers pulled up by the kerb a short distance ahead, and a number of shadowy figures jumped out. A confused battle ensued.

After a minute or two Wegener's attackers came running back, hatless, with their mackintoshes in shreds, hotly pursued by the men from the lorry. Serban hesitated another moment and then turned down the nearest side-street.

The next day he made ready to depart. He booked a seat on the night train and was busy packing his bags when Frau Bergmann came to say that someone had called to see him. Before he had time to ask who it was Nita Ghita had thrust her aside and silently entered the room, looking thinner and more white-faced than ever.

" Are you going away? "

" Yes, I'm leaving."

Serban tightened the straps of his valise. Nita Ghita had a violent fit of coughing. He looked hard at Serban and said:

" If you're going to the West you'll stay there."

" I'm not going to the West. I'm going back to Bucarest," said Serban.

This news evidently pleased Nita, but his awkward titter, that of a man who has never learnt to laugh, was painful to hear.

" So you'll be seeing Fanica Nicoulesco. You will go and see him, won't you? And please don't think I'm angry with you. You're young and you're looking for God. You'll find Him with *us*, among *us*, there's no other way."

" I wish you wouldn't say things like that, they simply horrify me," said Serban, reaching on to the wardrobe for another valise.

" With us you'll be able to live a true life. You'll learn a new kind of ethics—the ethics of heroism and sacrifice—Roumanian ethics based on Roumanian truth! " Nita rolled the " R " in Roumania like a stage character. " Be sure you go and see him."

" What's your connection with Professor Nicoulesco? " asked Serban.

" Go and see him and he'll give you what you're looking for," said Nita, in a tone of such sincerity, such evident conviction, that Serban was dumbfounded. A thought passed through his mind—" The professor listened to me, raised objections, commented on what I said and on what other people had said; but he volunteered nothing of his own, nothing personal to himself. He talked of two fundamental truths which he did not tell me."

Nita Ghita was overtaken by another fit of coughing. When he had recovered he went on:

" You'll find brilliant men in our country, philosophers, theologians, sociologists. You'll end by being convinced that our nation is destined soon to proclaim its truth to the world."

" Truth has nothing to do with nationality," said Serban with a sigh. " It belongs to the universal order of things."

" No! We must have our own truth, belonging solely to ourselves—our own religion of Roumanian orthodoxy, our own Roumanian metaphysics, our Roumanian State purged of parliamentary corruption, and purged of Jews! That is the truth to which our people will presently give birth in blood and suffering —just as the Germans are giving birth to their own truth and the Italians have given birth to theirs."

" Are there many of you? " asked Serban.

" We are the leaven in the loaf," replied Nita Ghita. " We grow more numerous every year. And you will be one of us! "

Serban said no more. He called to Frau Bergmann, paid what he owed her and sent one of the maids for a taxi. Nita watched him, smiling.

" You're a preposterous little boyar," he said, " infatuated and absurd. But I'm fond of you. Only, you must be careful. If you don't prove yourself worthy of my affection you will die! "

" Why on earth should I die? "

" I'd kill you myself—with a pistol or a knife. We're entirely logical. You'll get your deserts, regardless of whether we love or hate you. We don't indulge in tepid, mediocre sentiments. Be worthy of our love! "

Serban turned to the door, feeling that he must get away quickly, escape from this man who made him feel physically sick. Nita Ghita stayed where he was, with his hands in his pockets.

" You're bursting with cash," he said. " Let me have a couple of hundred marks. Can't you see I'm half starved? "

Serban had only just enough money on him for his journey. He apologised, trying to explain, and Nita said with an acid smile:

" Never mind. We'll assume you aren't lying. If I die there'll be ten others to take my place. But don't forget, you've got to choose. You mustn't think you can escape! "

4

Upon his return to Bucarest Serban lived very quietly, avoiding every chance of meeting Professor Nicoulesco. He spent his days reading, but with little of his former eagerness. He did however write a critical study, which appeared in a philosophical review published in Halle, on *The New Scepticism in Contemporary Thought*. It was favourably commented upon in Germany and in Bucarest.

Late one afternoon towards the end of the summer Serban, clad in a pale-grey shantung suit, went out for a stroll. He had no particular destination. He walked with hands behind his back, his air of abstraction, knitted brows and lustreless eyes in marked contrast to the brightness of his attire. And at a moment when he was thinking, " I have got to find a solution, I mustn't accept defeat," Madame Valentine Scarlat appeared round a corner coming towards him. She did not look well, and was not very smartly dressed. She seemed unhappy. But at the sight of Serban her face lighted up and she greeted him with evident pleasure.

Serban bowed and smiled, somewhat embarrassed by the recollection of the state he had been in when they had last met. She asked him what he was doing and finally took his arm.

" Let's walk along the Chaussée. I'm feeling thoroughly wretched. You're so strong and vigorous—so different from the men I usually meet! " She looked admiringly at him with a clear-eyed directness that said more than her words.

They strolled together under the lime-trees of the Chaussée Kisseleff until it began to grow dark, and presently, as they passed the Châteaubriand, one of the most elegant restaurants in the avenue, Madame Scarlat gave a sudden shake of her platinum-blonde head and exclaimed:

" Oh, bother them all! Let's have dinner here." She added, laughing: " But you must promise not to drink too much! "

An hour later they were beginning to feel like old friends. Valentine Scarlat talked about the empty life she led, made up of bridge-parties and interminable gossip over cups of coffee.

" You don't know how I envied you when I saw you with that plaster on your cheek! I so longed to be a young man, playing rough games and fighting and getting drunk. Instead of which I'm a respectable married woman with a respectable husband and respectable friends whom I invite to respectable dinner-parties—and sometimes I have to invite the children as well, because they're as old as I am! Oh, sometimes it's more than I can bear! " Then she looked inquiringly at him, very like a child. " But perhaps you're respectable, too? "

" Yes. . . . I mean no, not in the least. Why should I be? Time enough for that when I'm past forty."

" How old are you, exactly? "

" Twenty-nine."

" And I'm twenty-three," said Valentine, with a gravity and sadness that were no less childlike. " But I can feel myself getting older every day. I'm beginning to look old. It's all on account of being so respectable."

Serban laughed.

" You're not to tease me," she said. " You mustn't be unkind. I know you're terribly intelligent and a great scholar. Anyway, that's what people say when—when your name happens to crop up. . . . But me, I'm just silly, or so everyone tells me."

After a number of similar meetings and increasingly surreptitious meals in out-of-the-way restaurants, they became lovers. At the beginning Valentine said:

" It's terribly wrong of us! "

Serban did not reply. He felt, indeed, that it was profoundly wrong. Finding him silent she said quickly:

" Never mind. We won't think about things like that."

Later she said: " At first I thought that it would just happen a few times and then it would be over. But now I think of you every minute we're apart. I'm falling more and more in love with you. I'm not myself any more, not a free person—I'm becoming your slave! "

And on another occasion: " Sometimes I try to imagine what it would be like if we were never to meet again, but I simply can't. It would be like dying. I can't picture it at all."

Utterances of this sort had a profound effect on Serban. He even went so far as to say to himself, " This, at least, is one kind of certainty." It was not enough, but he felt that it was a beginning.

He was deeply in love with Valentine. She was his first love, and, although he did not know it, his last. He forgot Leonardo, read nothing serious, sought out his friends, went to parties, theatres and concerts—anything to kill time until their next rendezvous.

He wanted her to get a divorce. Scarlat, her husband, was " dreadfully tiresome," and had lost interest in love-making after the second year of their marriage; in any case he had from the first proved distressingly inadequate in this respect. But Valentine was terrified of a scandal, and moreover she had a son, the fruit of their first year of marriage.

Plunging into the fashionable world, Serban became known as an amusing young man capable of the most engaging flights of fancy when he had had a few drinks.

" He's changed enormously for the better," said Titel Negruzzi. " Really he's splendid company when he's a bit lit up. And how right he is when he says that he can't be bothered to talk about politics and crises—Hitler, Mussolini, war and all the rest of it. Why do we have to let ourselves be obsessed by that sort of thing, as though we had nothing else in our heads? There's still art and literature and travel and so forth—why bother about anything else? Serbanica's dead right. But he always was a sensible chap, with more brains than most of us."

5

When Titel Negruzzi, being fairly drunk, used the word " cuckold " in connection with Valentine's husband, Serban felt his heart stand still. He had to keep a tight grip on himself; but it soon became apparent, from Titel's subsequent remarks, that he was not the person referred to. If Titel was right, Valentine was deceiving him as well as her husband. His first reaction was one of utter disbelief.

" You say Scarlat's a cuckold? "

" My dear boy, and how! Horns a foot high. It's a wonder he can still keep his hat on his head. Cut to me, dear boy," said Titel, passing the pack.

Serban cut the cards with a hand that shook, and Titel began to deal.

" His wife . . ." said Serban. " That pretty little thing—Valentine . . ."

" Oh, she was pretty as a picture when she came back from Switzerland, just out of finishing-school. Now she's beginning to look like a horse. No charm at all, but madly keen on you-know-what."

" Really? " Serban was now very pale.

" My God, yes. . . . Hey, what are you doing? Haven't you really got any hearts? "

" I'm sorry. . . ."

" That's better," said Titel. " One time I was in Capsa's, and I saw her across the street, skipping along on high heels dressed up to the nines. She went into that house opposite, next door to the telephone-exchange, the one where there's a brothel on the fourth floor—a *maison de rendezvous*, I should say. You must know the place."

" I've heard of it," muttered Serban, with his eyes on his cards. " Well? "

" Well, that's all. I waited to see how long she'd stay there. She came out about three-quarters of an hour later, not a hair out of place, and off she went."

Serban had the feeling that his heart had started to beat again after a long pause.

" And because of that you think she's nothing but a layabout ? "

He was enormously relieved, and Titel looked at him in surprise.

" But what more do you want? Isn't that enough? How many times does a woman have to go to a place like that to be a layabout? "

" You're talking as though you actually saw her go into that particular place," said Serban harshly. " But there are six floors to the house. It's full of offices and apartments."

" You've lost, Serban. You're playing like a fool tonight. Aren't you going to shuffle? "

" Do it yourself," said Serban, throwing the pack on the table. " You're like a gossiping housewife."

" No, but seriously, I went across and had a word with the concierge. I asked him if he'd noticed a platinum blonde in a grey suit. . . . Serban, aren't you going to cut? "

" Go on with what you're saying."

" I don't know what's got into you. I thought you were a good loser. All this fuss about a hundred lei——"

" What did the concierge say? "

" Well, he didn't exactly put it into words. He just winked and leered, the old swine. Concierges are all crooks, besides being police narks. . . . But now what are you doing? What on earth's the matter with you? "

" I don't know. I think I'll be going home. Good night."

For a time when he got home Serban paced his bedroom; then, feeling the need of space, he went downstairs and opened all the communicating-doors between the reception-rooms. He spent some hours striding up and down those vast, chilly apartments with their furniture in dust-covers, the carpets rolled and the chandeliers wrapped in tissue-paper. He would have to see her

and get to the bottom of this business. Titel was a notorious liar.
A nice enough chap, but the sort that would say anything for a
laugh. Anyway, he had been drunk. He was capable of inventing
the whole story simply on the strength of having seen Valentine
go into the house, which she might have done for a dozen reasons.
As for the bit about the concierge, the man might have winked
out of sheer bloody-mindedness, just to take a rise out of a well-
dressed young man keeping tabs on his girl-friend. . . .

Serban marched up and down the empty rooms and suddenly
came to a dead stop as a thought occurred to him—" She's been
deceiving her husband, so why not me?" . . . He went on walking,
but more slowly now, and presently he dozed off on one of the
covered couches.

He rang Valentine next morning before she was awake. When
finally he was able to speak to her, he simply said that he must
see her as soon as possible. Valentine, unsurprised, said that she
would come at five that afternoon.

She arrived looking upset, kissed him quickly, and as she
undressed began to talk about the strikes that were spreading
throughout the country.

" Everybody's very worried. We had some high-ups to lunch
today, and they were saying that this was just how it started in
Russia—strikes and strikes and strikes, and then . . . Oh, it would
be too terrible! Darling, come and kiss me!" Then she looked
at him and said: " But what's the matter with you? Aren't you
well? Are you tired?"

" It's nothing," said Serban.

He took her in his arms, but with little happiness. Even if
what Titel had said was a pack of lies, it seemed that something
had been destroyed. The innocence, the first unspoilt rapture of
their love, this was gone.

Later, as Valentine lay gazing dreamily at the ceiling, he asked
with his eyes on her:

" Do you happen to know anyone living in the house opposite
Capsa's, just before you get to the Rue Sarinder?"

" I don't think so," she said, still staring at the ceiling.
" Why?"

" Well, this is what Titel Negruzzi told me last night."

He repeated it all without ceasing to watch her, feeling that
now he must discover the truth. A flush or a paling of her cheeks,

the merest flicker of her eyelids, was all that was needed. But Valentine gave no sign. She did not even turn her head to look at him. She listened in silence and then said:

" And a man like that has the cheek to go accusing other people! "

A great weariness overcame Serban. " What do you mean? "

" A chronic drunk and man who goes in for parties with half a dozen women at a time—they do the most disgusting things."

" How do you know? " asked Serban, startled.

" There's no secret about it. Everybody knows the sort of thing Titel Negruzzi and his friends get up to—Petrigor Znago-veano, Cesar Lascari, Trixi Comnène and all that lot. They're unspeakable. And then he goes slandering other people! "

" So it isn't true? "

" Did you really think it was? Is that what you've been worry-ing about? My poor darling! " said Valentine with calm.

She was not outraged, not even angry. Yet it seemed that she knew all about the pastimes of Titel and his set. How did she know? And how coolly she had answered! . . . Serban thought of this, and then he thought: " But why shouldn't she be telling the truth? I'm jealous and suspicious. Why can't I trust her? "

6

Early the next morning Serban went out and bought an automatic pistol, and having done so stood undecidedly on the pavement. Was Valentine telling the truth, or wasn't she? People were clustered together in agitated groups, and the newsboys were dodging across the street between cabs and private cars. Suddenly realising that something was going on, Serban looked about him. A procession was passing, consisting of women in shawls with baskets, marching arm-in-arm in rows of eight or ten, and loudly talking and laughing, although their cheeks were blue with cold. There seemed to be an enormous number of them. At the end of a quarter of an hour they were still coming. They carried red-and-white banners, and called to the onlookers, " Why don't you join us ? Don't stand doing nothing ! Help us to get enough to eat! " They passed on without waiting for any reply, impelled forward by the hundreds behind them, no less noisy, gay and resolute.

" They're the cigar-girls from the Belvedere factory," said a man in a fur cap standing beside Serban.

Another man said: " Are they on strike too ? "

" New strikes are starting all the time," said the man in the cap; and a sturdy girl in the procession shouted: " Come on! Don't leave us to fight alone! "

Serban started slightly. The girl seemed to be looking straight at him. He had a feeling of terrible disquiet. " Are they justified or not? " he thought, gazing with dismayed eyes at the endless column. He was afraid to answer the question, just as he feared to answer the question about Valentine.

He hailed a taxi and told the driver to take him to the outer boulevards, where the factories were. The man was so astonished that he had to repeat the instruction. Serban was very tired. For some minutes he lay back in the cab; but then he leaned forward and looked out of the window.

The crowd was growing thicker. Increasingly compact groups of workers in leather jackets were obstructing the traffic and blocking the side-streets. The cab was forced to stop and the driver blew a long blast on his horn. They went on another hundred yards and then had to stop again. Serban finally got out and continued on foot, pushing past the groups of demonstrators.

" Watch out! Out of the way, everyone! Here comes the soup! "

A party of large, heavily breathing men went by carrying a steaming cauldron, and a minute later another cauldron followed, borne by muscular arms and heralded by shouts. A short distance ahead there was a high iron fence surrounding a factory, and Serban worked his way towards it through the surging crowd. A factory-siren was blowing, a shrill, ear-shattering blast.

" You can't bring that stuff in. Keep moving! Get back! " shouted a police-officer, stretching out his arms to intercept the soup-cauldrons.

The bearers exchanged glances and withdrew a little way. A

sudden clamour arose at another point along the fence, where some people started trying to climb over. Seeing this, the officer dashed in their direction, ordering his man to follow. The nearer portion of the fence was thus left unguarded. The soup-bearers hurried forward, made a " back " and hoisted the cauldrons over the fence, where they were grasped by grim-faced workers on the other side.

The police came running back, sweating and cursing, furious at being tricked. The soup-bearers were laughing even while they dodged their truncheons. The siren was still wailing. On the other side of the fence the sit-down strikers had gathered round two or three men standing on a stack of timber. One was addressing them, gesticulating with clenched fists. Jostled here and there in the crowd, Serban Romano was profoundly impressed by the solidarity of the workers, their resolution and their gaiety; but he was, he could only be, an onlooker.

A man in a trench-coat had climbed on top of a wall and was surveying the crowd. He seemed to make a signal to someone, and then he vanished. Two workmen passed by.

" The place is lousy with coppers," one of them said.

" Like this bloke," said the other, looking at Serban. " What are you doing here, mate? "

" Nothing," said Serban, and turned away and left. He thought suddenly of the automatic in his pocket, bought only an hour before. If the men had found it on him no one could have blamed them for assuming that he was an agent provocateur and beating him to a pulp. The man in the trench-coat had certainly been a police-agent. There must be dozens about.

When he arrived home he took out the automatic and, not knowing what else to do with it, put it away in a drawer and then forgot about it. That evening he went to call on his mother, having nothing better to do, but found that she was out. His stepfather was attending an emergency session of Parliament. Serban had no wish to go to his club for fear of meeting Titel Negruzzi and hearing more of things that he preferred not to know about. He decided to go to Serban Lascari's house in the Rue Culmea Veche where there were bound to be a lot of people, which would spare him the necessity of thinking. He went on foot, glancing absently at the detachments of gendarmes marching in close formation along the streets.

A number of cars were drawn up at the kerb outside the house in the Culmea Veche, and a policeman was keeping watch over them and chatting with the drivers. A man emerged from the house as Serban approached it, and at the same moment a Rolls with a coat of arms on its doors and a flag on its radiator drove into the courtyard. A footman seated beside the chauffeur jumped out and opened the door. The man got in and the car drove off.

The big french-windows were ablaze with light. Serban walked up the steps, very conscious of the fact that on the outskirts of the town the factory-siren was still wailing, crying its defiance into the night. " What do they want? What do they complain of? " Serban asked himself, and knew the answer without having the courage to put it into words. Profoundly depressed he handed his sable-lined cloak to the footman in the hall.

In the salon ladies and gentlemen in half-evening dress were talking excitedly, the words " strike " and " preventive measures " being constantly repeated. Vasilesco-Rimnic, the minister, was laughing loudly, standing with a glass in his hand under a chandelier which cast a yellow light on his bald patch.

" Dear lady, it's nothing for you to worry about. Go on dancing and enjoying yourself and leave it to us politicians to deal with the situation. . . . How does it strike you, *cher maître*? "

" I'm not a politician," replied Professor Fanica Nicoulesco serenely.

At the sight of Nicoulesco Serban had stopped short, so taken aback that for the moment he forgot his private troubles. The professor was looking as though he had passed his whole life, glass in hand, in the houses of the rich. He was better dressed than the minister, and his slight figure, his thin, pale face and white hair, were in striking contrast to the latter's flushed cheeks, bald head and enormous stomach.

" I'm the merest bookworm," he said, smiling and modestly lowering his hypnotic eyes.

Vasilesco-Rimnic also smiled, with a sort of envy and impotent hostility.

Serban, standing apart, watched while Serban Lascari and his son led the professor aside and began talking to him in a fashion very different from their usual attitude towards intellectuals, whom ordinarily they never invited to the house, and for whom they professed a polite but absolute disdain. Meanwhile General

"Telescope" Ipsilanti, the brother of Prince Bubi, had approached Vasilesco-Rimnic.

" Well, what are we going to do, my dear minister? " he asked in a voice of indulgent bonhomie, turning the monocle upon him. " My frontier guards are getting sick of being confined to barracks. They're used to an open-air life. How much longer are you going to keep them here? "

" Don't worry, General. The crisis will be settled tomorrow."

" I'm very glad to hear it. They've been talking about this damned crisis for years. A strong government would have settled it long ago."

" I didn't mean the general economic crisis," said the minister. " That's something we can't control—any more than the British or the Americans, for that matter. I meant the crisis in our own country, the state of industrial unrest."

Serban Romano was trying to catch the professor's eye. He now desperately wanted to talk to him, feeling that he was the only man with whom he could discuss the questions and uncertainties by which he was so oppressed. Fanica Nicoulesco gave him a passing glance, smiled and went on with what he was saying.

". . . Clearly it is a conflict between two philosophies, rationalist, materialist and atheistic Marxism on the one hand, and on the other hand European Christianity, which is idealistic and mystical. But at the same time it is something like the reverse—a conflict between a mass movement which also wears the aspect of a religious faith, and State necessity, cold, logical and almost scientific. It is the communists who foster the romantic concept, whereas our own approach is one of pure realism, outside good or evil. But that is a machiavellian position that cannot be openly acknowledged in face of the peasants, who understand nothing but their ikons, or the mass of workers and small shopkeepers whose minds are filled with prejudice."

Old Lascari, his eyes sparkling with alertness, turned in his gilt armchair and said with his shrewd Greek smile:

" So it might be better to foster another kind of romanticism— perhaps mystique is the right word—which for the time being, at least, could do us no harm? "

Cesar Lascari laughed, and the professor replied:

" I see I am dealing with men of intelligence. I need say no more. You have understood what is in my mind."

" I shall take the first opportunity of talking to the King," said Serban Lascari, writhing his fingers. " Don't you think it is time you made your peace with his Majesty? "

The professor looked at him but said nothing. The old man smiled benevolently.

" You don't answer, Professor."

" I shall be most happy if you can prevail upon his Majesty to alter his last decision affecting me."

" You two should be reconciled. It's obvious. What exactly happened? I have an idea that it was a friend of both of you who made the trouble."

Fanica Nicoulesco made no reply. He tried to change the subject, but Serban Lascari was determined to get at the truth.

" Do you still bear a grudge against Monsieur Vardala? "

" I bear no grudge against anyone," said Nicoulesco in a detached voice.

" But it seems that Vardala, who is jealous of your growing political influence, has managed to turn the King against you."

" That is simply a rumour."

After a brief pause Serban Lascari said: " It was foolish of the King to lose a man like yourself."

" Thank you."

" You're invaluable, and of all the men I know I find your views the most instructive. I'm not trying to flatter you. Beware of the evil eye! " Serban Lascari chuckled, like an old, experienced horse-trader who knows more than he lets on.

Serban had ceased to listen. He was thinking again of his own problems, in something like panic. Eventually he contrived to draw near Fanica Nicoulesco and murmur in his ear:

" I should very much like to come and see you."

The professor gave him an inquiring glance.

" By all means. I've moved, by the way."

He gave him the address, and Serban said: " I'd like it to be as soon as possible."

" Whenever you like."

" Could I come tonight? "

The professor looked startled but said: " Very well. But make it after midnight. I'll expect you then."

He turned back to the two Lascaris, who had now been joined by General Ipsilanti.

Serban left soon afterwards and walked towards the centre of the town. The factory-siren was still wailing in the distance. The streets were almost deserted, and the few hurrying pedestrians were being held up at the intersection to have their papers inspected by police-officers with armed gendarmes in support. An occasional large car rolled smoothly past, in which one might catch a glimpse of distinguished grey heads or women in full evening dress; but these were not stopped by the police. In the main thoroughfares there was a tramp of marching feet and the spectacle of contingents of cloaked and helmeted gendarmes, moving like spiked monsters under the gleaming points of their bayonets. Serban hesitated, wondering how to pass the time before he went to the professor's house. Despite the risk of meeting Titel Negruzzi, or perhaps because of it, he decided to go to Capsa's.

Titel was not there. Serban found an unoccupied table and, calling for brandy, emptied his glass without looking at the people round him. But he could not shut out the voices.

". . . The Belvedere factory's on strike, and I'm told the textile workers are coming out tomorrow. . . . It's a concerted movement—anti-Nazi. . . . Then there's the trouble at the central power-station, they're planning to cut off the electricity supply. . . . I thought the Army had occupied the power-station? . . . Not yet, but it's going to. . . ."

A gust of cold air caused Serban to look round. A man who had just entered was standing by the door, divesting himself of his overcoat and the fur cap which protected his bald head. Rubbing his hands together he nodded to one or two people and looked round for somewhere to sit. All the tables were filled except Serban's. The newcomer came towards him.

" Good evening, Romano. Do you mind if I join you? "

" Please do," said Serban.

The man was Nicolas Prodan, an old acquaintance in the sense that Serban had met him in the fashionable salons to which his birth gave him the right of entry, but from which he had been gradually excluded because of his political activities. He was something over forty, the son of an impeccably " correct " cavalry colonel and the grandson of a man who had gone in for " red " politics in the days when liberalism was regarded as red; that is to say, round about 1870, when there had still been revolutionaries and republicans in Roumania. His great-grandfather had been one of the revolutionaries of 1848. During three generations the spirit of revolt in that family of small landowners, book-lovers and art-lovers, had gradually died down, to re-emerge in Nicolas Prodan. Physically on the small side, he was sturdily built, muscular and vigorous, with a notable gift for political journalism. He had started his career as a young man by publishing articles about the King (Carol I, of Hohenzollern) containing truths of a kind that are better left unuttered unless the writer is prepared to risk his neck. Being constantly threatened with arrest he had gone to Russia in 1918 to meet Lenin and become acquainted with the workers of Petrograd. He was a friend of Barbusse and Romain Rolland and he had visited Gorki. He sat down, still rubbing his hands, and beckoned to the waiter, whom he had known for twenty years.

" Costica, bring me a really hot grog, I'm frozen." Then he turned his keen, penetrating gaze on Serban. " Well, have you been there? "

" Where? "

" Where? To the only place where there's any real humanity left in Bucarest—the factories and the homes of the people who make the things we live by. What else is there to do except vegetate—rot—die on one's feet? I can see what's happening to you, Serban. You'd better listen to what I have to say."

All this came pouring out of him, as though he had summed up Serban at a glance. He went on in a voice of absolute assurance:

" It's time you pulled yourself together. The place of every honest man in these days is at the side of the workers. They're the ones who matter, the indispensable men of our century, and they're suffering appalling hardships—thanks to people like these! "

He had said it loudly, with a contemptuous flourish of his arms at the other customers which caused a few heads to turn indignantly towards him.

" You're an intellectual. Your business is to look for the truth and find it and proclaim it. It is a duty that has been much neglected in these last years. Why don't you do it? "

He leaned across the table.

" Why don't you write an article saying what a thinking man feels about the callousness and cynicism of the people who let that siren go on wailing while they're mobilising their troops to drive the workers out of the factories? You should be writing and speaking—acting! At this moment there are only two possible courses—either you fight with the strikers or you help to destroy them. You should find out something about the people who are helping them, small people of modest means, clerks, shop-assistants, scribblers, all sorts, queuing up with baskets of food to give them a chance to hold out. And meanwhile the people in this place sit round drinking their coffee and pretending it's no business of theirs. They're really fighting against the strikers, and in their hearts they're hoping to destroy them."

The electric bulbs flickered at this moment, and then, amid a sudden hush, all the lights went out.

" So the men at the power-station have stopped work! " Nicolas Prodan's voice exclaimed in the silence. But his triumph was short-lived. After a minute or two the lights came on again.

" You know what that means, don't you? " Prodan said harshly. " Can't you picture the worker's hand on the switch, and the soldiers crowding in and the bayonet at his back—and the fight that's probably going on at this moment, the shattered skulls, the blood and guts? Simply in order that these gentlemen in Capsa's may go on drinking undisturbed! "

He glared again at the smooth, sleek crowd around them, and a powerfully built young man shouted, rising to his feet:

" You shut your mouth, you bloody Bolshy, or we'll stuff it with earth! "

His name was Christian Tell and like Nicolas Prodan he was descended from the revolutionary leaders of 1848; but unlike him he had become a leading Fascist. Prodan laughed jeeringly and said:

" It doesn't matter what you do to me—you can't stifle the revolutionary idea by stuffing it with earth. It will beat you in the end. Can't you hear the bell tolling for you outside? Don't you know what that siren means? "

There was a general uproar. " The man's mad! He's a Bolshevik! He ought to be shot! "

Christian Tell thrust aside his chair and came towards them with clenched fists, and Prodan sat calmly and scornfully awaiting him.

" The great-grandson of Tell," he said. " The Christian who

doesn't believe in God, the European who preaches tribal warfare, the civilised man who rewards murderers, the book-collector who advocates book-burning in the streets. Well, come and get me! But I shall see you wiped out in the end."

He sat with his arms folded while Tell stood hesitating over him, his fists still clenched. Serban Romano could stand the strain no longer. He rose, snatched up his overcoat and left. Out in the street someone gripped him by the arm.

" You, where are you off to in such a hurry? " But then the voice changed. " Why, it's Serban! But this is splendid! Where are you going? "

It was Titel Negruzzi, with a white scarf round his neck and a cane in his hand.

" I don't know where I'm going," stammered Serban. " I've got to talk to the professor. I wish to God that siren would stop."

" What professor? Do you mean Fanica? Is that where you're going? Well, that's fine—I'll come with you," said Titel.

" But he isn't expecting you," Serban said weakly.

" Who cares? I take it he *is* expecting you? You can say you insisted on bringing me. I'd particularly like to come. That chap gets more interesting all the time. He's just been made Balkan representative of the Siemens factories in the Krupp-Thyssen group, did you know? To say nothing of *Motorenwerke Augsburg-Nürnberg*, *Rheinmetall* and the *Allgemeine Elektrizitäts Gesellschaft*! Not bad, eh, for a professor of metaphysics? He's quite a chap. They say his mother was a fortune-teller, or a witch, perhaps. There's no end to the stories about him. It seems that Despina Ipsilanti fell for him in a big way—she's always been half mad, of course—and when the old fox wouldn't play, and I expect he's impotent in any case, she doused herself with petrol and set herself alight. And she isn't the only woman who's lost her head over him, not by any means. He's a public menace, old man Fanica. He's just bought himself a new house and I'm very curious to see what it's like inside. What sort of taste does a professor have, to say nothing of a professor of metaphysics? Terrible, I expect, but I'd like to see. What do you think of all these troops in the streets? But the showdown isn't going to be tonight. I'm delighted I ran into you, Serbanica. I've always been fond of you. You're not just a frivoller like the rest of us. You're deep. You take me into a different world, the world of

ideas and things that matter, and you needn't think I'm saying
that just because I'm drunk, in fact if I was really drunk I probably
shouldn't say it. But what the hell! Life wouldn't be worth
living if we always had to watch every word we said. We shouldn't
be able to talk at all. We shouldn't be able to do a damned thing,
make love or business or politics, and our relations with A.M.G.
and *Motorenwerke Augsburg-Nürnberg* would be a lot less cordial,
and that bloody siren keeps on blowing and if it goes on much
longer, old boy, it'll be the end of serious conversation. I say, I *am*
glad to see you! . . ."

Titel, with his hat on the back of his head and his eyes affectionately beaming, was in an astonishing state of euphoria. Serban
was now anxious to get rid of him, but in his distressed and preoccupied frame of mind he could not think of a pretext for doing
so. He was desperately tired, having scarcely slept for forty-eight
hours, and almost at the end of his tether. There seemed to be
nothing for it but to take Titel with him, and then, at a pinch, he
could find some excuse to talk to the professor in private. Anyway,
it was still an hour to midnight. If they went there at once Titel
might satisfy his curiosity about the inside of the house and depart
before the professor returned home.

They arrived arm-in-arm. The house had walls of grey *calcio-
vecchio*, a Gothic doorway, windows flanked by small, convoluted
pillars in the Venetian manner and a roof of Italianate tiles.
Above the threshold there was a coat of arms carved, after the
Spanish fashion, in the stone, and a Moorish lantern. A manservant, having surveyed them through a small grill, opened the
door.

" Good evening, messieurs. The professor telephoned to say
that you would be coming and to ask you to have the goodness to
wait for him."

Serban in his state of exhaustion paid little attention; but as
they entered the hall, floored with black and white tiles and
furnished with carved wooden chests and X-shaped chairs, Titel
murmured:

" It sounds as though Fanica was expecting someone else
besides you. . . Splendid! We'll play a joke on them."

Serban did not understand. Mechanically he allowed himself
to be shown into a big library around which ran a gallery some
ten feet above the floor. The indirect lighting from the cornice,

bathing the room in a subdued light, left the books along the walls almost in darkness. Serban was about to drop into one of the big leather armchairs when Titel took him by the arm.

" Let's go up and look round," he said with a chuckle that meant nothing to Serban.

He dragged him up on to the gallery, where there were books stacked on the floor. Serban, drowsily stumbling, knocked over one of these piles, and Titel picked up one of its calf-bound volumes and read:

" *Patrologiae Cursus Completus*—Migne. . . . He must have just bought these, he hasn't had time to arrange them on the shelves. . . . Here, you sit on this chair. We'll hide and give him a fright when he comes! " Titel crouched on the floor of the gallery and peered down through the balustrade. " Not much of a dump, is it? Just a ready-made new-rich house, not what you'd call a portrait of Fanica. Hullo—he's coming. That must be him at the front door. Keep quiet till I give the signal and then we'll both shout 'Stick 'em up!' ' "

He had spoken with his face close to Serban's, his breath reeking of alcohol. Serban uttered a murmur of protest, trying to get to his feet, but Titel pushed him back and frowned at him to keep quiet. They heard the sound of voices outside, and the professor entered the library with two men. Serban, acutely conscious of the absurdity of his position, again tried to rise and was about to say something when he was struck dumb by the fact that he had suddenly recognised one of them. It was Nita Ghita, looking more pale and wasted than ever, his eyes sunken and feverishly glowing, his hands trembling, seeming in the grip of some overpowering emotion. The other man was also comparatively young, with a short, muscular neck and a small head surmounted by tight rolls of hair like a Greek statue, that of Antinous; but his face was bony and hard, with a low, narrow forehead and pointed chin, and there was a strange remoteness in his manner.

The professor pointed to two chairs with a gesture of extreme courtesy, almost bowing. From the first words that were uttered Serban and Titel realised that something peculiar and remarkable was taking place. Nicoulesco was looking at the two young men with a kind of tenderness, and when he spoke it was in a calm and solemn voice. Nita Ghita sat with his quivering hands clasped tightly together, while his companion, now with a look of absolute devotion, never took his eyes off the professor.

" We wanted to talk to you first—before . . ." said Nita Ghita, speaking with evident difficulty.

" I shan't attempt to thank you, because you and I are one," said Professor Nicoulesco. " I suffer for you in your suffering. Kant, my friends, knew in his time what we are now beginning to learn. He wrote: ' The only motive principle of man is pain. Pain precedes all pleasure. Pleasure is not a positive thing, it has no existence of its own.' "

The young man with the curled locks said nothing but maintained a posture of terrifying intensity, as though he were carved in wood. Nita Ghita said in a low voice:

" That is a Christian concept. We are born to suffer and to find salvation through suffering."

" Yes," said the professor, " and bourgeois democracy in its moral decay seems to ignore the fact that the most terrible form of suffering is crime—*for the one who commits it*. . . . The conscience of the criminal must be fortified, for the criminal is a strong man, stronger than his fellows. Indeed, we need to remember that we instinctively despise the man who is not capable, in appropriate circumstances, of killing a man. Only the circumstances can determine whether murder is evil. It is not an evil *in itself*; and that which does not exist *in itself* does not exist at all; it has no transcendency, no absolute truth."

A silence followed these words. The professor continued:

" And I maintain, my children, my dear young friends, that from the moment when you have accomplished an irremediable act, one which time and circumstance cannot alter or repair, you participate in the Absolute. By accomplishing an absolute act you enter the absolute life. I do not say what the act should be. It is for you to find the way."

He paused again.

" In Italy, at the time of the Renaissance," he went on, " there flourished a particular type of man, the ' man of crime ' who possessed his own kind of virtue—virtue in the Renaissance style, *virtu* without ' moralism ' as Nietzsche says. It is dishonouring to our European civilisation that we should have come to despise crime instead of valuing its essential truth. But a time of terrible purification is coming, purification of the democratic and judeo-masonic corruption—a time of which the prophets will be men like yourselves. It will be an era of terrible wars which will restore our spiritual health, making us stronger, more apt for good and ill, and shape a higher order of men, a new aristocracy of which you are the progenitors. It is for you to be the pioneers of that dark, bloody and tragic future——"

" In which the Cross will shine amid the darkness! " gasped Nita Ghita, his face working like that of a child on the verge of tears.

They both rose.

" We'll go now," Nita Ghita said.

The professor reached out a hand to him and he seized it and kissed it. The other young man, stiff and pale-faced, was standing rigidly to attention. The professor kissed them both on the cheek and said:

" May God protect you, my children, wherever you go. My heart will be with you."

He went with them to the front door and returned to the library after a minute or two, looking tired and aged, his face grown haggard. He passed a hand over his forehead uttering a long sigh.

" Stick 'em up! " called Titel Negruzzi from the gallery.

The professor uttered a gasp and swung round as though a knife had been plunged into his back. Wide-eyed and open-mouthed, his face whitening with terror, he looked wildly about him, as though seeking a way of escape.

Titel came gaily down the stairs, stumbling over the piles of books and causing two to fall to the floor. Serban followed in a state of extreme embarrassment, confusedly stammering excuses for the behaviour of his friend, who had insisted on coming because of his enormous admiration for the professor, but who, as he now realised, had had rather much to drink. . . . Professor Nicoulesco recovered from his shock and stood intently regarding them. Titel, giggling foolishly, dropped into an armchair, while Serban remained wretchedly standing. After a moment's thought the professor said:

" I'm not sorry you overheard what I said to those two young men. I think perhaps it's a good thing." He uttered a queer little laugh, which seemed to be one of relief. " Perhaps a very good thing! "

" But what were they looking so solemn about? " asked Titel, still grinning. " What are they doing? Are they going abroad? "

" I really don't know much about their plans," said the professor with a faint smile. " I think they may be going abroad. That's probably it." He glanced at the clock on the chimney-piece, which pointed to a quarter to twelve, and then turned to Serban. " Well, and have you found the method? Have you found the truth, the certainty that you were looking for? "

Serban did not reply. He was ashamed of himself and afraid of what was going to happen. Should he confide in this man, in spite of everything? He looked at Titel and saw that his head was beginning to nod.

" Professor," he said, " do you really believe the things you were saying just now? "

" Perhaps it would be better if you told me the conclusions you have come to," said the professor, now seeming quite at his ease. " I shan't lie to you. I'll tell you afterwards what is in my own mind—the two great truths I promised you. . . ."

He took him by the hand and led him to the other end of the room, as far as possible from the armchair where Titel now lay slumbering. As he did so he glanced at his watch.

" I'm afraid that I shall never discover any truth, great or small," murmured Serban. " I'm even afraid that I'm no longer capable of grasping reality as it really is."

" As it really is? You surprise me. With your grounding in philosophy I had not expected you to be so innocent as to believe in any ultimate reality."

Serban gazed childishly at him. " You think that we can never know the essence of reality? "

" What do you think? "

" I . . . well . . ." Serban shrugged his shoulders.

The professor motioned to him to be seated and leaned towards him. " I've been waiting a long time for you to reach this point. You have exceptional qualities of mind. Since I first came to know you I have been saying to myself, ' This will be a splendid man when his eyes are opened—when he has gone beyond good and evil, truth and error. . . .' Well, now is the time for you to accept the fact that *philosophy can go no further*. The play is over, the curtain has fallen, the circle is closed. In the year 700, or thereabouts, Fredegisus de Tours wrote in his *De Nihilo et*

Tenebri that limbo, like all forms of darkness, is a real thing, a thing with a being of its own. His primitive and sanguine creative spirit went so far as to credit even nothingness with a positive existence. Today, twelve centuries later, Martin Heidegger sees *only* the void—nothingness, and nothing more. Even our crude life of everyday is something to which he can attribute no reality. . . . I repeat, the circle is closed. Today there is no European who can form a whole and valid picture of the universe, or say finally what is good and what is evil. Ethical values survive by the weight of inertia, a mere inheritance from our Christian past. But no one any longer believes in them with conviction, force and purpose."

" I know," sighed Serban. " I know. So what is to be done ? What good is it for me or anyone to try to put something where nothing any longer exists ? "

" It is quite impossible," said the professor calmly. " Listen. At the time of the Crusade led by Philippe-Auguste of France and the Holy Roman Emperor, Konrad von Hohenstaufen, the Christians were amazed and terrified by the Isma'ili sect of the Assassins, who, regardless of danger, and risking the most appalling tortures, attempted to kill the two Christian monarchs. Their emissaries, as you know, were drugged with hashish, from which the word ' assassin ' is derived, and their leader bore the title of the Old Man of the Mountain. When he had selected agents suitable for his purpose he interviewed them privately, and without offering them either hashish or the promise of a future life divulged the two great secrets. . . ." The professor paused, smiling at Serban. " I said that there were two more, did I not ? Two ultimate truths——"

He broke off and looked over his shoulder at the clock. The time was nearly midnight. Then he said, coolly and clearly, " Everything is false; nothing is true. That is the first truth." He paused for a moment. " And since all things are a lie, all things are permitted. That is the second truth."

" Then what is the point of living ? " asked Serban Romano.

" For the sake of what we can get out of life. For pleasure. For power. Above all, for power."

" But that's not good enough ! It's not a reason ! " cried Serban, springing up from his chair.

The professor looked at him with his bi-coloured eyes and laughed and said: " It doesn't pretend to be a reason."

" You mustn't laugh! It's not a laughing matter! " cried Serban.
" The destruction of thought by your sort of nihilism is worse
than the burning of books by the barbarians—and that is what it
leads to. Ever since I've known you, you've been saying the
same thing to me, and more and more unequivocally—that you
have abandoned the thinker's main task, the search for truth."

" Yes, I've given up," said the professor.

Serban could no longer restrain himself.

" What was it you were saying just now to those young men? I
don't know what they're doing, but I happen to know one of them
and——"

" Indeed? You know one of them? "

" I know that he's unbalanced and highly emotional. And
what you were saying to them was pure fantasy, a string of words
intended to whip up passion, not to impart knowledge or truth.
You say you've given up thinking. Where does that lead? It
leads to dementia, the unloosing of every kind of irrational instinct
—*bellum omnium contra omnes*—all against all, chaos and destruction! "

" Yes, that is where it leads," said Fanica Nicoulesco.

" But how can you accept that? " cried Serban in a voice of
utter despair.

Titel Negruzzi stirred and grunted, " What a noise! " and then
fell asleep again. The professor turned a tired gaze on Serban.

" Monsieur Romano, I have simply taken the thinking of our
time to its strictly logical and extreme conclusion. In the world
today there are only two positions that make sense in terms of the
philosopher's problem as a whole. They are irrationalism or
Marxism. *Tertium non datur*. I gather that irrationalism does
not suit you. Then why aren't you a Marxist? "

Serban stared at him open-mouthed, looking foolish, then sat
down again with a helpless gesture.

" I can't be."

Fanica Nicoulesco's voice became coldly sarcastic: " Because
you think you have found a better way? "

It might have been a harsh examiner quizzing a student who
has not read his books. Serban shook his head. The professor
said, without heat but with contempt:

" You have not the strength of character I thought you possessed.
You're neither hot nor cold. I was wrong about you."

There was a silence. The professor turned again and looked towards the clock. It was exactly midnight. He said nothing but continued to gaze at it as though his thoughts were very far away. . . .

At that moment the train from Cluj was drawing up in the northern railway-station, wreathed in smoke, bathed in the glare of yellow lights, accompanied by the sounds of hissing steam, the shouting of porters and the rattle of couplings. There were only a few passengers. While the first of these were making their way to the barrier a middle-aged man in a fur-lined coat got down from a first-class compartment followed by two other men, the first of whom carried a brief-case while the second kept his right hand in his pocket. Two young men appeared from behind one of the pillars supporting the roof. Advancing towards 'the man in the fur-lined coat they whipped pistols out of their overcoats and fired.

The crack of the pistol-shots produced a sudden, huge silence broken only by the distant, unbroken wailing of the factory siren. Then a crowd began to gather round the wounded man, who had collapsed on the platform, his arms and legs moving at first convulsively and then more feebly, while his lips were drawn back in a grimace which showed his teeth. His staring eyes grew slowly glazed, and a pool of blood spread from his body. The man with the brief-case was groaning with his hands pressed to his stomach, and the one whose hand had been in his pocket produced a pistol of his own which he levelled at the murderers, exclaiming, " Hands up! " in a voice that sounded choked with fear. The two young men obeyed with an astonishing docility. They stood looking at the dying or dead man on the ground. The escort took their pistols from them, put them in his pocket, and shouted:

" A doctor! Police! Don't just stand staring! It's a member of the Government, Monsieur Vardala. For God's sake, can't anyone do anything? "

Someone produced a newspaper and spread it over the minister's face. No one paid any attention to the two assassins, who might easily have escaped but stood as though paralysed, still gazing at their victim.

7

The news of Vardala's assassination was given over the radio the next morning (the third of the General Strike), but Serban did not hear the announcement. He lay plunged in the sleep of exhaustion and despair, and it was not until lunch-time that his manservant brought him the black-bordered special editions of the newspapers.

They contained the dead minister's portrait and obituary notices, accounts of the crime, and also photographs of the body and of the two murderers, taken in the glare of flashlights. Serban recognised Nita Ghita and his companion of the night before. But there were also photographs of their dead bodies, looking like bundles of old clothes, so smothered in blood as to be unrecognisable. It seemed that they had tried to escape while being transferred to the Malmaison prison after a preliminary interrogation at police headquarters. There were leading articles calling for more drastic measures to maintain law and order.

Serban did not leave the house that day, but spent it pacing the empty rooms. He ate almost nothing, saw no one, dozed occasionally in a chair, to awake with a start and continue his pacing until late into the night. He slept for a little while, but awoke again at dawn and resumed his pacing. It was the fourth day of the strike.

Suddenly he realised that something had happened. The siren had ceased its wailing. The silence of the town was terrible and immense.

A column of lorries passed along the street in the dim light of that February morning. They were evidently heavy lorries, for the house trembled with their passing; and there seemed to be a great many of them. One of them sounded its klaxon. The house had ceased to quiver, but the blare of the klaxon continued for some moments, like a call for help.

Serban went out on to a balcony to see what was happening. The column had vanished except for one lorry, directly beneath him, which had evidently broken down. The driver, a soldier, got out, followed by two blue-uniformed gendarmes with rifles. They raised the bonnet and peered into the engine.

The back of the lorry was filled with sleeping men—workmen, Serban supposed, without really thinking. They lay on their backs under a tarpaulin which in the main left their heads exposed, but which covered the faces of one or two. This did not seem to trouble them. " They must be terribly tired," Serban thought. One lay on his stomach, so that the back of his neck was visible, and all were bare-headed—in February! " Extraordinary how tough those fellows are! " But then suddenly it was as though Serban's heart had stopped beating, and a mist rose before his eyes. He thought: " I believe they're dead! "

Yes, they were dead. The lorry was packed with dead men, hollow-faced workers with several days' growth of beard on their cheeks. Some were open-eyed, and one, a good-looking youth with a broad, bony face, had a trickle of blood running from the corner of his mouth.

The engine was started again. The driver got back behind the wheel and the two gendarmes took their places beside him. A small group of people had gathered on the pavement, and a voice shouted something as the lorry moved off, leaving behind it the smell of its exhaust and a blue cloud hanging in the limpid air.

Serban turned back into the room, trembling violently. He shut the french-windows, drew the curtains and stayed seated for a long time. He sent his manservant away. He had to be alone.

At length he stirred. He went to the drawer where he had put the pistol three days before, got it out, loaded it, released the safety-catch, and put it to his temple.

It felt suddenly very heavy, as though it were made of lead.

" I can't go on . . ." he murmured, solitary in the big, curtained room, with the grey light of the winter's morning outside. " I can't go on. . . ."

He sat down, staring at the pistol as he held it loosely dangling between his knees. He raised it again, and again let it fall. A weak smile appeared on his lips, as though he were apologising for himself to some other person watching him. Then he shrugged his shoulders and laughed feebly, an unhappy, guilty laugh.

" I've got to die some day in any case . . . why be in so much of a hurry ? "

He ejected the bullets one by one into his hand until the pistol was empty, put everything back in the drawer, locked it, and tossed the key on top of a wardrobe. Then, moving lethargically, he flung himself on the bed. He slept like an animal for another twenty-four hours, and awoke feeling stiff and sluggish, still in his crumpled clothes. He had a bath, and as he was dressing to go out his manservant announced that Titel Negruzzi had called.

" Show him up," said Serban.

Titel entered, more voluble than ever, and threw his hat and gloves on a chair.

" It's damned cold in this house. Let's go along to the club and get warm. The boys are all making whoopee. Vasilesco-Rimnic's chortling with delight, and no wonder. Vardala was his biggest rival for the party-leadership. But Vardala made the mistake of intriguing with the King against the professor. . . . Not nice, is it, when you come to think of it—makes your blood run cold. . . . Provided that lot doesn't get on top! Well, anyway, it isn't going to happen just yet. For the moment everything's splendid. The strike's over. They liquidated a few dozen strikers—bang bang!—and old Telescope Ipsilanti has been promoted divisional general. Hurry up, can't you, and let's go and eat. I'm ravenous."

The manservant entered.

" Monsieur Nicolas Prodan has called to see Monsieur."

" Prodan ? " said Titel, frowning. " What the hell does he want with you ? Why hasn't he been arrested anyway ? "

Serban gazed round the walls and even at the floor as though he were searching for something.

" Show him up," he muttered.

Nicou Prodan burst into the room like a squall of wind, bringing with him a thin, bony-faced, sensitive-eyed young man in a loose raincoat.

" Monsieur Romano," he said rapidly, " let me introduce Comrade Eftimie Popa, one of the most gifted of our younger writers . . ." He paused for an instant to glance at Titel Negruzzi, who had not troubled to rise from the armchair where he sat smoking with his legs crossed, staring at the silk-lined walls; then he went on: " You have heard about the crime they committed, the massacre of the strikers? I've formed a Committee of Public Protest. We're going to send a letter of protest to all the news-agencies, all the leading European newspapers and all the foreign embassies. Two hundred intellectuals have signed it already. You have contacts in the German universities. I want you to add your signature and write personally to everyone you know who might be of help."

He was talking with his customary fervour and single-mindedness—everything positive and straightforward, everything to be done instantly, in the cause of liberty and justice.

Serban Romano again peered round the room as though in search of something and then thrust aside the document Prodan held out to him. He was clad in a green silk dressing-gown. Prodan had on a black overcoat with an otter-skin collar and held his fur cap in his hand.

"Why won't you take it?" he asked. "What does this mean?"

"I must ask you to leave me," said Serban, speaking almost humbly. "I don't want to be mixed up in anything. I have nothing in common with your aims."

"Nothing in common? But you're a man—a citizen—an intellectual!"

"No, I'm nothing at all," said Serban in troubled exasperation. "I only want to be left in peace. Leave me alone and let me go on living my own life."

"And you'll let the workers go on dying!" cried Prodan. "A fair exchange!"

"Monsieur Prodan," said the young man, Popa, "we aren't going on our knees for anyone's signature."

"No, I thought he was a man, but he's not. He's a different species—like all the rest of his breed." Prodan turned contemptuously and left the room, pushing the young man ahead of him and slamming the door.

"They're mad and they're insolent," said Titel Negruzzi. "They'll end up in prison."

Serban was striving to appear calm and unperturbed, as though no insult had been uttered.

"Lunch . . ." he said. "What do you say to some caviar and a *tournedos*, and perhaps a bottle of Chambertin?"

They went to the club. The first bottle was followed by others.

Prince Bubi Ipsilanti and Cesar Lascari, immaculate and beaming, came and joined them.

"My dear prince," said Cesar, "I hope you will tell your brother, the general, how greatly I admire the way he has handled the situation. No one will be able to say that we don't know how to solve our industrial problems. Anyone who has been buying shares is to be congratulated. The boom's terrific. Some issues have risen as much as ten points. Let me order champagne, and then we'll go along to a cabaret."

Serban Romano said, thick-mouthed: "Anything you like. . . . Just so long as we don't talk politics. Anything—provided it isn't serious. . . ."

8

Serban went next evening to a dinner-party for twenty guests given by his uncle, Serban Lascari. He arrived a little late. Passing through the wrought-iron doorway with its fading gilt he handed his cloak to Nicolas, his uncle's old manservant, and asked:

"Is everyone else here?"

"We're waiting for Monsieur Van Narredom, Monsieur Serban. But Professor Nicoulesco has arrived."

Serban gasped at this, but recovering from his shock he went upstairs to the reception-room, decorated with exotic plants and big Capo di Monte vases. Fanica Nicoulesco's hands were stained with the blood of Vardala and the two young men whom he had incited to kill Vardala, but this did not prevent Uncle Serbanica from inviting him to dinner. *Ainsi va le monde*, reflected Serban with a bitter smile.

And he bowed to left and right. Old Serban Lascari, his hands clasped on his round paunch, was twiddling his fingers and gazing about him in evident satisfaction. Vasilesco-Rimnic and General Ipsilanti were among the company, and Serban's cousin, Elvira Vorvoreano, and various other ladies, among whom, with a sudden beating of his heart, he saw Valentine Scarlat. Scarlat, the betrayed husband, was seated in an armchair looking more indolent and sluggish than ever. He was talking to another member of the Ipsilanti family who had been converted to the Catholic faith and had become an abbot. Fashionable Bucarest, always on the look-out for high-sounding titles, addressed him as Monseigneur.

Valentine was sheathed in a tightly fitting gown of lemon-yellow velvet, the skirt split at the knee, which stood out startlingly against the black coats of the men. Elvira Vorvoreano wore a backless black silk dress with long sleeves slit from shoulder to wrist, disclosing her round, slender arms bearing a cluster of large gold bracelets studded with red, green and blue stones— a barbaric adornment as striking as Elvira's language, into which there crept occasional, casual words of such coarseness that even the gentlemen were startled. These were followed by a brief silence, after which the conversation would be resumed as though nothing had been said; Elvira, knocking the ash off the cigarette which she smoked through a holder six inches long, her manner cool and distant, would glance through long lashes at the particular man she had sought to impress, who was doubtless saying to himself, " What a woman! "

At the moment she was talking to a tall, slim young man whose face was familiar to Serban, although for the moment he could not place him. She introduced them.

" Baron Ulrich von Heck. Herr von Heck has just joined the German embassy."

Serban then recognised the harsh, bony features and dull blue eyes of Ulrich of the Hopfenperle. For an instant he hesitated before shaking hands with him. He had thought to have finished with all that. Would it not be simpler to behave as though they had never met?

But then he held out his hand, bowing and smiling with an unctuous, levantine politeness which secretly outraged him.

" We've known each other a long time."

Ulrich responded with a stiff, military inclination of his head and a patronising smile. After a minute or two Serban left them, and as he turned away he saw Fanica Nicoulesco. The professor's face was grey and there were heavy shadows under his eyes; but he seemed to have no difficulty in confronting the gentlemen he was talking to, Serban Lascari, Vasilesco-Rimnic and General Ipsilanti; all of whom, knowing him to be at least morally responsible for the murder of Vardala, were gazing at him with a sort of awed fascination.

" I realise," Serban Lascari was saying, " that your political friends are an important element. . . ."

" They are the only ones who can preserve our country, our national integrity and our faith from Bolshevism," said Fanica Nicoulesco.

For an instant, as he said it, he seemed to be mocking his own words and those of the other men—deriding himself. He had an air of hectic gaiety, as though he were in the grip of some kind of intoxication.

" Precisely—our national integrity and our faith, as you so admirably put it," said Serban Lascari, smiling. He glanced at Vasilesco-Rimnic. " His Excellency has been telling me that if you and your friends were prepared to give certain assurances— in short, if you are ready to listen to reason—his party might be able to offer you an electoral alliance, a few seats in the Chamber. How does that strike you? "

Fanica Nicoulesco grinned sardonically. " I will pass the suggestion on to my associates. Certainly we're anxious to improve our political status."

Serban stood listening and smiling a few paces away. There was blood on all their hands, everything was covered with blood, but no one cared. . . . Old Lascari announced to the company:

" We have been waiting for Monsieur Van Narredom, but he telephoned a few minutes ago to say that he can't be here before midnight, so we might as well go in to dinner."

Serban was seated between Elvira Vorvoreano and Princess Ipsilanti, a woman of forty-five with a beaked nose, withered, small and ugly, whose dyed hair looked as though it were made of tow. Her arms rattled with the filigree bracelets, studded with diamonds, which she had inherited from her ancestress, the Princess Ralou.

" But think how brave they were," she said to Elvira. " The two of them alone in that crowded station! "

" Whom do you mean? " asked Serban.

" The men who shot Vardala," said Elvira.

" Oh, the murderers," said Serban vaguely. He was now gazing miserably at Valentine Scarlat.

" How can you talk of them like that ? " cried Princess Ipsilanti. " They were so good-looking and so young ! "

After this Serban kept his eyes on his plate, only raising them from time to time to glance covertly at Valentine, who was sitting beside Ulrich von Heck. She evidently found his conversation entertaining. Elvira remarked:

" Valentine is charming—and that young German is certainly a fine male specimen." There was nothing in her voice of the romantic exaltation with which the Princess had talked of the youth and beauty of the two murderers. She was more like a horse-trader looking over an animal to be bought or sold. She went on: " I once went to a concert at the von Hecks' castle in Bavaria. Well, not a concert exactly. It was an opera by Monteverdi, conducted by Toscanini. The hall was lit by candles, just as it must have been when the opera was first performed in Monteverdi's presence. It was wonderful. I simply don't understand how parents as cultivated as that could have produced such an oaf of a son. That lovely castle, the performance, the atmosphere, everything. . . ."

" It's more like a museum than a castle," said Serban savagely. " A museum where gorillas are allowed in."

After dinner he began to drink heavily. Others were doing the same. The voices grew louder and the laughter more strident. Serban watched a crystal chandelier gently swaying, and wondered if it was due to an earthquake; and suddenly Fanica Nicoulesco appeared at his side.

" Well, young man, are you still worrying about trifles? Have you begun to grasp what is *real* in life, or are you still preoccupied with theoretical values ? "

" Is there any—does any truth exist ? " Serban asked drunkenly.

" You must make up your mind. I've told you already not to waste your life on futilities. *Geld und Gewalt, Gewalt und Geld, der Rest ist Narrheit*—money and power, power and money, the rest is folly. Your health, my dear boy." The professor raised his glass.

" You know," said Serban between hiccoughs, " I'm beginning to admire you."

Monsieur Van Narredom, minister-plenipotentiary of a kingdom in northern Europe, arrived at one in the morning. He was enchanted with Bucarest. Nowhere else had he encountered such aristocratic gaiety, such light-hearted audacity, such sparkling defiance of convention and engaging arrogance. These Levantines had the heedless high spirits of the Athenians described by Thucydides, who had held high revel during a visitation of the plague, respecting neither things divine nor things human. When he was shown into the salon he stood staring on the threshold with an enraptured smile on his plump, pink face. The ladies were convulsed with laughter. The gentlemen had just removed their trousers, and, impeccably clad as to the upper half of their bodies, offered, as to the lower half, a rich and varied spectacle of under-pants and sock-suspenders. Fanica Nicoulesco had remarkably skinny and hairy legs; those of Serban Lascari were white and varicose-veined, those of General Ipsilanti thin and bony, those of Serban Romano muscular but flabby. Vasilesco-Rimnic's huge stomach billowed over a pair of knock-knees. Amid delighted laughter and applause Monsieur Van Narredom, with the aplomb of the seasoned diplomat who never strikes a false note, removed his own trousers, handed them to the footman, and advanced to take up his position at the right hand of his host.

VIII

Very Busy Men

I

Ionas Apostolesco, the younger brother of Gogu Apostolesco
(they were both grandsons of Walter Apostolesco and Cléopatra),
was in the habit of saying: " My dear fellow, I'm always so busy.
I get through an enormous amount of work. In fact, I never stop.
I live in a world of extremely busy and active people. You can't
make money by idling. You've got to sweat at it."

The busiest man in Bucarest after Ionas, who held the first
place as of right, was old Monsieur Gherson, the chairman of a
large industrial corporation, and after him came Monsieur Mayer,
his general manager. Compared with the cares and activities of
these three men, those of Pericles Mittesco, the well-known
Bucarest advocate who specialised in company law, or of Titel
Negruzzi, Cesar Lascari, Dimitri Coziano, Valentine Scarlat or
Madame Gherson, were almost trifling, although not wholly
negligible.

Monsieur Gherson was old. His body no longer counted,
whether in the eyes of others or in those of Monsieur Gherson
himself, to whom that frail and unimposing mechanism of bone,
flesh and liquid was no more than a source of obscure aches,
cramps, tics and anxieties. In the past he had derived exquisite
enjoyment from it, but now he was confined to the pleasures of
the table, in which he indulged in moderation. As all the world
knew, and not least the newspaper cartoonists, Monsieur Gherson,
with his dry, crumpled face and look of melancholy intelligence,
resembled an aged chimpanzee withering away in some provincial menagerie. But this is a daring and even improper simile,
for Monsieur Gherson had not grown old behind bars but in the
Kingdom of Roumania.

On a morning in November, in the year 1938, Monsieur
Gherson awoke at five, as he generally did, having gone to bed
at one-thirty. Being unable to get to sleep again, he picked up a

book (like so many men of his kind he was a great lover of art and literature) and then lay for three-quarters of an hour with it unopened in his hand. It was a newly published volume of poems by Tudor Arghezi, a poet whose merits were much discussed and who was often reproached for the indecency of his writings. Monsieur Gherson enjoyed them in the way that he enjoyed heady vines and highly seasoned dishes. But that morning he could not even read. He lay wondering, " Did I do the right thing? Would it have been better to give way? But since I have agreed to arbitration, would it not be prudent to try and make sure of Mittesco? "

The business was bothering him, he should never have got into it. He liked straightforward deals, openly transacted without risk of scandal. And now look what had happened! He could not even blame Ionas Apostolesco, who after all was only taking care of himself—anyone would do the same. Monsieur Gherson got out of bed, slipped his thin, white feet into bedroom slippers and put on a pleated silk dressing-gown in which he looked like the Emperor of China's favourite monkey clad in his master's robes of ceremony. Thus attired he left the small room which served him as a bedchamber, leaving the night-light burning at the bedside and the volume of verse open on the pillow.

He went into his study, a long room with a window at one end filling the entire wall, protected by a diamond-patterned iron grill, beyond which the street lights shone upon a row of chestnuts in a quiet street running into the Place Pache Protopopesco.

Monsieur Gherson turned a switch, lighting up the other walls on which were arrayed a large library of legal, literary and financial works which he was too busy ever to refer to, and in which Madame Gherson took no interest, any more than did her friends or the men of affairs who visited the house.

Crossing the room to the far corner Monsieur Gherson pressed a button concealed behind a picture by Patrasco of the Santa Maria della Salute, white against a metallic blue-green sea and an equally blue-green sky. A section of the book-shelves swung aside revealing other shelves behind them, loaded with files and bundles of documents. Monsieur Gherson got down a slim folder and sat in an armchair to study its contents.

The folder contained a document of which the replica was held by Ionas Apostolesco: a private agreement stipulating that in the

event of the Roumanian Metal Corporation (" Romecor ")
securing a contract from the Directorate of the State Railways
for the reconditioning of 1200 passenger coaches, Monsieur
Gherson, that is to say, Romecor, would pay Monsieur Apostolesco
the sum of 98,000,000 lei. To this document was attached a copy
of the contract in question, counter-signed by three Ministers of
State. But then there came a letter from the Director of State
Railways informing Romecor that the contract had been suspended, and finally there was a sheaf of newspaper clippings of
recent date.

The first of these asked: " *Is it true that the railway coaches
supposedly repaired by Romecor were stripped of all their valuable
components and then accepted by the State Railways as ' recondi-
tioned' although in fact they had been reduced to the state of old
iron?* " The second clipping, from a newspaper opposed to the
policies of the first, demanded: " *What part does the scoundrel
Ionas Apostolesco play in the outrageous swindles countenanced by
the Directorate of the State Railways?* " And a third clipping
ran: " *It seems that negotiations are in progress for the granting of
the concession for a large section of the fortifications in the Carol
Line to the Roumanian Cement Corporation. The Cement Corporation, like Romecor, is controlled by the Gherson brothers. One
wonders whether these fortifications will be as solid as the ' skeleton '
railway-coaches.*"

Monsieur Gherson sighed deeply. This last blow was the most
painful of all. It had resulted in the loss of a concession worth
several hundred million, perhaps as much as a milliard lei, with
a profit of—but it didn't bear thinking of.

What was more, his friends were displaying a marked interest in
the matter. Serban Lascari had taken him aside at an evening
party and asked:

" My dear fellow, what's it all about? What's going on between
you and Ionas Apostolesco? I thought you were the best of
friends."

" But nothing has happened," said Monsieur Gherson, with a
candid, slightly melancholy smile.

" Come, come. Do you think my son doesn't know? Cesar can
ferret out that sort of story in no time at all. Besides, the newspaper chaps have told him that the information was slipped to
them in the first place by Ionas. And anyone can see that you're

behind their latest story. You don't need me to tell you that we don't want any scandal at the present time. It would be bad for everyone, ourselves and the Bank of Roumania and the Government. The defence of the country is involved, and contracts for the fortifications have got to be settled without delay. A scandal might have most serious consequences. I must beg you to tell me the exact position."

Gherson allowed himself to be led into a corner and seated on a deep, luxurious couch. Here he related how, owing to one of those contretemps which sometimes arise, he had failed at the appropriate moment to suborn the Committee of Control, which oversaw the operations of the Committee of Estimates (the Committee of Estimates, he explained modestly, being already in the bag), with the result that the contract had been cancelled and, what was worse, Romecor was threatened with legal proceedings.

" Not only have I sustained a considerable loss, but Ionas is demanding his entire commission. I ask you, Monsieur Lascari, is that reasonable? I simply can't afford it. I have offered him two million—two and a half—but that is as far as I can go. The loss would be crippling. What would you do if you were me? "

Serban Lascari smiled in his little white beard and said with the utmost amiability:

" I wouldn't get involved in that kind of transaction. Why did you have to get on the wrong side of the law? You can't pretend that there aren't legal ways of doing business—even big business. The laws are not intended to make life impossible for us. They allow a certain latitude, thank God! "

Gherson blinked his eyes, humbly smiling.

"We haven't been in business as long as you, Monsieur Lascari."

Old Serbanica smiled again, but then said coldly: " You know as much about these things as I do. There must be something more, which you haven't told me. What are you really after? Are you trying to raise money to send abroad? What are you afraid of? "

Gherson sighed and said with melancholy wisdom: " We know what's happening to Jews in other countries—Germany, Austria, Czechoslovakia. We're threatened with the same thing here, through the Iron Legion."

" Well, yes. It's certainly possible."

" You'll take everything from us—our capital, our factories, everything we possess," murmured Gherson.

Serban Lascari patted him reassuringly on the shoulder. " Don't be too pessimistic. We shall try to arrange matters so that people like you don't suffer too severely. But in the meantime, do try to get out of this mess with Ionas. To tell you the truth, I think he's in the right. It isn't his fault if that business turned out badly for you. He had fulfilled his obligation."

" According to the letter, Monsieur Lascari, but not according to the spirit. It was not simply a matter of a contract but of an understanding. One has to show good faith."

Serban Lascari shrugged his shoulders. " Obviously good faith is essential in all business transactions, but here there's a difference of opinion. Ionas maintains that he acted in good faith and that you are the one who has gone back on your agreement. You should call in an arbitrator, my dear fellow, a man of acknowledged integrity."

Monsieur Gherson stared at the carpet.

" I shall not suggest anyone," said Serban Lascari. " Ionas is a distant relation of mine and you are a customer of my bank. I'm not taking sides."

Gherson looked up. " What would you say to Mittesco? "

" I think he would be excellent. But do, for Heaven's sake, get the thing cleared up. You're embarrassing everyone with these newspaper stories. The whole thing is most unpleasant and unworthy of a man in your position."

This conversation had taken place at the beginning of the week. Serban Lascari had had a word with Ionas and had secured his acceptance of Mittesco as arbitrator. The matter had at once been placed in the hands of that distinguished lawyer, who was to give his verdict tomorrow, Friday. Meanwhile, at six o'clock on the Thursday morning, when nearly all Bucarest was still asleep, Monsieur Gherson, seated in his magnificent dressing-gown with his spectacles on his nose and the folder on his knee, was saying to himself: " It isn't so much the 98,000,000. I can find that. But if I start giving ground I shall have everyone after me. That brute Apostolesco has even raised the matter of the fortifications. He's getting above himself altogether, he needs to be taken down a peg. The exasperating thing is that technically he is in the right, and Mittesco is too honest a man and too good a lawyer to

be influenced by anything but strict legal form. If he were a man
of business it would be different. He would understand that
morally I am in the right. But he isn't a business man and he can't
be got round—which, of course, is why we've called him in as
arbitrator, because he's known to be honest. So what am I to do?
Have I got to swallow it?"

He hated the thought of losing, the more so since this was
not a matter of some event outside his control, such as an unexpected fluctuation in exchange prices, when one simply wrote
off the loss and took steps to recover it. This was a case where,
with common justice on his side, he was being impudently
challenged and defied by a mere novice in business matters, a
man probably under forty. "I won't put up with it!" exclaimed
Monsieur Gherson, and rising from his chair he rang for his
breakfast.

Three-quarters of an hour later he got into the car which stood
waiting for him outside the house, its driver pale-faced and
red-eyed.

"I kept you up very late last night," said Monsieur Gherson
gently, "and here we are, starting off again at seven. It's unfair
to you, Stefan."

"That's all right, sir."

"I'm so busy, you see. I have so many things to attend to."
Monsieur Gherson fished in his pocket and thrust a hundred-lei
note over the man's shoulder.

"Thank you, monsieur," said Stefan, looking a little more
cheerful. He added: "You should try to get more rest, sir, at
your age."

"There's no retiring in my business," said Monsieur Gherson
sadly.

Stefan nodded in secret admiration, reflecting that he wouldn't
mind working as hard if he could earn as much money as his
employer. Meanwhile Monsieur Gherson was brooding—and
it was the cause of his melancholy—on the great, solid financial
houses which had existed in Germany and Austria-Hungary
before the war. The Barons Adler and Salomon, ennobled by
the Emperor Franz-Josef, represented Monsieur Gherson's ideal.
What men they had been! When the financier Kuproly had
called on Baron Salomon ("Monsieur le Baron, my name is
Kuproly and I am a Persian") to inform him that he had bought

fifty-one per cent of the shares in his bank and to ask him to surrender the Chairman's seat on the Board, the Baron had received him in a room with a magnificent Ispahan carpet. " *Mein Herr*," he had replied, " *ich bin gewöhnt auf Perser zu treten*—I am accustomed to tread on Persians." He had simply thrown him out, and within six months Kuproly had been completely ruined. What a man!

But since the war things had gone from bad to worse. Monsieur Gherson thought of his Uncle Poldi, in Vienna, in December, 1920. One afternoon the three of them—Gherson, his father and Uncle Poldi, who was his father's brother—had sat together in the Café Bristol. Although it was growing dark the lights had not yet been turned on. The old waiters moved in and out amid the buzz of talk with beer and coffee and the daily papers on their wooden frames. They had sat sipping *kapuziner* coffee and nibbling Viennese pastries; but Uncle Poldi had not eaten anything. He had talked without drawing breath, gesticulating all the time. Finally Gherson's father had said:

" Never mind, Poldi. Don't forget that you can always come to us in Jassy, and that you have a home there and a family."

" Bless you! " said Uncle Poldi feverishly, staring out of the window. " Let me think it over. Perhaps we might be able to work together in Roumania—it's a blessed land."

Then he left, and Gherson's father said sadly:

" So many people have been ruined in this crash. I've never known anyting like it."

The next day they had been summoned to identify the body of Uncle Poldi, in the villa which no longer belonged to him, since it had become the property of his creditors. He lay on an iron bedstead in the cellar, a dreadful sight, for he had shot himself through the mouth. But why in the cellar, when there were sixteen rooms in the villa, six of them bedrooms? Monsieur Gherson wondered at this again, while the car bore him to his office. " And since then," he thought, " there's been no end to it." Hitler was swallowing up Czechoslovakia, and here in Roumania they had the Iron Guard, Couza and Professor Nicoulesco. What a time to be living in!

The offices of the corporation were in the centre of Bucarest, in a new, ten-storey building full of lifts, marble corridors, doors with brass nameplates and rooms containing typewriters. Monsieur

Gherson was one of the privileged few who occupied rooms
of immense size, quiet and thick-carpeted, with huge windows
affording a view over the city, like a sea of white buildings, and in
the far distance, beyond the factory-chimneys, the green expanse
of the plain with its curtain of woods.

That morning Monsieur Gherson received a number of representatives of foreign concerns, a factory-manager and the head of
an import-export agency who produced a list of goods and equipment which were offered for sale and another list of goods for
which he could find a market. Monsieur Gherson called his
general manager, Monsieur Mayer, on the house-telephone and
asked him to come in. Mayer, who was Monsieur Gherson's
right-hand man and the best paid of all his employees, was thick-
set and nearly as broad as he was long, with powerful arms and
fleshy hands. He had a large, round face, always glossy and
smoothly shaved, a small hook-nose, and cold eyes behind his
glasses; and he wore admirably cut clothes and a large gold
signet-ring on his little finger. Monsieur Gherson was accustomed
to arrive at the office at seven or, very occasionally, at seven-thirty.
Mayer never arrived later than ten to seven, at which hour there
was no one but the cleaners in the building.

After some discussion with him and the agency representative
Gherson said:

" Well, then, we're agreed. Mayer, will you see to it? Have
the contracts drawn up right away and come back here when
you've finished."

Having dismissed the two gentlemen Monsieur Gherson rang
for his secretary who entered with a red leather folder filled with
papers awaiting his signature. He signed until the letters grew
distorted under his pen and then looked up at her.

" Is that the lot? "

She smiled. She was a woman of forty-five with dyed hair and
reddened lips who dressed quietly but with elegance. She had
always been plain, but for twenty years past she had been far
closer to Monsieur Gherson than the actresses who had been
his mistresses, and she was still his close friend and devoted
servant.

" Yes, that's all," she said. " You're worried about this arbitration business, aren't you? " He did not answer, and she went
on: " Shall I send for Monsieur Mayer? "

Gherson's eyes twinkled. " He's probably waiting outside. Go and see."

She laughed. The old man was always a jump ahead of anyone else; he was always the first to come up with an idea. Seeing the candid admiration in her smile Gherson felt comforted, and he greeted Mayer almost gaily.

" Sit down, my dear fellow. Try one of these excellent cigarettes. They were given me by our Argentine ambassador yesterday —he came home by way of Cuba. Well now, what are we going to do? "

" About what? " asked Mayer.

" Don't pretend you don't know. I mean this arbitration business."

" I have always said that we should honour our undertakings," said Mayer.

" Come, come," said Gherson. " That isn't the way one does business. The fact is, you've never been anything but an administrator, not a real business man. One respects contracts when one can't do otherwise, or when it pays to do so."

" We're in bad trouble," said Mayer. " This matter of the fortifications is causing a lot of talk. We should have done better to settle with Apostolesco."

" Ninety-eight millions! Are you really suggesting that we should throw away that much money? "

" Anyone can see that you're a self-made man," said Mayer, speaking stiffly and seriously. " If you had inherited a fortune you'd be more pliable."

Gherson looked hard at him and smiled. " He's not such a fool," he thought. What Mayer said was the truth, and it was with satisfaction that he reflected that he, Lazar Gherson, was the sole author of his wealth. His father, like Uncle Poldi, had lost everything, and had then lived at his expense.

" So you think we should have paid up? "

" I suggested that we should offer fifty millions, just over half. It would have been a generous gesture which would have been good for our prestige."

" In other words, we should encourage people to put shabby deals our way and then try to extort rich rewards which they haven't earned? "

" You asked my opinion," said Mayer without flinching.

" I know I did, and I thank you for it. But I can't allow Monsieur Ionas Apostolesco to lead me up the garden. Have you nothing else to suggest? "

" Well, if we could bring some sort of pressure to bear on the arbitrator . . ." Mayer said uncertainly.

" Aha! That's more like it. You may be slow, but you get there in the end."

" But it's no use thinking you can buy Mittesco. He's not that sort of man."

" You feel sure of that? "

" We'd be liable to find ourselves in even worse trouble," said Mayer steadily. " We certainly can't buy Mittesco."

" My dear Mayer," said Monsieur Gherson, " there isn't a man alive who can't be bought. Kaiser Wilhelm once said to an English diplomat, ' Every man has his price.' ' Even your Majesty? ' asked the diplomat. ' Yes, even me.' ' And may I inquire what your Majesty's price is? ' ' My price is the road to India.' . . . You see? The price is not necessarily money, my dear fellow. Now I want you to do something for me. I want you to go to Silberling and buy me a ten-carat diamond. Or perhaps it would be better if you didn't actually go yourself."

" You mean, you're going to offer . . .? " Mayer broke off and said: " I beg your pardon."

" It's all right. You needn't be alarmed. I have no intention of offering Mittesco anything at all, or even of hinting at it. Go and get me that diamond. I didn't think of bringing one with me from home. This is a notion that has just occurred to me, while I've been talking to you. You may be lacking in imagination, my dear Mayer, but you have an instinct for the sure way out."

Gherson had a number of other visitors that morning, including three newspaper editors who promised him their support in the matter of the fortifications and to whom he distributed successively three bundles of notes carefully wrapped in paper (he got them out of a drawer of his desk where he always kept such tokens in readiness).

He gave two similar packets to a gentleman in civilian attire, a colonel of reserves who had contacts with the Ministry of War; after which he looked up a number in his diary and put through a private telephone call to Madame Valentine Scarlat.

" Dear Valentine, how are you? And how is your husband, the future minister? . . . In Paris, is he? What is he doing there? . . . Yes, I see. Missions of that sort are a part of his duties as a deputy. . . . But no, my dear, it's you I want to talk to, regarding a matter that affects you personally. What's more, I must see you at once, before lunch. . . . Most certainly it's important. You can hardly suppose that I would waste your time—or my own!—for a trifle. I shall arrive in half an hour. I kiss your hand."

Monsieur Gherson hung up and rang for his secretary.

" Has Mayer come back? Ask him to come in."

Mayer brought with him a leather case lined with black velvet containing a large blue-white diamond, cut in the latest Amsterdam fashion. Gherson held it up to twinkle in the light, and examined it carefully through a magnifying-glass.

" It's a fine one," he said. He put it back in its case, put the case in his pocket, locked the drawer of his desk and stood up. " I shan't be coming back to the office today, I've too much else to do. But you're coming to us for lunch, aren't you? I'll see you then."

Monsieur Gherson went down to his car and gave the chauffeur Madame Scarlat's address. He was now in good spirits, delighted at having found a solution to his problem before it was too late, and confident of success. While he was being driven to the Boulevard Dacia he thought with sentimental melancholy of Valentine's naked body and of their liaison, which had lasted only a few months. Since then he had run into her occasionally at social functions, but had done no more than exchange amiable commonplaces. What had there been to say? Valentine had now and then asked a service of him, some use of his influence, and he had put her off as civilly as he could. She wanted too much; she had always wanted too much; she had thought, no doubt, that she could squeeze him dry. But Monsieur Gherson was not the man to be carried away by passion, and indeed he was not particularly sensual; his latest liaisons had been principally for show, because it was proper to a man in his position that he should keep a beautiful mistress in Bucarest. Valentine was ridiculous; one could not sustain a serious relationship with her. However, she was clearly the right person for use in the present affair.

Monsieur and Madame Scarlat lived in a handsome house near the Icone Garden. Valentine's maid showed Monsieur upstairs and he knocked and entered her bedroom. She was seated at her dressing-table clad in a voluminous gown of pink silk, with a pink silk turban on her head, a thick layer of beauty-cream on her face and neck, and long gloves, shiny with grease. Nothing was visible of her except her alert eyes, which gazed intently at Monsieur Gherson. He smiled, bowing with a calm politeness, sat down in a chair near her and sighed.

" What is it, Daddy? " asked Valentine, with no great amiability. " I let you come up because you said you had to see me at once. I've a very busy day ahead of me—lunch, tea and dinner dates. I've got to finish dressing and go to my dressmaker for a fitting before lunch, and then pay a quick call on my doctor."

" Aren't you well? "

" There's nothing wrong with me. I'm only explaining why I'm receiving you in this get-up. Would you care for something— tea or coffee? "

" No, thank you, nothing. As you're in such a hurry——"

" I'm sure you are too," said Valentine. " Life's becoming impossible in Bucarest. We shall all have to get out of this town.'

" I quite agree. I'll come straight to the point. You know Ionas Apostolesco? "

" Of course. He's a friend of Scarlat and me, and we've a lot of friends in common."

" Well, this is my problem."

Monsieur Gherson proceeded to tell her the story, glossing over the details and putting it in terms that could be followed by a person little versed in business matters.

" So the present position," he said, " is that my Government contract is suspended, Ionas hasn't had a penny out of me and we have asked Pericles Mittesco to arbitrate between us."

Valentine had listened with close attention.

" But what has all this to do with me? "

Gherson sighed again, got out the little black case, opened it and placed it on the dressing-table.

" I hope you will allow me, as an old adorer, to make you this trifling present. And I will give you three million if you can persuade our friend, Mittesco, to arbitrate in my favour. In any case I am in the right, as you will have gathered."

" Are you saying that to appease your conscience? " asked Valentine. " It's no use, Daddy. I'd never be able to influence Pericles. It would only end in a quarrel, and he'd despise me for trying. *Rien à faire, mon pauvre papa....* I don't know if I even ought to accept this diamond—although I think I will, all the same."

She laughed, and Monsieur Gherson, unperturbed, said:

" I don't want you to so much as mention my name, or even to hint at what I've been telling you. What you must say is that you're having great trouble with Ionas, who is always pestering you and won't believe that you love no one but Pericles. And now he has sent you this diamond, and you would like dear Pericles to tell you what you should do about it. Will you be seeing him today? "

Valentine was now regarding the old man with respect.

" You're not such a fool, are you, Daddy? You're an old fox! "

" Will you be seeing him today? " repeated Gherson, who disliked any kind of compliment.

" Yes—either this afternoon or tonight. But supposing he

just tells me to send the diamond back to Ionas and forget about
it?"

"You must pitch it stronger than that. Remind him what a
coarse, brutal creature Ionas is, and what a vile reputation he has
with women. Say he's insulted you, even that he tried to rape you.
Say anything you like that will drive Pericles into a frenzy and
make him want to tear Ionas limb from limb—provided you don't
breathe a word about business or arbitration. You'll manage it,
my dear. I have every confidence in your feminine resourceful-
ness. And if all goes well there will be three millions for you and
you will have done a great service to a man with a long memory.
Well, now I'll leave you. Ring me up whenever you like."

"All right, Daddy, and thank you for the lovely present. I'll
keep in touch."

Monsieur Gherson was well content. The day that had begun
so badly now held the promise of triumph. He drove to the
Turkish bath, where, while relaxing his limp, shrunken body
amid clouds of steam, he was accustomed to discuss the latest news
with other bodies, sleek, square-jawed faces, vast bellies streaming
with sweat.

"Well, and what about that Apostolesco business?" the bodies
asked. "Have you reached a settlement?"

"Not yet," replied Monsieur Gherson with calm. "Mittesco
is arbitrating. He's to give us his verdict tomorrow."

"You'll have to watch out. Apostolesco is a tricky customer,
and very tough. You remember the Skoda affair? It was Ionas
who had the best of it, although that was in Prague, not Bucarest.
You want to be careful."

"I see no reason to view the situation with alarm," said Monsieur Gherson.

When he had departed the paunches and double-chins returned
to the subject.

"The old boy's pretty formidable, you've got to admit."

"But so's Apostolesco."

"I wouldn't back his chances. There's no one capable of
standing up to Lazar Gherson, unless it's the King."

"I'm not so sure. Well, we shall know more about it tomorrow.'

Monsieur Gherson had invited a number of journalists and
politicians to lunch. Afterwards he rested for an hour and then

called at Lascari's bank to see the younger Lascari, Cesar, with whom he had a number of matters to discuss. Finally he returned home, changed into a dinner-jacket, collected his wife and went to dine with the Vasilesco-Rimnics. As ever he made an impressive entrance, small though he was, at the side of the graceful and elegant Madame Gherson, who looked so young for her forty years that she could afford to allow a few silver threads to appear as an added adornment amid the smooth, gold waves of her hair. They separated at once. Gherson moved to greet Prince Vogoride, who seemed bored, and Pericles Mittesco, who was looking as grave and distinguished as ever. Nothing, of course, was said about business, but Gherson had hoped to catch a gleam of sympathy and goodwill in the lawyer's eyes. He was met instead with a suave politeness in which there was no hint of any personal feeling. " Perhaps he hasn't seen her yet," Gherson thought. " Good God, supposing he doesn't see her until after he's given his verdict! But that's absurd. Valentine isn't going to run the risk of losing those three millions." Comforted by this reflection he went to shake hands with the diplomat, Jean-Pierre Haralamb, who was talking to Serban Lascari. Old Lascari seemed pleased to see him.

" So tomorrow you and Ionas are going to make peace? "

" So far as I am concerned," said Monsieur Gherson, " I am prepared to forget the whole business, whichever way it goes. It remains to be seen what your nephew will do."

" But what else would you expect him to do? It's true that Ionas is very hard, even ferocious, in business matters, but arbitration's arbitration, and the result has got to be accepted. I've no doubt at all that when it's over you two will go on doing business together as though nothing had happened."

" But then, nothing *has* happened," said Monsieur Gherson.

3

On the morning of that same day Madame Gherson had awakened at nine o'clock as usual. She had drunk a cup of coffee in bed, smoked a cigarette and gossiped for the better part of an hour by telephone with a woman friend. Then she had sent the car to fetch her masseuse, her manicurist and her hairdresser. At half past eleven she had gone into town to choose material for an evening dress and had then met Alexandra Lascari and Madame Mavromihali at the Café Nestor, where they had discussed plans for a trip to Paris in December. She had returned home at half past one to change her dress and supervise the preparations for lunch. The first of their luncheon-guests arrived just before two. It was Professor Nicoulesco, who now had his own newspaper. He was very much plumper than he had been in the days, some years previously, when Serban Romano had first made his acquaintance; he was also more weighty in manner but more suave, rendered glossy by the circles in which he now moved. He liked Madame Gherson, finding her handsome and distinguished.

The big drawing-room had been decorated by a fashionable designer with pink marble, light-coloured Smyrna tapestries, walls of *calcio-vecchio*, curtains of *faille vert nil*, chairs and couches in silver-grey silk; and it was furnished with a concert-grand piano at either end. Seating herself at one of these instruments Madame Gherson played a few bars of Mozart and then rose to greet her second guest, Ionel Haralamb, who was followed by Titel Negruzzi and the editor of a weekly paper which lived by blackmail.

" Did you read the professor's article this morning? " asked Ionel Haralamb. "*Cher Maître*, you are preaching nothing less than the total extermination of the Jews—like Hitler! I am amazed, madame, that you should still receive him."

The others laughed, including Fanica Nicoulesco himself and Madame Gherson.

" I'm sure he isn't going to exterminate me," she said, with her head coyly on one side while she fingered the pearls of her necklace.

" You're too beautiful for anyone to want to harm you," said the professor, writhing his lips in a smile and making his eyes sparkle.

" That's very nice to hear, but my husband is less beautiful. Are you going to exterminate him? "

" He's too rich not to be able to come to terms with any government," replied Nicoulesco. He turned to Ionel Haralamb. " As a man of the world you must surely know something of political strategy. What else should we play on, if not passion, desire, frustration, hatred—in general, the follies and miseries of men? If you were interested in anything except tennis I would talk to you about the *Idola Tribus*."

" It's true that I'm a tennis player," said Ionel Haralamb dryly. " But tennis at least is a game that doesn't threaten to turn into a massacre."

" Come, come, dear boy," said Titel Negruzzi. " So long as the professor's alive nothing will happen to the Ghersons, or to you or me or a great many other people."

" But when he's dead? "

The professor laughed strangely. " I shall never die," he said. " Haven't you heard of the Comte de Saint-Germain? Don't you know that he's alive even now? "

Meanwhile other guests had been arriving, also Monsieur Mayer, sober and laconic as usual, and Monsieur Gherson himself, in the happiest frame of mind. After greeting everyone he asked:

" Where's my little daughter? "

" She ought to be back at school," said Madame Gherson shortly.

Their daughter was not yet quite fifteen. But since she had taken to wearing high heels her father had insisted on her joining them at table when more or less intimate friends were invited, greatly to his wife's annoyance.

" Are you afraid she'll make you look old? " asked Monsieur Gherson, smiling but casting a swift glance at her with his shrewd, penetrating eyes. " But you're still young and beautiful, and after all, Ida's no longer in the nursery."

" I'm not worrying about anything of the kind," said Madame Gherson angrily. " But she's still only a child."

The truth was that Ida had for some time been an increasing source of vexation to her mother. She appeared at this moment, a slender, well-shaped girl with a full bosom, smooth fair hair and big green eyes flecked with gold. " She behaves like a screen vamp," Madame Gherson reflected. " At her age! She needs to be kept well in hand."

But the gentlemen were kissing her hand as though she were grown up, leering and looking her over like huntsmen sighting game. Standing at the side of Monsieur Mayer, who was coolly contemplating the scene, Madame Gherson was very conscious of this, but her husband seemed to be quite unaware of it. He remarked delightedly to Professor Nicoulesco:

" Don't you think she's charming? Quite the little lady already. You'd never dream she was so young. She ought really to be having lunch with her governess." He said to his daughter: " It looks to me, miss, as though you've been putting rouge on your lips. How dare you! If you don't wipe it off this minute I shall be cross."

Ida shook her golden curls. " But, Father, you know I belong to the depraved younger generation. And there's no natural colour in my lips today. I was up half the night writing an essay and I'm worn out. Besides which, this is kiss-proof lipstick. It doesn't come off. Look, I'll show you."

She came and kissed him, and then led him to a mirror. Monsieur Gherson, at once delighted and disapproving, noted that there was indeed not a trace of lipstick on his chin. He also saw the gay, fresh young face beside his own, and caught the scent of copper-tinted hair as it brushed against his cheek. A lump rose in his throat. To think that so much grace and beauty should be his, that he had created it! It was a miracle.

" Let's go in to lunch," said Madame Gherson. She was still standing beside Mayer, whose expression, as he watched these proceedings, seemed to be almost one of hostility.

At four o'clock that afternoon, when the guests had departed, Monsieur Gherson announced that he was going to lie down.

" And you had better do the same, miss," he said to his daughter. " Children ought always to rest in the afternoon."

" But I can't, Papa, I've got friends coming to tea. I can't even go to the cinema, although it's a Clark Gable film and I'm dying to see it. Please, can I go this evening? "

" Go where? " asked Madame Gherson, suddenly looking up.

" I shan't tell you if you ask like that," said Ida. " Anyone would think it was a crime. I only want to go to the pictures with two friends. They——"

" I won't have you going out at night, I don't care who it's with," said Madame Gherson.

Monsieur Gherson made a private sign to his daughter and she said meekly:

" Very well, Mother."

She smiled ravishingly at her father and turned towards the door. But he called her back, saying, " Come here, young woman! " He bent towards her and asked: " Who are you going with? "

She whispered in his ear and then left the room.

" You always let her have her own way," Madame Gherson said angrily. " You do nothing but spoil her, and one of these days you'll be sorry."

" Oh, come, it's not as bad as all that. She's still only a child. What are you doing with yourself this afternoon? "

" I've got to go and try on some dresses, and I'll come back here for a minute to see how Ida's tea-party is getting on, and then I promised to call on Nelly Varlan," said his wife, no less casually.

" Good. Then we'll meet here this evening. Try to be ready in time. I don't want to be late for the Vasilesco-Rimnics."

Madame Gherson drove off in her car and parked it outside the house where her dressmaker lived. But instead of looking in to try on dresses she went up to the tenth floor, where Monsieur Mayer rented a bachelor flat under the name of Goldstein.

An hour later, both clad in dressing-gowns, they lay side by side on a silk-cushioned divan, smoking and sipping the coffee Mayer had just made.

" I must be going," said Madame Gherson. " Ida's tea-party

will have begun by now, and I want to see who she's asked. I'm beginning to be seriously worried about that child. I don't like the way she's been behaving lately."

" I shall have to look in at your house for a few minutes," said Mayer. " And then I must get back to the office."

Madame Gherson looked at him. " How detached he is," she was thinking. " All these years, and still I never know what he's going to say or do next."

Mayer inspired her with a sort of terror, and it was precisely this that appealed to her. With Gherson, whom she had married solely for convenience, she felt safe and protected; but Mayer, who had first furiously seduced her in a room where anyone might have entered, gave her a feeling of delicious risk and insecurity. With him she felt that anything might happen, although he had never harmed her except inasmuch as he was brutal in his fashion of love-making, saying when she complained, " If you don't like it you can stay away."

" You weren't listening to what I said about Ida," she said with a slight bitterness. " You might at least pay attention when I'm talking about her. After all, she's your daughter."

Mayer glanced coolly at her and said: " I can't take charge of her upbringing. That's your affair. Anyway, I've too much else to think about. Who do you suppose is going to save you all—you and your family and your fortune—when Hitler gets here? It certainly won't be Gherson. He's getting more vain and silly and over-confident all the time. He believes everything his cronies tell him. I'm the only one who can take care of you. You can't expect me to worry about Ida and her misdemeanours."

Madame Gherson said no more. She was firmly persuaded that Mayer was a man of quite exceptional attainments, capable of the most wonderful and far-sighted stratagems, the more so since he mystified her more than anyone she had ever met. He could not be asked to waste his time on trifles. Yet they were not altogether trifles. She was genuinely concerned about Ida, and afraid for her. But she did not pursue the matter.

After leaving him she went down to her dressmaker and then returned home to make a brief appearance in the drawing-room, where Ida's party was in progress: to kiss the girls and take satisfied note of the open-mouthed admiration of the boys, who blushed to the roots of their hair and stammered when she spoke to them. Finally, after further kisses for the girls and distracting smiles for the boys, she said, " Well, enjoy yourselves, darlings, but mind you all behave," and went off to have tea with Madame Varlan who was the wife of a lawyer and prosperous man of affairs. Then she returned home again, changed, and accompanied her husband to dine with the Vasilesco-Rimnics. As they were getting into their car after this function Monsieur Gherson said:

" You know, I'd like to go and drink a glass of champagne at the Melody Bar."

She looked at him in surprise. " But you'll be so tired in the morning. It's nearly one."

" We won't stay long," said Monsieur Gherson. " Not more than a quarter of an hour, I promise. You can't say I often drag you to night-clubs."

" Very well, Daddy," said Madame Gherson, indulgently smiling.

This spark of life in the old man amused her, although it also caused her to wonder, with a momentary misgiving, if it heralded a renewal of his amorous propensities. But it was some years since he had troubled her in that fashion. Why shouldn't they go? She had spent a pleasant day and had had something of a success at the Vasilesco-Rimnics' dinner-party; and there were sure to be people they knew at the Melody Bar, and someone for her to dance with. So, all unsuspecting, she let herself be taken there.

And the first person they saw as they entered, on the far side of the dance-floor, was Ida in the company of two strange youths in dinner-jackets, neither of whom looked more than seventeen. The girl saw them at the same moment and turned pale. Madame Gherson strode over to her table and cried:

" What are you doing here? Get up this instant! And who might you two urchins be? "

The boys promptly rose and fled, leaving Ida to face her parents alone. Madame Gherson turned furiously upon her husband, who was suddenly looking very tired. He murmured to Ida:

" Come, my child, we must go home."

Madame Gherson was trembling. It seemed for a moment that

there was to be a violent scene. The people near them stared and whispered. But then the band began to play a rumba, the floor filled with dancers, and the Gherson family left without attracting further notice.

Nothing was said in the car. When they arrived home Monsieur Gherson seated himself in an armchair and said mournfully to his daughter:

" Why are you so naughty? "

Madame Gherson burst into a flood of scolding, shed tears and came near to boxing her daughter's ears. Ida said doggedly:

" But what am I supposed to have done? What crime is there in going dancing? I haven't killed anyone or robbed a bank. What harm was there in it? "

When at length she had been packed off to bed Madame Gherson rounded on her husband, blaming him for everything and accusing him of ruining the girl's character with pampering and over-indulgence. Gherson said after reflection:

" But surely the child's right. What harm was there in it? She wants to enjoy herself. She was only doing what we do. It's not so terrible."

" Can't you do anything but echo her? Haven't you anything of your own to say? " cried Madame Gherson.

He got up from his chair. " Anyway, let's leave it for the moment. We'll talk about it tomorrow. I'm tired. And tomorrow I'm going to be even busier than today. Good night."

4

Monsieur Mayer had worked in his office that morning from
seven o'clock until midday, only breaking off to go out and buy
the diamond at Silberling's. He had then gone in search of Titel
Negruzzi, whom he had long regarded as a man of reliability and
discretion, fit to be entrusted with private commissions. He had
found him at Capsa's, which was where they generally met, and
had asked him to sell a substantial packet of shares on his behalf in
anticipation of a fall. They were shares, owned by himself, in
"Romecor," Monsieur Gherson's corporation. It caused Titel
Negruzzi no astonishment to learn that the general manager of
the Corporation was thus stimulating the fall in its shares which
had been started by recent newspaper reports. He asked no
questions but went to the Bourse to carry out the commission.
Mayer also went there to hear the latest prices and publicly deny
any alarming rumours. He there encountered Ionas Apostolesco,
whom he greeted formally, not speaking but raising his hat and
holding out his hand, by which means he was able to pass him a
note asking him to be outside the Galeries Lafayette in a quarter
of an hour. So fifteen minutes later they stood together gazing
at a display of men's shoes and keeping a sharp eye on the reflection of the passers-by in the shop-window. Mayer said:
"The old man's trying to get at Pericles through his girl-
friend. He sent me out to buy her a present this morning—a
diamond costing twelve hundred thousand."
"Anything else?" asked Ionas Apostolesco.
Mayer glanced at him in considerable surprise, while Ionas
continued imperturbably to study the shoes. He was a vigorous,
well-built man who affected the low, rather wide collars worn by
artists. His large head, brown eyes and somewhat flattened nose
gave him a stolid, benevolent aspect. Mayer gulped and said:
"That's all."

341

" Well, thanks," murmured Ionas, and turned away. Mayer also swiftly departed.

Ionas Apostolesco had risen at eight that morning, and after doing a few physical exercises and taking a cold shower had gone along to the Bourse, where he had busied himself with his clients' commissions until closing time, only pausing to meet Mayer and then to spend a quarter of an hour, in a shop near the Exchange, with certain gentlemen who did not wish to be seen in his company. Later he lunched at Capsa's with his cousin, Dimitri Coziano, through whom he hoped to get in touch with certain personalities who had a large say in the matter of the Carol Line fortifications.

" I shouldn't be surprised if you wanted to contact them on Gherson's account," said Dim Coziano with a hint of malice as he attacked his jugged hare.

Ionas emptied his glass of burgundy, wiped his mouth and said: " Well, why not? Gherson's a very sound man."

" Have you made it up with him? "

" No," said Ionas, " but I shall."

" Is the arbitration over? "

" Not yet. Mittesco is to give his verdict tomorrow. Naturally I shall accept it whatever it is, and I'm sure Gherson and I will end by becoming friends again. After all, it's a small matter and really rather silly."

" Is it, by God? You aren't worried at the thought of losing ninety-eight million? "

" Oh, I wouldn't say that," said Ionas serenely. " But I think I've got a good case and that Mittesco will see it my way. And even if he doesn't, Gherson is too honest and too sensible not to do the right thing. When you come right down to it, the money means nothing to him. From his point of view it's far more important to take a generous line and keep the friendship of a man like me."

He said this so mildly, and with such an air of gentlemanly goodwill, that Dimitri burst out laughing.

" Really," said Ionas, with an expressionless face, " I don't know what you're laughing at."

Dim Coziano went off after lunch, leaving Ionas to drink another cup of coffee and puff thoughtfully at his pipe; and in the Calea Victoriei he ran into Titel Negruzzi.

" Dim, dear boy, how are you? "

" I've been lunching with Ionas."

" Ah, Ionas. A splendid fellow."

" Yes, but at the moment he seems to me to be making a fool of himself. Of course, one has to judge by results, but——"

" That's it—judge by results! Otherwise you might take Ionas for a half-wit, which, by God, he isn't! Old Ionas make a fool of himself? Well, let me tell you——"

" Titel, you're drunk again."

" Not drunk, dear boy, merely well lit. There is a difference. Are you coming round to the club for a game of ecarté? "

" No time. I'm on my way back to the Ministry."

" Well, I'll walk along with you and you can give me all the dirt. What's the latest about Hitler? Are we going to have another world war or is it just talk? "

Ionas, while they were discussing him, had finished his coffee and gone off to visit a lady whose rent he paid for reasons of health, as he put it. He then made a number of business calls and spent the evening at the theatre. He went to bed at midnight and slept the sleep of the just.

The next day Pericles Mittesco gave his verdict in favour of " Romecor," to the great surprise of all those who had supposed that a written agreement existed between the Corporation and Ionas, by the strict terms of which Ionas was in an unassailable position. However, since the eminent jurist had pronounced in the opposite sense there was nothing to be said.

Monsieur Gherson was content. His gratification could not, indeed, wash out the distress which his daughter's behaviour had caused him, or the restless night which he had passed; but he admired the calmness with which Ionas received the verdict.

" I've beaten him," he thought; and he was relieved to find that Ionas seemed disposed to accept the situation without making any further claim on him. Everything would now go smoothly. His prestige had been triumphantly restored, and henceforth no one would dare to try to get the better of him. The cost—one million, two hundred thousand for the diamond and another three million commission to Valentine—had been not inconsiderable, but it represented a saving of ninety-three million eight hundred thousand lei.

He walked down the stairs beside Ionas who, with his hands in his pockets and his pipe in his mouth, was looking as placid as ever—a ruminative ox at the side of an old vulture.

" The fact is," said Ionas meditatively, " we should never have let that situation arise."

" Well, who wanted it to arise ? " demanded Monsieur Gherson. " It was entirely your doing."

" Not entirely. You would persist in that absurd offer of two and a half million."

They had reached the foot of the stairs. Monsieur Gherson turned to face Ionas and said:

" You should have accepted it. As a matter of fact, I was prepared to go to three million. But now you get nothing at all. Can I drop you anywhere ? "

The porter opened the door for them and they walked out on to the pavement.

" I'll come with you to your office, if I may," said Ionas. " There's a matter I would like to discuss which affects you personally."

Monsieur Gherson looked sharply at him, but there was nothing to be discerned on his smooth, red face except an expression of dull-witted stolidity.

" Get in," said Gherson, at the door of the car.

" After you," said Ionas. " We must respect grey hairs."

" I'm bald," said Monsieur Gherson, chuckling. " So we're all square on that, too."

It caused Gherson's secretary some surprise when her employer entered the office in company with Ionas Apostolesco. However, the old man was looking pleased with himself, so she assumed that all was well. The two men went into Monsieur Gherson's room, and he invited Ionas to sit down while he wrote a cheque for three million, made out to his secretary, who was to cash it at the bank and convey the money to Madame Valentine Scarlat. With this matter attended to, he settled comfortably in his chair and prepared to listen to what Ionas had to say.

" What I want to talk to you about," said Ionas, " is strictly a private matter. As you know, I have a great respect and liking for you, and I do not forget our many satisfactory transactions in the past. Besides which, I believe that in this latest business you will end by paying me the sum we agreed. I can promise you that if you do you'll get it all back. I have very influential contacts. I can arrange for the scandal over the railway-coaches to be hushed up, and I think there's no doubt that the Government will reconsider its decision to suspend the contract. I simply mention this to make you realise how distressed I am by something I have found out. The facts are these. My brother, Gogu, the painter, a very wild character as you know, has an addiction for boys, youths of sixteen or seventeen. I'm sorry to have to tell you that your daughter, for whom I have the greatest affection, has got mixed up in that circle. I hate to think of the harm she may come to. If it were simply a matter of adolescent love-affairs it would be nothing to worry about. But it's far worse than that— drugs, among other things—and recently she has become involved with a young man who persuaded her to let herself be photographed in—well, I needn't go into details. I shan't tell you his name. When I heard about it I went to see the gentleman and after putting the fear of God into him I bought the negatives, eight of them, and the prints. I intend to burn them, but I think you should see them first."

Ionas got an open envelope out of his pocket and tossed it negligently on the desk. One or two amateur snapshots fell to the floor, and Monsieur Gherson bent and picked them up with a trembling hand. Ionas rose from his chair and went and stood tactfully at the window, gazing into the violet November mist that wreathed the town.

When he returned Monsieur Gherson was sitting with his elbows on the desk and his face hidden in his hands. Ionas picked up the photographs, put them in a large marble ashtray and set light to them, carefully crushing the ashes with the handle of a gold paper-knife.

" Those are the only prints," he said. " I have the negatives at home, and I shall burn those too. I needn't dwell on the consequences for that child if those photographs were to get into circulation. You should keep a sharper eye on your daughter, my dear Gherson. And there is another matter which, as an old friend and business associate, I feel bound to mention. The fact is that I am not at all happy—indeed, I am very much concerned —at the way people talk about Madame Gherson. Of course, we all know that any married woman may have a trifling affair now and then. That is of no consequence. The wise husband merely looks the other way. But a good deal depends on how long the affair lasts, and when it's a matter of fifteen—no, sixteen years . . ."

Monsieur Gherson's hands slid slowly down his face, uncovering his eyes. He stared at Ionas over the tips of his fingers, while the tears ran down his cheeks.

"Sixteen years," said Ionas. "That is to say, since a year before Ida was born. . . . But what is really intolerable is the particular man involved, a swindling, double-crossing scoundrel. The sort of man, I am bound to say, with whom I wouldn't want to have any truck at all."

"Who?" asked Monsieur Gherson in a voice that was scarcely a whisper.

"You really don't know? It's Mayer, your general manager. He offered some time ago to keep me informed of everything that went on at your board-meetings, and I accepted—of course, only out of curiosity, to see how far he would go. I've paid him nearly two million since May, and there's very little he hasn't told me. For instance, I know all about the diamond, costing one million two hundred thousand, you gave Valentine Scarlat, to persuade her to go to work on Mittesco. You really shouldn't have done that, my dear fellow, seeing that we'd agreed to accept arbitration. In general, I'm bound to say I think it's time you did a little tidying up. A man in your position can't allow these things to go on."

Gherson was still staring over the tips of his fingers. His expression was such that Ionas knocked the ashes out of his pipe, scattering them over the ashes of the photographs, and rising rather hurriedly from his chair said with less than his usual assurance:

"We shall have to have a talk about the Carol Line fortifications, but that can wait. I'll come and see you again in a day or two. Goodbye for the present."

He left the room without offering Gherson his hand, because he was afraid that the old man would not take it, and he did not want to strike a jarring note at the conclusion of an interview that had been so smoothly and delicately conducted. . . .

Monsieur Gherson spent the next fortnight in bed, and for another week did not go to his office. The thought of encountering Mayer made him feel physically sick. At the end of the third week Mayer received a note of dismissal, with a hint that he would do well to leave the country. It may be presumed that he did so, since no more was heard of him.

For some months Monsieur Gherson did not address a word to his wife or daughter, and rarely even saw them. He spent his whole time at the office, very busy indeed.

Madame Valentine Scarlat received her fee, and Ionas Apostolesco received a cheque for ninety-eight million. This news caused stupefaction at the Turkish baths.

" What! You really mean to say that old Gherson let Ionas get away with it? "

" No, my dear fellow, I don't think it was like that. They decided to make it up, that's all. A friendly understanding. You may have noticed that nothing more has been said about the railway-coaches, and in the matter of the fortifications . . ."

IX

The Career of Dimitri Coziano (I)

I

Shortly after the First World War there came into being in Bucarest a number of private clubs of which the existence was known only to their members. Among these was the one cynically referred to by its founders as " Roumanian Corruption," which included in its membership a number of persons destined to distinguish themselves or to acquire notoriety in Roumanian society between the wars. Ghighi Duca, the flower of the *jeunesse dorée*, arbiter of elegance and idol of the younger set, was one of its leading lights soon after 1918, although the fact was not generally known. Later Professor Fanica Nicoulesco, one of the leaders of the Roumanian fascist movement and the most exalted figure in the Faculty of Philosophy, a man whose life and death were equally tragic, became a member, although this too was kept secret. Another member was Dimitri Coziano, who before, during and for a year or two after the Second World War came to be numbered among the country's ruling élite. Younger men, of the generation of Serban Romano, did not even know of the club's existence, but there were yet others, younger still, who were destined to worship and admire certain of its members and who even to this day hold their memory in reverence: for nearly all those idols are now dead. The name of the founder of " Roumanian Corruption " is not known, but it is known that the club had its headquarters in a house belonging to Ghighi Duca. The 1920 agrarian reforms considerably reduced Ghighi's fortune, but thanks to his extensive house-property in Bucarest he was still, at the age of twenty-two or -three, an extremely wealthy young man.

The house in question was situated between two streets in the centre of the town, and had entrances in both. On the fifth floor, reached by way of a circular staircase, there was a dingy landing with plaster flaking off the walls. The visitor, feeling his

way in the darkness, came to a door which opened only if one of
the two or three persons possessing a key was already in the
apartment, and in response to a prearranged knock or password.
On the other side of the door was luxury—thick carpets, rose-
painted walls, divans draped with oriental silks, Venetian mirrors,
somewhat yellowed by time, reflecting the light of silk-shaded
lamps, old furniture and costly ornaments. In addition to the
main salon there was a dining-room with a long table where the
company was waited on by servants brought from Ghighi Duca's
house, a Turkish sitting-room and still other rooms. Not all of
them were known to all the members of the club, for certain were
kept locked. By standing on the furniture one could get a view,
through small, round attic windows, of the roofs of the town, the
Calea Victoriei with its crowded pavements and café-terraces, the
parks and gardens with their trees, and, in the distance, the girdle
of factory-chimneys.

The members of the club here forgathered for boisterous
evenings, or for parties of a more recherché kind, when, under the
influence of wine and drugs, the more lusty or exhibitionistic
celebrants elected to entertain the rest with displays of their
prowess, assisted by the town's most beautiful prostitutes. Only
members of the inner circle, perhaps half a dozen, took part in
these debauches. There were others who came to dine in company
with the ladies and then withdrew with them discreetly to the
bedrooms. Still others, the greater number, came simply to dine.

After his attack of scarlet fever, when he was fifteen, Dim
Coziano had turned into a taciturn and reserved young man, inclined to shyness but intelligent. He had entered the Army as
an officer in 1918, had been decorated, and subsequently had
taken a legal degree, showing brilliant promise. In 1920 or
thereabouts he became personal secretary to that great lawyer and
politician, Leon Popesco, at one time the bitter opponent of
Boniface Coziano, and now the country's Prime Minister. It
was with a sardonic satisfaction that old Popesco had bestowed the
appointment on Boniface's nephew.

Dim was in the habit of dressing quietly. He had dark eyes
deep-set under bushy brows, but his mouth was youthful, mobile
and well shaped. Until he was nineteen he had never known a
woman, but then Ghighi Duca, in Jassy, had introduced him
to one or two ladies of easy virtue. With the war over, Bucarest

had become the province of the new generation of expropriated boyars, the rising class of the new-rich, and a miscellaneous world of demobilised officers, entertainers, actresses, hangers-on of all kinds. As a qualified lawyer and secretary to Leon Popesco, Dim had this post-war world at his feet. With his influential connections he could scarcely fail to marry a girl from a family as good as his own, and there was every reason to suppose that by the age of thirty-five he would be a member of the Government, although in student debates even the mildest heckling had put him out of his stride. He was no orator, but the same could be said of Ionel Bratiano, and it was not important; given sufficient backing, even the dreariest of read speeches would pass. In the meantime he was twenty-three and spent two or three evenings a week in what was known as the " Leopard Room " of the club called " Roumanian Corruption."

On an evening in early spring a few members of the club were assembled here, and after a dinner given by Gogu Apostolesco sat lolling on the divans, smoking and chatting. Ghighi Duca was among them, Fanica Nicoulesco, Dodel Doudesco, Titel Negruzzi, Cesar Lascari and Dim. Cesar was telling the story of how by gradual degrees he had achieved the conquest of a teen-ager, the daughter of a schoolmaster, a little middle-class girl stuffed with idealism and prejudice,

". . . and at the crucial moment she suddenly said, ' You're the first—the very first man in my life. . . . You see how much I love you! ' "

Cesar mimicked the voice while his audience chuckled.

" So then I looked absolutely horrified and pushed her away. ' You mean to say you're a virgin and never told me! ' I said. ' What deceitfulness! Aren't you ashamed of keeping your virginity at fifteen? And now you want me to get rid of it for you. What do you take me for? Aren't there any corporals or errand-boys in your neighbourhood? You run along, my child, and grow up, and then perhaps I may have some use for you.' She was utterly shattered. She looked as though the whole world had fallen to bits."

Fanica Nicoulesco was the only one who did not laugh at this engaging anecdote.

" Little monster," he muttered.

Cesar Lascari turned to look angrily at him.

" Why, what's wrong with that? What would you have done? "
Receiving no reply, other than a sardonic smile, he went on: " The
trouble with you is, you've got such a chip on your shoulder
because you don't get asked to the best houses that you never miss
a chance of sneering at the rest of us."

Cesar lay back against the cushions of the divan in his elegantly
cut suit, his pearl tie-pin, silk socks and crocodile-skin shoes,
and grinned unpleasantly at Nicoulesco, ten years his senior,
whose shabby, ill-fitting jacket left his wrists exposed. Nicoulesco
turned pale, and Ghighi Duca said authoritatively:

" That's enough of that. Gogu, you were going to tell me
about that woman in Jassy. How is it I never met her? "

" You were fooling around with politics in those days, instead
of having fun like me. Anyway, Bubi Ipsilanti was keeping her
in the lap of luxury, and that's putting it mildly. But she was a
real dish, marvellous figure, bosom, thighs, the lot, and the sort of
mouth—well, she was the best performer in bed I've ever known,
she practically wrecked me! "

Gogu launched into a graphic description of his encounters
with the lady, his hands describing circles in the air, which
was received with general laughter not unmixed with envy.

" What was her name? " asked Ghighi.

" Fifi. Fifi Opresco. Bubi was crazy about her; I'll swear
he's hocked every bit of land he's got left. And she's had it all.
She's cleaned him out. So I suppose now she'll be looking for
another customer."

" Is she in Bucarest? "

" No, still in Jassy, I think—anyway, she was a couple of
months ago. That's where she worked during the war, although
she was born in a Bucarest suburb. I fancy Bubi's predecessor
was an officer who fished her out of a brothel. But, believe me,
she's terrific, one of the most beautiful women you ever saw, with
a dark, gipsy sort of face, and damned intelligent, too, and passionate—like a tigress! My God," concluded Gogu Apostolesco with
a sigh, " I wish I could afford her."

" You're making our mouths water," said Cesar Lascari.

" We'd better change the subject," said Ghighi, "or else we'll
all be catching the train for Jassy."

So much for the Leopard Room and its frequenters. The

history of that secret society, less aspiring but perhaps more effective than the Thirteen of whom Balzac wrote, may some day be related elsewhere. What matters for the purpose of this chronicle is that Dimitri Coziano was among those who listened to this account of Fifi Opresco; and so greatly did it stir his imagination that, returning home alone, he scarcely slept. He continued to think of her for several days and then forgot her. But one night when he thought he had quite forgotten he dreamed about her, a dream of simple, crude eroticism. Then again he put her out of his mind and passed his days as usual, attending to his duties as secretary and legal assistant to Leon Popesco.

One day on the Calea Victoriei, when he was coming away from the law-courts and looking for a cab to take him to Popesco's house, on the Chausee, a sudden craving for a cup of tea and a cake caused him to drop in at the Café Riegler. It was half past four of a warm, clear April afternoon. He entered the café, and finding it stiflingly hot went through to the garden at the back, a courtyard surrounded by high buildings. But in the doorway he came to an abrupt stop and stood staring as though spellbound at a dark-skinned woman seated alone at one of the tables. She wore a toque with a short veil, an admirably cut pale-blue suit, and a white kid glove on the hand holding her bag. She had very dark eyes with long, curled lashes, and her mouth was beautiful and firm.

"It's her!" Dim Coziano thought with a shiver. He stood motionless, scarcely in possession of his senses, while she beckoned to a waiter, paid for her coffee and came towards the door. As she passed by him she gave him a swift glance which she sought to make indifferent but which betrayed her awareness of the intensity of his gaze. Dim stayed where he was for a full minute, feeling slightly giddy, so startled to find her in Bucarest when he had supposed her to be in Jassy—not for an instant did he doubt who she was—that he had not even the wit to follow her. Then he ran madly through the café and up and down the Calea Victoriei, a hundred yards either way, without catching her. Finally he made for the passageway in which was the entrance to Ghighi Duca's bachelor flat, pushed open a door with dirty glass panes and climbed the stairs, muttering feverishly to himself, " My God, I hope he's there! "

As it happened, Ghighi was there. He opened the door wearing a red silk kimono with gold embroidery and a green sash.

" What on earth brings you here? I can't talk to you now, I've something else to attend to. You can wait, if you want to."

Ghighi turned away, but Dim grabbed the kimono, which opened to display a bare leg, and cried:

" Ghighi, I've seen her! Get rid of this woman, whoever she is, we've got something better to do. We've got to find her. She's here in Bucarest, do you realise? We've absolutely got to get her along to the Leopard Room! "

" What on earth are you talking about? " asked Ghighi, amused but slightly annoyed.

Dim Coziano had undergone a sea-change, cheeks flushed and eyes feverishly glowing, his customary reserve all shed.

" I tell you, I've found her. She's ours, if we handle it right. We mustn't let her get away. She's here. I've seen her, I swear I have."

" For God's sake, who have you seen? "

" Fifi Opresco, of course. The one Gogu was telling us about, who used to be Bubi Ipsilanti's girl."

Ghighi began to see daylight.

" Fifi Opresco—that girl in Jassy? Well, what happened? How did you find her? "

Dim told him and he burst out laughing.

" My dear boy, have you gone crazy? Dragging me out here with a yarn like that, and a girl in the next room without a stitch on, probably catching her death of cold! How the devil do you know this woman was Fifi Opresco? "

" Well, I—I'm absolutely certain, that's all. I'm positive! "

" You're nuts! Although I suppose Bubi Ipsilanti might have brought her to Bucarest, in which case he'll be here too. Well, we can easily find out about that. And now, if you don't mind, I'll get back to business. So long, and don't forget to shut the door."

He departed, but Dim, instead of leaving, dropped on to a divan and lit a cigarette. He could think of nothing except that Fifi Opresco was in Bucarest and that he must somehow get to know her and take her along to the Leopard Room. Time passed; it began to grow dark; and Ghighi, accompanying the **lady** on her

way out, paused on the threshold of the ante-room and exclaimed:
" Good God, are you still here? "

" Yes, I—I stayed, but I'm going now." Dim got to his feet and
went hastily to the door while the couple stared in astonishment.

" The boy's gone completely mad," Ghighi said.

The fact was that Dim had suddenly remembered that he
should have been back at Leon Popesco's house three hours
before. However, he decided on reflection that it was now too
late; so he went home and passed the night in dreams of Fifi
Opresco, without even dining.

2

Dim had turned instinctively to Ghighi for help in this situation
because he was too young and too poor to handle it himself. His
father, Manuel Coziano, was dead, and the land-reform acts had
left him with only a hundred acres of the Cozia estate, which was in
any case mortgaged, and a country-house and buildings devastated
by war. The Bucarest house, where Dim now lived with his
mother and two aunts, had also suffered. Ghighi was the only one
of his friends who was still rich, indeed very rich, despite the
land-acts. He had a whole wing of the Duca palace at his disposal;
he knew and was known to everyone in Bucarest; he was one of
the leading lights of " Rumanian Corruption " and the owner of
the Leopard Room. He seemed to Dim to be the only person
capable of putting him rapidly in touch with Fifi Opresco, and
to Dim this was all that mattered. As to the possible outcome, or
the part Ghighi himself might play in the affair, these were things
he did not trouble to consider.

The next day Ghighi encountered Bubi Ipsilanti in the Calea
Victoriei. Indeed, he had strolled out for the purpose, half
convinced by Dim's story, and knowing that if Bubi was in
Bucarest he would be bound to meet him somewhere. They stood
chatting on the pavement, the tall, elegant Ghighi and the ageing

Prince Ipsilanti, something over fifty and grey-haired, who turned to look at every woman who passed.

" Bubi this is splendid. It's so long since we met. What brings you to Bucarest? "

" A woman, the most lovely creature, she insisted on coming here and I'm just realising how much it costs. I can't even afford to buy her a present. The war has been absolutely ruinous for me."

" My poor old Bubi! I hope I may be allowed to meet the lady. But are you completely tied to her apron-strings? I'd like you to come to dinner at home, but I can't ask her as well because mother simply won't allow ladies in the house who haven't been properly introduced. I've got two men coming, cousins of mine, one's a talented painter and the other is Dim Coziano, Popesco's private secretary. He's a chap who might be useful to you if you're having trouble with your property. And afterwards we can go into town. Perhaps we might join up with this proud beauty of yours, if that would suit you."

" I can't manage tonight, I'm afraid."

" No, no, tomorrow night," said Ghighi, who in fact had not arranged anything at all. " Tomorrow night at eight."

" That would be delightful," said Bubi Ipsilanti.

And on the following evening he dined at Ghighi's house in company with Gogu Apostolesco, plump, sleek and wearing a stock, and Dim Coziano, pale-faced and tense. Ghighi had ordered dinner for four to be served in the library.

At the conclusion of the meal they moved to armchairs to drink their coffee. The huge room contained fifteen thousand volumes, ranged from floor to ceiling. Ghighi rose and rang for a servant to close the windows. Then he re-seated himself with a cigarette dangling from his lips and one leg over the arm of his chair.

" What was it you were saying, Bubi? "

" We were talking about the land-acts," said Gogu Apostolesco.

Here Dim Coziano chipped in with a quite unaccustomed eagerness:

" You mustn't worry, Prince. I'm quite sure something can be arranged. I haven't studied the legislation in detail but I know there are escape-clauses. Special allowances are made in the case of vineyards, newly planted timber, model farms and so forth, and of course the law can always be stretched a little. There's sure to be a way round it. If necessary I'll have a word with my chief. The land-reform acts were never intended to ruin people like you."

" Do you own land yourself? " asked Bubi Ipsilanti.

" Yes, but I've lost all mine," said Dim, laughing. And then he was plunged in confusion as he realised the gaffe he had made. Bubi Ipsilanti was looking at him in some astonishment.

" You mean, you weren't able to save it? "

" It wasn't enough to matter," said Ghighi quickly, giving Dim a sharp, quizzical glance. " Dim's family fortunes are mostly invested in other kinds of property."

" Oh, I see," said Bubi Ipsilanti, quite satisfied.

Dim avoided his eyes. He was reflecting in amazement— " Has he really swallowed all that? Doesn't he realise there must be a catch in it? " He had still to learn that a man who is not looking for a catch is very easily deceived. But Bubi Ipsilanti suspected nothing. He sat calmly enjoying his brandy and cigar, smiling contentedly at the three younger men.

Ghighi changed the subject. Getting to his feet he said:

" Did you know that we had our dinner on a gaming table? It's a very old and beautiful one. I'll show it to you, because I don't think any of you have seen it before. As a painter, Gogu, you'll be particularly interested."

He had slightly stressed the word " painter," although Gogu was a notorious gambler. Ghighi enjoyed such trifling ironies, just as he enjoyed the smoothness and air of innocence with which he had held out a bait to what he also knew to be Bubi Ipsilanti's ruling passion.

The table was indeed a fine one, with an ancient wind-rose inlaid at its centre and a sunken recess in each of its sides.

" What are these for? " asked Gogu, running his finger round one of them.

" To put your money in, my lad, in the days when people played for real money—*louis d'or*, ducats, thalers or whatever."

" It's a beautiful piece," said Dim, looking at the table. " I don't think I've ever seen one quite like it."

" Neither have I," said Bubi Ipsilanti, whose eyes were beginning to light up, " and I've lived a lot longer than you."

" We might have a game, if anyone feels like it," said Ghighi casually, the courteous host prepared to humour his guests.

Gogu and Dim smiled and looked inquiringly at Bubi, who laughed and said:

" Are you leaving it to me to choose? Well, why not? Just a short game to try out the table."

Accordingly Ghighi rang for cards and side-tables on which to put their coffee and brandy, and they settled down to play, all in the best of spirits.

An hour later Bubi Ipsilanti's aspect had greatly altered. He was feverishly sipping brandy and exclaiming with strained good humour at Gogu's run of luck.

" But it can't last. It's bound to change. We must go on a bit longer."

Gogu smiled and dealt another hand. Ghighi was neither up nor down, and Dim, although he said nothing, had lost nearly as much as Bubi.

By midnight Bubi was finding it difficult even to smile.

" I've never seen anything like it. It's perfectly extraordinary."

" I've gone down quite a few times," protested Gogu, " and once or twice pretty heavily."

" But, by God, you've got it all back! I've played a good deal of cards in my time but it's years since I've seen a run of luck like this. In fact, I can only remember three occasions. The first was a complete novice, just a case of beginner's luck. The second time it was a professional card-sharp, as I discovered later. And the third time it was a man who was an absolute fool at the game but whose luck was always fantastic."

" Whose deal is it? " asked Ghighi, with the cool intentness of the born gambler.

" It's mine," said Bubi, " but I've run out of money."

" That doesn't matter in the least," said Gogu. " I wouldn't dream of stopping now, when I've taken so much off you. You've got to have your revenge. Besides, we all know your credit's good, particularly if Dim's going to help you out with this bit of trouble over your land."

" How nice you all are! " cried Bubi, his happiness restored. He promptly dealt, while Ghighi rang for more brandy.

By two o'clock that morning Bubi Ipsilanti had lost about 200,000 lei. Dim had lost 45,000 and Ghighi 5,000. Gogu Apostolesco was the sole winner. Of Bubi's losses, 180,000 were on credit.

" Whose deal? " Bubi demanded in a voice of suppressed fury.

" It's mine," said Gogu.

" Do you mind if we have the cards reshuffled? "

" My dear fellow . . ." murmured Ghighi, laying a hand on Bubi's arm.

" Not in the least," said Gogu coolly. " But I should like to know what you're suggesting."

Bubi was struggling to keep his self-control. " I'm not suggesting anything. I'm simply saying this run of luck's a bit over the odds. We should all feel happier, I think, if someone else dealt for you."

" And do you propose to go on staking by word of mouth? " asked Gogu, his manner coldly insolent.

Bubi started up. " If you talk like that I shall get really angry."

" You've made a grossly insulting insinuation regarding my play, and then you expect me to accept your word. I must ask you to pay up if you want me to go on playing."

" Gently, Gogu," said Ghighi, unruffled. " I'll go bail for Prince Ipsilanti."

" I'm very sorry, but it's a matter of principle. Prince Ipsilanti owes me a hundred and eighty thousand. I must at least have his I O U."

" I object to this kind of talk in my house," said Ghighi, still with calm.

But Bubi Ipsilanti was now beside himself with rage.

" It's all right. Where's a slip of paper? I'll give you an I O U if you'll agree not to do any more shuffling."

At this, which amounted to a direct accusation of cheating, the party came very near to breaking up. Only with difficulty did Dim and Ghighi succeed in calming the two antagonists and persuading Bubi to apologise. He signed an I O U for the present amount of his losses, and Dim, who was also cleaned out, tactfully insisted upon doing the same. After which, at Prince Bubi's urgent request, the game continued.

It ended in daylight. Bubi, very pale of face, had played for the last hour in silence. While Dim and Gogu attacked the cold collation brought in by a servant he murmured pathetically to Ghighi:

" Your brandy was so good, my dear fellow. . . . I'm afraid that's why I got rather carried away."

" You really mustn't blame me," said Ghighi. " It was your own doing. Why did you insist on going on when the luck was dead against you? You could have had your revenge some other time."

" I was so furious. . . . A run of luck like that. . . . I still don't understand it, if the fellow wasn't cheating."

" I lost quite a bit myself, but I'm quite sure there wasn't any cheating. It's an outrageous suggestion. How much did you lose altogether? "

" I'm not sure. I signed a second I O U. About three hundred thousand."

" That's a devil of a lot. You've been very rash, to say the least."

" I thought the luck was bound to change," moaned Bubi Ipsilanti. " The devil of it is, I don't know where I'm going to find the money. How can I possibly raise it in twenty-four hours? I shall have to blow my brains out."

His hands were trembling. Ghighi looked at him with a smile.

" Listen, my dear Bubi. Invite me to dinner tonight with this charmer of yours. And then it might be a good idea if you took a little trip—to Vienna or Carlsbad or wherever you like, provided you go alone. After all, you'd be bound to tire of her in the end. An old wolf like you doesn't stay long with any woman. Well, if you'll do that I'll buy your I O Us from Gogu. I'll allow you six months' grace, and then we can arrange for repayment by instalments, if by that time you haven't retrieved your fortunes. What do you say? "

Bubi Ipsilanti met his eyes.

" Supposing I say no? "

" You don't need me to tell you what will happen. Your I O Us will be posted up in the Jockey Club. You won't blow your brains out, but you'll have to resign from all your clubs, and fashionable hostesses will no longer receive you. You'll even find it embarrassing to show yourself in places like Capsa's. In fact you'll be in much the same position as my uncle, Colonel Duca, who changed sides during the war; but at least he has sufficient private means to be able to live comfortably in Germany. I shall be delighted to lend you the money for a trip to Carlsbad."

Bubi continued to gaze at him and finally heaved a deep sigh.

" Very well," he said.

" Won't you have something to eat? "

Prince Bubi shook his head. But then he paused at the table to nibble a morsel of caviar on toast; and in the end he made a hearty meal before leaving.

3

Gogu Apostolesco, delighted at being paid on the nail, handed over all the I O Us and went off to celebrate. Ghighi met Dim Coziano at Capsa's and returned the one he had signed.

" I bought it back from Gogu. You can tear it up and pay me when you're rich. I know you aren't earning much at present."

" It's very good of you," said Dim, doing his best to appear grateful, but in secret despair. He knew very well what was in store for him. From the moment he had seen that woman in Riegler's café he had known what was going to happen. He knew that he was lost.

" My dear boy, it's only natural, between friends," said Ghighi. " Incidentally, Bubi has asked us both to dinner to meet this sweetie of his. I'm glad you told me about her."

And he patted Dim on the cheek and went lightly off along the Calea Victoriei, with his hat on the back of his head and his cane under his arm, dapper, immaculate and with an air of gay insolence which caused every woman to glance at him.

They dined together that evening at Capsa's—Ghighi and Dim, Bubi Ipsilanti and Fifi Opresco. Bubi, thankful at having been rescued from a desperate situation and philosophically resigned to the loss of a mistress, and Ghighi, enjoying one of the most agreeable triumphs he had known for some time, were the only ones to do much talking. Dim was trying not to stare too openly at Fifi, and failing so often that his struggle was apparent to everyone. As for Fifi, she replied modestly and with intelligence in her slightly husky voice to the remarks addressed to her, while she summed up these new acquaintances. The one, with his hard, brilliant eyes, was very' sure of himself, too sure; an irritating, intolerable young man. The other, thin and dark, with a red-lipped mouth, too full, too mobile, had most evidently fallen for her. This was no new experience, but Fifi had rarely encountered it in so acute a form. " He's mad about me," she thought with pleasure. She was enjoying his presence at her side, the feeling of his eyes on her face and neck and bosom.

At midday the next day a fiacre drove into the courtyard of the Duca palace and stopped at the main door. Fifi, dressed in her best, got out and rang the bell. A footman informed her that his Highness lived in the right wing, which had a separate entrance. Accordingly she dismissed her cab, walked the length of the façade of the huge mansion, and rang another bell at a less imposing doorway. Another manservant asked her tó wait in the hall, and after an interval of ten minutes Ghighi Duca appeared, dressed for the town.

" Dear mademoiselle, how very nice to see you. I was just going out. Can I drop you anywhere? "

Fifi Opresco was looking pale and intense.

" I wanted to ask you something. It will only take a minute, but——"

" You can tell me in the car, or if you like we'll go and have a drink somewhere," said Ghighi amiably.

" Not somewhere where there are a lot of people," said Fifi. She still showed signs of wanting to enter one of the rooms, but Ghighi took her by the arm and led her gently but firmly outside. After they had gone a few yards she detached herself and turned to face him. " Why don't you want to let me into your house? "

Ghighi smiled. " It belongs to my mother, who is elderly and straitlaced. She doesn't allow me to entertain ladies who are not on her visiting list."

" I get it," said Fifi, and the sudden anger in her dark eyes made her look more alluring than ever. " Aristocratic. Well, you can tell her what to do with her bloody coat of arms! "

This delighted Ghighi, as did her furious look and the rich play of her mouth. She went on plaintively:

" I thought you were a friend to whom I could come for advice."

" And so I am," said Ghighi, opening the door of the car.

They drove to the Calea Victoriei and thence towards the Chausee. "Well," said Ghighi, "and what's the trouble?" He knew very well what it was, but all this was giving him great amusement.

She looked suspiciously at him. "Do you know where Bubi is?"

" I? I've no idea, if he isn't with you. I'm surprised that you should ask me."

"You honestly don't know?"

"No, I assure you. What made you think that I would?"

"Well, all I know is that the bastard's stood me up. We had two rooms at the Grand Hotel, and when I woke up this morning I found that he'd cleared out, taking all his baggage with him. He hasn't left me a bean, and no message, no address, nothing. He just walked out on me. I didn't like to ask at the desk, because of looking a fool, but the fact is, I can't even pay my bill unless I sell something. If you do know where I can find him, I think you might tell me."

" I really can't, and I fancy you'll have a job finding him if he doesn't want to be found. But is Bubi so much worth chasing after?"

Ghighi looked at her with a twinkle in his eye that caused her suddenly to burst out laughing.

Dim Coziano passed the next few days in what amounted to a state of trance. He lived his life as usual, attended to his secretarial duties, visited the Law Courts and was to all outward seeming what he had always been, the well-conducted, capable young man of good family for whom a brilliant political career was assured since he was already the protégé of Leon Popesco. But in the evenings he could remember nothing of what had happened during the day, no thought in his mind except of Fifi and Ghighi Duca, and what must surely be going on between them.

Then Ghighi invited him to spend a week-end in the country, at a place not far from Bucarest where the Duca family owned a country mansion, a pseudo-classical monstrosity built about 1840, with a Palladian front surmounted by a Gothic tower.

"We'll take Fifi along," said Ghighi. And he added lightly: "I haven't laid a finger on her yet."

Dim might perhaps have blackmailed him into surrendering her by an effusion of gratitude, by a show of trusting innocence followed by protestations of eternal friendship and devotion, to the point of tears, if necessary. That is what he would have attempted at thirty or forty: but he was only twenty-five and besottedly in love. His heart nearly stopped beating. What did Ghighi mean? Was he going to give her up to him? He half believed it but dared not ask.

And on the Friday night he discovered his mistake. The bedrooms occupied by Ghighi and himself were on either side of Fifi's room. Dim said good night in a voice that trembled, and the first thing he saw, on entering his bedroom, was that there was a communicating door and that the key was on his side. " Ghighi is the best and truest of friends," he thought. " I shall never cease to thank him." His first impulse was to rush to the door, but then he reflected that it would be tactful to allow the lady time to disrobe. He stood for some time waiting and listening, hearing nothing at first but the beating of his heart. Then he heard a soft creaking of floorboards and thought he caught a whiff of perfume, for the door was old, with a wide gap at the bottom.

He began at length to turn the key, slowly and cautiously. He did not know what he was going to say to Fifi, or what he was going to do. He got the door unlocked, and gently turning the handle opened it a fraction of an inch. " Now! " he said to himself, but as he still hesitated, with his hand on the handle, he heard Fifi's husky voice say something in a low murmur. He stood rigid while a tremor passed through his body, and now he heard the voice of Ghighi. Although it was no more than a whisper he knew what he was saying and what she said in reply. He knew everything; but still he stood there, listening to all that passed, sick with helpless misery, shame and humiliation, but unable to tear himself away.

4

" After all," Dim said to himself, in the sleepless nights and days of agonised lucidity which followed, " why should I have expected him to give her up to me? He couldn't have known that I'm in love with her. He doesn't know it now. He did what I wanted. He kept her here and got her out of Bubi's clutches, although he lost money in doing so. I lost even more, but that was my own fault, and there was no reason why he should have paid my debts. But he did it, and he even gave me a fair chance with her by leaving the key in the lock. And I did nothing. I just waited too long. I stood there like a fool until he decided that it was his turn. Why, oh why, didn't I go in a minute sooner? "

Outwardly Dim was unchanged, as silent and discreet as ever. But it happened now and then that he failed to answer a question, or did so as though his wits were wandering. On two occasions his chief asked him the time, and after looking at his watch he forgot to reply.

" What's the matter with you? Have you fallen in love? " said the great man, laughing. But eventually he grew serious. " You really must pay more attention to what you're doing. You've become extraordinarily absent-minded."

Even so, Leon Popesco did not suspect that his secretary was neglecting his duties, putting aside or filing away everything that was not of immediate urgency. He discovered this later. For the present only Ghighi was aware of Dim's state of moral disarray. He invited him out constantly with Fifi, to restaurants, theatres and night-clubs; and Fifi, laughing in seeming delight at Ghighi's jokes, darted curious glances at the tense, unhappy young man who accompanied them.

This went on for nearly a month. Then one evening at the beginning of May, when the cousins were alone together in the Leopard Room (where Fifi had never yet set foot), Ghighi said:

" Listen, Dim, you're my closest and dearest friend. I have a particular favour to ask you."

He said this with the utmost gravity, his blue eyes candid and clear, although secretly he was highly entertained. Dim listened in extreme alarm, guessing that some terrible request must be forthcoming.

" I've got to take my mother to Paris and then on to Cannes," said Ghighi. " I shall come back here as soon as I've got her settled. Obviously I shall have to leave Fifi behind, and I want to ask you to look after her while I'm away—take her out and keep an eye on her and see that she's happy. Will you do that for me?"

He continued to look gravely at him with the same air of trusting candour, and Dim was overwhelmed with dismay, at once terrified at the prospect of being alone with Fifi and irresistibly allured.

" You're the only man I would dare trust with her," said Ghighi, with difficulty restraining his laughter. " Can I rely on you?"

Dim, all unsuspecting, murmured, " Yes, I'll do it," and Ghighi clasped his hand and said simply, " Thank you, dear friend."

He left two days later; and to the profound astonishment of his family and friends Dimitri Coziano, that promising young barrister and rising star in the political firmament, began to be seen in theatres and night-clubs with Fifi Opresco. The ladies pretended not to notice him, or responded only distantly to his salutations. The gentlemen, on the other hand, greeted and congratulated him with ribald enthusiasm. Dim was unconscious of all this. " She doesn't know that I love her. I've got to tell her. . . . No, I must never tell her. Even if I did it would mean nothing to her. . . . I'll tell her today—no, not today, tomorrow. . . . Yes, I'll tell her tomorrow!"

As for Fifi, she dined with Dim, danced with him, sat beside him at the theatre and bestowed smiles on him with white pointed teeth in a fierce, voracious mouth; but her looks grew increasingly tender. She teased him gently, touching his hand or knee as though unconsciously with her own, so that sometimes she robbed him of his breath.

" Why have you stopped talking? Go on with what you were saying."

And finally, one night a week after Ghighi's departure, she

caused him to drink far more than he was accustomed to, and herself drank a great deal, so that in the end they woke up in her bed in the Grand Hotel. Dim was in a state of exaltation such as he had never known before and was never to know again.

"We'll get married," he cried. "My loveliest and most beautiful, I've never been so happy in my life! I'll make you happy. I'll make a career for you that will turn all those half-wit society bitches green with envy."

She stroked his hair, gazing at him with half-closed eyes.

"I love you," she murmured. "You're young and sweet and passionate, and you don't know how to make love. You're miserly in love—but I'll teach you. . . . The men in this town are all too old, even Ghighi, who's older than any. Why do you let him make a fool of you? I've never known anyone so cunning or so callous, he's rotten through and through. But you're everything that is sweet and gentle, and I love you."

There was an interlude, and then they talked again about Ghighi.

"He's a wonderful friend," said Dim. "You don't know him."

"What a great goose you are! Can't you see that he's playing cat-and-mouse with both of us?" And she went on to explain Ghighi's manœuvres after her own fashion. "He's perverse and cruel. He gets a thrill out of watching people suffer. He's bored without it. To be bored is his destiny in life, as though it were a curse laid upon him."

"I just don't understand," muttered the bewildered Dim Coziano.

By the time Ghighi returned from France, towards the end of the month, Dim and Fifi had fallen into the habit, after dining in the garden restaurants of Bucarest, of spending their nights in the Leopard Room, of which Ghighi had left Dim a key.

It was here that Ghighi found them, having arrived at dawn and only stopped at his home to bath and change. They were lying entwined on the divan when they heard the sound of his key in the lock, and they had only time to slip on wrappers before his tall, lean form appeared in the doorway of the room. He stood motionless, stonily regarding them. Early sunshine was streaming in through the attic windows, lighting up the red carpet and drawing gleams from the chiselled edges of the Venetian mirrors. The room smelt of French perfume, tobacco, coffee and human sweat.

Ghighi said quietly: " So you broke your word. You have betrayed your trust."

" It wasn't his fault! " cried Fifi, springing up. " I made him do it. I love him. I don't need you or anyone—only Dim! We're going to marry and be happy. I won't let you go on tormenting him for your own amusement. I love him. I could never love you because your heart's like ice, and there's no blood in your veins. I love him! "

She was a picture of health and vigour as she stood fiercely confronting Ghighi, her skin fresh and glowing, her bosom beneath the wrapper half exposed; but he brushed her aside.

" I don't want to talk to this creature, but I must have a few words with you. Let's go into the next room."

" Don't go! " cried Fifi.

But Dim followed Ghighi, after clasping her in his arms and kissing her on the lips.

" You needn't be afraid," he said.

Ghighi seated himself on a couch in the ante-room, crossed his legs and looked at Dim, who remained standing.

" Why don't you sit down? " he asked mockingly.

Dim blushed and did so.

" My dear Dim, I'm very distressed indeed. I thought you were my friend, I trusted you completely; but you've behaved like a dirty little rat."

" What about you? " growled Dim, agitated but aggressive. " You talk about friendship. You've been laughing at me the whole time. You seem to think you can do whatever you please with me."

" I don't know what you're talking about."

" You knew damned well I was in love with her."

" Well, but I gave you your chance, and you didn't take it. Was I supposed to let her go for no reason? And if the lady was in love with you why didn't she turn me down in the first place, instead of waiting until now? Do, for God's sake, have some sense. You must surely realise that she's the worst kind of trollop."

" Don't dare to talk like that! " shouted Dim. " I won't have her insulted."

" All right," said Ghighi, unperturbed, " we'll say no more

about her. But she said something about marriage. Have you
gone clean off your head? "

" That's my affair." Dim got up and moved towards the door.
" It's none of your business."

" Wait! " said Ghighi. " I want to perform one last act of
friendship, because after today I shall have nothing more to do
with you." He was silent for a moment while he savoured his
secret delight in the situation. " After this I've finished with you
for good. But I do want to urge you to think what you're doing.
Don't you realise that if you marry this woman you'll destroy
yourself? You'll outrage everyone, you'll be cold-shouldered by
society, you'll lose your job and have to start again from nothing.
Your career will be ruined."

" I disagree. I shan't be destroying anything—and if I do,
it's still my own affair." Dim plunged back into the Leopard
Room, where Fifi, who had been listening behind the door, flung
her arms round his neck. " Let's go, darling," he said. " We've
nothing to keep us in this place."

They dressed and passed through the ante-chamber under the
sardonic gaze of Ghighi, who had not moved.

" What are you grinning at, pig? " demanded Fifi. " You're
trying to pretend you don't care, but you're mad with rage underneath, you're livid! "

" Darling, don't talk like that," said Dim in embarrassment.
" It's too ugly."

" Don't you try to stick up for him, the rotten bastard, he can
go and——. And don't you start preaching at me either or you
can do the same," screeched Fifi.

As they went down the stairs they heard the key turn in the
lock behind them.

5

" You'll be rich! " said Dim. " You'll live in luxury like my aunt, Olga Duca, or Elvira Vorvoreano."

" Darling, as if I cared. I love you. All I want is for us to go on making love," said Fifi.

But Dim did not doubt that this was only a form of words, and that she was as fond of luxury as every other woman he knew. He had to consider what his next move was to be. He was already in danger of losing his job. In his present preoccupied and over-wrought state he was incapable of carrying out his duties efficiently, and the Prime Minister had several times rebuked him severely during the past few weeks. He would have to think of something.

After some thought he went to see his uncle, Serban Lascari, at the bank, where he was received with all the ceremony due to a brilliant and promising nephew. They sat together in a sombre office with brown-tinted walls and worn, leather-upholstered armchairs.

" Uncle Serbanica, I need your help. It's a matter of a loan. I want you—that is to say, the bank—to allow me a credit of two millions. I must have it within the next two days, and I'll pay it back in three or four days' time."

Serban Lascari stroked his grey imperial beard, modelled on that of the late King Edward VII of England.

" Are you hoping to make a big killing on the Bourse? " he asked.

Dim smiled but did not answer.

" You've got very thin, my boy. Is anything wrong? Aren't you well? " asked Serban. After a brief pause he went on: " As you know, we're very chary of personal loans. It's not at all our line of business."

" Yes, I realise that. But you know me, Uncle Serbanica, and that I'm to be trusted."

" Of course. But you must bear in mind that I have to persuade my co-directors. You have recently been seen rather often in company with a lady who is known to have swallowed up at least one fortune. I'm not lecturing you on morals, my dear boy, I'm simply mentioning something which the Board will be bound to take into account if I put the matter before them."

" But there's Cozia," said Dim, who was beginning to be alarmed. This was his only chance; he would be lost without it.

" The Cozia estate is already mortgaged, and in any case it is not solely your property. Your mother has a share. Besides, we're not an agricultural bank. And, finally, even if we agreed to the loan in principle, it would be subject to a satisfactory report by our agents, and that would take a little time. You say you want the money within two days."

" At the latest! "

Serban Lascari shook his head.

" I'm very sorry, but it's out of the question. I might be disposed to lend you something out of my own pocket, but you're asking for a large sum. Even I would want some security, and I'm afraid Cozia would not be enough for me. I should want something more substantial than that."

Dim was closely watching his uncle while he wondered whether to risk what he had in mind. But he had no alternative. He was on the verge of disaster already.

" Look, Uncle Serbanica," he said, " in return for a loan of two million I'm prepared to give you certain information. But only on the understanding that you don't make use of it to the extent of more than four or five million. Otherwise you'd be liable to ruin everything, and you'd be risking a serious scandal."

" You're making conditions? " said Serban Lascari, raising his eyebrows.

" I'm making you an offer," said Dim, getting up. " You can take it or leave it."

" Now, now, don't get excited. Sit down and tell me what it's all about. Would you care for some coffee? "

" No, thank you, I'm not interested in coffee at the moment. You must listen and then forget what I've said. At what rate are Transylvanian Austro-Hungarian kronen being quoted at present on the market? "

" They're very low and still falling. Do you mean that you know what is going to happen to them? " Serban Lascari was suddenly very alert.

" There's to be a revaluation. I know the new official rate, which will be announced the day after tomorrow, Thursday."

There was a brief silence.

" I see," said Serban. " Well, of course, that puts a new complexion on the matter. I take it the official rate will be higher than the one currently quoted? "

" Why else should I be trying to raise money? " asked Dim dryly.

" Quite so. So you propose to buy two millions' worth of kronen, and what do you expect to get for them when the new rate comes into force—three million? "

" Four."

" As much as that? Well, that's most interesting. I think we may say, my dear Dim, that our little piece of business has been satisfactorily concluded. I congratulate you. I only wish my son, Cesar, would display a similar degree of perspicacity and initiative. I foresee that you have a great career ahead of you."

The new rate was duly announced on the Thursday, and on the Friday a young man dressed with quiet elegance pushed his way through the crowd thronging the counters in the National Bank. Entering the assistant manager's office he asked him to sell the holding of Austro-Hungarian kronen, now worth four million, standing to his credit at Lascari's bank.

" It's a large sum, Monsieur Coziano," the assistant manger said. " Are you aware that you may be asked to explain how you acquired it? Lascari's bank also has an exceedingly large holding of kronen which they bought at the old rate. No doubt their long experience told them what was likely to happen. But an established financial house may be allowed to do things which are not permitted to a private person."

Once again Dim Coziano felt himself on the brink of disaster. At any cost he must have the money—for the sake of Fifi and his life's happiness. He took another chance, well knowing the risk he ran. Smiling with the utmost calm he said:

" Even if the private person is the Prime Minister's secretary? "

He saw the other's expression change.

" I see. Well, of course, that is another matter. If you'll come this way we'll attend to the formalities at once."

By midday Dim had cleared a profit of two million. But that afternoon the Governor of the National Bank, having had the matter reported to him, telephoned the Prime Minister.

" This kronen transaction, your Excellency. It's a little awkward. We can't prevent the facts from becoming known. If I may say so, it should have been more discreetly managed."

" Kronen transaction? " exclaimed the startled Leon Popesco. " What are you talking about? "

Realising at once what must have happened, the Governor gave him the facts. There was a long silence at the other end of the line, and then the great man said:

" I'm grateful to you for informing me, but the gentleman in question is no longer my secretary. I have dismissed him."

The same evening Dim received a note from the Prime Minister's office. " Sir, I am instructed by his Excellency the Prime Minister to inform you that your appointment as his personal secretary is herewith terminated. . . ."

Dim went the following week to pay another call on his uncle. Serban Lascari received him standing, his manner cold, and did not ask him to be seated.

" I'm exceedingly sorry to hear about this business with Leon. You should really have been more careful. You put him in an impossible position. And is it true that you're proposing to marry this woman you've been going round with? "

" We can discuss that some other time," said Dim stiffly. " I have come to ask you to arrange for my credit with you to be transferred to the Deutsche Bank in Berlin."

" You're going abroad? Well, it's probably the best thing, until this business has blown over." Old Lascari was relieved. He was reflecting that although the boy had undoubtedly done for himself in Bucarest it did not follow that he was irretrievably ruined. He might bob up again as a man of affairs in Berlin or Paris. Plenty of young men had launched themselves on prosperous careers in this fashion. " Sit down, my dear boy," he said more amiably, " while I give the necessary instructions."

Dim did so and lit a cigarette. " And won't you offer me a cup of coffee, Uncle Serbanica? "

" But of course, of course. Just let me ring the bell. And so you're going abroad? "

" I'm hoping to launch my wife on a film career in Berlin," said Dim calmly.

Serban Lascari started.

" You're already married? "

" We were married yesterday."

" I see. . . . And when will you be leaving Bucarest? "

" Quite soon. We shall go first to the Côte d'Azur and to Berlin towards the end of the year."

" I see . . ." repeated Serban Lascari. . . .

The next day Dim's mother called at the hotel where he was staying with his wife. They received her together. Ignoring Fifi, Madame Coziano said to her son in a trembling voice:

" I want to talk to you alone."

" I have no secrets from Felicia. Felicia, this is my mother."

The two women gazed at each other in silence. Then Madame Coziano burst into tears and sank into an armchair. She cried to Fifi:

" Don't you realise that you're ruining my son? You aren't suited to each other. You can only do him harm. He's my only child. The whole of Bucarest is talking about him. I beseech you, I implore you on my knees, do not take him away from me! "

She would indeed have gone on her knees if Dim, in acute distress, had not prevented her. Fifi, very smart in a pale-grey suit, with her hair cut short, was white with anger and alarm. She said venomously:

" Look at the old cow! What's the good of her anyway? " She turned furiously upon Dim. " You'd better get her out of here before I hit her! "

" Mother—Fifi——" babbled the distracted Dim. " Darling, you mustn't say such things."

" Go on, get her out! " shouted Fifi. And when Dim made no move she cried: " Aren't you going to? Well then, I'm off, and you can sleep with the old biddy if you like! "

She made for the door. Dim rushed after her, and as he grabbed her by the arm she turned and smacked his face. Then she went for his mother, who was huddled in terror in her armchair.

" Out you get, you old haybag! "

Madame Coziano was seized by the hair, dragged from her chair and thrust out of the room, while Dim stayed motionless, rooted to the spot where he stood. But when Fifi turned back after slamming the door, cheeks flushed and eyes sparkling, more beautiful than ever, he fell upon her and beat her soundly. . . .

Within a short time every night-spot in Bucarest had come to know Dim and Fifi Coziano. They were the last to leave, the heaviest drinkers and the most open-handed of customers, as unrestrained in their public show of affection as in their quarrels, which often ended in the smashing of crockery and mirrors. They went to Paris and the Riviera during the summer, but returned to Bucarest before going to Berlin. In the streets heads were turned to gaze at them, except those of persons belonging to the social world from which Dim was now excluded.

At about six one September evening they drove in a fiacre along the Colentina road, passing small houses and half-ruined buildings guarded by lean, rapacious dogs. Dim, worn out by the life Fifi compelled him to lead, was gradually sinking into despair. He had failed in his attempt to make a lady of her, and he was wondering how they would live after they had run through all his money, of which there was still enough to last another two or three years, but no more.

Fifi, in high spirits, kept up a constant flow of chatter. She pointed and said:

" Look, that's where the priest lives. And there's Mirica's café. And there's Papa! Hullo, Vasily, how are you? Driver, stop! "

" I must be drunk," said Dim, in bewilderment. " You say, there's your father, but I can't see anyone."

" Use your eyes, silly! There he is—up there! " She pointed to a telegraph-pole.

Halfway up the pole a grey-moustached workman with climbing-irons on his boots was looking down at them.

" Vasily," called Fifi, " this is Dim. I wrote to you about him. Come on down. Dim, move over and make room. We're all going home."

Dim Coziano was in a state of stupefaction. Later that evening as they drove back into Bucarest, bumping over the ruts in the road, he attempted to get his thoughts in order and to recall what he could of the small, squalid dwelling he had just left, the fat mother who had embraced Fifi, the coldly unwelcoming father, and the brother, a taciturn youth with side-whiskers and a small black moustache, who had gazed at him with intense dislike. Fifi alone had seemed happy and at ease, and she had never stopped talking. " God help me, what have I got into? " Dim pondered, seated in silence beside her while she babbled on. And suddenly she flung her arms round him and began to murmur hoarsely in his ear.

" Now, darling! Now, this minute! I can't wait! "

She continued to plague him all the way back to their hotel, in the lift and to the very moment when they scurried into their room; and as they lay panting, locked in each other's arms, she whispered:

" You see? This is why you'll never get rid of me. You can't live without me."

Dim shivered; wrenching himself free he went into the bathroom. He had a cold shower and came back streaming with water.

" You'll find that you're wrong," he shouted. " I can manage very well without you."

Fifi turned pale. She pulled the eiderdown over her body and sat looking at him with her large, dark eyes. The next morning Dim went out alone. When he returned he found their room deserted. Fifi had gone, no one knew when or where. She had taken a few thousand lei and vanished.

Dim shut himself in and never left the room except to eat. He stayed there for two weeks, meditating suicide. Then one morning the door opened and Fifi reappeared. Standing in the doorway she said harshly:

" So you don't need me, eh? "

He went on his knees to her, weeping; then took her in his arms and carried her to the bed.

When they were on the point of leaving for Germany he ran into Titel Negruzzi, one of the few of his former friends who still spoke to him.

" What's happened to you? You look like a dried fig, dear boy! That woman's eating you alive. You'd better take it a bit easier or she'll burn you to ashes. You're going to Germany? What, *now*? It's a fine time to choose. Have you any dollars? "

" I've got quite a lot of marks in the Deutsche Bank," said Dim. " Why do I need dollars? "

" Don't you know what's happened? The French have occupied the Rhineland because the Germans defaulted on reparations, and the Germans are trying to get rid of them by torpedoing their own currency. The maddest inflation the world has ever seen, dear boy! You should at least wait until the mark is stabilised. I can see you've been living in Lotus land, and good luck to you, but you really ought to glance at a newspaper now and then! "

Dim sold his marks the same day. They realised the sum of 575 lei. He was completely ruined.

6

In a suburban side street, on a site where later a modern block of apartments was to be built, there was at that time a row of old bungalows with a wretched strip of garden at the back. The occupants were minor employees of one sort or another. The owner of the property, a Madame Eliza Vasilesco, widow of an army captain killed on the field of honour, also lived there. And Dimitri Coziano and his wife occupied two rooms in one of the bungalows, with a door opening on to the street.

Behind drawn curtains Dim, with several days' growth of beard, and a tousled Fifi lay exhausted in each other's arms. Rain was drumming steadily on the tin roof. They had not left the room for two days.

" What shall we do? " murmured Dim. " Shall we stay where we are or go out and eat? "

" What's the time? I'm hungry."

Dim looked at his watch and found that it had stopped. He got up, blew out the oil-lamp and went and drew back the window-curtains.

" It's a filthy day. If we'd got anything here I wouldn't want to go out."

" I'm hungry," Fifi said again. " Aren't you? "

" I'm starving, and no wonder. You condemn me to hard labour and then don't feed me."

They both laughed and she put her arms round him.

" Stop it! " said Dim. " Stop kissing me like that, it makes me giddy. I've had all I can take."

" Me too." Fifi yawned and lay back against the pillows. " I must have something to eat."

Dim shaved with cold water, shivering. They got dressed, then stripped off their clothes again. It was nearly dark by the time they left the house.

They dined at a cheap restaurant in the Obor district, drinking a very thin soup and stuffing themselves with bread and gherkins. Cart- and lorry-drivers were talking loudly around them in an atmosphere thick with smoke and kitchen smells. The walls of the place were grimy, the floor muddy and littered with crumbs and cigarette-ends.

" Hey—waiter! " shouted Fifi. " Let's have some of that sausage."

Dim winced, for the hundredth or the thousandth time.

" How often have I asked you not to call out for what you want. You should tell me and let me do the ordering. And you don't have to wave and smile at the man like that. He's here to serve us, he isn't one of your pals."

" Oh, stuff it! " said Fifi. " I behave the way I like, and if you don't like it you know what you can do. There are plenty of other men in Bucarest. Anyway, who's paying? "

He subsided in furious silence, finding her detestable. An hour previously, holding her in his arms, he had adored her. Now he was thinking, " I wish she'd die! If only to God I could get away from her! " And he looked at himself, Dim Coziano in leaky shoes, eating vile food in that dingy place, and living on the proceeds of the sale of the last of Fifi's jewels and furs.

" Let's have the bill, boss! " cried Fifi, shouting at the top of her voice to make herself heard amid the din of customers and hurrying waiters in dirty aprons, bellowing orders through the service-hatch.

There was nothing for Dim to do but go back to work. Two years had elapsed since his marriage. Returning to the bar he began to plead minor causes, looking out especially for commercial disputes which did not call for oratory but for solid knowledge and sober argument. As time passed Madame Vasilesco, their land-lady, became familiar with the sight of a lamp burning in the small hours behind the drawn curtains of the Cozianos' sitting-room, and she would see Dim emerge with his brief-case at eight in the morning, haggard and pale-faced with his clothes hanging loosely on him.

" What do you do all night? " she asked. " Are you studying something? "

" I'm working, that's all," said Dim with a faint smile.

" But do you have to work so hard? There's time for that later. You're young. You should go out sometimes and enjoy yourself."

" I'd like to," said Dim, " but we've got to eat." And grimly repeating, " We've got to eat," he went on foot to the law-courts, filled with harsh thoughts for the woman he had left in their bed, sleeping peacefully as a child, and even more beautiful asleep than awake.

He began to earn money, not much but enough to enable them to feed less often at that squalid establishment in the Obor district and more often at second-rate restaurants in the town. They even went to the theatre, but only once or twice a month, since this was all Dim's means and his nightly labours permitted.

It was at the theatre one evening that Dim caught the eye of his cousin, Alexandra Sufana. Instead of looking away, as he generally did in such circumstances, he waved to her and she returned the greeting. She was in a box with a girl who was also known to him, Colette Arnota, a little blonde with clear, innocent eyes. He greeted her too, and she smiled. Fifi asked:

" Who are those two floozies? "

" A cousin of mine and a friend."

Fifi said no more. Without intending to Dim glanced again towards the box and saw that the young women were looking at him. They were probably talking about him. At the interval Fifi said furiously, " Let's get out of here! "

" Why? It's not a bad play."

" Well, I'm going anyway," she said, rising.

Dim followed her, muttering under his breath. She hailed a fiacre and they got in. It was cold and a few flakes of snow were falling. Fifi suddenly burst out:

" I saw you staring at those two mares, you bloody aristo! "

For a time Dim bore her abuse in silence, while the cab creaked over the cobbled streets, but finally exasperation overcame him.

" For God's sake shut up, you mad woman," he said.

" So now you're insulting me! "

She slapped his face. He tried to grab her wrists, but she hit him again, scratching his cheek with her long finger-nails. He punched her in the ribs.

They were nearing home and he was terrified of what he knew would happen, the shouting and brawling on the pavement and in the house, the delighted disapproval of the neighbours. Directly the cab stopped he jumped out and ran for it. But Fifi also jumped out and taking off her shoes ran after him, screaming at the top of her voice, " Help! Stop thief! He's stolen my bag! "

Dim ran like a hare, forgetting that the police-station was just ahead. The policeman at the door had only to put out a hand to stop him. Fifi caught up a moment later, and a crowd of spectators began to gather round.

" I haven't stolen anything, officer," said Dim, panting and dishevelled. " This woman's my wife. She's mad."

Fifi screamed: " You'd like to get rid of me, wouldn't you? You think you're going to do a bolt! I'll show you! "

The battle was resumed with still greater violence when they got home. Dim slapped and punched her and she flung the lighted lamp at his head. He dodged, but it set the curtains on fire. There were cries of alarm and the neighbours rallied round with buckets of water. Finally the commotion died down and they were left alone together in the damp, chilly sitting-room. Dim stood gazing in despair at his wife while she sat warming her feet, reddened by her barefoot chase in the snow.

" If you'd only let me work! Can't you see that you're wrecking my nerves? Do you want us both to starve? Have pity! Have some sense! "

Fifi said nothing.

The next day Dim lost the case he was pleading. When he told her she said, " It's your own fault for staring at those whores." He looked at her with disgust, and thought at the same instant, " How beautiful she is! . . ."

And life pursued its course, always the same, for another year and yet another. Their physical passion was unabated. Dim felt that he hated Fifi more and more; he would have killed her if he could; but whenever he drew near her his loathing was transformed into desire. During this time, despite the strain of these continual scenes, he continued to work furiously and began to earn more money.

On one occasion, after a particularly violent quarrel, he fled for refuge to a place in the country. He stayed there contentedly for several days, but then desire gripped him by the throat and he boarded the next train for Bucarest, scarcely knowing what he did.

7

Five years after his marriage Dim began to see his relatives and former friends again and to show himself in reputable places with Fifi, clad in the first, rather scanty mink that he had been able to buy her. He forgathered with Professor Fanica Nicoulesco, Titel Negruzzi and Ionas Apostolesco, the last of whom had given up sport (he had been an amateur boxer and wrestler) in favour of the Stock Exchange. These and a few others visited him occasionally in his home, but Fifi was not always present. She went out a good deal in these days, leaving Dim to entertain his guests alone.

On one such occasion the guest was Fanica Nicoulesco, at that time a lecturer at Bucarest University. Although he was still young, Nicoulesco's hair was almost entirely white. His suit was readymade and his tie a glaring colour. Thin and dark of face, with black, tufted eyebrows, he carried his head low, which made him look more mephisthophelean than ever.

" Yes," he said, " you had the world at your feet, unlike myself, who long for the chance of success and have never had one. You had your chance and you threw it away. Why? "

" Perhaps," said Dim, " because I wasn't ready for it."

" Perhaps. But are you now? "

Dim did not answer.

" Power . . ." said Nicoulesco. " By now you might have been a man of some importance in this country. As it is you have neither power nor money, nor——" He broke off.

" Nor what? "

" You have nothing. You were a young man of great promise, but today, at thirty, you're simply an obscure lawyer. And you seem to me to do nothing about it. I hate to see these failures. I want to share in victories and triumphs. But you young men are all the same. I'm thinking of those of you who formed our little group in Jassy, and had dreams of ruling the country, as I had. You're all frittering away your lives with drink and women and easy living. None of you has any courage or purpose or will-power. You're spineless and negligible, and it sickens me. I'm the only one with any ambition, but I have no family and no fortune. I've never had your chances. I don't know why it should be so."

Dim was staring out of the window. There was still a glow of light in the garden, although the room was almost dark.

" You're wrong about me," he said. " Wait another five years and you'll see. I'll show you that I'm not negligible. Five years . . . not even so long."

" I hope it will turn out to be true," said Nicoulesco.

There was silence, and then Dim said: " You broke off just now. You were saying that I had neither power nor money nor . . . And then you stopped. What were you going to say? "

" Nothing."

" Oh, but you were. What was it? "

Nicoulesco did not reply.

" Neither power nor money nor . . . Nor what? " Dim persisted.

There was silence.

". . . nor a faithful wife. . . . Was that it? " Dim asked in a low voice.

Still no reply.

" Do you know who the man is? . . . Is it Ionas Apostolesco? "

The professor spoke at last. " If you know, why do you ask me? "

" I didn't know," murmured Dim. " But I suspected. . . . I wondered. . . ."

" Mark you, I can't swear to it."

" No. No, of course not. I understand—I understand. . . ."

In the autumn of that year Fifi left home, and two months later
Dim discovered that she was in Paris with Ionas. He went after
her and fetched her back. In the spring she went off again, and
this time he did not trouble to pursue her. One morning a large,
handsome car pulled up at his dwelling and a gentleman with a
white imperial beard descended from it. Dim opened the door
in response to his ring.

" Why, Uncle Serbanica, what brings you here? "

" I'm very much upset, my dear boy," said Serban Lascari,
sitting down without taking off his overcoat. " Very upset indeed.
It seems that that wife of yours, after wrecking your life, wants
to destroy the rest of the family. She's in Prague with my son
Cesar. He seems to have completely lost his head over her. He
was always weak and foolish. And from what I hear she's behaving
abominably, making scenes in public, covering him with shame
and ridicule, which reflects on us all. I do beseech you, dear boy,
go and rescue him. After all, she's your wife. It's your business
to look after her."

He gazed pathetically at Dim, who smiled and said:

" I've no intention of doing anything. She can stay in Prague
for the rest of her life, for all I care. I'm thankful to be rid of her."

He had some difficulty in persuading Uncle Serbanica that he
really meant it, but he did so in the end, and escorted him politely
to the door. " It looks as though that boy's pulled himself together," the old man reflected as he got back into his car.

8

Some time after Fifi's departure Dim met his cousin, Alexandra, strolling along the quay of the Dimbovitza with her friend Colette Arnota. It was a mild, sunny afternoon, and Dim was feeling free, cleansed and light of heart as he had not done for years, like an invalid regaining strength. He had had a good day at the law-courts. He was filled with hope and vigour. The two girls in their low-waisted, short-skirted dresses looked fresh and gay, and he went up to greet them.

" How are you, Dim? " said Alexandra, smiling. " Is it true that you're single again? "

Colette Arnota raised her head and looked at him with childlike blue eyes.

" No such luck," said Dim, and was surprised at the ease with which he said it.

" Where are you going? "

" Nowhere special. I'm just out for a stroll."

" Then let's all go and have a really cold glass of beer. I can drive you. My car's parked over there."

The car was a low, gleaming Hispano-Suiza. " It's very handsome," said Dim as he opened the door.

" It'll do a hundred with someone else driving, and if I'm not there," said Alexandra. " But I intend to live to a ripe old age."

She let in the clutch with such a jerk that Dim and Colette rolled backwards, both laughing. They spent an hour in light-hearted conversation at a café and then Alexandra offered to drive Dim home. Colette said that she wanted to go on walking.

" I can't, my dear," said Alexandra. " I promised to call on Madame Mavromihali. But perhaps Dim . . ."

" Of course," said Dim.

Colette was again looking at him with a sort of wondering candour, like a child examining a grown-up. " These girls of good family," he thought, " do they know anything at all? " A vague image passed through his mind—" What are they like in bed? "

He brushed the thought aside. They walked a long way together, talking about his work at the law-courts, and suddenly Colette Arnota exclaimed in a tone that was almost one of reverence:

" You're a man who knows how to love! "

" Good heavens! " said Dim. " Is that what I look like? "

" Everybody knows what you did. You sacrificed everything for love."

He smiled at this innocence. " First I get tied up with a vixen," he thought, " and now I'm landed with a goose! "

But he had no objection to being admired. They arranged to meet again, and did so. He allowed himself to be not only admired but loved. After a month or two, not from love or desire, but largely out of boredom and curiosity, he became Colette Arnota's lover. Then he secured a divorce from Fifi on the grounds of desertion.

They went for a walk along the quay one autumn morning, beneath the reddening plane-trees and chestnuts.

" You ought to go back into politics," said Colette, not for the first time. " They were talking about you yesterday at Elisa Vogoride's, and everybody said that you were a very able young man who ought to be putting his gifts to better use."

" Do you want to be a minister's wife? " asked Dim, smiling.

" No," she said gravely, " but I want you to be a great man. I want people to respect you as you deserve."

He thought her foolish, but was gratified none the less.

" Very well, Madame Coziano," he said, squeezing her arm.

She looked at him with limpid blue eyes and said: " You know I don't like you to say that."

" Why not? We're going to get married, aren't we? "

" Of course."

" Well then! Are you filled with superstitious terrors, afraid of the evil eye? Don't worry, darling. We'll be married in the

New Year. We——" But suddenly he broke off, staring at a party of people who were approaching.

"What is it? Who are they?" asked Colette, alarmed by his sudden change of expression.

He did not answer; and instantly Colette guessed the identity of the dark-skinned young woman in a Paris suit, straight and slender as a wand, who was coming towards them accompanied by two men. She was gazing with an unnatural intensity at Dim, and as she drew near him she stopped. He too stood motionless. The young woman gave Colette a single, brief glance, dismissing her as though she were no more than a bundle of old clothes, and took Dim by the arm.

"I've only just got back," she said, "I've been looking for you. Take me home."

And they went off together, leaving the others in a state of stupefaction. The two men exchanged glances. "Of course, she's quite mad." Then they gazed at Colette. "Mademoiselle, may we not hope to console you?" She turned from them and ran, and burst into tears in the open street. . . .

As for Dim, he sat on his bed listening distractedly while Fifi told him about her latest adventures in Paris. She had learned to speak French fluently and had been to plays by Cocteau. He listened without hearing, and she examined him critically and said:

"You're looking wonderful, darling, and I like your suit. You're very smart these days. That woman's no use to you. You want something livelier—hard liquor, not lemonade. I'm the woman you need. Why don't you say something? You know you're the only man I really care about."

She went on her knees and put her arms round him, and Dim submitted apathetically to her embrace.

But he did not long remain apathetic, and they lived together for another three weeks. Then Fifi went off again without a word; explanations bored her. She departed one day when she knew Dim would be out for some hours.

He came home to find her gone, with all her belongings, and for the rest of that day he remained closeted in his room. "Never again, I swear it! Never, never again!"

He made it up with Colette and married her in December. The

Cozianos, Lascaris, Apostolescos, Vorvoreanos and Sufanas were all at the wedding.

In January Dim obtained an important Government appointment and went to work in a massive office building near the Calea Victoriei. The post had been secured for him by Serban Lascari and Colette's father, a former Minister of Justice.

And one day in that same January the commissionaire at the main door was startled to see a strikingly handsome and elegant young woman get out of a taxi and come running towards him.

" Hullo, Daddy! " she said. " I'm looking for Monsieur Coziano." She had slipped past before he could stop her, and ran upstairs calling, " Dim! Dim !" in a melodious and penetrating voice which caused secretaries, messengers and high officials to stare in amazement as she opened one door after another.

She burst like a whirlwind into Dim's room, despite the efforts of his secretary to restrain her. Dim got to his feet quivering, and said to the dignitaries with whom he was in conference: " Gentlemen, I must ask you to excuse me for a minute."

He took Fifi by the arm and led her through the ante-room on to the landing and down the stairs, dragging her along by force and in complete silence, his face absorbed. He dragged her down the street under a fine rain. Fifi was talking without a break.

" Well, I've come back, I can't live without you, you're the only one I give a damn for, although you're cruel and heartless and a bloody little aristo, but it makes me go weak all over when I think how it used to be when we first met, oh, Dim, you can be so'sweet and I need you so much, and I'll tell you what we're going to do, we'll meet at a friend's flat, she'll let us have a room whenever we want it and no one need know a thing, and I won't try and come between you and that woman any more because I quite see how it is, you need her father to help you in your career which you ruined for my sake, but now——"

Dim came to an abrupt stop on the muddy pavement and swung her round to face him. They were standing beside a newly dug trench where workmen were laying an electric cable. He spoke steadily at first, but with an increasing lack of self-control.

" Now listen! I loved you very much and I came very near to

wrecking my whole life on your account. You cheated and made a fool of me. You're utterly worthless. But now it's over. It's finished for good and all. And this is what I want you to get well into your head. I'd sooner spend the night in that ditch than in bed with you!"

Fifi uttered a sort of wail and turned and fled. Hatless and coatless, Dim walked slowly back to his office in the rain.

X

The Career of Dimitri
Coziano (II)

I

Some twelve or thirteen years after his second marriage Dimitri
Coziano was a departmental head in the Ministry of Finance, a
Counsellor of the National Bank and a director of several companies. He had matured into a tall, dark-haired, bony man with a
big, over-red mouth and dark eyes set deeply beneath heavy
brows. He dressed quietly but immaculately, and women found
him amiable and well-mannered but a dull dog.

" How did he ever come to lose his head over that dreadful
woman, and what does poor Colette see in him? "

" But don't you see, my dear, they suit one another exactly.
The one's as boring as the other."

But in Dim's case this was a matter of policy. For years now
he had deliberately set out to make himself appear colourless and
self-effacing, both in word and in deed. He had come to be
known as a person deserving of confidence, and by rejecting
several offers which, although immediately profitable, were not
otherwise conducive to his advancement, had further enhanced
his standing. His break with Fifi and marriage to Colette had
established him in the eyes of the world as a man who, when it
came to the point, had made his choice between the way of
pleasure and the way of duty. No hint of scandal had since been
associated with his name, and any trifling adventures he might
indulge in were conducted with a discretion that did him honour.
Moreover Colette was still in love with him and gave every sign
of continuing to be so. She was a woman much given to good
works who, besides attending the usual social functions, was an
active member of several charitable organisations. Husband and
wife met normally at lunch-time and in the evenings, although
quite often they went out separately.

Dim, for example, always went alone to the house of his friend,
Monsieur Gherson. Colette could not abide Madame Gherson

who, she considered, ran after men in a way that was positively indecent, and she found Monsieur Gherson tedious because he could talk about nothing but business.

One afternoon in the winter of 1940–1 Dim went to take coffee at the house of Monsieur Gherson, with whom he had just concluded a business transaction as discreet as it was profitable. The time was about half past five of a cold, dry afternoon, without snow or ice and with a scent of smoke in the air. The car which brought Dim (a Ministry car, since his own was being used by Colette) drew up outside a high, solid wall, beyond which, sheltered by a row of leafless poplars, a tiled roof was to be seen, a grey façade and the barred windows of Monsieur Gherson's study. Another car was drawn up outside the house, a long and elegant but somewhat old-fashioned Horch which caused Dim to wonder whose it was. He went up the steps and rang the bell, to be admitted by a maid with the smile she reserved for regular visitors.

" Is someone with monsieur? " he asked as he took off his coat.

" Yes, a gentleman."

" You don't know his name? "

" It's Herr Faber."

" Thank you."

Faber was the representative of a number of German commercial houses, one of the many German men of affairs who had appeared in Bucarest in recent months, together with army instructors and the first troops in grey-green uniforms and steel helmets. He was a regular visitor at the German Embassy, and he paid frequent visits to Constantinople, Ankara and Salonika, always returning to Bucarest, where he placed discreet but substantial orders with Roumanian commercial and industrial concerns. He also subsidised one or two newspapers and was a friend of Professor Fanica Nicoulesco and the leaders of the Legion. But why was he here? What business had he with Gherson?

The maid returned and asked Dim to follow her, and he did so with a slight hesitation, wondering if it was altogether prudent for him to let himself be seen in Gherson's house by a man whom he knew to be a German agent. It might lead one of these days to a paragraph in the *Buna Vestire* referring to the " Jew-friendly official, Dimitri Coziano." The point would have to be borne in mind. At the door of the study he met Gherson's daughter, Ida, in the act of leaving it. He greeted her with a smile and she gazed ardently at him with large green eyes. " The child's in love with me," he thought. " How old is she—eighteen? " The thought left him cold. He found her quite uninteresting, as he did most women in these days.

He went in and Monsieur Gherson rose to greet him. The old man, now white-haired and bowed, was looking very tired.

" Do you know Herr Faber? Herr Faber, may I introduce——"

" We've met already," said Herr Faber affably.

They shook hands. Herr Faber was so squat-figured as to be almost a perfect cube, broad-shouldered and deep-chested, his small hawk-nose lost in a massive, smooth-shaven face, like polished stone, that revealed nothing when he talked. He never laughed or raised his voice.

" You must take my word for it," he said to Monsieur Gherson as he sat down again. " If you do as I suggest you'll find that it's best in the long run." He turned to Dimitri. " Have you heard that since our air-attack on Coventry the English have invented a new word—to coventrate? London, for example, is going to be ' coventrated.' " He said it with an air of mild amusement.

" I've heard the word," said Dim. " And when is the invasion of England to be launched? "

" Oh, we're in no hurry. Being masters of the situation we can choose our own time."

Herr Faber then looked at his watch and said that he must be going. Monsieur Gherson saw him obsequiously to the door, like a whipped child or an under-nourished slave. Having done so he rang for coffee and came and sat beside Dim. He sighed.

" Well, what's the latest news? "

" There's nothing much. Everybody's wondering how the struggle is going to turn out between the Legion and General Antonesco. I daresay it doesn't look to you as though it will make much difference which of them gains absolute power, but it matters a good deal from my point of view. Antonesco would probably go on working with the existing civil service personnel, but the Legion would bring in their own people and very likely murder the lot of us, just as they'll murder you Jews."

Gherson looked at him, sighed again and said:

" Do you know what that German wanted? "

Dim could guess, but he replied:

" No. In fact, I was surprised to find him here. Are you doing business together? "

" He wants to buy up ' Romecor ' and ' Roumanian Cement.' You can imagine the sort of price he's offering."

There was silence while the maid brought in coffee. Neither man touched his cup.

" I'm afraid that looks rather bad," said Dim. " He works with the German espionage service and the Legion police, which means that he can have anyone in this country murdered whenever he likes—or almost anywhere else, for that matter. But does he want to buy you out completely? Wouldn't he be content with a share? "

" I don't know. I didn't attempt to bargain, I simply refused point-blank. He then gave me a long lecture on the war, which according to him the British have already lost, and about the New Order in Europe, and he went on to say that before long there'll be no room for me in this country or anywhere else in Europe, or even in Africa."

" That is certainly possible if they decide to go to the help of the Italians in Tripolitania. And they won't be far from the route to India."

" Exactly. He advised me to go to South America, and he undertook to procure passports for me and my family. But what would I do in South America at my age, with scarcely any money? "

Monsieur Gherson looked at Dim and then said bitterly: " They'll pay for it one of these days. This isn't the first persecution of the Jews, and probably it won't be the last. They all fail in the end. The day will come when they'll be on their knees to me, instead of me to them! Good God, the insolence of these people, with their thousand-year Reich. They think they can make a beggar of me—I who have handled as much money as any man in this country! I've made and unmade ministries and governments, I've been as much a ruler as Carol or Corfiotu or Max Auschnitt. And they want to make a beggar of me. Well, I'll beg. I'll sell nails, bootlaces, women's underclothes, anything! I'll beg—but I'll survive! "

He ended with a cold, hard laugh, while Dim Coziano thought

of the vast profits that must have been accumulated by the corporations he controlled, particularly since 1938. In the past three years Gherson's personal fortune had grown till it was as large as any in the country. But what had he done with it? This was what Dim was anxious to find out.

" It won't come to that," he said soothingly. " But I admit the prospect isn't very hopeful. If the Legion comes into power you'll have to leave everything and simply bolt for it, without wasting any time. If it's the General things will be a little less desperate. You still won't be able to stay indefinitely in this country, but at least you'll have time to transfer funds abroad, to Switzerland and then to Lisbon, and you'll leave when you're ready. It seems to me that your best course would be to try to gain time by negotiating with Faber over terms, while you start to make your private arrangements."

Dim sat quietly sipping his coffee, and Gherson murmured, " Yes, I shall have to think about it. You may be right." Then they went on to talk about recent political happenings. Nicolas Iorga, the eminent historian, had just been assassinated, together with certain lesser-known persons who had been involved in the sanguinary events of the last two years of Carol II's reign.

" It has now come to an open break between General Antonesco and the Legion," said Dim. " It's all a question of which of them Hitler intends to support."

" Yes, that's the question," said Gherson, his eyes vague.

Some days later he invited Dim to lunch, and somewhat to his surprise Dim found that they were to be entirely alone. At the end of the meal the old man asked him point-blank if he would help him with the transfer of funds abroad.

" What I would like you to do, when next you have occasion to go to Switzerland on official business, is to get in touch with Raphael Mercado, the Zürich banker, and open an account with him on my behalf. There will be a key-word and a number, without which no money can be withdrawn from the account. I shall arrange for funds to be paid in by someone belonging to one of the foreign Legations, and Mercado will let me have private confirmation through some other channel. As you see, I have thought it out carefully. My trouble is that only people on official duty can leave the country, mostly people whom I don't know or else don't trust; and, of course, I shall be very much at the mercy of the person knowing the key-word and the number." Gherson smiled resignedly, looking more than ever like an aged, melancholy monkey. " That is why I am asking you. We have known each other a long time and worked together on many occasions. There is no one else I would care to trust."

Dim Coziano's heart was beating heavily. This was precisely what he had hoped for, and now he had to find something to say which would confirm Gherson's confidence in him and deliver the old man into his hands. This did not mean that he intended to rob Gherson of his money, not all of it, but he certainly proposed to get hold of very much more of it than Gherson would be likely to concede of his own free will. As to how this was to be done, since all funds were to be paid into the account by some third party, that problem would have to wait upon a solution. For the present he had to consider what attitude it would be most judicious for him to adopt. He gazed in seeming tranquillity at his host while he thought the situation over.

" Well," said Gherson, "what have you to say? "

Dim made up his mind. He said in a cool, matter-of-fact voice:

" I think you're wise. I shall be quite ready to help you if I can. But, if you'll forgive my putting it so bluntly, what is there in it for me? "

He saw Gherson relax at once, almost to the point of sighing openly with relief, and he could almost read the thoughts in the old man's mind—" So I picked the right man! Well, it's no wonder. When have I ever been mistaken in my judgement, except in the case of the wretched Mayer? This is a man one can do business with. He might be a Jew. He wants to know what he's going to get out of it. No protestations of friendship or devotion, no flummery, no beating about the bush—a plain, straightforward, sensible question, worthy of a sound business man. Yes, I was right."

Gherson smiled and said benevolently: " Suppose you tell me what you want."

" Very well," said Dim. " In view of the exceptional and very difficult circumstances I am bound to ask more than I would otherwise do. However, if you feel that it's too much we will simply forget that this conversation ever took place."

" How much? " asked Monsieur Gherson, his voice hardening slightly.

" I should ask for a high percentage in any event—not less than one per cent. In the circumstances I think I am entitled to three."

Gherson's benevolence returned.

" Very well, in the circumstances I will agree to three per cent. You have only to open an account of your own with Mercado's bank. It will be credited with your commission as each payment is made. So that is settled. When will you be going to Switzerland? "

" Before Christmas, certainly. As soon as I possibly can."

" It can't be too soon. I can't go on holding off Faber much longer," said Gherson with a malicious grin. " He's at me the whole time."

" I'll do my best." Dim was still contriving to appear calm, although it cost him a great effort to master his delight. " And you must work fast. You should convert everything you can into gold or dollars. It looks as though the war in Albania is going to end after all in a Greek defeat. I've heard that the Germans want to move forces into Greece to occupy the aerodromes for their African campaign. It won't be healthy to stay here much longer."

" And you? " asked Gherson, with a shrewd glance at him. " How long are you proposing to stay? "

Dim shrugged his shoulders.

" If I'm not a member of the Government within a year I shall be forced to do what you're doing. In other words, either I shall be in power or I shall have to bolt to save my skin."

These words caused Gherson a feeling of vague disquiet. " A queer fellow," he reflected. Had he been mistaken in him after all? This Coziano was an impassioned climber and careerist, a type of man whom in general it is dangerous to trust. But he had said, ' What is there in it for me? ', and those were not the words of a trickster. Where another man might have leapt exultantly on his prey he had reacted like a sober man of affairs, an honest merchant exacting his fair price. Perhaps the truth, after all, was simply that he was not solely a business man. He had other sides to his nature, and political ambition was one of them. He was a native Roumanian with powerful connections, friends and relations in high places, who might go very far. No doubt he knew what he was doing. He was ambitious, bold and intelligent. And what became of him was none of Gherson's business. All that mattered was that he should open the account with Mercado's bank.

2

Dimitri Coziano left for Switzerland a week later and stayed there three days. He called upon Raphael Mercado, managing director of *Mercado und Sohne* (founded 1876), opened two accounts and returned to Bucarest. A telephone message from Zürich, in the form of a birthday greeting, notified Monsieur Gherson that the necessary arrangements had been made, and he began to divert funds accordingly. By mid-January the entire liquid assets of the Gherson family had been transferred to Mercado's bank, one-thirtieth part of them to the account of Dimitri Coziano.

Dim, meanwhile, continued to perform his official and social duties, always with an eye to the next upward step. January was for him a month of feverish activity during which he made two air-trips to Berlin and attended conferences with the representatives of the Deutsche Bank, newly arrived in Bucarest. In addition he busied himself strenuously with routine problems, showed himself at official receptions—including one at the German Embassy and another at the German Institute to celebrate the opening of an anti-Soviet exhibition—and visited the homes of Elisa Vogoride, Prince Mavromihali, Serban Lascari and other houses closed to the new place-seekers who had come up with General Antonesco, but still open to him because he was related to everyone. During that month of January, 1941, Dim saw some hundreds of people; he talked to former members of Parliament and ex-ministers, generals, chiefs of the Legion, ladies being kept by persons of importance, Jewish business men terrified by the prospect of a huge pogrom and Roumanian business men who hoped to step into their shoes when it happened. Whenever he could find the time he dropped in at Capsa's to exchange gossip with journalists of high and low degree, all of them on the verge of becoming the glory of Roumanian letters, or else of finding themselves behind bars for blackmail, fraud or incitement to crime. He was at Capsa's on the afternoon of the 20th of the month, and since there was no one there of interest he had to put up with the company of his cousin, Cesar Lascari, a tedious, thick-witted fellow who worked in his father's bank, and Titel Negruzzi, still the play-boy but endlessly involved in shady Bourse transactions. Shortly after Dim joined them Serban Romano entered, now so fat that his big buttocks showed through his overcoat. He greeted them with a grunt and came and sat at their table, and Titel Negruzzi murmured in an aside to the others:

"He must have a monumental hang-over, considering the amount he put away at Aurelien Sufana's last night. I took him home and he was sick in the car."

Serban called for lime-juice and soda and asked glumly:

"What were you all talking about?"

"Hitler," said Cesar. "Personally I don't think he's going to win this war. The thing I don't understand, Dim, is why you're risking your whole future career on the assumption that he is."

"For one thing I'm not the heir of Lascar Lascari," said Dim with a grin. "I've got nothing but my bit of land at Cozia. You can't really expect me to live on a hundred acres."

"Come off it! It's no use pretending that's all you've got," said Cesar.

"But apart from that," said Dim, "how can you possibly imagine that totalitarianism isn't going to win? Even if you disregard the military situation, look at the way things have gone— first in Italy, in 1922, Germany in 1933, Spain in 1939, to say nothing of Portugal. And now France! It's a political trend that has been gaining ground for years, and it seems only logical to assume that it will end by engulfing the whole of Europe."

"So you're banking on the total victory of totalitarianism?"

"I don't bank on anything—I just look about me and try to see which way history is moving."

"History is moving in the direction of European decadence," said Serban Romano harshly. "And the totalitarian States are nothing but symptoms of decay, like the philosophy of unreason which gave them birth. Writers like Thomas Mann have pointed out the relationship existing between democracy, political liberty and rationalism on the one hand, and between irrationalism and tyranny on the other. Rationalism is now vanishing from European thought, just as democracy is vanishing from the political map. The same thing happened in the Greek city-states in the day when the Nietzsches of the time were philosophising with more taste and style, being Greeks, than Nietzsche himself did—for instance, Thrasymachos, whom Plato brings into his *Georgias*, if I remember rightly, although I'm pretty hazy now about all that stuff. But don't you realise? Don't you see that these tyrants who are cropping up like mushrooms all over Europe are indications of the disease, the disintegration of a society? Athens had become a sick State when the presence or absence of Alcibiades, or of Cleon or Phocion, from the seat of power could completely change her policies and lead her to disaster or away from it. In the case of Sparta, there was never any one man who either made her or ruined her. There were only men pursuing a traditional policy, and by the time she came to have tyrants, whether they were good ones such as Agis or Cleomenes, or bad ones such as Nabis, it was too late. Rome, too, in the days of her prosperity produced successive groups of men capable of following the policy demanded by the national interest, not by their own. If one died there was always another to take his place. But who will replace Hitler or Mussolini when they die? There is no one. It will be chaos. Surely you must realise that? Was Florence in better health under the Medicis or Savonarola than in the days of the battle of Montaperti? Was Milan healthier under Lodovico Sforza's rule than at the time when he defeated Barbarossa? The presence of a tyrant is always a sign that the State is in its death-throes, whereas the existence of a group of statesmen striving to pursue a consistent policy is a sign of health and even of invincibility. That was the case with Rome after the battle of Cannae. A State may be destroyed by force of arms, but if the political and social structure is sound it will re-build itself. There is nothing, indeed, that needs to be replaced. The men are already there, occupying all the posts, guarding the key-points. But is that the case with Germany or Italy today—or with ourselves? Of how many countries in Europe can it be said? Perhaps the Russians——"

Here Serban Romano broke off. He called abruptly for his bill and then said, leaning across the table:

" Dim is one of Antonesco's men, but I hope he won't hold it against me when I say that I hate ' saviours.' Do you understand what I mean? When a Ptolemy Soter appears in Egypt it means that Egypt is already rotten. Men of that kind, ' unique ' men, are the ones who bring disaster. It is better to do without them, above all when they exact total submission, intellectual as well as political. Believe and do not question! *Mussolini ha semper ragione.* . . . Well, that is when I prefer to take up my hat and depart."

He started to do so; but having put on his coat he came back to the table.

" But where is one to go? It's too late—the Peloponnesian war has begun. Europe is in its death-throes. Titel, let's go somewhere else and get drunk, I can't bear being clear-headed. We live in an age ruled by frenzy and I want to have at least the sensation of power."

He ended with a little feverish laugh, and Titel said:

" It's not a bad idea, but why take things so tragically? What do you care about Europe? "

" I happen to live in Europe—otherwise I shouldn't give a damn."

They went off together, and Cesar Lascari said, gazing after them:

" Poor Serban, he's going to bits, I'm afraid—drink and all his other vices. It's sad to hear a man as educated and intelligent as he is talking all that rigmarole, like a student's nattering."

" It's pure Spengler," said Dim. " But so muddle-headed. He's much more amusing when he's drunk. I find him intolerable when he's sober."

" Perhaps that's why he never stays sober," Cesar Lascari said.

They talked for a time about the war reports from Albania and North Africa, and then Dim remembered that he had an appointment. He left Capsa's, nodding to various acquaintances, and getting into the car which was waiting for him had himself driven to the home of Professor Nicoulesco. As he stood at the door after ringing the bell he noted the vaguely Italianate style of the villa, the stout door with its decorative metal-work, studded with large nails, and the fact that the three or four very small windows on the ground floor were all heavily barred. " How does he get any light? " he wondered absently.

Then he became aware that someone was peering at him from a window directly over the door, which closed as he looked up. Again he wondered, " Why all these precautions? They're in power—or at least they share it with the General. . . ."

The door was opened by a man with a hard, deeply lined face whose aspect caused Dim to reflect that he looked no more like a manservant than he himself resembled an archbishop. He gave his name and was shown into the library, one of the largest private libraries in Bucarest, where the professor was awaiting him. The big, lofty room, with its gallery, was in half-darkness, lighted by a single lamp in a corner. Fanica Nicoulesco had grown a little thinner, but his manner was calm and he seemed to be in good spirits.

" My dear friend, I'm very glad to see you. What's the latest news? Have you been in town? What are people saying? "

" There are troops in the Calea Victoriei, I believe, and a demonstration of some kind outside police headquarters. It seems that the body of a murdered German officer has been found, and your friends are staging a protest. But I came by car and didn't see very much. In fact, I don't think there's much to be seen."

" Ah," said the professor. " And how are you? "

" I'm getting ready to serve my new masters," said Dim Coziano, smiling.

" Whom do you mean? "

" Yourself, for example."

" You expect me to become your master? " said the professor gently.

" I shan't object if you do," said Dim. " I don't care for your acolytes, but I regard you as a remarkable, a unique, man."

As he said this he surprised himself by recalling what Serban Romano had said only a little while before. " ' Unique ' men are those who bring disaster."

" My acolytes, as you call them, are admirable instruments. They don't think; they are content to believe and to carry out orders. I have taught them that instinct is superior to reason, science and art, and in doing so I have set them free. The ones who killed Iorga genuinely despised him because he was a man of learning."

" If anyone except myself heard you say that, Professor, I think they would be horrified."

" I say it to you because I know you. It is humiliating for anyone whose thinking extends beyond good or evil to be obliged to wrap up his meaning in terms of newspaper clichés and the language of the public platform. One can't be for ever indulging in that kind of hypocrisy. Now and then I have to say what I really think, and it is a great relief." Fanica Nicoulesco smiled. But his voice was weak, and he was looking aged and worn.

" I'm honoured that you should confide in me," said Dim.

" Oh, but I know that I can do so. We had a long talk some time ago at a party given by Elisa Vogoride. Do you remember? "

" Yes, I do."

" And do you remember what you said to me—' The man who is content to be smaller than another man doesn't deserve to be alive at all.' Do you remember that? "

" No," said Dim, lightly. " Did I really say that? I'm surprised."

" Why are you surprised? "

" Because I don't much like saying things of that sort. I've been thinking them for a long time, but they are things that are better left unsaid."

The professor laughed softly.

" I like you. You're the sort of man I can work with. Do you remember our meetings in Jassy? Such foolishness! And of all the young men who came to them you are the only one who today amounts to anything. Negruzzi is negligible, Duca is dead and the rest are mediocrities. Duca might have done great things if he had been cast in a different mould, and so might Serban Romano. But they were all weak and purposeless, self-indulgent, brought up without cares or responsibilities, in too much comfort and security. I so badly needed strong men, but I've had to make use of clods and petty adventurers—Calibans. But what Prospero wants is Ariel, not Caliban. Ghighi Duca might have been Ariel if he had lived."

" Or Lucifer. . . . He would have dominated you, Professor. It's a good thing he's dead."

" Did he do you so much harm? " Dim Coziano did not reply to this. The professor went on: " You're more simple and less exceptional, but you're stronger than men like Duca. Let us see what we can make of you."

" You must feel yourself to be in a very strong position if you can talk to me as openly as this."

" By tomorrow we shall have gained power," said Fanica Nicoulesco in a low voice.

" As soon as that? Tomorrow? "

" Yes. What you saw in the streets today was merely the prologue. *Prolog in der Hölle*—Faust back-to-front. The assault will begin tomorrow at dawn, on all the key-points in the town. It should have happened already in the provinces."

There was a moment of silence. Then Dim murmured:

" I'm glad I came to see you this evening."

" I'm sure you are," said the professor, smiling. " I'm glad, too."

" When I think of Jassy! " said Dim, marvelling. " It's strange to think what has become of the rest of them, while you're on the way to becoming Dictator of Roumania."

" Not dictator—patriarch," said Nicoulesco seriously. " The Grand Pontiff. It is necessary for the new order to be a theocracy. Our peasant masses are Orthodox Christians."

Dim had difficulty in restraining a smile. The professor looked at him with his two-coloured eyes and said: " You are right not to laugh."

Suddenly Dim was alarmed. He was alone with this man, and his solitude seemed too great, in that empty house in its quiet quarter of the town, while elsewhere the crowds were massing and howling. He uttered a few commonplaces to bring the conversation down to a less exalted and irresponsible level, and then rose to take his leave.

" I wish you success with all my heart," he said as they shook hands.

" I cannot fail," said the professor calmly.

Realising what was expected of him Dim again took the other's hand and bowed low over it as he might have done over the hand of the King or the Patriarch of the Roumanian Orthodox Church. Fanica Nicoulesco raised his other hand with its long, thin fingers over his head in a gesture that was almost a benediction.

" Come and see me again," he said paternally.

3

" What a man! What a terrible man! " Dim said to himself as he
was driven back to the centre of the town. He sat staring absently
at the crowds on the pavements, the passengers on the trains, the
lighted shop-windows. . . . " They don't look as though they
realise that they live in the same town as Fanica Nicoulesco, or
that one of these days they'll be making a pilgrimage to the Piatza
Mare to go on their knees for his blessing. . . ." He wanted to
laugh, but he was too afraid. " The man's mad! " But then, so
was Hitler: as Serban had said, it was an age ruled by frenzy, and
the only thing to do was to look for a share of the power. " Serban's not such a fool, after all. . . ." But what was the best course
to take at this moment? Dim knew, but still lacked the courage to
act. The thought had come to him as he got into the car, but he
needed time for reflection. Perhaps he should ask advice—but of
whom? Whom could he trust in the present situation and in the
face of such risks? He had gone more than once to his uncle,
Serban Lascari, but he knew that he would not do so in this case.
In matters of this sort it was better not to confide in anyone. . . .
He sat in the car furiously weighing and calculating, and with an
almost physical sensation of the turmoil around him, the fever
mounting in this city of Bucarest, the massive powers which might
crush and destroy him or bear him upwards, higher than he had
ever been, even to the topmost heights.

" To the Culmea Veche," he said to the chauffeur.

During the rest of the journey he paid more attention to the
crowds, which seemed to be moving towards the centre of the
town, and presently he noticed that small, organised groups of men
were stopping people on the pavements and at street-corners. They
were clad in what might be called civilian uniform, green shirts
and a sort of padded jacket of grey material. The car drove past
all this and turning into the empty side-streets drew up at the

monumental grill of Serban Lascari's house. The place looked dead. Only at a second glance did Dim discern a faint streak of light escaping from behind the thick curtains that masked all the windows.

He went in, and handing his coat to a manservant glanced at the other coats hanging on the hall-stand. It seemed that Uncle Serbanica had a number of callers. In the main salon the chandeliers were unlit, and only a few old china lamps—Sèvres, Nymphenburg or Russian porcelain of the 1840 period—lighted the big room. A little group was seated round the armchair of Serban Lascari, who, now aged over seventy, his hair completely white, his face pale and shrunken, still had the same alert, intelligent gaze. Vasilesco-Rimnic was there, corpulent and sagging, destroyed by over-indulgence in food and drink; Cesar Lascari, well-dressed as usual but looking completely lethargic, incapable of being seriously concerned about any serious matter; Pericles Mittesco, his grey hair carefully brushed, his manner grave and stern, neat and master of himself, with his elbows tucked into his sides; and lastly Grigore Balota, a State Under-Secretary in the Ministry of National Economy, a short man, still young, who wore high heels, dressed with exaggerated fastidiousness and powdered his face like a woman. Dim greeted them and sat down.

" Have you been in the town? " asked Serban Lascari.

The others looked at Dim without speaking. They had fallen silent when he entered.

" Yes. But why is it that everyone I've met today has asked me the same thing—' Have you been in town? ' "

" Who else has asked you? " asked Cesar.

" Well—all kinds of people. And why do *you* ask? " said Dim, forcing a smile.

" They must have been people who are in the know," said Cesar.

Dim decided that it would be foolish to pretend ignorance.

" Well, of course, everyone knows that something's going on. There are crowds everywhere, and I believe there's been some sort of demonstration outside police headquarters. Besides, there's a different look about the people in the streets, a different feeling. Something is obviously going to happen."

" And what's more," said Vasilesco-Rimnic, his breath coming fast and his lower lip trembling, " I believe it's going to happen tonight."

" What, exactly? " asked Dim.

" They're going to murder the lot of us, the way they murdered General Argeano, Gabriel Marinesco, Madgearu and Iorga! There'll be a mass round-up tonight of all the parliamentary opposition to Antonesco's dictatorship, and by tomorrow we shall all be dead. And you people will be responsible! " cried Vasilesco-Rimnic, turning upon Grigore Balota, with a hint of politician's rhetoric in his manner, but in genuine terror, fat, flabby, grey-faced and lamentable, dribbling over his cigar.

Balota said loftily: " I've told you already that the Chief of State disapproves of the crimes that have been committed, and that we are taking steps to ensure that they won't be repeated. Everyone in danger of attack by the Legionaries will be protected. When you go home, my dear sir, you will find your house surrounded by a military guard." He concluded with a serene smile.

" I find that amusing," said Serban Lascari. " To hear you talk, my dear fellow, one would think that the ground wasn't trembling beneath your own feet. But what will become of you if the Legion takes over the country? "

" I can assure you, Monsieur Serban, that isn't going to happen," said Balota, still smiling.

" Did you listen to the seven o'clock news? " old Lascari asked. " No."

The others had not heard it either.

" It said that Brasov had been in German hands for two hours and that the Moldavian army-corps is marching on Bucarest."

" Well, there! " cried Vasilesco-Rimnic in a shrill voice, wringing his hands. " You see? " He turned upon Serban Lascari. " You see? This is your work—you and Auschnitt and Gherson! Don't you remember what I said to you six or seven years ago? I warned you against subsidising the Nazis and the charlatans working for them in this country. But you wouldn't listen to a man of experience. You had to get mixed up in politics —a pack of business men. And this is the result! "

Balota was scarcely less shaken. His effort to preserve his smile was unsuccessful. Serban Lascari looked contemptuously at Vasilesco-Rimnic.

" I wouldn't have supported your lot in any case," he said.

" Only a thorough-going military dictatorship can save this country."

" I must be going," said Balota abruptly, rising from his chair.

Dim and Pericles Mittesco also rose, and Mittesco took Balota aside and in a low voice implored him to arrange for a guard to be posted outside his house. He had quite lost the calm, imposing dignity that Bucarest had associated with him for so many years. He was in a fever of alarm.

" Of course, of course—you needn't worry," said Balota, rising and falling nervously on the tips of his small shoes. He managed at last to get away and crossed to the other side of the room, where Dim came up with him.

" Under-Secretary," Dim said in an undertone, " the Legion is preparing to carry out a *coup d'état* tomorrow. I have it from a reliable source." He knew that he had spoken too late, but still he tried to give the information a dramatic importance. " This is not a spontaneous or disorganised uprising," he went on. " There's a plan and a definite objective. They mean to seize power."

Balota, a head and a half shorter, turned only part of the way towards him and stood listening with his head bowed, staring at the point of the silk handkerchief in his breast pocket.

" May I ask what your reliable source is? " he asked with an equivocal smile.

" It's a woman—the mistress of one of the leaders of the Legion."

" Ah, in that case . . . Very well, I'll pass your message on to the Prime Minister," said Balota smoothly, and departed.

Pericles Mittesco also took his leave. Vasilesco-Rimnic growled:

" Well, anyway, it was amusing to see the worthy Pericles in that state. He was shaking in his shoes! And that pipsqueak, Balota, wasn't much better."

" They hadn't heard the news from Brasov," said Dim.

" No. Well, I think I'll go and inspect my guard of honour," said Vasilesco-Rimnic, raising himself laboriously out of his chair with his hands on his thighs. He laughed weakly, his own alarm all too apparent.

Serban Lascari, who had been contemplating the scene with an occasional shrill titter, went with him to the door and then returned to his nephew.

" And what do you think of it all? "

" That's what I came to ask you, Uncle Serbanica," said Dim.
" I'll tell you tomorrow. You'd better come to lunch."

Suddenly the house began to tremble slightly, and there was a grinding, rattling sound outside, like that of blocks of metal being carried by the stream along a river-bed of iron. They went and drew back the window-curtains. Massive vehicles were passing along the street, looking, in the dim light of the lamps, like monstrous tortoises or crabs, each with an hexagonal carapace and a huge phallus.

" For God's sake, what are these? Are they ours? " cried the old man.

But Dim had seen the swastika painted on their sides. " They're the Germans," he said, " making for the Danube on their way to Bulgaria."

" If that's the case, they won't want any disorder on their lines of communication," said Serban Lascari, letting go the curtain. He returned to his chair and sat down again, staring fixedly at Dim. " If the Legionaries start to make trouble now, they'll be finished."

" Yes," murmured Dim. " I must go, Uncle Serbanica. Colette's expecting me home, and she'll be worried."

4

But he did not go home. There was somewhere else he wanted to go. The thought had occurred to him when Vasilesco-Rimnic had said, " Tomorrow we shall all be murdered." One of those to be murdered might well be Monsieur Gherson. On the other hand, he might escape. He might have an armed guard. Even if he had none he might be overlooked, although it seemed improbable, since he was one of the best-known and wealthiest Jews in the country. But suppose he were to be overlooked? The chance could not be ruled out. Men sometimes escaped what looked like certain death in the strangest ways.

If Gherson died his fortune in Switzerland would be at the mercy of the possessor of the secret number and the key-word, the man who had opened an account on his behalf at Mercado's bank, despositing a specimen signature on a small piece of cardboard. His whole fortune. . . . The stacks of bullion, the bundles of shares. . . . There were few such fortunes in Roumania, and they had been rare even in the days when Boniface Coziano, Dim's uncle, had grown rich. But if Gherson survived (and surely he would have seen to it that he was provided with a military guard) the whole of this money would go sooner or later to his wife, a foolish, extravagant woman of promiscuous habits who would run through it all in ten or fifteen years. It would be squandered on gigolos and playboys, on every kind of folly, when it might otherwise be used to further a great political career. And Gherson was an old man, unlikely in any event to last more than another two or three years.

The car bore Dimitri Coziano towards the centre of the town, where the streets were now almost deserted, the shop-shutters lowered. They were brought to a stop by an endless column of tanks, army-trucks and artillery that roared and clattered along the boulevards, to be followed by other columns, all painted a dull green and marked with a white cross on a black background. Helmeted motor-cyclists in long capes stood by their machines controlling the traffic at the cross-roads, each with another man armed with a sub-machine-gun in his sidecar. The columns were heading for the Giurgiu road.

" You'll have to try some other way," Dim said to his chauffeur. " I've got to get to the Athenee Palace somehow."

One street after another was barred to them. The Bucarest police had vanished, and at every corner there was a motor-cycle with a machine-gunner in its sidecar. Dim's chauffeur so far forgot himself as to murmur:

" They're on their way to attack Yugoslavia, Monsieur."

" Yes," said Dim. But his thoughts were elsewhere and he had no wish to exchange commonplaces, particularly with servants. Everyone knew that the Germans were going to attack Yugoslavia.

By eleven o'clock that night the rearguard of a column twenty miles long had passed through the town and left it by the Giurgiu gateway. The first tanks of another column were at Ploesti, while its tail was leaving the mountainous region of Cimpina. But this,

too, was of no interest to Dimitri Coziano. He had reached the
Athenee Palace at last and was telephoning Gherson's house. An
agitated woman's voice answered.

" Is that Madame Gherson? I kiss your hands, madame. This
is Dimitri Coziano. May I speak to your husband? "

Madame Gherson was clearly in a state of panic. Dim pictured
her pacing with clasped hands up and down the vast empty
drawing-room with its grand piano at either end; he imagined
the daughter realising, perhaps for the first time in her life, that
she had a father who was a human being, fragile and easily destroyed. Perhaps at that very moment she had her arms round the
old man's neck, the handsome girl with long, red-gold hair. . . .
" Bitches, the two of them! They're thinking of the money and
their own skins . . ."

" Good evening, Monsieur Coziano." Gherson's voice over the
line sounded faint and exhausted.

" Good evening. I rang up to ask if your house is being
guarded."

" Yes," said Gherson. " They've sent me two soldiers." Dim
could picture his mournful, disillusioned smile. " It seems more
than enough where I personally am concerned, but scarcely
enough if it becomes a matter of dealing with resolute marauders."

" It's better than nothing," said Dim, now in a state of great
tension. He had learned what he wanted to know, and he knew
what he intended to do. " It's some protection, at least, but I
agree that it's not enough. I'll arrange for more men to be sent to
you, a dozen at least. Meanwhile, don't leave the house."

" I've no intention of doing so," said Gherson with a small
laugh. " I shall die on the barricades."

" What nonsense! You aren't going to die," said Dim with a
feverish heartiness. " I must ring off now, but I hope I'll see you
tomorrow. Good night."

He hung up and looked feverishly about him while he stood
thinking. The plan had occurred to him the instant Vasilesco-
Rimnic had spoken. Of course, it might fail, and that was why
he would have to cover his tracks with the greatest care. But he
knew precisely what action he proposed to take, and with whom,
in order to ensure that the wealth stored away in the vaults of
Mercado's bank should become his property and his alone. This
was why he had come to the Athenee Palace. There were plenty

of ways in which the plan might go wrong. Faber might not be there, or perhaps the guard of two soldiers would prove all that was needed to scare away any hooligans sent by the Legion to force their way into Gherson's house. But Faber, from what Dim knew of him, would undoubtedly be taking his own precautions, and in that case . . . But suppose Gherson were to give him, Dim Coziano, away? " No matter, I can look after myself. If Antonesco's beaten I go with the professor and no one can touch me; and if the general comes out on top I'm one of his men." He was thinking at furious speed, but with the clarity and precision of a chess-player. If Faber was available, if he could be prompted to do what Dim wanted, and if he brought it off, then the game would be won. If, on the other hand, he was not to be found, the plan would have to be abandoned. There would be nothing for it but to wait and see what happened, and if necessary run fresh risks with a new plan.

Going over to the reception-desk Dim asked if Herr Faber was in the hotel and was told that he was in the restaurant. Almost dizzy with relief he got rid of his hat and coat and went in search of him. The restaurant was nearly empty. There were one or two parties of German officers, youthful, gay and meticulously well-behaved, a table or two of people who might be Roumanians or foreigners, and, at the far end, the table at the head of which Faber was seated with a party of eight or ten people, ladies, officers, and a couple of fair-haired young men from the German Embassy. They were evidently in high spirits, loudly talking and laughing, with the champagne-coolers close at hand.

Dim nodded to Faber from a distance. Then he got out a visiting-card from which he had effaced his name so thoroughly that nothing was visible except a dense smudge of ink, and on which he had written (in English, because his German was not good enough), " I would like to have a word with you about a matter of great importance." He handed it to a waiter.

" Will you give this to Herr Faber and tell him I shall be waiting in the lounge."

He went and sat in an armchair, and two minutes later the huge man appeared with a cigar between his teeth, his face flushed and greasy, his eyes bleary with drink.

" It's you, is it? Why don't you come and join us? We're celebrating. Yugoslavia will be finished in a week."

" And in this country our friends will be in power," said Dim with a taut smile.

Faber's expression went suddenly blank. " I don't know anything about that," he said.

" No matter," said Dim. " I came to talk about something else. In a word, our friend Monsieur Gherson is in process of liquidating his entire assets and transferring the money to Switzerland."

Herr Faber took his cigar out of his mouth and looked hard at him, his eyes now alert.

" He asked me to help him do so, and I have been instrumental in arranging for the transfer of part of the money." Dim had decided that a frank avowal would be the best way of persuading the German that he was telling the truth.

" I see," said Herr Faber. " And how much is left? "

" I've no idea. There are his factories and industrial plants, which as you doubtless know are among the largest in the country. But he should be stopped before he goes too far, or it may turn out that the control in all his various enterprises has passed into foreign hands, Swiss perhaps, and no means of knowing who's behind it."

Faber gazed thoughtfully at Dim, evidently speculating as to his interest in the matter. But not much guessing was needed. Obviously Coziano was hoping to get his hands on the part of Gherson's fortune which had been transferred through him.

" Well," said Faber at length, " I am obliged to you for the information. And now, if you'll excuse me, I must be getting back to my guests. Good night."

They separated without shaking hands, and Dim went out to his car and ordered his chauffeur to take him home. Driving along the deserted boulevards they saw a number of empty trams. There were four on the Place Rosetti, blocking the view of Bratiano's statue and the end of the Boulevard Carol. It looked as though they had been deliberately left there to serve in the morning as barricades.

Entering his house he found the drawing-room lighted but the room empty. There were also lights in the dining-room, where the table was laid for two. Colette appeared in a dressing-gown in the doorway of the small salon, slim, fair-haired but a little faded. She came and clung to him.

" Where have you been? I was so worried about you."

" Why? There was nothing to worry about."

She gazed at him with anxious blue eyes.

" Are you all right? You don't look at all well."

" Of course I'm all right. Stop fussing."

He began to pace in a preoccupied fashion up and down the room.

" Your face is so flushed," said Colette. " And there's a big vein on your temple. You look terrible. You're working too hard. You ought to try to get some rest."

" I daresay."

" Don't you want anything to eat? "

" No . . . yes . . . If you like. But don't bother me."

She took him by the arm and led him into the dining-room, sat him down and served him herself. After a while she laughed and said:

" Well, there! You said you weren't hungry, but you've eaten a huge meal. Didn't you have dinner in town? "

He did not answer until she repeated the question, and then he thought it over and said doubtfully:

" No. . . . At least, I don't think I did."

" Dim, you're frightening me! " cried Colette. " You're overstrained. You must take more care of yourself. And what's going on in the town? Everybody's terrified. You ought to stay at home tomorrow. Everybody says something's going to happen."

" We shall see," said Dim. " I'm tired. Have you any sleeping-pills? "

5

He was awakened at eight the next morning by the sound of Colette's agitated voice.

"Dim, get up! Get up at once!"

She was shaking him by the shoulder. He opened sluggish eyes, heaved himself out of bed and asked crossly:

"What's the matter? Why are you shouting at me?"

As he spoke a series of detonations shook the walls of the house. It was gunfire. Where did it come from, and who was firing at whom? Then he heard the rattle of machine-guns a long way off.

"There are some men at the front door wanting to come in," said Colette. "I don't like the look of them."

Dim suddenly awoke to the situation. He heard voices in the street shouting threats, followed by a furious pounding on the door.

"They're shouting for you," cried Colette, clinging to him. "What do they want you for?"

Dim began to tremble. He had to clench his jaws to prevent his teeth from chattering. "They've come to arrest me," he thought. "If they get me, I'm done for. But why me? What makes me so important?"

In the act of asking the question he guessed the answer. Ambition is a disease of the imagination. Dim Coziano had a lively imagination for things and people. What a fool he had been to think he could make use of a man like Faber! If he had had any judgement he would have steered a hundred miles clear of him and everything that concerned him.

He ran to a lemon-wood chest, fished in a drawer with small gilt handles, found his revolver and dashed out of the room.

"Where are you going? What are you going to do?" cried Colette, running after him.

He did not hear her. He was thinking, "I've been rumbled. They must have tortured the old man and made him talk, and now

Faber knows that I can put my hands on the money. So he means to get it out of me. But, by God, I'll fight! I won't let him have anything, not a bean. I'll die fighting!"

Trembling all over, gritting his teeth in fury and despair, he opened a french-window and went out on to the balcony. There were four of them, armed with automatic rifles and banging on the door with the butts. He aimed shakily and fired, and the banging ceased. One of them shouted, "Watch out!"

Dim leaned over and fired again. They were now all huddled below the balcony. He went indoors again, shutting the window, and an instant later the pane was shattered. A man was firing from the opposite pavement. Dim darted across the room, keeping clear of the windows, and ran down to the hall, where he found his chauffeur and two maids huddled under the stairs. He said hoarsely, "Don't move, any of you, or I'll fire." He put four bullets through the woodwork of the front door, and then heard a click—his magazine was empty. There was the sound of a groan outside, and an instant later a burst of return fire. Keeping under cover Dim crept upstairs for more ammunition. He was panting, his throat very dry.

"Dim, are you hurt?" moaned Colette. She was lying flat on her stomach beside the bed, having been unable to crawl underneath it because it was too low. "What are you doing!"

He took no notice. After wiping the sweat off his face he was struggling to re-load the revolver, doing it so clumsily that half the bullets fell on the floor. The idiot that he had been! Gherson was probably dead by now, and he himself was done for, all that vast fortune lost to him for ever. . . . He heard further shots from below and went out and crouched at the head of the stairs, whence he could cover the door if they broke it down. At least they did not seem to have any hand-grenades.

There was a brief pause and then another bullet came through the door. The sweat ran down Dim Coziano's body. He raised the revolver, but his hand was shaking so violently that he had no hope of hitting anything. "I'm done for," he thought, and crouched there waiting for the next assault. But nothing more happened. There was silence except for the distant sound of gunfire and the rattle of machine-guns in the town.

After waiting another minute Dim left the landing and gingerly approached the french-window giving on to the balcony. He peered through it at the street, hastily withdrawing his head. But then he looked again. A file of khaki-clad soldiers in shallow steel helmets was moving in front of the houses across the way. Dim came near to weeping with relief. He went out on to the balcony. A similar file was passing beneath him, in front of his own house. An officer with a drawn sword followed, and then came more soldiers, one carrying an automatic rifle by its butt as though it were a stick of wood. Dim went back to the bedroom, feeling his legs weak beneath him. Colette, still lying half under the bed, moaned, "What's happening now?" but he paid no attention. He went downstairs to the telephone and dialled a number, failing at the first attempt because of the trembling of his hands. When finally he got a reply he said:

"This is Dimitri Coziano. I've rung up to ask if Monsieur Gherson is all right."

A woman's voice which he did not recognise answered, with a sob: "He's been taken away." Then she hung up.

After a fruitless attempt to re-establish the connection, Dim put down the receiver. Colette came downstairs, keeping close to the wall.

"Dim, what's happening?"

"We were saved in the nick of time. They've cleared out. The army's arrived."

"Who were you ringing up?"

"Gherson," said Dim, avoiding her eyes. "They've attacked his house and taken him away."

"They'll kill him!" Colette cried.

"Oh, not necessarily. Perhaps they'll let him go."

But they did not let Monsieur Gherson go. His naked body was found hanging by the chin from a hook in a meat warehouse. He was not the only one. The other hooks were occupied by the bodies of lesser Jews, tradesmen, shop-assistants and the like. . . .

Thus it was that Dimitri Coziano came into the possession of a large fortune, unknown to everyone except himself and Herr Faber. He and Faber met from time to time after the revolt of the Legionaries, at receptions at the German Embassy or those held by the Head of the Cabinet, Mihail Antonesco, brother of the dictator. But they did not speak. They nodded distantly and that was all.

Professor Fanica Nicoulesco was rumoured to have been found in his house, dead of a heart-attack, on the third day of the revolt. According to another report he escaped under the protection of the S.S. and died in Germany soon afterwards, also of a heart-attack. In any event, he was never seen again in Bucarest.

Dim Coziano discovered that he was under vague suspicion of having been a Legionary, which was something he would never have expected. But Grigore Balota and Mihail Antonesco had both received information of his visit to the professor on the eve of the revolt, and this was enough to render him suspect and debar him from promotion to the highest offices. Nor was his position improved in 1943. Looking ten years older, consumed with the restless, unappeased desire for power, he was bitterly indignant at the injustice of his treatment. Finally he had a show-down with Balota.

" Why am I not offered anything? Why is everyone else promoted and rewarded for their services to the Marshal "—General Antonesco was now a marshal—" while I'm always passed over? I did far more than most of them."

Balota gazed at him, reflecting, " Well, certainly I've thrown a good many spanners in the works where he's concerned. He's not a serious rival any more." So he promised to help him, saying, " I'll do my best to try and get you something more worthy of your talents. I agree that you have not been treated as you deserve."

6

During this period, that is to say in 1942 and 1943, Dimitri Coziano changed in another respect. He spent his energies, which the directorship of a ministerial department did little to absorb, more and more in riotous living, letting himself be borne on the tide of extravagance and sexual promiscuity that was sweeping through the wealthier sections of Roumanian society. Both men and women were plunged in a fever of dissipation, exchanging mistresses and lovers, husbands and wives, almost openly and with tolerance on either side. Women of good family married to rising men were prepared to offer themselves for the furtherance of a business transaction, or to enable their husbands to gain promotion or a Government concession, and this increase of amateur competition was severely felt by the professional harlots. In the summer months the scene of these festivities was transferred to the country. A century earlier, when Manuel Coziano, the grandfather of Davida, had been a young man, debauchery had taken place in the monasteries; in Davida's youth people had gone to the big country houses, or to Paris and Nice. This had been the case until 1915, and for the next quarter of a century the wealthy Roumanians, idle and pleasure-loving, had sought distraction all over Europe. During the latter years those who had acquired fortunes under King Carol II had built themselves villas along the road from Bucarest to Brasov, more or less rustic in style, surrounded by vineyards, orchards, flower-beds and vegetable-gardens. Here it was, sufficiently far from the town to be secure from prying eyes, but within a day's journey, that the masters of Roumania came to divert themselves during the war years.

Early in the summer of 1943, Dim Coziano, having acquired a reputation as a lover of these diversions, was invited to a luncheon-party at the villa of Monsieur Corfiotu. It was a wonderfully fine day, with a scent of flowers and aromatic herbs borne on the breeze over the sun-warmed fields. A steady stream of cars raced along the tarmac road, its grey surface polished by the daily passage of innumerable tyres. Contrary to his usual habit, Dim wore a light-coloured suit. He had said to his wife, " I'm going to be very busy all day. I'll get a bite to eat wherever I happen to be." To which Colette had trustfully replied: " Well, take care not to eat anything too indigestible. You know how it upsets your liver."

Leaning back in the car Dim thought pleasurably of the day that awaited him, but not with unalloyed pleasure. He also thought, resentfully and with dislike, of the people he would be meeting; indeed, in these days he thought bitterly of every man he knew. Corfiotu, for example, a vulgarian who had got rich by toadying to the King and manufacturing arms—he would patronise

his guests as though they were a troupe of strolling players hired
for his amusement; and it was pretty much what they were.
. . . The imbecile Cesar Lascari, forming a trio with Alexandra
and Ionel Haralamb, who was certain to make a fool of himself
by letting some cat or other out of the bag. . . . The half-wit
Giurgea-Roscano, who was now a member of the Government
whereas Dim was still only a departmental chief, although he
possessed ten times as much ability; but then, that was why they
made use of Giurgea-Roscano, because he was so stupid as to be
harmless. . . . The fool Scarlat, who would be invited because
he was Valentine's husband; and Valentine, who would be invited because Corfiotu was hoping to get something out of Pericles
Mittesco (also invited) and wanted to keep him happy. . . . Then
there would be Balota, who had made a better career for himself
than Dim, although he was two years younger; but of course he
hadn't squandered the years of his youth on a woman like Fifi
Opresco. . . . And incidentally, what had become of Fifi? Dim
had heard of her last from Titel Negruzzi, who had run into her
in Paris, where she was flourishing as a *poule de luxe.* She had
been married for a time to a Frenchman, fairly rich, but then had
walked out on him, being insatiable in her craving for variety.
Dim made a mental note to ask Titel if he had heard any more
news of her. Titel was sure to be there. He cropped up everywhere where there was free food and drink, or financial pickings. . . .

At seven o'clock that evening the party was still in progress.
Corfiotu, Scarlat and Mittesco were drinking port together;
Cesar Lascari had gone for a stroll among the vines with Valentine
Scarlat; and Dim had gone to lie down on a divan in one of the
guest-rooms. Through the communicating-door he heard the
murmuring voices of Alexandra Lascari and Ionel Haralamb in the
next room, and presently sounds of a more specific kind. Un-
settled by these he got up, but as he was about to leave the room
Valentine entered. She was then about thirty-five. Her beautiful,
silken hair, light walnut in colour, hung loose over her shoulders
and she wore a very low-cut dress with a fringe of lace showing
beneath the hem of the neckline. Her calves were round and
supple, her gaze forthright, shameless and voracious.

" Why, what are you doing, resting? " She came and sat beside
him on the divan, her hip touching his. " You shouldn't be so
lazy."

Dim put an arm round her. " I'll show you if I'm lazy."

" You mustn't," she murmured, delighted and half apprehensive. " Someone might come in."

" All the more reason for not wasting time."

Presently, after Valentine had repaired the disorder of her dress
and vanished with a smile and a grimace, Dim slipped cautiously
out of the room. The three gentlemen were still seated at the table
with their glasses, gravely discussing the prospects of victory or
defeat for the Third Reich. Titel Negruzzi and Cesar Lascari
were lounging in wicker chairs on the terrace, drinking and
smoking. Madame Corfiotu, a celebrated Bucarest beauty, was
conversing with Balota in a corner, and he was saying something
in an urgent undertone which caused her to smile. Everyone was
more or less drunk. Scarlat said loudly:

" They haven't a hope of winning. They're beaten already."

" But what about the Japanese? " said Mittesco. " Look what
they've done to the Americans and British."

" It makes no difference. The Germans lost the war at Stalin-
grad."

" Do you hear that, Balota? " cried Corfiotu. " It seems that
your German friends are defeated."

Balota got up and came over to the table, and after listening
said:

" Haven't you heard of the German secret weapons? "

" What do you know about them? "

" Merely that they're secret," said Balota with his superior
smile. " All I can tell you is that the marshal, when he visited
Germany and the Führer's headquarters, was greatly impressed
by what he saw and heard."

Dim passed by the table and approached Madame Corfiotu.

" Do you know that I'm the only man here who has never
visited your orchards? Won't you do the honours of your estate?
I'll return the compliment at Cozia."

He gave her his arm, talking, as they strolled off together,
about the beauties of Cozia and the manor-house built by his
grandfather, Eustache Coziano; but when they were out of sight
of the house he embarked upon quite other topics. They returned
three-quarters of an hour later in the warm tranquillity of the
falling dusk.

" How enchanting you are," he said, kissing her hand.

She smiled and drew close to him.

" And will you return the compliment at Cozia ? "

" Here and now, if you like. Let's go back."

" No. It's getting dark. I might dirty my dress and not notice till I came under the lights."

" Well, then, in Bucarest——"

" You mustn't expect too much," said Madame Corfiotu gently but firmly. " We mustn't get serious. This is just a game that everyone plays." She laughed softly.

" Yes," said Dim, and kissed her hand again.

Back in the house Balota said rather crossly:

" Coziano, where did you get to ? I've just had a phone-call from the Ministry. We've got to go back to Bucarest at once. Something important has come up."

" We ? The two of us ? "

" Yes, you and I."

Dim thought, " A pity. I might have caught Valentine again," but he said: " Very well. I wonder what they want."

7

What " they " wanted was to effect the transfer of twenty truck-loads of gold to Portugal by means of a bank clearing operation, since the removal of the bullion itself would never be permitted by the Germans. The decision had been taken by the Head of the Cabinet, Mihail Antonesco.

" I know how resourceful you are," he said to Dim, " and you have contacts in Switzerland. I want you to try to find a bank there which will carry out the operation on our behalf."

" You must realise that the chances are very small," said Dim.

" That's up to you and Balota," said Antonesco dryly; and he went on with a smile which he sought to make disarming: " The Marshal himself is interested in the matter. He fully appreciates the difficulties and will be particularly grateful to anyone who pulls it off. I told him you were Balota's right-hand man, and he said he knew you and was sure you were the right man for the job."

" It's true that I was once presented to the Marshal at the house of my uncle, Serban Lascari."

" Ah, yes. And how is Serban Lascari? " asked Antonesco affably.

" He keeps remarkably well," said Dim, wondering whether Uncle Serbanica had ever done this mountebank the honour of inviting him to his house.

He left for Zürich the next day, and during the journey asked himself repeatedly, in a cold rage, " Why should I go back? Why not stay in a neutral country? They've all cheated me, Balota, Antonesco, every one of them. Why should I trust them and their precious gratitude? " Nevertheless what Mihail Antonesco had said sounded hopeful. The Marshal—the General as he was then —had been a regular visitor at Serban Lascari's house. It was quite possible that he did really remember him, in which case there might be a marked improvement in Dim's affairs, even the ministerial portfolio he had so long coveted. . . . " Yes, but if Hitler loses the war? In that case I should be far better off in Switzerland. But then, if they win with these new weapons of theirs, or manage to make a favourable peace, it would mean that I could never go back to Roumania and my career would be ruined. No, I shall have to wait a little longer and see which way the cat jumps."

The banker, Raphael Mercado, received him the day after his arrival with the reserved courtesy which he had shown on each of their former encounters, and listened attentively to what he had to propose. The Antonesco Government was offering generous terms for his assistance. When Dim had finished, Mercado sat silently reflecting for some moments. He was a man of something over fifty, his hair prematurely white, his face narrow, lean and pale. He wore gold-rimmed spectacles and kept his hands constantly clasped in what was either a gesture of perfect relaxation or the effort to conceal some incurable physical weakness. When he spoke he did so calmly and without raising his voice.

" Yes, Monsieur Coziano, I could carry out this transaction for you, although I am perhaps the only banker in this country who would accept the risk."

" I'm delighted to hear you say so. My Government will be——"

" Wait! I said that I *could*. Not only does your Government persecute my co-religionists in the most barbarous fashion, but it is allied to a country which is murdering them in thousands every day. Why should I do your Government a service, however great the financial reward? It would be an act of betrayal on my part."

Dim, considerably taken aback, smiled at him in embarrassment, shrugging his shoulders.

" My dear Monsieur Mercado, there are a great many Jewish men of affairs who continued to do business with us and even with Germany, by way of Switzerland and Sweden. I myself am acquainted with several."

" I know none," said Raphael Mercado coldly. " In any case, what they do is their affair and I have no wish to imitate them. However, I am prepared to do what your Government asks on one condition, which is that you will secure the release of one of the most illustrious of my co-religionists, the Rabbi Emmanuel Rubinstein, of Cernowitz. I understand that he has been deported to a concentration-camp somewhere in occupied Russian territory. He must be brought safely to me here in Zürich, and once this is done I will undertake to carry out the operation."

Mercado was seated with his legs crossed, his hands clasped on his knees, sallow-faced and motionless. Dim thought—" What an extraordinary type! Why on earth does he bother about a Galician rabbi who's probably dead by this time in any case? It's as though I were to pass up real money to save the skin of the Bishop of Rimnicu-Vilcü! " Aloud he said: " Very well, Monsieur Mercado, I'll do my best. But you had better give me all the details you can, including a physical description, to make sure I don't come back with the wrong man."

He laughed loudly, but Mercado's expression remained unchanged. He was looking, at that moment, as though he had never laughed in his life.

Dim returned to Bucarest by plane, and after seeing Mihail Antonesco had inquiries put in hand to discover the exact whereabouts of Emmanuel Rubinstein. He was finally located in a small prison camp behind the German lines, which were then being driven steadily westward. After several days' negotiations the

German authorities agreed to hand him over to the Roumanians, and it was arranged that a Roumanian army officer should be sent to escort him to Bucarest. But then, when the matter seemed to have been settled, Balota sent for Dim and said:

" Listen, my dear Coziano. I've been talking to Mihail Antonesco. There's a possibility that Faber—you know who I mean, Faber, the German agent—may get wind of what is going on and arrange to have this Jew murdered on the way here."

" Faber is at present in Istanbul," said Dim.

" No, he got back yesterday. I can't help feeling that someone with special authority ought to go along to deal with the Germans on the spot—someone able to take a stronger line than a mere junior officer."

" You mean me? "

" Yes. Of course, only if you're willing to go. But it does seem to me that as you're in charge of the whole business you would be the right person——"

" I quite understand, Minister."

" I'm most grateful. I may add that the Marshal is personally very much interested."

" Quite so."

Dim was by no means sure that Balota was not lying, or that it would really be worth his while to make the perilous journey to the front. But he could scarcely refuse; and perhaps—who knew? —the outcome would be beyond his highest hopes.

" I'll leave tomorrow," he said.

8

On an afternoon three days later Dim was seated in the back of an olive-green army car beside a youthful Roumanian officer, promoted captain at the front and decorated with the German Iron Cross. Another officer, attached to Army Headquarters, was sitting in front with the driver to show them the way.

The late sun, sinking at their back, sent a red glare through the plastic windows, and ahead lay the endless rolling plain dotted with shrubs and thickets, armed with large, spiked thistles and aglow with lilac-coloured flowers. The cloud of yellow dust raised by their wheels was blown back over them by a hot following wind so that it penetrated every crack and silted up in the folds of their collars, in their cuffs and on their shoulders. Dim could feel its grittiness in his mouth, and there were crusts at the corners of his eyes which re-formed as often as he wiped them away. Was there no end to this plain? Indeed, there was none. It stretched all the way to the Pacific coast.

The surface was very bad, and the small army car with its stiff springs was being driven as hard as it would go, bounding and swaying over pot-holes and ruts along what looked like a broad river of dust. Each successive jolt jarred Dim from his heels to his head, causing him to long for less speed, although there could be no question of slowing up. They were progressing too slowly as it was. They had arrived at the last minute. Everything behind the front line was moving hurriedly back to avoid being cut off by the Russian armoured columns. Three days previously Camp 308 had been a fixed point on the map: now it was in process of being removed by special train to some unknown destination. " Can I hope to find him? " Dim was wondering. So much peril and discomfort for the sake of a man who was perhaps already dead, his body flung into a common grave. . . . But there was nothing for it now but to go on. He sat in a half-daze, exhausted by the shaking, with his feet on the black, dust-coated barrel of a sub-machine-gun.

They overtook a long column of supply trucks driven by elderly, moustached soldiers, and their driver left the road and cut across the open country to save time. Out of a dense cloud of dust there suddenly emerged a self-propelled gun on rubber-tyred wheels, followed by more lorries and officers' cars. Then they got back on to the road which now stretched wide and empty ahead of them, losing itself in a flat horizon as vast as the globe itself. Presently more trucks came in sight and then tanks, from the turret of one of which a fair-haired officer in a black uniform gazed impassively at them. They passed through a devastated village with signposts bearing the names of other villages in German and Ukrainian, distances in kilometres, and obscene drawings. As they emerged from it they saw a party of children at the side of the road, who stood with their caps on their heads and their hands in their pockets gazing apathetically at the hurrying car with its load of enemy officers.

Dim was nearly asleep. Whenever he opened his eyes it was to see the same endless monotony of plain and gathering dusk. " I'm very tired," he thought. Oh, to be at home, seated at his ease in an armchair! But then he gave himself a shake. This was no moment for repining. He had to find the Rabbi Emmanuel Rubinstein and convey him safely to Zürich. Sitting upright he forced his eyes to stay open, and they drove into another village amid a furious barking of dogs.

" We'd better stay the night here," said the officer at his side, Captain Dobresco. " The driver's had all he can take and the rest of us are pretty exhausted."

Dim nodded gloomily. They drove down a side-street, seeing some old women in a courtyard, and then some trucks and a field-kitchen with Roumanian soldiers standing round them. They pulled up at the command-post and got out under the eyes of a German sentry who stared at them without moving. Dobresco, leading the way in, asked to speak to the officer commanding the detachment, who turned out to be a bespectacled warrant-officer, aged about forty, short and square-shouldered with a mouth as tight and thin-lipped as the slot of a money-box. Dobresco produced the document given him in Bucarest by General von Röderer as well as his own papers, Dim's (Captain Dimitri

Coziano, of the Roumanian General Staff) and those of the lieutenant who was escorting them. The German studied them in
silence, and Dobresco said heartily, in an effort to thaw him
out:

" What's the food like in this place? Horseflesh, I suppose,
as usual. And how about girls? Anything doing in that line? "

The German remained perfectly unresponsive. Perhaps he was
deaf. Like Dobresco he wore the Iron Cross, first class; and
Dobresco pointed at this and shouted at the top of his voice:

" Where did you get it? I got mine in the Kuban."

This, too, evoked nothing but a stony stare. The German then
glanced at Dim and said, scarcely opening his mouth:

" You'll be sleeping here. I'll show you to your quarters."

He led the way along a whitewashed corridor, its floor newly
scrubbed. Dobresco followed, muttering under his breath, then
came Dim, saying nothing, and the lieutenant and the driver
brought up the rear. The German showed them into a room with
an oil-lamp on the table, saluted and left them there.

" God almighty, what a clot! " exclaimed the indignant
Dobresco. " These Germans! What dull-witted animals they
are."

But Dim had no desire to talk or even to eat. He was worn out.
Pulling off his clothes he tumbled into bed and within a minute
was sound asleep.

He was awakened during the night by a sound of human wailing
and bellowing which caused him to start up on one elbow, trembling as he listened. It sounded like a paroxysm of terror. He heard
voices talking in German.

" What the hell was that? " asked the lieutenant, still half
asleep.

Dobresco, cursing, was groping in the darkness for his boots.
" I'll go and see," he said. He went out, but now there was
nothing more to be heard except the barking of dogs, at first near
at hand, but then more distant and finally a long way off. Dobresco
came back.

" I couldn't find out anything, damn it. All they would say
was that nothing's happening. So I asked, ' Well, what was all
that yelling about? ' and they simply said, ' Nothing.' "

He got back into bed with a sigh. But the next morning, as
the car was leaving the village, he said suddenly to Dim:

" That row last night, you know what it was? I asked our chaps, the ones with the field-kitchen. Well, it seems that it was that German warrant-officer, the clot who let us in. It seems that for a time he was on the staff of one of the concentration-camps and it was too much for his nerves. He's not a bad chap, so they say, but he gets these nightmares and screams as though he was having his throat cut. Poor fool! "

" It seems they even killed children at that camp," said the driver.

" What? How do you know? Where did you hear that? "

" That's what the lads with the field-kitchen told me."

" Good God! " said Dobresco, but then he added: " Still, I dare say it isn't true. They very likely invented it."

" You never know with the Germans, sir," the driver said. " They're not the same as us."

" Do you think you'd get on better with the Russians? " asked Dobresco sarcastically.

" I don't know," said the soldier, startled by his tone. " But the Russians—after all, they're mostly country folk."

" Well, yes—peasants. Yes, that's true."

9

At about midday German bombers began to pass overhead in a steady stream, travelling from west to east and back. After a time it seemed that their general direction had altered, but Dim was not paying much attention. The heat was stifling. Eventually, however, he noticed that the lieutenant, seated beside the driver, was growing restless, leaning constantly out of the car to look up and down the road. At the next crossroad he told the driver to turn to the right, and a minute later they stopped.

" What's the trouble? " asked Dobresco.

" I'm afraid we've come the wrong way. We shall have to turn back."

" For God's sake don't waste time," said Dim, his voice suddenly on edge. " We've got none to spare. This isn't a pleasure trip." He sat upright listening to a distant rumbling. " What's that—artillery-fire? "

" Yes, those are the guns," said Dobresco sourly. " Bless their little hearts."

They turned back, and half an hour later, under the ceaseless drone of aircraft, took another road of which the surface was so bad that Dim, under the violent jolting, was on the verge of telling the driver to slow up. He hesitated to do so, since it was he who had been calling for speed, and then, just as he made up his mind, it was too late. The car thudded into a particularly deep pot-hole; there was a clang of breaking metal beneath their feet and they pulled up in a cloud of dust.

They stood waiting at the side of the track while the driver crawled underneath the car to inspect the damage.

" Well, what is it? " Dobresco asked furiously.

" The cardan-shaft, sir. Snapped clean through. One spring's gone as well."

There was a silence.

" Well," said Dim through his teeth, " it looks as though we're stuck here. There's not much you can do about that."

" No, sir, it's a workshop job."

Four fighter planes roared overhead, going east. The thunder of gunfire was now so close that it set up a quiver in the air.

" Hey, you there, get down! " a voice shouted from somewhere not far off. They looked round but could see no one. " Get down, can't you," the voice repeated, " and crawl over here."

They then saw a low parapet and a helmeted head that seemed to emerge from the earth. They ran towards it, bent double, and dropped into the trench. It was a gun-emplacement, U-shaped, with a short-barrelled 47 Bofors at its centre and a row of shells beside it, standing neatly on end in their brass cases with their fuse-caps painted red. They were the only clean things in the trench. The gun was served by four sweating, dust-stained soldiers under the command of an officer as begrimed as themselves, a dark-skinned, thick-lipped lieutenant with a small black moustache and very white teeth. He welcomed them with a sardonic grin.

" Why were you standing about like that, Captain? You could be seen for miles."

" And who might you be? " asked Dobresco. " What are you doing here? "

" We're occupying the front line," said the lieutenant and introduced himself—Martinesco, of the Forty-sixth Artillery Regiment. They could tell at once that he was a reservist. He went on, speaking in the same familiar fashion: " And where are you off to in your motor-car? "

" To divisional headquarters," said Dobresco, pointing. " Over there."

Martinesco burst out laughing.

" But Division's moved that way, about seven miles to the right. The Russians are in the direction you're heading for and they'll be showing up any minute now." He pointed to a pink eddy on the horizon. " You see that cloud of dust? Those are their tanks."

" Oh lord," said Dobresco.

" Well, that's it," said Martinesco, grinning.

There was something unreal in his voice and movements. The soldiers were smoking, their eyes vacant. They were all waiting, simply waiting. Dim gazed to right and left over the parapet; nothing to be seen but the endless, empty expanse of the plain. Dobresco asked:

" But why have you chaps been left here on your own? "

" We're blocking the road—as though the Russians didn't know how to come any other way."

The soldiers laughed.

" But with no infantry to support you? " said Dobresco. " No machine-guns, nothing? "

" There weren't any to spare, I suppose."

" Well, there's no point in our stopping here," said Dim. " If divisional headquarters is only seven miles away we can walk it in two hours. We'd better go."

" Good luck to you, Martinesco," said Dobresco. " And to you lads."

" At your orders," the soldiers murmured.

The four of them set out to walk across the plain, picking up their sub-machine-gun as they passed the car. The lieutenant and the driver were silent. Dobresco cursed under his breath until he had exhausted his vocabulary. Dim walked fast, saying to himself, " I've got to reach headquarters. I must. I must."

Once he looked back, but there was nothing to be seen of that hole in the ground where five lost men crouched waiting.

They had been walking for about half an hour when, as they were climbing a slope, a grey-green object suddenly appeared above the crest of a small hill a short distance ahead—the turret of a tank. " This is the end," Dim thought, and frozen with horror gazed wildly about him. There was nowhere to run to, no shelter of any kind. The tank had reached the crest of the hill and others were appearing behind it.

" They're German! " cried the driver.

" We'd better stay upright," said Dobresco, " and let them see who we are."

More tanks were coming into view, dozens, perhaps a hundred, causing the earth to tremble. The leader, descending the slope, passed close by them so that they could see the force-commander standing in the open turret with his hands on the sides, a thin, fair-haired man with a bony face, wearing a black beret. He was staring straight in front of him and did not seem to notice them.

" It's Count Ulrich Brederode," Dobresco shouted in Dim's ear. " He's just been brought across from France with an armoured division. The Germans call him *der Panzergraf*."

Deafened by the vibration and the roar of the engines, Dim scarcely heard. The dust was growing so thick that they were almost blinded. When at length the column had passed and the cloud began to subside they stayed still for some moments, motionless and dazed.

" Let's hope they don't run down our poor blokes in the gun emplacement," the driver said.

" Come on," said Dim, rousing himself. " Keep moving."

They covered another mile and came to a road running between deserted meadows. The steady rumble of gunfire was now behind them, at times sounding so close that it was surprising that there was nothing to be seen. 'Nor did it grow any less as they moved away from it, although they were hurrying at their utmost speed. " Why the devil did I let myself in for this? " Dim thought. There was still a chance that he might bring it off if he could reach divisional headquarters before the Russians got there, but he was beginning to feel that it was a forlorn hope. There was too much against him. If the German tanks had not come along he might already be in Russian hands.

" Hurry—hurry! " he cried.

He presently glanced over his shoulder, paused for an instant, and then broke into a slow run. A tank was coming up with its turret askew and its gun pointing sideways, followed by another with smoke pouring out of it. Dobresco and the others had also seen them, and they all began to run, panting and gasping, with the sweat streaming down their bodies. Again the air was filled with the roar of engines as another column of tanks, about twenty, appeared over a low rise. They were Germans, the retreating survivors of the column they had seen going into action, and many had black-shirted men clinging to them, belonging to the tanks that had been knocked out. One of them, already carrying several passengers, passed close by the four Roumanians, travelling slowly and reeking of petrol fumes. Dim yelled:

" Take us with you! "

The young lieutenant, who had been close beside him, ran forward to jump on board. He was met with a burst of machine-gun fire from one of the Germans already installed. He crumpled and lay motionless, dead. Dim shouted to Dobresco and the driver, " We'd better get out of here! " and they ran.

Later they returned to the road, and after a time were overtaken by a large vehicle with a canvas cover, emerging from a cloud of dust. Dim snatched the sub-machine-gun out of their driver's hand and ran into the middle of the road, followed by Dobresco. The truck stopped, and they saw that it had red crosses painted on its sides. The uniformed driver got out and stood stiffly to attention; and from the back of the truck there emerged a small, slender woman in khaki with a white headdress.

" I want you to take us with you," said Dim.

" I've only room for two people in front," the driver said.

" We'll get in behind."

" You can't. I have twelve stretcher cases," said the woman, speaking with a strange calm.

She was young and very pale, with a big, well-shaped mouth and eyes like lapis-lazuli, hard and shining.

Dim said: " Surely I know you? "

It was Isabel Giurgea-Roscano, who had amazed Roumanian society by leaving her husband to his civilised pastimes in Bucarest while she went to serve at the front as a nurse—a madwoman, in short. And there she was, not by any means ugly—indeed, disturbingly beautiful—but bundled up in a shapeless military uniform, dirty, dishevelled, and so white of face that she might have been one of her own casualties.

" I'm Dimitri Coziano," said Dim. " I've got to get to divisional headquarters with all possible speed."

" That's where we're going, because these men will die if they aren't flown back to base. They're all badly wounded. But we've only room for two."

" We don't care if we stand on the running-boards or cling to the roof," said Dim. But there was no need for this. Dobresco had occupied one of the front seats already. " In you get," Dim said to their driver.

He helped Isabel Giurgea-Roscano to climb in at the back, and followed her. The ambulance started off again. The wounded, swathed in bloodstained bandages, were lying on stretchers, their faces grey and emaciated, covered with black stubble.

" They'll all die if we don't get there quickly," Madame Giurgea-Roscano said, huddling in a corner to make room.

" Oh, come. They don't die as easily as all that."

" Two are already dead."

" Which ones? " Dim asked casually.

She pointed. The two dead men lay staring into nothingness, their mouths open. Dim was thinking, " This war's going bloody badly. The Marshal's getting ready to clear out, with all his gang. The Russians are moving in. It's not a time for showing too much zeal. The question is, how am I to get in on the next Government? " He said aloud: " That one there—I think he's dead too."

She corrected him in a low voice: " No. He's in the act of dying."

Dim thought: " Well, what's the odds? I could have sworn he was already dead." He glanced at Isabel Giurgea-Roscano, crouched beside him with clasped hands and half-closed eyes. " She's praying. . . . I wish I could make up my mind if it's really worth my while to do Mihail Antonesco and Balota the favour of getting this gold transferred. I suppose I might as well see it through, having gone so far. There may be something in it for me after all." Isabel Giurgea-Roscano's lips were moving. " She's really beautiful," he thought. " The lovely line of her forehead and nose. . . . A beautiful woman, and she chooses to watch over the dying. How strange! Well, she's mad, of course, religious mania or something—how else can one account for it?" He knew very well that there might be other ways, but these he preferred to dismiss from his thoughts. He had to think of his career.

10

General Tortoreano stood angrily muttering in the corner of a room congested with suitcases, kit-bags, typewriters, box-files, cases of field-telegraph equipment and soldiers who were hurriedly packing up everything in sight.

"Have you no idea of the position? Do you really expect me to spare you a car, now of all times, when we're liable to have the Russians on top of us at any moment? You must be out of your mind. And whoever it was in Bucarest who sent you here on this damned, lunatic mission must be as big a fool as you are." He lowered his voice almost to a whisper. "Do you realise that we may be cut off by tomorrow?"

Dim marked a brief pause and then said formally:

"Nevertheless, General, I must request you to allow me the use of a staff-car. The Marshal himself is interested in the outcome of my mission. You can, of course, telephone to Bucarest for confirmation, but that will cause a delay for which you may be held responsible. I have shown you the letter signed by the Minister for War and the Chief of the General Staff. Surely that is all you need?"

Tortoreano started to bellow, "Captain, I——" but Dim coolly cut him short.

"In the first place I'm not an army captain, I'm the head of a ministerial department. Let me strongly urge you, General, to let me have a car at once, if you do not wish to jeopardise your own career."

Tortoreano gasped and spluttered, his eyes almost starting from his head, but eventually he cooled down.

"All right," he said resignedly. "I suppose I've got to do what you ask."

"I shall make sure that the Marshal is informed of your helpful attitude," Dim said smoothly.

"My dear boy . . ." the general rumbled. "Only natural in the circumstances . . . an important mission. . . ."

He turned away to give the necessary instructions, and Dim thought, "He's scared out of his wits. They all are. The German Panzer divisions—a hell of a lot of use they've been. This war's as good as over. The Germans are whacked and so are we. I've got to make up my mind what to do."

Half an hour later he and Dobresco were speeding across the moonlit plain, by-passing roads where possible to avoid the congestion of tanks and trucks, vehicles of all kinds, some wrecked and overturned, some still burning and surrounded by their dead, all the litter of disaster and rout. The summer night was aquiver with the chirping of crickets near at hand and the rumble of guns in the distance; and Dim sat considering the course of prudence and calculation in this war that was almost certainly—no, quite certainly—lost. Should he accept a more important post under the present government, and thus commit himself, or would it be wiser to get discreetly in touch with the Opposition through his father-in-law and Uncle Serbanica? And the communists? They might well become the dominating factor. But no one knew who their present leaders were, not even the Secret Police. Nothing to do but wait for them to show themselves—and then what line should he take? . . .

He fell asleep at length, to be awakened in the dawn by sounds of shouting. Some Roumanian soldiers, swarming over a tank, were fighting the Germans already clinging to it, using their rifle-butts. Later they passed a tractor-drawn gun, its carriage loaded with men without belts or arms. Finally they got clear of the obstructions and Dim fell asleep again. When next he awoke they were entering a forest of pines with a clean scent of resin. They came eventually to a stockade, a heavy gateway in a high fence of barbed wire with wooden towers on which were armed guards. Here they stopped and Dobresco produced their papers, including a document signed by the German commander in Bucarest. The S.S. men on duty opened the gates and they drove into an open space surrounded by long rows of army huts. Four big diesel-lorries were being loaded by a party of men in striped prison uniforms wearing clogs on their bare feet. Isolated shots sounded somewhere in the distance.

" *Den Herrn Lagerkommandanten!* " said Dobresco sharply in German. " Hurry it up! "

After a further inspection of their papers a sergeant led them along an alleyway of tangled wire, while the guard on one of the towers kept an eye on them with his machine-gun crouched like a dog at his feet. A heavy stench of excrement hung over the place, gradually dying away as they left the hutments behind until they could smell the pines again. The sound of shooting went on for a little while, curiously hollow, as though blank ammunition were being used, but then it stopped. After ten minutes' rapid walking they came to a clearing some hundreds of yards in extent, beyond which was a further zone of trees. Armed guards, their tommy-guns slung from their shoulders, made a large circle within this space, and on a low hillock a little to one side a group of officers and non-commissioned officers, with black ribbons on their caps and pistols at their hips, stood in casual attitudes chatting among themselves while they watched something that was in progress.

In the middle of the clearing was a large ditch. A bank of newly dug earth some four or five feet high ran along one side, with picks and shovels lying against it. Along the top of this bank, with their backs turned to the group of officers and to Dim, stood a line of about twenty men, their striped uniforms hanging in tatters from their emaciated bodies. As he walked towards the officers, too fascinated to pay any attention to the German sergeant or Dobresco, Dim made out the scene more clearly. Two S.S. men went up to the line of prisoners, one approaching it from either end. The one on the left was the nearer, a large, beefy man, almost bursting out of his uniform. He climbed on to the bank of earth, pistol in hand, and standing to attention, back arched and bottom protruding, laid his left hand on the nearest prisoner's shoulder and thrust the heavy automatic against the back of his head. There was a dull report. The man's knees crumpled and like a sack he fell forward into the ditch, propelled by his executioner's left hand. The soldier then moved on to the next man. Meanwhile the same thing was happening at the other end of the line.

Dimitri Coziano came to a stop and stood staring in wonderment at the row of victims, like sheep in a slaughter-house, waiting motionless with their heads bowed. " Why the devil don't they do something? Hasn't even one of them got the guts to turn round and try to kill the chap? " The ceremony took its course, one dull report after another; the bodies tumbled into the trench. " It's queer," thought Dim. " I don't feel a thing." Indeed, he felt absolutely nothing—interest, a sort of fascination, and that was all. But suddenly he thought: " My God, suppose my man's in this lot! "

He almost ran towards the officers, and stood waiting in extreme anxiety while the S.S. sergeant saluted and made his report to the colonel commanding the camp. The colonel turned to look at Dim and Dobresco, and the latter handed over their documents. " For God's sake ask him to stop the shooting," muttered Dim. " Our man may be one of these." After giving him a startled glance Dobresco translated the request. The colonel, a lean, wrinkled man, gazed coldly at them, said, " What on earth are you talking about? " and turned his back.

They had to wait until the last of the prisoners, a very small, unclean man who wept like a child, covering his eyes, had gone the way of the rest. Then a whistle blew. The guards started to form up, and the men nearest the trench set about shovelling earth over the bodies.

" This way," said the colonel.

Dim followed him, thinking: " It's no use. He's bound to be dead. It has all been a waste of time."

But in the event they found Rabbi Rubinstein still alive. Telephone calls had been put through from Bucarest to Berlin and from Berlin to the eastern front. The Rabbi was a short, slightly built man, yellow-skinned, his head shaved, his beard black on his hollow cheeks. Dim and Dobresco tried to talk to him but he could only wag his head, since he understood none of the languages they spoke. Dim sought to reassure him with smiles and friendly pats on the shoulder, but there was no sign of gratification in his huge, desolate eyes. He seemed wholly indifferent to what became of him. They took him to the car, and as it started he put his head out of the window and spoke a few words in a harsh, strange tongue, after which he relapsed into his seat beside Dim. " Would that have been Hebrew? " Dim wondered, without much interest. Thereafter he forgot the Rabbi and returned to the consideration of his own affairs, emerging occasionally from these painful calculations to take note of their surroundings—the endless plain, the ravaged villages and, ceaseless on the horizon, the rumble of guns. Presently they were caught up again in the torrent of traffic, cars, carts and lorries packed to overflowing with dust-caked, bloodstained and exhausted men. The confusion grew steadily worse. There were constant traffic-blocks caused by wrecked vehicles. Capless German soldiers were riding on cows, discharging their rifles into the air; and scattered on all sides over the plain, extending to the horizon itself, were the forms of men, an infinite multitude of men.

They were brought finally to a dead stop. " I've never known a shambles like this," said Dobresco. " Something pretty bad must have happened. The Russians must have smashed clean through. I'll walk on and see if there's any way through or round. If we get bogged down here we'll be sunk."

He jumped out and strode off, slamming the door behind him, while Dim sat contemplating the tens of thousands of men scattered over the plain like a handful of dust blown by the wind, tens of thousands of little vertical lines, like sticks of tea, moving with a terrible slowness over the huge expanse of the land. " It's all no use," he thought despondently. " All this trouble for nothing. Even if the marshal offered me the job of Prime Minister I wouldn't take it. He has no power to reward me now, even if he wanted to. My only chance is with the people who come after him." And then hope revived in him. " But there are the German secret weapons. We still don't know what they can do. Perhaps they'll work a miracle after all."

He turned to glance at the man he had come so far to rescue. Rabbi Emmanuel Rubinstein was also staring at the horde of soldiers in flight over the plain. He uttered no sound, and there was no expression on his face, no pleasure, no grief. He simply stared.

I I

In Zürich a week later Raphael Mercado, the banker, handed Dimitri Coziano a scrap of paper no larger than a big postage-stamp on which were inscribed certain groups of figures in red ink.

" This will serve as an introduction in Lisbon to the gentleman whose name I have given you."

" Thank you," said Dim, and placing the fragment in his wallet he prepared to take his leave.

" There is someone who would like to say a word to you," said Monsieur Mercado with a faint smile.

He led Dim into the next room, and here a small man rose from an armchair, wearing the black satin surtout and white silk stockings of a Galician rabbi, with a round, flat-brimmed hat on his shaven head.

" Ah, my protégé! " exclaimed Dim in a tone of exaggerated cordiality.

The small man spoke a few words in his own outlandish tongue.

" Rabbi Emmanuel," said Monsieur Mercado, " asks me to make his excuses for the fact that he has hitherto been unable to speak to you. He only knows Hebrew, Aramaic and Yiddish. He wishes to thank you for having saved his life."

" You're the one who saved him," said Dim.

The rabbi gazed at him with huge, dark-ringed eyes and spoke again.

" He wishes to bless you."

Dim bowed his head. The rabbi laid his hands upon it and in a sing-song voice uttered a long string of words.

" He has prayed to God on your behalf," Monsieur Mercado said.

" How strange! " thought Dim. " I don't feel anything at all.
I never do feel anything. The rabbi has tears in his eyes, I wonder
why. Perhaps I should be able to weep too if I were master in
my country—a patriarch, for instance, like Nicoulesco." But he
refrained from laughing, partly from politeness but perhaps mainly
because he was tired and bored. . . .

The same weariness oppressed him throughout the rest of 1943
and the beginning of 1944. He spent his time at parties of the
more recherché kind and in meaningless love-affairs. But he
never took his eyes off his career. " When this Government goes
there'll be a parliamentary set-up on Anglo-Saxon lines. But
however strong American and British influence may be the pre-
ponderance of power will be on the left, with the socialists and
communists." He put out cautious feelers among the people with
whom he believed the future to lie. The communists were the
only ones he could not contrive to meet. They did not belong to
his world, and were so closely pursued by the police that they
dared not show themselves. " Well, but they aren't so important,"
he reflected. His calculations went with him everywhere, in bars
and bedrooms, in his office, in the trains which bore him to and
from Lisbon or Zürich or Istanbul, on missions which he performed conscientiously but with no excess of zeal. He was offered
a better post but refused it.

" I'm tired. I've been working too hard these last few years.
I need a rest," he said coolly to Mihail Antonesco.

But there was no rest for him. He was sent again to Zürich
and returned by train, being due back in Bucarest on April 5th.
But the train got no further than Chilita. He had not spoken to
any of his fellow-passengers in the wagon-lit. They had come by
way of Austria and Hungary, then through Curtici and Arad,
travelling all night through stations with dimmed lights and towns
plunged in darkness. When they reached Chilita the sun was
shining in a blue sky. Dim heard voices on the station platform,
and the sound of his fellow-passengers talking more loudly than
usual.

" When did it happen? "

" Yesterday at about midday."

" Does it mean we've all got to get out? "

" It looks like it."

Then the conductor appeared in the doorway of Dim's compartment.

" All change! All passengers are asked to leave the train. This is as far as we can go."

" What's wrong? " asked Dim. " What has happened? "

" A heavy air-raid on Bucarest. The station's still out of action."

Dim got down from the train and joined the excited crowd on the platform. A fat man was saying, " They might have had the decency to choose some other day! " Smoke was visible on the horizon, in the direction of Bucarest.

" The town's still burning."

" The Grivita district's completely gutted, and so is the station," a railwayman said.

Dim was not unduly perturbed. This was something that had been bound to happen sooner or later. The war was closing in on them. Italy had surrendered and enemy airfields were getting nearer. He handed his bags to a porter and went to telephone his house for the car to come and fetch him. His wife's maid answered, and he realised that she was in tears.

" What's the matter? " he asked sharply.

" It's Madame," the girl said, sobbing. " She—she's very bad."

Dim knew instantly what she meant, but could not at first believe it.

" What do you mean, she's very bad? "

" She's dead, monsieur. She was killed yesterday in the air-raid."

Dim was silent for a moment, and then asked: " And the house? "

" The house hasn't been touched. Madame was invited out to lunch, and a bomb fell on the restaurant."

Another pause.

" I see," said Dim. " Well, ask Vasily to come and fetch me. I'm in Chilita, at the station."

He hung up and left the booth. People were swarming like ants over the platforms in the brilliant light of the spring morning. " Wonderful weather," thought Dim. Then he remembered that Colette was dead. " How strange! I don't feel anything at all." And it was true. He did not feel anything.

In Bucarest he found a number of houses still smouldering, others with their façades ravaged by blast like faces assailed by smallpox. Dust and charred embers and a reek of destruction lay over the town. The car had to take a circuitous route because many of the streets were blocked by craters or wrecked trams. Three houses in the street where Dim lived were now no more than piles of rubble. His own was intact, with everything in order, everything in its proper place. Colette's room still retained her scent; her furs and dresses were hanging on their hooks, her shelves filled with underwear. " How strange. You'd never think she was dead." One or two things were locked, including her writing-desk, which slightly complicated matters. Dim left the house and returned to his car.

" Which restaurant was Madame lunching at? "

" The Florea Soarelui, sir."

" You'd better take me there."

Dim sat silent in the car. The Royal palace had been damaged and there were craters in the Place du Palais. Columns of smoke were still rising in the direction of Grivita. The Hotel Splendid was a blackened ruin with blue sky to be seen through the gaps in its walls. The Athenée Palace had lost all its windows. There were shattered walls and shop-fronts all round it, and the pavements were deep in broken glass. A crowd was gathered round a party of soldiers searching for the dead amid a pile of rubble. Somewhere amid that debris Colette must be lying, with her keys. Dim stayed watching for a quarter of an hour and then went back to the car.

Returning home he sent for a locksmith to open the desk and make a new set of keys. Then he had a bottle of wine brought to the library and drank it all, sitting by himself in an armchair. " How strange. No more Colette. It's as though she had never existed at all." He thought of moments in their life together, moments of warmth and married intimacy. Now it was over. No more Colette. His manservant entered and said:

" Monsieur Serban wishes to speak to you on the telephone."

" Which Serban? "

" Monsieur Serban Romano."

" He can go to hell. Tell him I'm not here."

Other people rang up, but he did not want to see anyone. He wanted to think. What were the German secret weapons really worth? North Africa and Italy were lost, and the Russians were in Poland and on the river Prut. How was it going to end? All that mattered was to be on the winning side, even if it meant starting again at the beginning, a man his age, over forty. " No matter," said Dimitri Coziano. " If we must we'll start all over again."

THE END